By JOHN TERRY MOORE

Black Dog
A Nice Normal Family

Published by DREAMSPINNER PRESS
www.dreamspinnerpress.com

A
Nice Normal
Family

JOHN TERRY MOORE

Published by

DREAMSPINNER PRESS

5032 Capital Circle SW, Suite 2, PMB# 279, Tallahassee, FL 32305-7886 USA
www.dreamspinnerpress.com

A Nice Normal Family
© 2016 John Terry Moore.

Cover Art
© 2016 Maria Fanning.
Cover content is for illustrative purposes only and any person depicted on the cover is a model.

ISBN: 978-1-63477-545-8
Digital ISBN: 978-1-63477-546-5
Library of Congress Control Number: 2016906158
Published September 2016
v. 1.0

Printed in the United States of America
∞
This paper meets the requirements of
ANSI/NISO Z39.48-1992 (Permanence of Paper).

To Russell.
An achiever.
Much smarter and wiser than you once thought.

Life is like a jigsaw puzzle.
We search for ages, not really knowing why or what we are seeking.
And suddenly, we find the very last piece of the puzzle.
It fits easily and quickly
Because it was made for that empty space.
And life is complete.

—John Terry Moore, April 22, 2008

Chapter 1
In the First Place

I'M A married man, in my late thirties, and we come from a regional city in Australia.

However, we don't live there much these days.

We have two great kids: Kate is nearly ten and Max is eight.

We're just like any other family, yet we seem to thrive on adversity, considering our backgrounds and the way we started our life together, including living in this bloody great house that doesn't even belong to us.

We've faced some unique challenges in life that we want to share with as many people as possible because we reckon it's a bloody good story.

WRITING OUR story is difficult for me, firstly because my spare time is almost nonexistent, but also because I'm dyslexic.

I have a voice-recognition PC that does most of the work for me—I yap away and the bloody thing types by itself, even checks its own spelling, which is amazing because I can't spell anyway. But my other half supplies the encouragement and does the editing, which is why you're able to read this and enjoy it—and the farther you go, the more you'll realize what a lucky man I am.

So I hope our yarn reminds people that hope is a finer emotion than despair. Why? Because of life's most precious emotion, the true regard of one human being for another—love.

I DON'T think I'm that unique—most new-age Australian guys think the way I do these days.

But I guess they don't make an issue out of it like I bloody do.

Because when my life changed for the better, love made it happen.

Love was both the catalyst and the motivation, and I don't want anyone to forget it.

Least of all myself.

Love has no boundaries and no rules; it's perfect the way it is.

Love inspires us to rise above our ordinary lives. In fact, love is never ordinary.

Love is the only imperative we should teach our children because the lessons of life won't work without it.

In our case, love was waiting for us when we least expected it.

And we realized our former lives had just been a rehearsal.

But having received the gift of love, reality told us we had to work at it.

Just like any living thing, it needs a good feed every day.

A kind word, a knowing wink, a plaster on a cut finger.

And a responsibility to share our good fortune and experiences with others.

Chapter 2
Dyslexia

JACKSON SMITH, the youngest of the Smiths, that's me.

But being Australian, with our predilection for shortening names, I'm usually called Jacko. Only when I'm in trouble with the other half do I get the full title, but that's rare, thank Christ; I'd rather ride out a tropical cyclone than face up to that.

My older siblings are Travis and Alison, and they're also married with kids; I'm nine years younger than Trav and five years younger than Ali.

We three are closer than ever, and we'll always stay that way because we like each other. Nothing like an ongoing shitstorm to bind siblings together.

Even though it was a long time ago, I remember I first realized I was a bit different from other kids when I was five years old.

When I couldn't read the bloody kids' book that Trav and Ali had been reading as babies, suddenly I wasn't the perfect child any longer, my pleasant childhood memories overtaken by the feeling I was an idiot.

Mum called me stupid, dull, and moronic until Dad intervened, told her to cool it, and arranged a visit to the local GP who sent me to an expert in the field.

I was diagnosed as dyslexic, quite profoundly so. Evidently my IQ was in the normal to high range, but I needed specialized teaching aids and teachers with a lot of patience, all of which were available. A special school was being set up for the purpose in Melbourne, an hour away from home.

I can remember Mum screaming and shouting at the time, but as a little tacker I didn't understand what it was all about. Trav and Ali told me years later that Mum was hung up on me being a "special child" who needed remedial teaching. As my own brother and sister explained to her, I had nothing to remedy, I was simply born that way, but I needed expert help to unjumble the words on a page so I could understand them and read properly. Dyslexia is language based, and the inability to read was common to most kids like me.

I never did go to the Melbourne school; Mum was adamant I didn't need to.

Dad was upset, and I can still hear him shouting, probably arguing my case while I wondered what all the fuss was about.

My attendance at kinder confirmed Mum's worst fears, and I can still remember crying as she dragged me home so I wouldn't "make a fool of myself anymore." Mrs. Pearson, the teacher, simply said I was a kid with special learning needs, not a kid with a disability, and help *was* available.

But Mum held firm. When it came time for Year 1 at primary school, I would attend classes with all the other children, and I would "learn along with them because no child of mine is disabled," she'd said.

I didn't understand what she meant, but I soon found out.

JUST LIKE my experience at kinder, I couldn't read at all.

I was no good at writing, and I couldn't spell either.

I was a good listener, but I got bored easily because the other kids seemed smarter than me. My attention span was limited, depending on the subject.

And kids sometimes said shitty things, which Trav and Ali said they shouldn't do; it was wrong, they said.

Some of the teachers were really nice and showed me stuff.

Others yelled at me, like Mum.

One day Ms. Watson screamed at me in rage, calling me lazy and stupid. She dragged me to the front of the classroom where I wet myself in terror. The other kids laughed at me openly, with my pants soaked through. I was only six years old and I cried like a baby, I was so upset. Ali took me home and changed me before Mum came home from work, and washed my shorts, so she wouldn't tell me off. I wanted to do well at school for Mum, but the harder I tried, the worse my results were. The words "slow learner" repeated over and over in my head.

By Year 2 I was even deeper in the shit, and I stopped trying because even then I thought I'd never catch up. I became a naughty little bugger, totally disruptive in class, and the bad reports and complaints rolled in. Finally a letter from the headmaster arrived, and Mum opened it just as I was putting my school bag away. She cracked it big-time, and for the first time in my life, I was truly scared. I didn't understand what was going on, but Dad stepped in, as did Trav and Ali. Somehow they calmed Mum down, and Dad told her she was overdue for her visit to her "specialist," whatever that was.

Mum always seemed a bit strange to me, even as a little kid. But I listened to Dad, Trav, and Ali talking, and they said Mum had a problem. A problem that became worse on Sundays when she spent a long time at church.

So my father, brother, and sister decided to take over my education without Mum's knowledge, and the benefits were explained to me. I could stay at my current school, so Mum wouldn't ask any questions, but I would have special books and several hours of tuition every week at school from a teacher experienced in learning difficulties. But I wasn't to tell Mum because she wouldn't be happy "and I didn't want to make Mum unhappy, did I?"

Is the Pope a Catholic? I was only seven years old, but I knew what I had to do. Dad paid the special teacher, Mrs. Hutton, and Trav and Ali would monitor my progress.

Trav attended the high school next door, but Ali was in Year 6 at my school, and she was just like another little mother. My big sister, lovely and caring. Years later I realized Trav was also looking after me when he often missed footy training just to make sure I was doing okay—no wonder we've stayed so close.

MRS. HUTTON was great—all these years later and we're still in each other's lives. She's a lovely lady and obviously went far beyond her normal teaching duties at the time to make sure I had a good learning foundation.

She said dyslexia was a gift because it made people like me think on a different level than other people. That many of us became high achievers because of that ability.

She reminded me constantly that some of the world's most famous people were dyslexic. In later years I actually repeated some of those names out loud to myself. To help me understand it was a blessing rather than a curse.

Leonardo da Vinci, Albert Einstein, Alexander Graham Bell, Sir Richard Branson, Walt Disney, Jay Leno, Whoopi Goldberg, Nelson Rockefeller, Agatha Christie, Steven Spielberg, Harry Belafonte, Winston Churchill, and Richard Strauss were among the people so affected. Tom Cruise belonged to one of those funny religions and he was publicly dyslexic, yet Mum's church didn't believe that God could create people like me.

Mrs. Hutton said that dyslexic people were all different to each other, just like other people, but as a group we were up to 13 percent of the population.

But one thing that was common was that we were usually brainy buggers.

With an above average to high IQ.

At first she focused on improving my confidence. When I looked at a printed page, the numbers and letters seemed so mixed up I sometimes felt sick as my brain tried to rearrange them and read them. "It's quite normal for that to happen," she said, and I started feeling less like a freak. After a few weeks she began gently probing my capabilities, focusing on what I could achieve rather than what I couldn't. Using all the little written symbols and stuff, she taught me to write, but I found printing was easier, so she let me continue that way. She seemed really pleased at my speed and neatness, although I spelled phonetically and still do to this day.

I could be a fiery little prick as well. My family thought being short-tempered was just my nature, but Mrs. Hutton said it was also sometimes part of being dyslexic. I had a really short fuse and could go from a nice little person to a screaming idiot in seconds. The good thing was I forgot about my tantrums as quickly as they occurred. In later life people would be standing around feeling pissed off and with injured feelings long after I'd cooled down, making me wonder what was wrong with them!

Mrs. Hutton was adamant that I had to practice my "social skills," as she called them, because I could so easily offend those who were trying to help me.

Later on I did upset people, and that contributed to my low self-esteem, which my mother had kick-started as a kid. I knew I should apologize, but I couldn't for some reason. But as time moved on and with help from my other half, I did.

MY BRAIN has always programmed information going in, and once it's there, it's impossible to alter it. So inside my head there is often stuff that's wrong, but if I was asked a question, it always came out as it went in. I sometimes found words hard to pronounce and stumbled around coming up with the nearest phonetic sound. Like mince for mints. Inexhaustible would come out sounding like inexorable, nonessential as nonsensical, and so on. Numbers sounded silly to me. If I were asked how many there were of anything, I'd usually answer the number on either side. If the answer was twenty-five, I'd say twenty-four or twenty-six, even though I knew the answer was twenty-five.

Frustrating.

From my earliest recollection, I became very adept at hiding the facts.

On test days, even as a youngster, I pretended I was ill so I didn't have to take the test and flunk out, but Mrs. Hutton was always a step ahead and gave me an oral test, which was recognized by the school.

Chapter 3
Sammy

MY REPORT card in Year 2 was, for the first time, enough to satisfy Mum.

I'd somehow nearly caught up to Year 1 standards, and while I couldn't read properly from a conventional book, my comprehension was improving.

Mrs. Hutton made sure of that.

I managed to bump along the bottom somehow until Year 5, when Mrs. Hutton sounded a warning. She told Trav and Ali that I needed to put more hours in than she had to spare, simply so I could be where I should be.

That meant homework that no other ten-year-old would normally do. Homework that needed supervising by someone who was bright enough to understand the issues and continue my education out of school hours.

It was Mrs. Hutton herself who provided part of the solution.

She'd grown up with Isobel Collins and they'd remained close friends over the years.

Isobel's husband had passed away suddenly and she had moved back to our area to be closer to good schools, with her son, who was brilliant scholastically and able to help out.

ENTER ONE Samuel Collins, the newest student at Northern Primary.

He may have been only ten years old, but when Mrs. Hutton showed him what to do, he was happy to take over, one ten-year-old teaching another.

I was introduced to him after school.

I couldn't believe my eyes—Sammy was so *different*.

Everything and everyone around me suddenly seemed so black and white compared to Sammy, who was in Technicolor, he was so bright.

Even though we had regulation school uniforms, Sammy accessorized like no one else. There was bling in his ear—and he wore a colored scarf, which he casually threw around his neck, and he just looked so *special*.

Trav, Ali, and Dad reckoned he was ace, and Dad offered to pay him, but Sammy just thanked Dad politely and shook his head.

Because I was Sammy's first real friend.

And he was mine.

Someone helping me because he wanted to.

Sammy never talked down to me, ever. While so many adults and other kids were busy pissing on me because they said I was dumb, Sammy treated me like the brother he never had. "We're equals," Sammy said and spoke to me like I was the most important person in the world. For the first time in my life, I had a friend who liked me the way I was, and I can still remember his smile when I'd open the front door in the mornings and he was waiting there for me.

We walked to school together, usually hand in hand. We had bikes but left them at home because we liked to talk to each other before school, and it was his way of preparing me for the day ahead.

Years later I marveled at his maturity—he was always so organized.

Sammy seemed like a permanent fixture at our place; even Mum realized he was helping me, and didn't bother us. My progress at school started to pick up, and Mum seemed to forget she had a son with "learning difficulties."

BRIGHT, BREEZY, and just amazing, Sammy had these wonderful funny sayings and he made me laugh. I was "Jack the Crack" before we realized it might have some vague pornographic implications, and he was "Slammin' Sam," which was also a bit risqué but went completely over our heads.

At school our close friendship continued. In general classes we sat together and spent other periods in the rec room where Sammy focused on me alone. Without falling behind himself, he got me through assignments and I flourished.

It was a great life lesson for me, and for the first time, I actually began to enjoy the school experience. Dad, Trav, and Ali couldn't believe a young kid like Sammy could be so generous and unselfish. Years later I found out Dad had insisted on a financial arrangement with Sammy's mum, and the money was put into a trust fund for our future education—for both of us.

Dad was smart; with my dyslexia it was unlikely I would ever be a captain of industry or an Albert Einstein—who was also dyslexic—without attending the special school in Melbourne, so a future fund set up with Sammy and me going through high school together was a great solution. I would get a good education because Sammy would be there to help me all the way.

Chapter 4
High School

PRIMARY SCHOOL was one thing, high school was another.

For one thing my lovely sister was in Year 12, and as much as she tried to keep tabs on me, she was so busy with her final year she had to look after herself. So we didn't see as much of each other. Trav had finished school and was well into his apprenticeship as a plumber.

As a result Sammy and I became even closer.

I quickly realized the gateway from primary to high school was, unfortunately, puberty.

We didn't know it back then, although I suspect Sammy did, but not only did our bodies begin to change but so did our attitudes.

I got pimples around my dick, which worried the shit out of me, but then they sprouted hair. "Pubic hair," Trav gleefully told me, which only made me ask more questions in my new, deeper voice. Too terrified to ask Mum, I plucked up courage and asked Dad. He filled in most of the blanks for me, but it was Sammy who knew it all. Isobel, Sammy's mum, understood how important this subject was, so Sammy had this amazing picture book that highlighted all the changes we were going through, the why, the how, and the when. So we compared notes, and then we compared dicks.

I had a nice long dick even then, curved to one side, uncircumcised. Sammy was cut, but he was huge, like a bloody python. A smaller bloke than me, and he was hung like a bloody horse.

The kids who attended high school with us in Year 7 at Northern High were mainly our old classmates from primary school, most of whom were cool.

But something else had changed.

Two little blokes at primary school, one of whom was a smart, high-achieving academic coach of the other, could be excused for walking to school hand in hand.

But at high school, no way.

Puberty, ignorance, and mob rule fucked that notion up completely.

THE FIRST week of high school was confusing.

Sammy and I were as close as ever, we were able to walk to our new school so we left our bikes at home, finding interesting things to talk about as usual.

But when we arrived at the school yard we were suddenly the center of attention.

Some smartasses suggested we were an item, like boyfriends, which left both of us amazed, mainly because we'd never thought of it first.

Suddenly it all got a bit nasty, and we were ambushed on the way to school one morning with more name-calling. A group of Year 8 kids decided we needed to be taught a lesson, and the harassment continued until within earshot of the school buildings. The next step would likely be physical, so I enlisted Dad's help. He was furious but decided a formal complaint wouldn't resolve anything. Sammy and I would be taught to defend ourselves; it was the law of the jungle out there, and this was the way we'd handle it.

Trav took us to a local gym where boxing lessons were available, but we both hated it. The guys were thugs and we felt intimidated. So Isobel took over. She had a Thai friend who taught Thai kickboxing nearby, in a shed behind his home. Chart was in his forties but looked twenty years younger, a product of Asian agelessness. He had a very gentle nature, and when we explained our predicament, he was shocked. People didn't behave that way in the country of his birth, and to seek training to protect oneself at such a young age was unusual. So he focused on defense rather than attack for the first few lessons. Sammy was a much better student than me; I was fascinated as he swung around and dived in harmony with our teacher. The insults continued to build every day as we walked to school, so much so, Trav walked with us most days just to ensure our safety. He warned the idiots, but it seemed to make them worse, the taunts by now openly insulting and awful just because Sammy and I had held hands.

About six weeks later, one of the goons threw a punch at Sammy.

My mate was as cool as ever; he just grabbed the guy's wrist and twisted, stepping to one side and allowing him to fall in a heap on the footpath.

We continued on, but we'd insulted them. The two blokes who thought they could walk along hand in hand had put one of their number on terra firma, and they wanted revenge, to teach us a real lesson.

They shouted at us now, totally out of control, screaming their angry filth, their footsteps rattling on the loose gravel as they caught up with us.

I tried to remember what Chart had made me practice and, as we turned around to face them, I kicked the guy in the nuts. He screamed and doubled up, so I chopped him under the chin with both fists together. He went down like a bag of shit and the others magically lost interest.

Sammy and I high-fived each other as the remainder of the gutless gang looked on, and then we walked on toward school—hand in hand just to rub their noses in it.

Chapter 5
Lily

WE WERE still outcasts and the name-calling persisted.

We were addressed as fags, poofs, and queers every day, even though no bastard dared come near us for fear of physical retribution. The stories had grown exponentially to protect the Year 8 cowards who, in the end, exaggerated our fighting ability to protect their own reputation.

Then nirvana arrived in the form of Lily Sanchez.

Sammy and I were drawn to her immediately.

Lily was wonderfully different. She had more tats, piercings, and hardware hanging off her body than anyone I'd ever seen. Lil was alternative in the best possible way because she looked far tougher than she actually was.

She frightened the shit out of the other girls, and the boys didn't know how to handle her. We enjoyed their discomfort.

Yes, Lil was a girl, and a very good-looking girl at that.

Part Spanish, part Asian, she lived with her father, not far from school but in the opposite direction from Sammy and me.

Outside the school gates, she overheard the group of Year 8 bullies who stood around us, still trying their best to harass us.

"You mongrels look like you've all got a dose of the clap and gave it to each other."

She pointed to a cold sore on a guy's lip as evidence.

He self-consciously touched his mouth as we turned away, trying to keep a straight face, and we were never bothered by them again.

NOT ONLY did Lil intimidate our schoolmates, but after that particular confrontation, the questions over our sexuality just melted away.

Which was a shame because Sammy was proud of who he was, and I was proud of him too. And so was Lil. A few brave souls started to drift in our direction at lunchtimes, and soon Sammy was holding court. There were smartasses, too, but Sammy seemed to grow in confidence. I thought

Lil was vehement enough, but Sammy had a tongue like a viper, particularly when someone had a crack at me for being a slow learner. When I got angry, I got tongue-tied. When Sammy got angry, he became even more articulate, and it clearly wasn't worth the trouble to take him on.

One poor bastard found out the hard way.

We were at lunch in the canteen and there were sniggers at the next table from Simon Green, a big, overweight Year 8 kid. Sammy was suddenly on full alert. Among other accomplishments he was a skilled lip-reader, and it was obvious he'd "overheard" something crass.

"So you don't like sharing the school with so-called disabled people like Jacko. That's what you said, wasn't it, Simon?"

A hush came over the canteen as everyone focused on the entertainment. Simon Green broke into a sweat, his pudgy face a picture of shock.

"Lost your voice, Simon? What a waste of space you are," Sammy said in a chilling tone. "Your lack of manners and revolting appearance are only exceeded by your ignorance. You see, Jacko has more intelligence in his little finger than you have in your entire body, so why don't you fuck off and haunt a house or something."

Sammy's outfits grew more outrageous by the day; in fact he and Lil seemed to have a competition going. They still wore school uniforms, but it was the accessories that highlighted their presence.

Rings and studs hung off Lil's nose—I told her she'd better take them out if she had a cold. Sammy's sparkling ear studs ran around his left ear, and his hair was a beautiful rainbow shade.

"It pays to advertise, dude," I told him. "You'll get all sorts of invitations," and he just laughed his nice, musical sort of laugh.

When he was eventually questioned by the headmaster out of curiosity rather than censure, Sammy was straightforward.

"It's a statement of who I am, sir," he said. "The colors in my hair are the same as the gay community's flag. We've won a few battles both literally and metaphorically; my friend and I were physically attacked on several occasions, and we've also suffered verbal abuse but we fought them off. So it's a celebration for me."

The head was shocked. Not only was he unaware of our misery, he was amazed how our parents had paid to train us in the martial arts to defend ourselves.

Mr. Mostrop turned out to be a lovely man and, like Mrs. Hutton, is still in touch with my family all these years later.

He acted quickly, without involving Sammy and me, and within a few days, attitudes began to change. The guys who bullied us were threatened with expulsion, and Mr. Mostrop encouraged Sammy to start up a Gay-Straight Alliance.

BY YEAR 10 half the school belonged to the Alliance.

And the other half wished they did, because the Alliance brought with it a sense of pride that saw Northern High School receive community awards for interaction and support of the gay community. Mr. Mostrop pointed to the improved academic results, a direct result of students feeling relaxed, and thereby more productive.

The only problem was the Parents and Friends Association, which was critical of the school's stance. An association led by a newly elected president—my mother.

Suddenly, our profile as part of the Alliance was in question. Sammy had gone from a nice friend helping her son to being persona non grata at our house, and Dad erupted. Mum was immoveable, and Dad apologized to Sammy. So did Trav and Ali.

We all felt betrayed, and poor old Dad started sleeping in another room. Insult was added to injury when Mum announced she was standing for state parliament as a Family Priority candidate.

Her church was driving this stuff, as was her attitude to gay kids through the Parents and Friends Association. Poor Mum thought she was a certainty to win the seat because Jesus and his earthly mates were sponsoring her campaign. But Dad had other ideas. As much as Mum was giving all of us the shits, the one fact that escaped Mum's attention—and her church— was her mental well-being. Or lack of it. Somehow Dad got her back to her specialist, and she went back on her medication. A few well-chosen words from Trav to the Family Priority organizers, and her nomination was withdrawn on the grounds of ill health. Poor Mum. The Parents and Friends Association suddenly realized their president had some mental health issues, and Mum was advised to take an "indefinite leave of absence." Besides, there was mounting pressure for the association to support students as per the association charter, and their previous antigay stance was abandoned. Thank Christ! We could all breathe again, and I had a smile on my face once more because Sammy wasn't censored out of my life.

Chapter 6
Growing Up Tough

ONE THING changed because of Mum's illness.

Lily started spending more time with me in the period Sammy wasn't allowed at our place. And one Sunday when everyone was out, Lil made it happen and I lost my virginity. I was naïve, but I was smart enough to let Lil show me how everything worked because she certainly knew her way around. I thought girls wanted romance and candlelit dinners, but Lil told me pointedly she wanted a fuck and that was all. I knew I wasn't gay, but I also knew I didn't want to upset Sammy, and I told Lil so.

She understood, but before I could talk to Sammy, she told him.

"Hey, thanks for the heads-up," Sammy said, and we were cool.

So Lil and I started dating, but it was unconventional, to say the least. She lectured me on the subject; she hated the girlfriend/boyfriend tag; she wanted sex but never promised to be monogamous. Even back then I knew her behavior was a bit strange.

I suppose I was a bit strange as well because I insisted Sammy come with us on our dates, and she readily agreed, as if it was never in question. So Sammy came along and we had even better times than before. I was a happy bloke, getting a bit on the side, yet my two best mates were still around me.

We realized very quickly that social activities required cash and so, having explained our dilemma to Dad, agreed there was but one option.

Work part-time at weekends.

Dad was a builder specializing in kitchen renovations, and both Trav and Ali had worked for him in the past. Now it was my turn, but Sammy needed help as well. And Lil also, who always insisted on paying her way.

When I look back on that time, Dad was deliberately creating work for all of us, while he could have done most of it himself.

We loaded old cupboards and junk onto the truck, shoveled plaster into the wheelbarrow, and generally cleaned up the work sites so Dad was ready to go again the following week.

Dad praised us, which was great; we felt we were doing something really cool.

While earning money was highly commendable, and volunteering to work for it was even more amazing for kids our age, *how* we spent it was even more important, Dad said.

Christ, I knew what we'd do with the money: we wanted to go out and have a good time. End of story.

No it wasn't, Dad said.

Up until this time, I hadn't realized how much trust Dad had placed in Sammy, because what followed was amazing.

"Sammy," Dad said, "I want you to be treasurer. You guys must learn to live within your means. I want you to teach the others what responsible fiscal policy entails." I looked at my father as if he'd completely lost his marbles.

"The wages you've earned are precious because I can only pay you while the work is available. So with Sammy's guidance, you need to save your dollars for a rainy day. Any ideas how you'll achieve that?" Sammy nodded and mentioned opening a joint bank account, and the light went on in my brain.

"We could eat at home before we go out," I said, and Sammy nodded.

Dad sounded impressed, even though he'd be paying for the food.

"And Mum could drive us when she's free, that would save bus fares," Sammy replied.

Lil looked bored. "I've got a better idea."

Before she could say anything, Sammy cut her off, because we both knew what she was about to suggest. "No, Lil, we won't be doing that," Sammy said with murder in his voice, and my heart sank. To be fair, Lil had always told me where she was at, and that was okay. But suggesting she pull a few tricks to grow our funds wasn't even funny. Dad would've been horrified if Sammy hadn't stopped her in midsentence. I suppose it was another chapter of my life education, but I never felt the same about Lily ever again. I was disappointed. I was also wary because Sammy suggested Lil could be using some extra funds for drugs, and while there was no direct evidence, I wouldn't have been surprised if she was.

Chapter 7
Moving Forward, Going Backward

THANKS TO Sammy I began to catch a glimpse of my future life because I was no longer dragging behind. *Leonardo da Vinci, Albert Einstein, Alexander Graham Bell, Sir Richard Branson*, I thought, wondering at what point in their lives they'd left underachievement behind and begun looking forward with a little confidence and even hope.

I could now read almost anything, thanks to Sammy pushing epic tomes at me that weren't even on the compulsory list for school. Like *War and Peace*. Christ, I struggled, but in the end I was hooked because it was such a good yarn. Sammy questioned me every morning for ten days until I knew more about nineteenth-century Russia than Leo Tolstoy did. It was after that particular exercise that I realized with some shock and a little pride that my attention span seemed to match the other kids' in class. Because I was interested. When our English teacher asked what we'd been reading and I modestly told him, he just grinned at me, thinking I was full of shit.

I wasn't; I was full of Tolstoy as I gave him and the class a synopsis. The smile on Sammy's face was worth it all; his star pupil was indeed that, a bloody star.

Writing and spelling were still difficult, but I used the little laptop Dad had given me, and the spell checker was in constant use.

THE RELATIONSHIP between Lil and me had cooled, but not in a nasty way. I just put it down to my own feelings not being as strong, something she seemed to pick up on. Then abruptly she stopped having sex with me at all, and I realized she must be getting it somewhere else. Which was cool, because there was no shortage of other willing participants if I was interested.

But she'd been missing for two days, and both Sammy and I worried about her. She didn't answer her phone, and we decided to pay a visit after school. In all the time we'd known Lil, we'd never been invited over to her place, and we'd only met her father once, a swarthy guy, Latino in appearance with a big handlebar mustache. He'd been pleasant enough, but Sammy had a funny feeling about him, and I agreed, he made my flesh creep. We knew Lil's mother had passed away some years ago and that Lil was an only child. No discussion ever about relatives, although I knew the family originally came from Brazil.

As we rounded the corner, police cars and flashing lights from an ambulance lit up the street. We ran the last few meters, but a policeman stopped us in our tracks.

"No further, boys," said a kindly but firm senior constable. "Move on please, there's nothing to see."

We turned and walked back to the end of the street and then glanced back as two covered stretchers were carried out and slid into the ambulance. We knew something awful had happened and we'd probably never see Lil again.

I walked in the door, and Mum spat the dummy. "Peter," she shouted, "please deal with your son. There's been no phone call, and he's over an hour late."

Dad glanced at my face and could tell I was in trouble. "What on earth's wrong, mate?" he asked.

"It's Lily. I think she's dead."

I bawled my bloody eyes out; talking about it made me feel even worse.

Somehow this all seemed linked to the coldness that had developed between Lily and me, and I blamed myself for not paying attention, for not being a loving boyfriend.

The doorbell sounded and it was Isobel and Sammy. Ali and Trav were horrified and tried to help, but it was Sammy who organized the Smith household that night. He stood over me as we ate, then dragged me outside for a walk before bedtime. Then he showered me and pushed me into bed. I tossed and turned, and then a sweet-smelling and lovely Sammy slipped under the sheets with me and, exhausted, I fell asleep. I dreamed of Lil and when we'd first discovered each other, our relatively uncomplicated life, and our pleasant coupling together.

The following morning was, as expected, terrible, because daylight brought reality. Dad called us into the dining room and closed the door. If there was trouble, Dad was a great listener; we kids told him everything about our lives because we knew we'd never be judged and he'd be the first to help us.

And I appreciated him then more than ever.

"Boys, I'm sorry to confirm your worst fears," Dad said. "Lily and her father are both deceased. The police are treating it as murder-suicide.

"There was a gun used, and both appeared to have died instantly."

I cried on Dad's shoulder, but Sammy amazed me with his strength. He said we had no option but to accept what had happened, as awful as it was, and move on with our own lives. That there was nothing we could have done to have prevented this stuff happening and we should never, under any circumstances, blame ourselves for it. I wanted to believe him, but I couldn't let go of the feelings of guilt that enveloped my mind. Sammy reminded me that together we'd probably given Lil joy and friendship in her life for the first time ever. That if it weren't for us, this may have happened earlier.

I listened to what he was saying, and realized I had to be strong also.

Blaming myself was wrong and wouldn't achieve anything. I had to let Lily go to wherever she'd gone. There were obviously many unanswered questions remaining, and in a way it was healthy for us to understand why this all happened, and more importantly, why it occurred at this particular time.

THERE WAS no funeral because there was no family or relations to say good-bye. Just Sammy and me. And a few brave souls at school who got past Lil's unfriendly exterior and found the real person underneath, as we had. So instead there was a memorial service for Lil at school.

Mr. Mostrop was amazing. I'm sure he knew Lil and I had been lovers, but he didn't patronize me, just treated me like the adult I was fast becoming.

Because what Sammy and I'd experienced forced us to grow up faster than any two sixteen-year-old kids should ever have to.

Rather than alleviate our angst, the facts from the postmortem made it worse.

It appeared that Lil's father had been having sex with her, but over what period was unknown. What was conclusive were the drugs involved, ice in particular; traces were found in both bodies. Sammy always reckoned Lil was on something, I remembered him saying so. At the time I was so obsessed with getting my rocks off, it didn't register.

I was a total mess, but as expected, Sammy was there for me. We walked to school and I'd start blubbering, and he'd take my hand just like when we were little kids, and I felt better immediately. No one at school hassled us. The train of events was so horrible that even our worst detractors felt sorry for us, and many of them actually said so, which was amazing.

The memorial service was to give us all permission to move on with our lives, the celebrant said.

But I couldn't. It was all too hard, and I started feeling like shit, all day, every day.

Even though I knew it was stupid, and even though Sammy never left my side, I still felt this awful blackness. Mr. Mostrop had insisted we both have counseling as we were Lil's closest friends, but we thought we were okay, trying to move on ourselves. Eventually Dad and Isobel stepped in, and we were sent to the recommended school counselor, Mr. Fisher.

Within minutes we both realized Sammy had a kindred spirit on board.

Mr. Fisher ("call me Pete") was lovely and made us laugh for the first time in many weeks. He sashayed around his office like a one-person entertainment team, and we were just fascinated with him. Underneath all the color and movement, I could tell was a loving, compassionate person who set out to win our trust. And he did, in our first session together.

He told us that the scariest cases were people who hid their grieving and sadness away, while they attended to those close to them.

"Like you, Sammy," he said, and my heart nearly turned over.

Suddenly I realized Sammy had suffered equally through all this horror just to protect me. I fussed over him like an old mother hen for the next few days, and in the end he put his head up and looked me in the eye.

"Thanks, Jacko," he said. "We look after each other, don't we?" Then he burst into tears, and I was adult enough to realize that's exactly what he needed to do when this first happened. But he'd been so focused on me, he'd forgotten about his own feelings. So I cuddled him some more and did special things for him without being asked, and we seemed to grow closer than ever.

Chapter 8
Year 12

INSTEAD OF walking home with Sammy every afternoon, sometimes one of the girls would invite me home, and I went with them. They were interested in one thing only, as I was, and I kept several of them happy, but not one knowing about the other. Sammy knew, of course, and gently chided me about my exploits, but being typically Sammy, he even said it was none of his business.

Attitudes had certainly changed in the last two years or so. The Alliance meetings were not only a hotbed of gossip; they were a hotbed for both straight and gay sex. Sammy was much sought after, although he seemed to politely decline all invitations. He'd grown even better-looking, but he was quieter, and notably less flamboyant. And that troubled me just a little because I was so attuned to Sammy being the sparkling center of attention everywhere.

We'd kept up our kickboxing training with Chart and actually entered a local competition. While the need to protect ourselves had almost disappeared, Muay Thai had served us well as a fitness regime.

Sammy was really into it and it showed.

So many people, male and female, gay and straight wanted to bed him. But Sammy just wasn't interested. I even tried to set him up with some guys but he turned on me, and I thought for a few days I'd lost my best mate, he was so pissed off. Some of us, including me, took life as it came, hormonal urges intruding on common sense and hard work, but Sammy was very serious about this final year of school. He finally lectured me, leaving no room for misunderstandings. I realized the effort he'd put into me was about to come undone because I was so "dedicated to fucking anything warm and with a pulse," as he put it most succinctly.

His words were shocking because it was the first time Sammy had ever raised his voice in anger to me. And I knew I richly deserved it. He'd put everything into my education, he'd been there through the black times of losing Lil, and now I was blissfully throwing it all away. I'd been rescued from illiteracy and Sammy stuck at it for no other reason than he was my friend.

I felt like shit, and I had to agree that the only person who could do something about it was me. "I'm really sorry," I said. "I really have to get my shit together, don't I?"

I saw a glimmer of a smile, something near the old Sammy. I knew I had to do it, for Sammy and for myself.

I wanted to succeed, but I wanted Sammy's approval even more.

SAMMY WAS honest. "Your only hope is to work your arse off and hope you complete your remaining three units on time."

I flew home from school, ignoring pleas from Michelle, my sort-of girlfriend, and made a start at my desk. *Walt Disney, Jay Leno, Whoopi Goldberg, Nelson Rockefeller*, I thought. *I remember these names easily, but I forgot what they achieved didn't come easily. They had to work hard at it and so do I.*

Dinnertime was terse, and after questioning from Dad, I let it all hang out. He wasn't as pessimistic as I was, but I knew I had to put the time in and time was short. That would effectively rule me out of weekend work on Dad's work sites, for which I apologized. "You don't have to apologize to me," he said, "because you're working towards your future at last, instead of burning the candle at both ends. But you should demonstrate your gratitude to your best friend who's pushed you to get this far."

As if on cue, the doorbell went, and it was Sammy, with a big smile across his face. Mum, as usual, stuck her nose in the air and flounced off, while Dad made the biggest fuss of him. Sammy pointed to my bedroom and the desk, and I knew I was forgiven. I felt liberated again, even though there was a focus on hard work for the months ahead. But with Sammy leading, I was following close behind, and I didn't want to disappoint him again. I also wanted to do something for myself; I knew without my Victorian Certificate of Education I was dead meat in the jobs market, slipping into that category had no future. Four hours later, when I was close to mental exhaustion, he went home. Somehow we'd reconnected, and there was a kiss on the cheek good night and he was gone.

TIME FLEW past, and final exams drew near. I'd already sat for the GAT—the General Achievement Test, covering written communication, mathematics, science and technology, humanities, the arts, and social sciences. In a broad sense, the test measures a student's overall grasp and balance of the various disciplines, very much forcing the issue of left brain versus right. Mine was mostly an oral test, but I was able to demonstrate my ability on my little laptop for the written segment, being allowed more time.

To my amazement, and to Sammy's delight, I aced it and did very well.

But October arrived and the finals loomed, and frankly I was shitting myself. The only public diagnosis I'd had of my dyslexia was through my family GP when I was five years old, and to convince the Victorian Curriculum and Assessment Authority that I was eligible for special treatment was difficult. Our headmaster, Mr. Mostrop, was amazing and intervened on my behalf. Like all students, there had been ongoing assessments, including the GAT, which counted toward the finals result, but the fact remained, I had to sit for the finals in the four units. Except mine was to be largely an oral examination. Mr. Mostrop insisted I was eligible for the Derived Examination Score to be applied to me, which meant if I failed I could apply for special assessment consideration, given my so-called learning disability.

IT WAS all over, so both Sammy and I decided we'd better help Dad.

He'd been so supportive, and was busier than ever with Christmas not far away and everyone wanting their new kitchens finished before the holiday season. We worked hard and we enjoyed it.

The physical activity awakened something inside of me long repressed, not, I thought, by design but by circumstances.

We went to the pictures together several times, and there was always a kiss good night at my door or his. But my favorite time was in the kitchen at his place, talking with him and Isobel; it was so warm and welcoming.

Some days poor Mum wandered around the house so full of her medication I don't think she even noticed I was there, so I inevitably ended up over with Isobel and Sammy, sometimes even staying the night.

It was a lovely relaxed few weeks. There was no pressure to study any longer, but our free time had a defined end to it, because sometime before Christmas we'd know our results. What next year and the future held for us was the elephant in the room; we both recognized it was there, but life was so perfect at the moment we didn't want to talk about it.

By the second week of December, results were being progressively posted online. I couldn't bring myself to log in, and instead I ran over to Sammy's house and we accessed the data together. We sat in front of the screen, hearts thumping.

"Look," I said, "you've got two credits."

"And you with two passes in the same subjects. How amazing you are, and I don't think you'll even need the Derived Examination Score."

Three days passed, and we couldn't sleep or eat properly.

Sammy wasn't worried about himself, but about me. His results were enough to propel him into university, but I'd been the work in progress for so long. All I wanted was a score good enough to get me a job because I was burnt out and I knew I had very little left.

Applied Mathematics was there the following morning; Sammy had yet another credit and I had a pass. Pretty good stuff. Shortly after arriving home, my phone rang. "Get over here now," he said, and I sprinted there. Sammy looked emotional and Isobel cried.

"Oh," I said, "I stuffed up in English, didn't I?"

Sammy gave it away, his lovely musical laugh ringing out. "You aced 'em, Jacko," he said. "You got a credit in English and I got a pass. You blitzed 'em, including me, congratulations!"

"Party time," I roared, totally excited. "At my place." Trav and Ali came over, Dad tore into the whiskey bottle, and I just slipped up close to Sammy, not really trusting my feelings at that stage, although I'd had a few drinks and was really relaxed.

He always fascinated Trav and Ali, a special link existed between them because Sammy took responsibility for my education.

Tonight, Sammy glowed; the bling in his ear sparkled, as did his personality. While Sammy had put on bulk and strength through Muay Thai, he was very obviously a proud gay man, and I loved him for it.

The party was in full swing when the noise stopped suddenly and everyone's eyes swung toward Sammy and me. I frowned, pissed off that good drinking time was being interrupted.

There was a noise behind us and I turned around to meet the piercing eyes of my mother boring into me. Before anyone could intervene, she started screaming, as if standing on a pulpit delivering a sermon. "Homosexuality is the ruin of the world," she ranted. "It's against God's word, and you two will burn in hell for your sins."

For the second time since we'd known each other, we felt cheated because we hadn't really thought about it first. We'd probably thought about it, but other events in our lives had overtaken it.

Dad had certainly enjoyed himself that evening; the pressure of educating me to a good standard was over for now, and even Mum's tirade couldn't dispel his good mood.

"Dad," Trav said, "where's Mum's pills?"

"I know where they're kept," Ali said, helping bundle Mum up, pushing her toward the bedroom as she screamed about Sodom and Gomorrah.

Twenty minutes later she was sound asleep under heavy sedation. Sammy always knew what to say at these awkward moments, and as Dad returned to the lounge room, Sammy cuddled him. "Sorry you had to see that, Sammy," Dad said, "after all you've done for us."

"Mr. Smith," Sammy said, "don't let it worry you. It's not like it's the first time, and it won't be the last. You're a saint for looking after Mrs. Smith the way you do and for encouraging Jacko and me in our studies. The experience has inspired me. I'll be training to teach people like Jacko as a full-time career."

Sammy smiled mischievously at Dad, who was looking a little downcast. "Mr. Smith," Sammy said, "no apology is necessary because I'm as gay as Christmas anyway."

Chapter 9
The Real World

WE STILL managed to see each other several times a week, even though preparation for university kept Sammy busy, and we texted each other every day. Always silly stuff, but we had our own language. I managed, with Sammy's help, to get myself a job working for the local city council. Michelle Brown also helped; we'd been at school together and knew each other quite well. She'd done work experience at the depot over several months and was now girl Friday in the Operations office, working for Craig Murray, the operations manager and also my boss. One of the things I could do well was to drive and operate various types of machinery, thanks to my time helping Dad in his business.

Mowers, graders, even garbage trucks were relatively easy for me to master, and I already had an endorsed license, so I could legally drive heavy vehicles.

By mid-January I was working full-time on the mowing gang.

Dad was disappointed that I hadn't gone further with my education, but as I explained, I was over it. Totally burnt out by the extra effort required to get me over the line. Sammy extracted a promise from me to study at TAFE in the future when I found a profession instead of a job. "Because," he told me, "you are wasting your natural talent."

I UNDERSTOOD what Sammy meant, but I actually enjoyed what I was doing.

I was on the zero-turn mowers, cutting the grass up to fences and around trees in the sporting reserves. Some of my new workmates said I was too fussy and threatened me with union action because I took a little line trimmer with me and cut the grass in places the mowers couldn't reach. I felt terrible until the phone calls started, praising the work ethic of the mowing gangs, and Craig Murray was made to look good. Craig told me to keep going, but my detractors wanted to call a strike on the issue. I was torn. I was always politically aware, but here I was on the side of the bosses when my heart was in tune with the working man. I don't know where the thought came from, but when Mr. Davis, the CEO of the City, became involved, I suggested a performance bonus.

And from being in deep shit with my workmates, I was their hero.

Our hourly rate actually dropped, but when other indicators were factored in, there was a sizeable monthly bonus. With everyone now busting their gut to get the work done faster and with higher quality.

I'd been in the job only six months, and at nineteen years of age, management was talking about where my future lay.

"I'm so proud of you, Jacko," Sammy told me.

His praise meant everything at a time when I was still developing my skills base, mentally and socially. I felt good around people now, and I felt more confident.

But Sammy wanted me to focus on the future even more.

"Jacko, I know you probably don't believe me, but you have to understand what's happening to you. You're still developing."

He reminded me of Mrs. Hutton's words: that people with dyslexia often think outside the square, that our minds are sometimes on a totally different level to people around us. And to expect that type of lateral thinking and problem-solving ability to show itself again. *Agatha Christie, Steven Spielberg, Harry Belafonte, Winston Churchill, Richard Strauss. I wonder if they ever worked a line trimmer.*

Sammy himself, thank heavens, had been accepted at the local university for a Bachelor of Education degree, and he'd continue to live at home, which suited me. Home for me was increasingly with him and Isobel anyway, because my mum was still driving me crazy. I felt guilty with Dad having to put up with the barrage of righteousness, but he seemed happy for me spending much of my time just two streets away.

Sammy borrowed Isobel's old Peugeot on a regular basis, and to save me a bus fare, he'd drive me home. We were desperate for cash, one of the reasons I hadn't been dating for nearly a year. I didn't think much about that sort of stuff anyway because my life seemed so full. The normal bodily urges were still there, but as long as Sammy was around, I didn't seem to care, even with Michelle dropping heavy hints every time we talked to each other.

SAMMY WAS flat strap at uni and I'd been upgraded to foreman at work, with a big pay rise. So with Dad's help I bought my first car, an old Ford

Falcon. The Ford became our transport to and from university for Sammy and to work and home for me. It was both freedom and independence. We liked going to the movies and some parties at uni. But Sammy and I were usually bored with them, or at least with the kids that attended. They were immature, naïve, and seemed totally focused on themselves to the point of selfishness. And these were the people being trained to teach the coming generations! We reckoned through our life experiences—my dyslexia, both of us being bullied, and finally the shock of Lily's death— we had been forced to grow up much faster than most young people.

But our life changed early in the new academic year, just before both of us were about to turn twenty. Sammy had texted me a friend was driving him home and he'd see me there.

I walked in the door and was on guard immediately. Isobel had a distracted look on her face as I was introduced to Matt, a somewhat campy, but otherwise good-looking fellow student.

My innards turned to ice water, and while I wasn't surprised a bloke as good-looking and fit as our Sammy would find a partner, I was surprised how upset I was. They were obviously an item—how the facts had escaped me until now puzzled me—but I knew my association with Sammy was quickly changing, probably forever. Matt grinned openly at me as if to claim Sammy as his own, while Isobel shook her head silently.

I was pleasant to Matt and helped Isobel with the vegetables as I usually did. The last thing I wanted to do was alienate Sammy and spoil our friendship just because his boyfriend was a fuckhead. After dinner I helped clean up, kissed Isobel good night, and left for home. Sammy pecked me on the cheek as he always did, and I saw a shadow pass over Matt's face, which gave me some satisfaction. Because I didn't like the prick, and I'm sure the feeling was mutual.

Chapter 10
A New Home, a New Life

FOR THE first time in years I began spending more time in the family home, and Mum decided my life should be enhanced by Christian values, being critical of everything and everyone I was associated with.

Not that she'd treated Travis and Alison much differently, they just managed to both get married early and move out as soon as possible. But as the last kid living at home, I was now the target. Only Dad defended her and spoke of her "nervous disposition."

As we grew up, Mum became even stranger. Ali and Trav said it had something to do with us reaching puberty; the very mention of sex would send her right off, and she'd go into the bedroom and pray for hours. Fancy having a mother that was praying you wouldn't have sex, and Trav, Alison, and I were praying for the opposite.

We all put it down to the God-botherers she mixed with; if ever there was a bunch of crazies, they were it. A born-again group, they were led by a guy who preached damnation for all those who strayed from the path of righteousness. Their version of Christianity didn't allow sex before marriage and even frowned on sex during marriage outside of procreation. For those participating in homosexual acts, they recommended stoning to death. Laughable and ludicrous, the threats were unlawful but enough to keep the police and press people on their toes. *How Christian of them*, I thought. *My best friend in all the world is a beautiful gay guy and my poor mother is a bloody believer of all this shit.*

Unsurprisingly they arrived one Saturday, all full of piss and importance, dressed up in suits and ties, with the Palmolive glow about them, gleaming with self-righteous mania, bursting through our front door without even knocking. They stopped outside my door, calling on me to come out in the name of the bloody Lord. Dad was furious; he grabbed their bloody leader by the scruff of the neck and walked him back out the front door with his suede shoes tapping on the carpet like he was treading on ants, and the two ugly-looking women with long faces who came with him just ran after them moaning and crying out.

The old man slammed the door on their backs with some words of advice: that if they came anywhere near his kids with their bullshit ever again, they'd need to find another fucking Lord because the one they were talking to wasn't fucking listening to bigotry and bullshit.

Mum finally came up behind him and hell on earth had no equal to her.

For the second time in his life, poor Dad was relegated to the spare bedroom as Mum prayed nonstop for days, hardly stopping to eat or sleep.

STAYING AROUND home under those circumstances wasn't an option for me.

I was between a rock and a hard place, however. Had Sammy been single, I would have asked Isobel to rent me a room, and I would have been more than welcome. But Matt had moved in and they were busily renovating the little bungalow at the rear of their house where he and Sammy would live.

Clearly there was enough space, but I knew being around Matt for lengthy periods wouldn't do either of us any good. And I didn't want to cause my mate any grief; this was his chance to bond with his new partner, and he didn't need me hanging around like a stale bottle of piss.

The following day I spoke to Michelle, or rather I found myself answering her questions.

Since our little fling at school, she'd done very well as Craig Murray's girl Friday.

She was literally pushing herself out there and never stopped coming on to me. So I surrendered and we started dating.

I was very honest. I knew I didn't love her and I told her so, but it didn't seem to deter her, she seemed even more determined to march us toward relationship status. But she did make sense in one aspect: a girlfriend and her husband had been transferred to Queensland and their house was available for rent. I thought about the angst I was suffering with Mum, so I promptly agreed and we signed a twelve-month lease. I knew it wasn't just a change in environment but a change in status for both of us, which concerned me, but Michelle seemed to take everything in her stride.

The place was furnished with the exception of the main bedroom. Before we moved in, she took me shopping with her and picked out a queen-size bed with all the nice trimmings. Over the following days we moved our personal stuff in, and by lunchtime Saturday, we had our first meal in our new home together. It felt pretty good. I was at last living independently, but I realized being part of a couple meant I had responsibility for another person, as well as myself.

I was a reasonable cook because I'd had plenty of practice, often helped by Sammy, who was magic in the kitchen, because my mother was often out of it. So I fed us mostly, although Michelle sometimes wouldn't eat for days. I worried about her. Eating good food every day was much smarter than starving yourself to lose weight, then pigging out on shit after the scales gave a better reading.

But it seemed to work; we were good in the bedroom and seemed compatible enough everywhere else. Michelle had always been an outgoing person, where I was the opposite, happy in my own company, particularly if I had a mate around, like Sammy. But Michelle loved a few drinks, the bright lights, and a good time. I was drawn into that lifestyle and, surprisingly, I began to enjoy myself. Dyslexia, through my short attention span, made it difficult to concentrate, so over the years I'd taught myself to speak using shorter sentences. But when fueled by alcohol, I seemed to string a lot more stuff together—whether I made sense or not was another thing,

I'd wake up many Sunday mornings remembering not much about the night before, only to find we'd been invited out for Sunday lunch, leaving little chance for me to dry out.

No way could I afford to lose my driver's license; it was my living, so I left the Ford at home, much to her annoyance. But I was drinking ten times more than I had in the past.

Michelle loved the social whirl, though sometimes I felt like another accessory of hers.

I met a whole new group of people. Almost all of them were products of the private-education system, some were at university, and others like myself were in the workforce. Michelle told everyone I was in middle management at the council office, which was bullshit, of course, because I was the mowing-gang foreman. Suddenly I understood my girlfriend had the potential to be the world's worst social climber, and I told her so after a big weekend when the grog had weakened my judgment.

She cracked it big-time. "You have no ambition," she said. "You have to face the realities of life—one has to move in the right circles to get on in this world, and the connections we've already made will prove invaluable in the future."

I did my standard thing and agreed with her, and she calmed down.
But it didn't end there.

Michelle sensed she had the upper hand and used the opportunity to outline my shortcomings as she saw them.

"I've felt deeply embarrassed on many occasions," she said. "How you seem confused and slow when counting anything, particularly money. You can't write properly, and you ramble on at times in front of people."

I was thunderstruck because she knew all about my learning difficulties, having been in the same year as Sammy and me.

Yet here she was, trying to shove my dyslexia in my face.

Whoopi Goldberg, Nelson Rockefeller, Agatha Christie, Steven Spielberg, Harry Belafonte, Winston Churchill, Richard Strauss.

At work, rather than progressing further, my "career" seemed to plateau, and while my mowing blokes seemed to like me and we worked well together as a group, there seemed little else to stimulate my mind. I knew I should be thinking laterally as I once had, looking for different ways to do things, but somehow I couldn't give a shit.

THE EFFECTS of my excessive lifestyle began to show; my weight increased, my system became sluggish. It was time to slow down, even if Michelle was oblivious to my physical problems.

At last I rang Sammy. He'd continued working out with Chart twice a week, even though Matt didn't approve. I smiled to myself; both Sammy and I had partners who preferred the bright lights and a good time while we enjoyed the basics of life. Keeping fit for Sammy and me wasn't a chore, and with Chart it had been fun. The following night I turned up for training after a four-month absence, Chart just shaking his head at me.

My body hurt, physically and mentally, without the discipline of Muay Thai and the respect it taught for both my body and my opponents. It was impossible to recover all my fitness in one night, but I still punished myself. Chart put Sammy up against me, I suspect to teach me a lesson, and I found myself on the mat and totally winded. Sammy picked me up, almost carried me into the locker room, and threw me under the shower. It wasn't a patronizing act, because despite our differences in size, we were usually evenly matched in the ring. This was caring, even loving behavior, and our past rocketed me back to earlier days. Sammy wanted me fit again, and I committed on the spot to the same days as him.

At least that would be two nights a week that I didn't have to worry about my social standing in the community.

Chapter 11
Losing My Mind

I MANAGED to keep my cool, and my domestic life settled down again.

Michelle was smart enough to understand that I could only tolerate a certain amount of shit before I exploded, and with our social life ever expanding, she didn't need me sitting around at home sulking and pissed off.

I was happy enough, but money was always short; often the Ford stayed home because I couldn't afford to run it, and there was no way I was risking any more on my credit card.

I tried to include Sammy in our social life, and we did go out with him and Matt on several occasions.

But while she didn't say so, Michelle was uncomfortable for some reason.

Not because they were a gay couple, but in my mind because neither Sammy nor Matt individually or collectively could advance her social aspirations.

I also had to admit that I still couldn't take to Matt. He was nice enough and we remained civil toward each other, but all he seemed to want out of life was a party. And usually a party full of screaming queens, which really frazzled my nerves.

WE HAD just signed a second one-year lease on the house, as the owners had decided to stay on in Queensland.

I had to admit Michelle and I settled into a pleasant enough routine, but I always looked forward to my two nights a week with Sammy, working out with Chart. I'd regained much of my fitness, and Sammy and I were evenly matched once again. For many people Muay Thai seems a bit basic and animalistic, but not when someone like Chart teaches it. Chart had such Asian wisdom that Sammy and I both found ourselves looking forward to the conversation with him before, during, and after the workout. And then there was Solada, Chart's wife. She had two young kids to look after, a home to run, and she worked part-time as a receptionist for a nearby clinic. Yet the moment Sammy and I turned up, she was there with drinks, smiles, and encouragement. So much so we looked forward to her company as well as her husband's training regime. Many nights there were snacks, even some amazing Thai soup that I loved so much Sammy reckoned I was addicted to *tom kha gai.*

I'd always thought when people got married a lot of bullshit went on.

My brother's wedding five years previously was out of control, his wife so appalled at her mother's antics and stage management they didn't speak to each other for months afterward. Poor Trav felt totally sidelined through the whole process, but Sally, his wife, made sure he felt part of the action. Swanning up the aisle, showing off to everyone wasn't what Sally wanted, so they walked on together. Same thing nearly happened to Ali, my lovely big sister. At least our mum was so zonked out of it she didn't much care what went on, but Ali had to tell her mother-in-law-to-be to fuck off two months before the wedding because she wanted to take over. Ali and Simon ended up doing their own thing, and we had a ripper party instead of a pissy reception.

So I had all this running through my mind when Michelle decided we should get married. I never even had a chance to propose; she just put it in such a way that it sounded sensible.

But then she started overorganizing and telling me how it was all about to happen. I had to remind her that we were already in credit card hell, and she'd best start saving our money, otherwise nothing would happen.

"That's what parents are for," she said, and suddenly Amanda, her mother, was in there with her ugly nose stuck into everything. When they told me who was to be my best man, I finally spat the dummy.

"There's only going to be one best man and that's Sammy," I said, "and if you don't like that, there won't be a wedding because I won't be there."

Amanda tried to be her sugary self and commented that "Samuel unfortunately has no connections at all and of course his orientation is not really all that nice."

That did it. I directed both women to sit down at the table while I had my say. My frustration and anger poured out unchecked for once in my life. Where I was normally rendered mute when rage overtook me, this time I found my voice in a big way.

"Firstly, if either of you ever speak about Sammy in that way again, you won't see me for dust, do you understand?"

They both stared at me and then nodded, round one to me.

"Secondly, when a marriage happens there are two people up there in front of the celebrant, because it takes TWO people to get married, not one, so it's logical that those two people make the decisions about what's going to happen, before, during and afterwards. That means Michelle and me; do you understand, Amanda?"

When I'd finished they sat there and Amanda decided to turn on the tears to see if that worked.

"I suggest you leave, before I forget I'm a gentleman and really say what's on my mind." Michelle reacted quickly and ushered her mother outside, the tears evaporating as she left the room.

Michelle sat quietly in front of me, her hopes dashed for a social wedding.

From a cathedral wedding, we'd gone to an open-air affair under an old fig tree at the reception rooms. The reception itself was to be finger food and a few drinks instead of a sit-down affair.

The guest list of 150-plus had shrunk to fifty.

Strangely enough I didn't feel an ogre, that I'd done something wrong, because it was common sense. We simply couldn't afford any more, and most of it was bullshit anyway.

Michelle became permanently depressed, not sleeping well, and despite her protestations, I refused to allow her parents to pay for anything more than the basics. Her father was a good bloke—he and I got on quite well together—but fucking Amanda and I were at the other end of the planet to each other. It was clear where Michelle's attitudes came from, and I wasn't going to budge for any bastard.

I began to have my doubts.

Dad was lukewarm, and so were my brother and my sister.

Sammy just sat there with negative body language. We knew each other so well, I didn't have to ask further. He finally looked at me with sorrowful eyes and spoke gently. "It's your business, Jacko," he said, "but you're so young, it's given me such a shock. Don't worry," he went on, "if anyone can make a go of marriage, you can because you're so loyal. And I'm most honored to be your best *person*," he said, hating the original ocker title as I knew he would.

FORTUNE SMILED on me for once and some extra hours at work came my way, so we could save some money. Within six weeks the credit card had been paid off and we started saving for the wedding in earnest. We both worked for Craig Murray, the operations manager, and Michelle's promotion as his PA came just at the right time.

She wanted to go out and celebrate with our "friends," but I put my foot down. A few quiet drinks at home seemed a good idea under the circumstances, but she thought otherwise.

"You're a cruel, thoughtless person and you'll never amount to anything because you don't mix socially."

Someone dropped her home at 2:30 a.m., and I wasn't impressed.

The next day she had the mother of all hangovers. I left her holding her head as I rode my trusty bike to work.

While Craig Murray had rewarded my missus, he appeared to take it out on me, as during the week I always pulled the shifts in the outer suburbs even though I was mowing foreman.

But the extra pay and the severely restricted social life did the trick. Michelle just couldn't believe where all the money came from, and I was able to reregister the Ford and begin using it again.

The offers for financial assistance were coming in from her family and were insulting. I had another altercation with them, this time with both her parents.

I laid it on the line. They could pay for her dress and the wedding cars; that was it. I was paying for the celebrant, and my father was helping us with the reception.

When Amanda decided to interfere again, I refused to listen.

"Amanda," I said, "we're not having any more than fifty people. We're not inviting people I've never met before just because you think they're nice and may improve your social standing."

I thought maybe I'd gone too far, but I had an ally I hadn't counted on—Geoff, Michelle's father. We appeared to be on the same page even though I'd thoroughly insulted his missus.

"I reckon you're ace, mate," he said. "I really admire your independence."

Amanda went a lovely shade of puce, and it was obvious our Geoffrey would be short on nooky for quite some time.

Something told me not to get in over my head financially. Married life was hard work, and the tales of couples splitting up because of financial hardship at this time were clearly understandable. I didn't want to be in that category.

Chapter 12
The Big Day

THE WEDDING day arrived at last and with it a sense of relief. I just wanted to get it over with so life could return to some sort of normality.

Some women became different people immediately when the word wedding was breathed. Illogical people, with a string of "simply must haves" for the special day. I thought Michelle at last had calmed down and become more sensible; she spent the final night back with her parents, so I stayed over with Sammy and Isobel, and we had a ball together, with Matt nowhere to be seen.

Sammy and I sat in the groom's room at the reception center, cooling our heels; we had nearly an hour before the ceremony, but we both couldn't stand being late for anything, let alone today.

Michelle, on the other hand, would be fashionably late—fucking Amanda would see to that. Amanda informed me that only cretins and lower-class brides arrived early, so I had to suck it up for once. She and her daughter were totally in sync with each other on the day, so while I'd been victorious on the things that cost money, they were determined to show off in front of as many people as possible. To the point where poor bloody old Geoffrey was trussed up like a turkey so he could walk Amanda up the aisle first! Then return to escort his daughter.

Sammy looked pensive, and suddenly I realized I hadn't seen Matt out front.

"Matt sends his apologies," Sammy said wistfully, no doubt knowing we hadn't exactly been close. I nodded and thanked him, not willing to pursue the matter further and spoil Sammy's day.

The time rolled on, three o'clock came and went, as I knew it would, and, my nerves on edge, we decided to have a quick scotch each, served by a really nice young waiter who looked sympathetic. "Don't worry," he said. "I've only ever seen one bride on time since I've worked here."

I'd just taken a nice sip of my drink when there was a tap on the door and the manageress of the reception center put her head in the door.

"Someone to see you," she said.

Sammy and I looked in astonishment as a disheveled Joanne Murray almost fell in the door brandishing a mobile phone in her hand.

"Sorry to do this to you, Jackson, but I thought you should see this before you get married. At least you can make up your own mind about things, where I didn't have that opportunity."

I tried to absorb her words but wasn't doing so well.

I didn't even know her all that well, except she always seemed a nice person, someone to chat to at work functions when she attended with Craig.

But Sammy was streets ahead. "What do you have there, Mrs. Murray?"

"My husband has always been an egomaniac," she explained. "He went out last night for a short while and left his phone on the kitchen bench. It chirped, a text message had come in, and I picked it up in case it was urgent. It was Michelle but nothing to do with work. Not the sort of message a PA has for her boss unless it's really personal."

Suddenly Joanne Murray had my complete attention.

"I'm glad I snooped and looked further, because while it's all too late for me, at least you still have the element of choice, Jackson. I found this video when I looked at his photos. There's no doubt who the players are. Fancy recording a sordid little affair like this and deliberately leaving it there for your personal titillation afterward." She handed the phone to Sammy, who passed it over to me. There was my missus, her face visible for a second or two, then it focused back on what Craig Murray had to offer as he had his way with Michelle. I showed it to Sammy so he would understand completely what was happening.

Just then there was another tap at the door.

"Your bride has arrived," the manageress said sweetly.

I turned to Joanne Murray, who was now looking forlorn, and I felt sorry for her. "Thank you so much, Mrs. Murray, what you've done must have been difficult. When this is over and things have calmed down, I promise I'll be in touch."

I turned to Sammy. "Can you please copy that video onto your phone and then give it back to Mrs. Murray?"

Brandishing Sammy's phone, I charged out to where the limousine had pulled up in the gravel driveway, the photographers taking happy snaps.

Take a pic of this one, I thought, *and you'll see someone very fucking unhappy.*

"What are you doing here?" Amanda hissed through her teeth. "You're supposed to be with the celebrant."

I waved the phone in her face. "Why don't you fuck off, Amanda, unless you'd like to see what your fucking daughter has been doing in her spare time, or maybe even as part of her work duties as Craig Murray's PA."

I turned to Michelle, who was smart enough to know it was all over, but the information didn't stop her from trying. "This is so embarrassing for all of us, but why can't we be adult about this, go ahead with the ceremony, and have a nice no-fault divorce afterward? After a few months of course, just tell everyone it didn't work out."

I didn't have a chance to reply. Magically, Sammy was there and turned to me first. "Why don't you go back to the room and just wait for me there," he said, smiling that bloody Sammy smile that puts everyone at ease. "There'll be no wedding," he said to the limo driver. "Would you kindly drive the bridal party home."

A short time later Sammy's voice came over the public-address system.

"Ladies and gentlemen, thank you for your attendance today. Michelle and Jackson have made a mutual decision not to proceed in marriage, so there will be no wedding today. We apologize for the inconvenience."

As he was finishing up, Dad walked in the door, and I bawled my bloody eyes out on his shoulder. Then the rest of my family arrived; poor Mum looked more confused than ever, but both Trav and Ali looked triumphant.

Dad and I settled the account with the reception center, loading up with enough tucker to feed an army, and we went back to my parents' house for a party.

Before I could do anything else, Isobel was there, her face full of concern. She and Sammy wanted me to move in with them, and they wanted me to do it today before Michelle and her bloody lot could interfere.

"I hear you, and thanks so much, but what about Matt, Sammy?"

"We broke up, Jacko," Sammy said, "several weeks ago. It was, unlike your situation, completely amicable. We're still good friends. Matt's living with his dad again, whose health isn't good, so things have worked out much better than expected."

I looked at Isobel, who was beaming at me, and I thought how lucky I was to have this surrogate family who cared for me no matter what, and promptly burst into tears again, my emotions raw from being pulled in several directions all at once.

Three hours later, using Isobel's old Peugeot and the Ford, there was no trace of me at my former residence. The lease was up for renewal in just three weeks, so I left an e-mail for the agent that I was moving out. I would go in and pay my share of the rent personally—I had no intention of leaving any money around the house for Michelle to lay her hands on.

Isobel and Sammy looked on in admiration; I'd become a good manager by default.

Chapter 13
A New Start

WE ALWAYS enjoyed each other's company, so it was no surprise how quickly Sammy, Isobel, and I settled in together. Craig Murray and Michelle both disappeared, and we assumed they'd gone off together once Joanne blew the whistle on them. It seemed unbelievable that the person I seemed to know in Michelle could be so deceitful, coldly planning to keep her affair going with Craig Murray after we were married.

I kept my word and rang Joanne Murray, calling around with Sammy, with a nice bunch of flowers and something for her two kids. They were only small, one six, the other four, and it was clear Joanne was battling to make ends meet.

This was my first chance to speak to her since that horrible day two weeks ago.

"Thank you again for your honesty and your bravery, but I guess in helping me, you're now the breadwinner."

"I hate deceit also, Jackson. I just hope the kids can grow up with me as a good role model, regardless of our circumstances. Mum and Dad are helping us until I can find full-time work, my current part-time job isn't enough to pay the mortgage and feed and clothe them."

Sammy had been following the conversation, and he excused himself to make a phone call, returning soon after. "My mother knows the welfare system, Mrs. Murray. You should have immediate help and a sympathetic ear at Centrelink if you ring this person."

I'D BEEN dreading returning to work, with the grapevine working overtime. The operations manager had disappeared without trace, as had his PA. No resignations, no forwarding address, just skipped town leaving the cuckolded fiancé behind—me.

I'd returned earlier than expected because without a honeymoon, I thought working was preferable to sitting around.

The shed was quiet, the machines lined up in readiness for the day ahead, but I wasn't happy. The mowers were dirty-looking, and when I looked at the service sheets, I realized very little had been done since I went on leave.

With no one supervising, and no clerical backup, the maintenance blokes were uncertain of their priorities, and I knew we'd start having breakdowns in the field if it continued.

The guys began to arrive for work, and I waited for the smirks, the limp-dick jokes, and the embarrassed silences, but to my amazement, none of that happened. Instead they responded with respectful handshakes, some very un-Australian male cuddles, and offers of everything from accommodation and food to sex with their sisters.

I wondered who would be running the place in Craig's absence because there were signs of neglect everywhere. I soon found out.

Before I had a chance to start work properly, Mr. Davis arrived at the depot.

Our CEO was a great guy, and he asked me to join him in Craig's former office.

"Jacko, I'd like you to take over on a temporary basis, until we can establish whether Craig Murray is likely to return. Then the City will go through the normal selection process to fill the position permanently."

His eyes softened when he understood he'd probably hit a raw nerve, but I hastened to put him at ease.

"It's okay," I said. "I'm over it, and to be honest I reckon I'm in a better place right now. I'm living with a friend and his mum, they're wonderful, and they've given me a great place to go home to. The guys here, at least the ones I've spoken to, are 100 percent on side, and that's shocked me."

"Why should it shock you, son? In two years you've managed to build a team spirit that never existed. Our turnover of staff in this area was worrying, but not one single person has moved on since you've been foreman. With the exception of your ex-boss, of course."

"Yeah, and with my ex-missus," I said with a laugh.

He stood up and threw his arms around me, as many of my workmates had done. "You're an extraordinary young man. I don't know what it is, but after all you've been through, there's a fire in your belly once more and a desire to excel, I suspect. Anything you need to get the job done, just ask. You'll need someone to get the wages done, to—ah—replace Michelle?"

He was right, I was enthusiastic once more.

My mind cleared, and I seemed to have put Michelle behind me so easily I almost felt guilty. I'd never loved her, but I'd been lonely at the time and had capitulated. Many people around the world had married for lesser reasons, but I knew it had been wrong for me to agree.

I'D BEEN living with Sammy and Isobel for some time now, my spirits lifting as time passed. For the first time in years, I was really happy, and I enjoyed the sensation.

Sammy continued working long hours in the final year of his degree and also coached kids with learning difficulties, just as he'd done with me. Isobel also had a busy schedule, running night courses at the local TAFE, so I took over as cook.

I was so content in the Collins home. Everything I did was appreciated, and the place roared along like a well-oiled machine, each of us supporting the other.

Sammy moved back into the big house, and the little flat he'd shared with Matt remained empty. Isobel gave me the room next to his, but I only slept there. I made sure I was around when they came home, supper made and a bright warm kitchen. "Don't ever leave," Isobel said. "I could get used to this."

I gave Sammy the spare keys for the Ford, which surprised him, but I insisted. So he dropped me at work most mornings and kept the car during the day. Either he or Isobel were there to collect me from work every evening.

Sammy took on more clients as a result of his increased transport mobility and made some serious money without even a full-time job. When he showed me his savings account, I nearly fell over. We were both doing very nicely, thank you very much.

As I was locking up only two days later, my phone buzzed, and it was Mr. Davis. "We have a replacement for Michelle, and I think you'll like her. Her name is Barbara Shields, and she'll be there first thing tomorrow morning ready for work."

Barbara Shields was everyone's mother.

I did like her immediately because she was approachable and understanding, the very qualities a dyslexic person needs around them in a work situation.

I explained how it affected me and why I found it difficult to do certain things, particularly writing stuff. She nodded sympathetically, and I wondered how she seemed to catch on so quickly. "My eldest boy has similar learning difficulties, but he's really fortunate that he has a wonderful part-time teacher, Mr. Collins. He's transformed his life," she said, as I sat there with damp eyes and explained we had something in common in our lives—Sammy.

Mrs. Shields had the payroll done in record time each week, and the office running so efficiently she regularly sought out other projects. The workshop was cleaned out, as was the parts store. The service and maintenance guys were terrified of her and found it was easier to do what she wanted rather than argue.

Mr. Davis commented on how well the place ran along "from the bottom up," he said with a smile. Somehow I was increasingly involved in making decisions on stuff for which I'd received no training at all. Mrs. Shields counseled me when I asked for help, and Mr. Davis was a phone call away.

I was smart enough to insist on a meeting with Mr. Davis every Monday, and Mrs. Shields always sat in with us.

It was at one of these meetings, and after a stressful previous week, I lost it.

There were discrepancies in the fuel account; the usage had slowly increased every week, but the information I had was incomplete. We'd started to log fuel use on the garbage trucks because I suspected that's where it was going. The drivers were asked to keep records of usage for each vehicle, and suddenly there was a strike threatened.

And here we were in our meeting, with Mr. Davis grinning broadly at me as I spat the dummy. Mrs. Shields also smiled, and it felt like they were laughing at me. I felt like I was back in school, struggling to make sense of something obvious, and I reacted angrily.

"Congratulations," Mr. Davis said. I stopped my ranting and stared at him.

"You're the first person around here to wake up to the few who use the good guys in the union as a front for some extra pocket money. I grew up in the bush not so far from here," he continued, "and we had a problem with black snakes around the house. My mother would pour a bucketful of boiling water down the holes near the back door, and they'd come charging out, mad as hell so my dad could fix 'em with a shovel. That's what you've done with the garbos, and that's why they're threatening to go on strike."

Mrs. Shields chuckled at the analogy and I felt better.

"So do you have any idea who the ringleader is?"

"Yes," I said, "I've had my ear to the ground. There's one guy who has a mate with an earth-moving business. He evidently stops during his round at about 5:30 a.m., and they pump out one of the truck's tanks. All done in a few minutes. He's tried to con the other drivers without success, and he's the guy who has the ear of the union. The other guys are too scared to say anything."

Mr. Davis took the address of the earth-moving business, and a week later the driver quietly resigned.

Mrs. Shields and the yardman, Bernie, were issued keys, and the three of us logged fuel usage on everything with a diesel engine.

The fuel bill dropped like a stone; even I was amazed.

I'd somehow managed to find the good guys in the union as a result, and I felt I'd achieved something. But I was tired, bloody tired, as I prepared to take some time off.

I went with the blessing of Mr. Davis and Mrs. Shields; they would keep the place going with some technical input.

I DRAGGED myself home. I didn't know exactly why I felt so tired, but I had a sneaking suspicion. More to do with my personal life and mindset. As happy and well balanced as my life had become, I knew I had to make some profound changes regarding my future.

Chapter 14
A Holiday

I NAGGED Sammy to the point where he was probably sick of me, but it was clear he could do with some time away, as I certainly could. September school holidays meant he had a clear two weeks off, and I had Mr. Davis's blessing for the same period.

Together we applied for our passports. We were going to Phuket, and we were going to have a ball. Sit under a palm tree and drink martinis all day. Eat Asian food, which we both loved.

With the bonus of our two most favorite people visiting their family in Phuket Town at the same time—Chart and Solada.

I felt guilty leaving Isobel behind and said so. But in her beautiful, unselfish way, she wanted Sammy and me to do our own thing, and we didn't need an old woman hanging around.

Sammy began to unwind. Even with over seven hours to Kuala Lumpur and a further two to Phuket, he was madly hyped up when we arrived. As we waited for our bags at the carousel, Sammy slipped his hand into mine, and he squeezed my fingers. A rough-looking woman with a strident Australian accent took a swig out of her first stubby for the day and just sneered at us with a look of pure hatred on her face.

Jesus, I thought, *I need to have that talk with Sammy as soon as possible, but I'm frightened I'll lose my best friend.*

I found the hotel bus and we rode for another hour or so, staring out the windows at the exotic landscape going past. The colors were so much brighter than home, the vegetation tropical and lush.

We came over the hill down into Patong Beach, and the sea gleamed an azure blue, sparkling through the trees along the foreshore.

Finally we were in our room, and because the hotel was overbooked, we were upgraded to a bigger room at the same price. With its own lounge room and little kitchen. A huge bedroom with a king-size bed and a bathroom big enough for a party.

"Gentlemen," the manager said, after escorting us to the room, "I'm sorry for the mix-up. Can we put another fold-up bed in there for you?"

We looked at each other and shook our heads. "No, that's fine," Sammy said. "We're quite used to sharing a bed. The room's lovely."

We unpacked our stuff—or rather Sammy unpacked both cases—and we changed into shorts and sandals. We made contact with Chart and Solada and agreed to meet them in two days' time, giving them some space with their extended family.

Outside it was a different world, exciting and colorful.

"Look." Sammy's eyes shone. "Muay Thai, Patong version."

"Tonight, tonight," the speaker intoned, "Muay Thai team battle, Thailand versus the rest of the world. Tonight, tonight, Monday night."

There was a one-ton ute with a portable stage built over the load area, which they'd turned into a mini boxing ring, and two guys were slapping each other around in a desultory fashion, but enough for spectators to get the general idea. Chart had given us the background on this stuff and assured us it was just playacting, just like the wrestling on television back home.

Then we turned into the Bangla Walking Street. It was early and the street wasn't closed to vehicular traffic just yet. But it was still its own place, lined with bars and full of Australians, English, Americans, Europeans, and ladies of the night determinedly working the day shift. The girls—and a few boys—seemed focused on the target market: senior-aged guys probably, looking to resurrect their sex life and live out their dreams for a while.

There were stalls selling everything from naughty objects through every type of souvenir imaginable. At every step, we faced a passionate plea to buy this wonderful whatsit because life couldn't proceed without it. I liked some of the stuff, but Sammy had other ideas. "No, Jackson, save your money. If you take any of that shit home, you know where it'll end up, don't you?" I agreed glumly; I knew he hated the stuff, but bugger it, some of it was really different, and I could imagine it sitting on my chest of drawers in my bedroom, a reminder of our first holiday together.

We found a great seafood restaurant across the road from the waterfront, and to my delight they had a seafood variant to tom kha gai: *tom kha talay*. With some steamed rice it was stunning. Solada had given us a deep appreciation of Thai food, while Chart had been our teacher of Thai culture.

On greeting, thanking people, and recognizing the majesty of another human being, Chart demonstrated the wai to us: hands clasped together, brought to near the nose, and performed with a little bow. We were received warmly by all the local people, but noticed that many other foreigners or farangs were rude and ignorant, and I thought how fortunate Sammy and I had been to have Chart and Solada in our lives.

Sammy took my hand again as we walked back to the hotel, and it felt just like going to school again as ten-year-olds. The odd stares came from farangs, but the Thai people just seemed so cool. No way was I going to let Sammy down; we'd traveled too far through so much shit together.

How am I going to broach this bloody subject without Sammy cracking the shits on me? Misery in paradise, all this beautiful tropical splendor, palm trees, golden sand, clear blue water, lovely people, and I have to fuck up the only meaningful friendship I've ever had.

We walked into the room, and I asked him to sit next to me on the big comfy sofa in the lounge room. He looked at me with those big puppy-dog eyes, and I knew I had to do it.

"Look," I said, "there's something on my mind. It's been that way even before Michelle and I got together, and I need to spit it out."

"Well, spit it, then."

I cleared my throat and the doorbell shrilled.

Cursing it, I threw the door open, and there stood Matt.

"What are you doing here?" I snapped.

I looked from one to the other without waiting for an explanation, and then I lost it.

"Well fucking enjoy yourselves," I shouted, running out the door like a maniac, my self-esteem in tatters and my temper as hot as a gas barbecue.

Moving fast, but not far, I found myself at a bar on Walking Street. The ladyboys had begun parading up and down in their finery with huge tall feathered headdresses, charging punters for the opportunity to have their photograph taken with them.

I watched them for a moment, forgetting my own misery. Then reality set in again as I sighed, working out how I could get myself out of the situation I'd found myself in. Probably catch another flight home tomorrow afternoon.

"Jesus, you can bloody run."

Matt stood there, but before I had a chance to say anything, he pointed to a stool at the quiet end of the bar. Something in his manner suggested confidence and authority, and I did as I was told and waited until he came over with two beers.

"What did you do that for?" he asked bluntly.

"Well you two are obviously an item again, and I didn't want to get in the way."

He shook his head sadly and smiled what I thought was a wistful sort of smile. "Some people are as thick as a brick, and you're no exception, Jacko. Sammy and I broke up because on his own admission, he couldn't get a certain person out of his head—you."

Chapter 15
True Paradise

WITH MATT'S help I found a stall selling magnificent orchids, and after explaining their purpose, the owner giggled and put them together into a stunning presentation vase.

Then I bolted for the room, peace offering in hand.

I arrived outside the door realizing I'd left my key card behind, so I rang the bell like a florist with a special delivery.

The door flung open. He'd been crying, and my heart nearly broke in two.

"Jacko, where have you been? I was so worried about you I was nearly sick."

I couldn't say anything much because I too was choked up, but I managed to thrust the flowers into his hand and say, "These are for you. I'm sorry I made a dick of myself."

His eyes shone.

Sammy always loved flowers; he loved growing them, displaying them, and I knew he loved them as a gift.

"Well," he said with a grin, "they're beautiful, thank you, but really I'm as much to blame as you are."

"No, you're not," I said, deciding I had to ramp up the stakes. First I had to wipe away his tears, very unromantically, with my thumb. Then I did what I have should have done many years ago and kissed him, on the lips. Beautiful, full, puffy pillows they were, and suddenly the world lit up, it was like someone had just turned the lights on.

We stood there gazing at each other in bloody wonderment as we leaned in and did it again. There was love in Sammy's eyes, but I could see the concern also, one of the benefits of some dyslexic people seeing things on a different level.

"Matt told me everything," I explained. "He found me at a bar about to drown my sorrows." Sammy had the decency to blush and put his head down, looking embarrassed. "The fact is we've both been idiots," I continued, "because I was too stupid to admit I was in love with my best mate. I tried to move on without you and look what happened."

I took a deep breath and told Sammy the truth. "I think my orientation is still straight, but the fact is that I've never loved anyone except you, period. When we finished school and we had those few months helping Dad and hanging with each other, the feelings intensified. But then Matt came along, and I knew I'd left my run too late. So I let Michelle have her way. But I never loved her, and I told her so."

Sammy's frown cleared and I relaxed, knowing I'd probably made my point.

"Jackson"—I understood the formality meant he was about to say something profound—"if you say you love me, then that's enough, because your character is such that I trust you implicitly. I love you, Jacko." I smiled at my mate.

"I bloody love you too," I said. "Now can I have a cuddle?"

We were on the bed together and somehow all my concerns about intimacy with a bloke evaporated on the spot. Because it was Sammy, my Sammy.

Those beautiful, puffy pink pillow lips were there and I sank onto them, and I was in heaven. Sammy's kisses were like velvet, and when our lips connected, it was like bloody heaven on earth. Soon there was a naughty thrust of tongue from Sammy and the game went up a notch. My shorts and undies went flying against the wall, dragged off me so Sammy could look at his new play toy. I was hard as a rock, and he looked at it with a puzzled expression on his face. "You've always done that to me," I said, "particularly lately. I should have taken more notice of Mother Nature, shouldn't I?"

It was his turn as he tried to be delicate and get rid of his gear, but I became impatient. I ripped the things off him and they joined my stuff on the floor.

Sammy was beautiful. But at this moment I tried to take a snapshot in my brain so I'd remember always what he looked like without clothes.

The work with Chart had turned Sammy into an athlete. The soft, smoothly contoured body that was Sammy as a young kid had been transformed. Yes, I'd seen him many times in the raw before and after training; the difference was that Sammy was now mine. We were a couple, and I gazed with wonderment at that enormous appendage that was complemented by Sammy's Muay Thai training and his body.

Because Sammy had grown more masculine in looks while remaining the same beautiful person, and that turned me on like nothing else.

"Jacko," he purred, "just relax and let me show you. Nothing is all that different. Concentrate on enjoying yourself, and it'll all come naturally."

I thought I knew my way around but I nearly jumped off the bed when he went down on me. I begged him to stop after a couple of minutes because all sense of control had disappeared.

It was so new to me I didn't think I'd know what to do—yet it all just fell into place.

It was my turn; I was disappointed I could hardly get the huge thing in my mouth, but after a while I really got into it and Sammy started moaning. Then we sixty-nined and came together in a rush, yelling out in sheer pleasure.

At no stage in my life had I experienced such intense passion with anyone.

Sammy echoed my thoughts; it was the same for him.

We slept like babies for a few hours and did it all again, even though it was by now the middle of the night.

I finally woke the next morning, with Sammy's head on my chest.

"Are we dreaming?" he asked, and I shook my head.

"It's reality, all right, welcome to the first day of the rest of your life."

WE WERE in danger of missing breakfast, so we threw ourselves under the shower.

I pulled the door shut and simply couldn't help myself; I pushed him against the wall outside our room in the warm air and passionately kissed him, which was returned with fervor. There was a giggle from the Thai girl who was cleaning the room next to ours, and we turned politely, giving her a wai.

I gave her a tip, asking her if she would clean our room as soon as possible, and she nodded, smiling. I couldn't tell what she said exactly, but it was something to do with "so beautiful"—Sammy heard it as well.

We roared into the breakfast room with a few minutes to spare and raced over to the eggs—fuck the fruit, we needed a protein fix and fast.

I was aware I'd lost my mind, I was so much in love, and I was enjoying the experience. I sat at our table outside on the patio eating, talking, and staring at my new partner, completely oblivious to everything and everybody around us.

"Poofter cunts."

I didn't know where the shout came from but I copped a biff under the ear.

Then screaming as Sammy kicked a tat-covered, dirty-looking bloke in the nuts.

The noise continued but from two spaced-out, dirty-looking females who saw their nightly root quickly disappearing in a blur of pain.

A second bloke, also a tattooist's wet dream, was full of apologies and was trying desperately to keep the peace and get the group of misfits out of the breakfast room.

"Ice," Sammy muttered, "but no bastard hits my boyfriend and gets away with it. You all right, darling?" I nodded, a broad smile on my face. Sammy probably thought I was mad, but I was now both his boyfriend and his darling, and as far as I was concerned, life couldn't get any better.

Chapter 16
Playtime in Paradise

WE WENT back to bed after breakfast, and if anything our libidos accelerated.

Sammy showed me how to make myself nice and clean with the douche hose, part of many Asian toilets. "All gay boys should practice cleanliness this way," he explained, and I nodded stupidly, full of raging hormones.

He stood up over me on the bed, then sat down, impaling himself, and I went on another trip to heaven. "Your education is proceeding to plan," Sammy told me happily as he allowed me to swing over on top of him, and we finished in a sheen of perspiration, with the air conditioning running flat-out. We showered again and slept in each other's arms.

It simply didn't matter to me what I did in bed, as long as it was with Sammy.

Simple. It all felt so natural, so *right*. But I was in love. It surprised me with its intensity, and I suspected Sammy's equally enthusiastic response deepened my feelings even further.

Sammy talked me through tops and bottoms. Typical of Sammy, he was logical and full of loving information—because it was me. I now understood that the douche hose wasn't just for show. He read my eyes, knowing I had a lot to process, but also I wanted to experience everything, bottoming in particular.

"Jacko, don't concern yourself. That can only come when you're ready and not before. I could hurt you with my big boy." Sammy pointed at the bloody monster, which had climbed skyward again, but I was on a mission.

"I want to try it and I want it now," I said with a pout.

"Get dressed, darling, and we'll go shopping."

I looked at him as if he'd lost his mind.

"Shopping?" I raised my eyebrows, worried we were losing good, productive rooting time.

"Yes," my beautiful bloke replied, "and it is also time for some food, some more soup, and an extra helping of rice." He grinned at me. "Because we need to keep our strength up, don't we?"

So we went bloody shopping. I stamped around like an angry pissant, desperate to get back to the bedroom and the new delights I'd discovered.

The shopping expedition involved something quite specific, I felt, as I ran after Sammy. So I thought I'd better calm down, my normal, impatient self shouting in my head to "do it now."

He turned suddenly and walked into a market, still quiet at this time of day because the heat was steadily increasing. To my horror he stopped at a stall with every known sex toy for sale. He looked thoughtfully at me as he picked up several dildos, finally choosing three of them, plus a huge tube of lube.

I looked wildly around, in case there was anyone looking, my mother's religious mindset hanging around in my subconscious, even though I'd rejected that stuff years ago. Then I saw the amused look on Sammy's face, and the world righted itself again. I smiled inwardly; I was always the first to walk hand in hand with Sammy for all those years when I was supposedly a straight boy; why should an armful of dildos make any difference now we were an item?

As we walked back to the hotel, I was shitting myself, my heart pounding in my ribs. Sammy grinned at me, reading my mind again, and took my hand, calming me down. A middle-aged American couple walked toward us, scowling, their accents a contrast to the soft tones of the Thai people around us. I braced myself for criticism, imagining they came from a Bible-bashing enclave somewhere in the Midwest, but I stumbled and nearly fell over on the broken cement of the footpath. Immediately they reached out and steadied me, and the woman's voice, softer now, said clearly, "You guys just have to watch your choice of footwear. Stilettos were not meant for Thailand, my dears—even the ladyboys stay off the footpaths."

We laughed at them and with them, the tension broken for me. All that was needed was for the shopping bag to break and for the dildos to spill out onto the footpath, and we'd keep them entertained for hours.

We ran into our room and locked the door with the security chain. Without being asked I went into the bathroom and completed my ablutions, my boyfriend looking on approvingly.

Over the next few hours, my body was prepared for what was now the main event. Finally he used the largest of the dildos on me, and the peculiar, unfamiliar feeling was there again, and I nearly lifted off the bed.

"That's your prostate," Sammy said with a smile, and at last I began to understand a little why many gay boys choose anal intercourse to satisfy their libidos.

More than curious now, I took charge.

"I want to be a power bottom, so lie on your back so I can sit on you."

He smiled broadly, his huge thing beautiful in its sleek hardness.

It hardly hurt at all; I had this sense of fullness as I slipped farther and farther down, breaching the final barrier with a soft "plop."

I used my muscles the way Sammy had taught me, but the position was awkward for me. I turned onto my back, he put a pillow under my bottom, and he was in again. This time he hit my prostate and I roared with lust, the light switching on in my stupid brain. Because this was meant to be. My previous view of the world was that Sammy would bottom for me because he was smaller in stature, but I hadn't counted on the fact that I now found I loved being fucked. I adored it, and Sammy did everything right, a thoughtful and considerate lover focused on giving me an enjoyable time as well as himself. We just fit together so well, and I surprised myself by hardly feeling sore at all. We were at it for hours; both of us were insatiable, it appeared.

We stopped when our bodies told us to, and when we needed more fuel by way of the beautiful Thai food.

We were meeting Chart and Solada the following day; somehow time had just run away from us, and we reluctantly agreed that it would be rude to cancel.

"What would you like to see for the remainder of our holiday?" Sammy asked. "There's some nice temples and stuff up the coast, I believe."

"No."

"No?" he echoed.

"I'd like to see plenty of ceilings, and the missionary position is the only religion I need."

Chapter 17
Friends in Paradise

WE WALKED into the family home in Phuket Town, and Solada embraced us, followed by Chart. Then to our initial embarrassment, Chart exchanged a look with his wife and gave us a wai. Most Asian people display very little emotion, but when our Muay Thai teacher turned to us, the tears flowed down his cheeks. "At last," he said, and Solada gave a little shriek, embracing us again, making enough noise to bring their family around, watching as Chart and Solada danced around us, clapping their hands and hugging us. "When did this happen?" Chart asked seriously.

"The magic of Phuket," Sammy said, and I agreed, feeling a bit overwhelmed.

They led us into a comfortable room at the rear of the house, and Chart introduced his aged parents, Pa and Ma, his brother and sister-in-law, and several children and grandchildren. All living, I guessed, quite harmoniously together.

Chart brought out a fiery liqueur of sorts to toast our health, and only then, with just ourselves and Solada present, did he elaborate.

He took his wife's hand, who was still sobbing and laughing at the same time, and began speaking. "From the first time you boys came to me all those years ago, I wondered if this would happen. We prayed for it because we felt it was meant to be, and we knew you were both unhappy at various times when you were separate from each other. Our prayers have been answered, and we will thank the Lord Buddha because you have given us great joy. But never again will I have you two fight each other. Muay Thai is also about loving, and a couple should not fight each other. Life for you now is a shared path together, not a battle in the ring. Do you understand?"

We nodded, both of us speechless for once.

The family wanted us to be their guests for a celebratory meal, so they booked a theater restaurant in Phuket Town a week away, a few days before we left for home.

Back at the hotel, I crashed on the bed and was only awoken by a hot-looking guy who slipped under the sheets with me. So many years ago, a sweet-smelling Sammy had slipped into my bed at home to comfort me when Lily died. This was similar, but without the tragedy, quite the opposite. But it was Sammy again, a consistent presence in my life and a reassurance that someone loved me more than anyone else in the world. I knew what I wanted now and I knew it was forever, but what lay immediately ahead was my responsibility to put together.

THE BELL chirped and Sammy answered the door to our hotel room.

Matt crouched to one side in the doorway and grinned at us both. "Do I need a crash helmet this time, or maybe a parachute?"

"Depends," I said, "you might need both if you're going to be a bloody bitch about it." He and Sammy looked at each other, then laughed at me as I qualified for queen status. I went over to Matt and cuddled him—after Sammy he'd become my best mate, simple. No one had ever been so kind, loving, and unselfish to me, ever. I'd apologized over and over for being such a dick over the years, but he understood. Poor bloody Matt was by sheer coincidence in Phuket working on a hotel chain's website for a few extra dollars. And I thought he'd taken up with Sammy again. I told him quietly what I was planning and he understood, pleased at his part in the little performance.

The door buzzer sounded again, and I thought how we might as well be in the middle of a marketplace, with everyone coming and going. I opened the door to find Scott, the guy who'd apologized for his mate's actions when I was given the big biffo in the breakfast room. He'd visited our room the same day, admitting he'd been dragged into the Phuket holiday at the last moment.

He found his mate had become an ice user, and the whores who came along for the ride were so vile he couldn't bear to be in the same room as them.

The management kicked the dickheads out, and Scott took over the room. He'd given us a magnificent magnum of champagne to make up, which we thought a bit strange, and according to Sammy, his taste was impeccable. It simply didn't fit with Scott's lifestyle in Sydney's western suburbs. We knew he was a sparky, but spending a few dollars didn't seem to worry him.

He seemed different today, however, the tattoos overshadowed by smart shorts, a well-pressed tee, and the latest shoes.

I was about to start shit stirring when Sammy introduced him to Matt, and we had our answer. It was like a bolt of electricity arced between them, and we watched as they eyed each other up and down.

Our Scott was family.

And Matt looked like a lovestruck teenager.

Chapter 18
Choreography in Paradise

AS HAPPY as we were, there were still moments where Sammy looked thoughtful, just as he'd done a few days ago when our worlds collided and we became a couple. I wondered how some of the famous dyslexics of history would have handled a situation like this, to have the most important thing in your life within your grasp but not quite able to seal the deal. I simply had to keep going and trust my judgment; there was no easy option.

I explained to Sammy that Solada wanted to take me shopping.

She actually fronted Sammy to seek his permission and said she knew he would understand because he was a kind and thoughtful person, someone who allowed his partner some flexibility.

Jesus, girl, what an ace fibber you are.

Before Sammy could respond, Chart was there to take him out on a mission of his own. Sammy grinned at me and shook his head; this was the price of a relationship, we had to share each other around, so we accepted their kindness and agreed to meet later in the day.

Solada and I finished our business in record time, and I had the goods hidden in a place where they simply wouldn't be found. Chart had taken Sammy to the boxing stadium, where Sammy'd been coerced into a practice bout with one of the local boys. Sammy came away shaking his head. "It's not sport here. This was thuggery," he said, "all show for the tourists, and the kids are paid a pittance. They even tried to sign me up for the international team. But the Australian boys who are here to learn Muay Thai are everywhere."

THE RESTAURANT was quiet when we arrived, a teak-timbered place with a vaulted ceiling in thatch, looking as if it had been there for a hundred years. Chart's family was there already.

I knew something of the Thai mindset regarding sexuality. Ladyboys had been part of the culture for hundreds of years, yet to have a gay son or daughter was still frowned upon by some traditional families. Not this family. Pa had a gay brother whom he loved dearly, as did Ma, and the remainder of the family followed. So when Sammy and I were outed by Chart and Solada, it became a big deal in a very positive way. Pa was clearly excited, his rheumy eyes sparkling behind gold-rimmed spectacles as he waved us over so he and Ma could say hello.

It was quite obvious we were the guests of honor, our seating arranged at the head of the table where we sat side by side with the family stretched away on either side, including most of the children.

Matt was there with Scott. Even after a few days, we had the feeling that this wasn't just a holiday romance. Scott talked of moving south; his electrician's business was quite portable, and we assured him he'd easily find work in our town. Matt and he just beamed at each other. They were also seated together—Pa hadn't missed a trick.

MATT'S CAREER had bloomed as an IT manager, so much so it was now clear that pursuing teaching as a career was never going to give him the returns that IT would. His few weeks' experience with the hotel group in Thailand confirmed that fact.

The lights dimmed slowly. Chart, Solada, Pa, and I exchanged glances as Matt said "Show time!" and a previously hidden monitor lit up.

I watched Sammy's face as the camera scanned the figures on the screen and they changed from shadows to real people on Skype.

"Mum," he said with disbelief, as Isobel's lovely smiling face lit up the screen. Then it was Dad's turn. "Mr. Smith," Sammy said, then turned to me; my other half wasn't stupid. "What have you been up to, Jacko?" he asked. "Care to enlighten me?"

"Just trust me," I said, and he smiled that beautiful bloody smile of his, and my heart turned over several times like a pancake.

Chart stood up, almost a regal presence, slim and fit with beautiful graying hair at the temples, dressed simply and elegantly, but with an air of gentle authority. He took over a microphone and made sure the figures on the screen could hear him. "Isobel and Peter, how lovely to have your company."

In the background, my mother, brother, sister, and their families tried desperately to be quiet. Chart spoke slowly and clearly. "Tonight, we have a family gathering, one half in Australia, the other here in

Thailand. Samuel and Jackson have honored us tonight by adopting Thai ritual and the Thai way of life in many ways, so we have ensured our ways are appropriate for their needs."

Sammy listened to Chart's words, but it was clear he didn't have the faintest idea what Chart was talking about.

"Jacko, it's your show now," Chart said smiling, and I decided I'd bring the boys on early just to get everyone's juices flowing. Matt dropped in a CD, the lights faded to black and the darkened stage had some movement and muttering going on.

The music blared. Matt and Scott left their places at the table, and in wonderful tutus, they led the dance group on stage. Chart's younger brother, Sert, and his teenage son Tic were in the group, as were two Australian boys in Phuket learning Muay Thai, invited by Chart and Matt to make up the numbers. Two lovely straight guys who thought what we were doing was amazing, and an experience to tell their grandchildren one day.

It was bump and grind; Scott, complete with tats, was the leading lovely, followed by Matt. It was unadulterated fun; everyone enjoyed themselves, particularly the two ring-ins from Australia.

At home our families held their sides, and Trav tried to sing a local version.

Then Ali became really sentimental, and it was time for the headline act.

I thanked the dancers, quietened everyone down, and knelt in front of Sammy, who looked more perplexed than ever. I held his hand and looked into his eyes, speaking slowly so every word was enunciated clearly. "Samuel John Collins, will you marry me?"

The world seemed to stop. Not a sound from anyone.

Sammy was struggling, and I whispered for him to take his time, because I knew it was the last thing he expected.

But he knew why, and his face told me so. Gone completely was any concern, replaced by a look of love, nothing else.

He stood up and smiled his beautiful smile, slipping his arms around my shoulders. "You're a good man, Jackson Smith, a smart man, and the most loving human being I've ever met. Everything you do is for us, and in one question you've set up our future together. Of course I'll marry you. I accept your proposal with pleasure." With that we slipped into lip-lock, and I thought he'd never let go.

At home and in Phuket, everyone was well-mannered and quite silent, giving us our space. Even Mum made the effort; the fact she attended willingly meant so much.

Pa and Ma came forward and laboriously made their way on to the stage. "In Thailand the bridegroom gives the bride a gold necklace," Solada said. "The necklace is a sign of commitment of one to the other. It must weigh an even number of baht. Baht is our measurement of weight, as well as our currency. Being an even weight signifies that two people are involved in the gift, not just one: the giver of the gift and the one who receives it."

Not a word was spoken, but Sammy's lip began to quiver, a first for him. I was the crier normally, but this time I surprised myself—because I had the responsibility to make it happen and to see it through.

Pa and Ma passed the necklace, still in its case, between each other. Then it was handed to Chart, the next generation, who passed it on to Solada. She kissed her husband, and she passed the necklace on to me, her partner in crime.

I placed it around Sammy's neck, and he began quietly weeping.

"It's beautiful, Jacko," he said. "I'll remember this forever. But I don't have anything to give you."

"Yes, you do," I said to him. "It's coming your way now."

Old Pa and Ma looked naughty and pretended to keep it for themselves. This time they passed it to Solada, who handed it to her husband, who bowed and presented my necklace to Sammy.

He had enough presence of mind to ask me to marry him, and I agreed as he fastened it around my neck.

Absolutely identical, same even weight, same heavy-duty clasp so they were likely to last well into the future without much maintenance.

Sammy's eyes were like saucers. I knew I'd get asked the how-much question, but it didn't matter as he slipped it around my neck.

It felt good on, not ostentatious but in good taste, and I knew when we had manual work to perform they would go into their boxes for a few hours for safekeeping.

That was it. We'd promised to marry each other, but there was pandemonium at home in our town and certainly in Phuket.

Cheers, tears, and celebrations.

My mother seemed genuinely happy that the dreadful gay man was going to marry her son. She'd clearly lost the battle but seemed happy about it. I assumed the relationship with her church had changed because since my first failed attempt at marriage, she'd actually made Sammy welcome. Dad always believed in Sammy, and thinking back, he always believed in us as a couple. My sister and brother were ecstatic; Sammy was like a brother to them, and saving me from illiteracy was just part of the reason they loved him. Sammy loved me, always had, and now it would be formalized, to their great joy.

And Isobel, my lovely mother-in-law-to-be and all-round caring person, a great loyal supporter of me, finally had her chickens where they should be.

But this was Sammy, and it was meant to be. It had taken me a few years and several near fuckups to get where I should have been all along. But we got there.

Chapter 19
Back to the Grindstone

WE TRIED our best to sneak home quietly but to no avail; a continual stream of visitors slipped through as the word spread. Isobel pointed to Sammy's bedroom—now our bedroom—so we could put our heads down. Sammy's beautiful soft bed felt like heaven after the hard Thai beds, and we were asleep in seconds.

The next thing I knew, Sunday morning rolled around. Sammy slept on like a baby, so I left him there.

After my morning ablutions, I joined Isobel in the kitchen. She admitted she hadn't come down off her high as yet; she'd been so excited by our news she'd found it difficult to sleep. I was on my second coffee when Sammy padded in, a big grin plastered over his face, kissing me good morning.

Isobel had begun telling me about her plans for the house, and I needed Sammy to decipher it all for me because it was too early in the day.

Isobel smiled patiently and Sammy laughed. Some things never change; it took a while to get my brain going in the mornings, and I was still on autopilot. Suddenly she had all my attention. She'd been able to subdivide the property and would extend the little unit out the back for her own use, leaving us the big house, which she'd sell to us at a bargain price.

Dad would be her builder and he'd be starting work in a few weeks.

I couldn't believe anyone could be so generous and kind; even Sammy was in awe of his mother. In less than a week, she'd moved with lightning speed, giving us an amazing start to our life together. She admitted she'd begun working on the project just after I came to live with them permanently, and thought it might "hurry us along a bit."

We stared at each other: first Chart and Solada, now Isobel—they had us worked out before we did.

"Anyone else with the ability to read our minds that we don't know about?" I asked.

"Your father, of course." She giggled. "He's already organized the planning permit."

The new arrangement ensured our privacy as a couple, but with the bonus that Isobel would always be close by. She'd been such a close influence in my life, particularly when my own mother had been busily rejecting me. Isobel would still be there, every day, and I was a happy bloke.

I ASSUMED life would return to normal, but it didn't.

It got better.

Everything glowed; it was like looking at the world through a golden haze. The feeling touched everything I did, and Sammy admitted he felt the same way. We were in our own world, but somehow we began to understand that becoming a couple was more than just being in love.

We'd always worked well together, but now it came so easily. From the moment we committed to each other in Phuket, our individual lives ceased to exist because now there was an "us." We'd both noticed the change, and it was change for the better. My ability to think in a linear fashion at work reasserted itself, and I started a business degree at TAFE in the evenings, while chairing a major project committee involving garbage disposal for the City, a project I'd initiated myself. A new special school opened on the campus where we'd spent our high school days, and Sammy had been appointed to run it. It was teamwork, working for the common good of our little family, and we loved the way our life was going.

Anything we put our collective mind to seemed achievable, even helping Dad with the renovations to Isobel's new home, where he just let us take over certain parts, secure in the knowledge it would be finished properly and in good time.

We had a visitor one Saturday morning, Mrs. Hutton, my first remedial teacher, an all-time believer in Sammy and me as a couple. Another one.

She and Isobel were like sisters, their friendship made even closer now by the excitement of our news.

Mrs. Hutton embraced us and turned to me with a twinkle in her eye. "Remember the list of dyslexic people, Jacko?"

Albert Einstein, Alexander Graham Bell, Nelson Rockefeller, Winston Churchill, Steven Spielberg, etcetera.

"Most of the famous dyslexics through history had dedicated partners, who were smart and loving enough to provide a fertile environment for their other half to grow and develop, as you two do for each other. Don't be surprised where this leads you," she said. "Any two people who love each other as much as you two, have the power to improve and develop each other. The world isn't populated by individuals who are high achievers, but by people who achieve excellence by supporting and growing each other in a strong partnership."

In the background Isobel smiled at her friend; she no doubt couldn't have put it better herself.

I BOUNCED into work one Monday morning to find our CEO waiting with Mrs. Shields in the office. I was early enough, but they were the early birds for once.

He handed me a key to my office, with both a warning and a request. "Please," he said, "there's some nasty stuff going on, so I've had the locks changed on your office door. I need you to keep it locked at all times, even when you're working, okay?"

I was naturally confused, but then it dawned on me.

Craig Murray was trying to slip back into his old job, and possession would be nine-tenths of the law if he was able to access his old office and pretend nothing had happened.

And if Craig was back in town, so was Michelle.

Shit.

"What we've done is to change the job specification," my boss said, but I was hardly listening.

Bloody Michelle.

Why come home? Why couldn't they keep their ugliness to themselves without flaunting it in our faces? I immediately thought of Joanne Murray and her kids and wondered if she'd also had the locks changed.

"Because if Craig wants his old job back, it doesn't exist anymore," Mr. Davis confirmed through his teeth, his displeasure clear.

Our CEO had my sympathy; we were all trying to avoid the unpleasantness that Craig would undoubtedly create, knowing he'd never resigned, just walked out, leaving a legal vacuum.

THE WEEK went from bad to worse, drama seeming to follow us everywhere. Isobel's old Peugeot shit itself beyond repair, Mum had another minibreakdown, and Travis cut his hand badly at work. I ran from one house to another achieving absolutely nothing. Mum's doctors finally stabilized her condition with the help of some new medication, but Dad worried because he felt there was something else amiss and wouldn't say what. Trav was off work for at least two weeks, and I'd volunteered to help finish two plumbing jobs for him at the weekend with him supervising and me doing the grunt work.

We'd been grocery shopping, one of the thankless tasks of any household. Loaded with plastic bags, we approached the front door, Sammy out in front, both hands full. Isobel was at work and unlikely to be home for nearly two hours, as one of us would have to collect her in the Ford.

I handed the front door keys to Sammy, but he didn't have a spare hand as I looked on uselessly. He spat the dummy big-time.

"Jackson! You can't rely on me every fucking minute of the day, so if you can't remember which key it is, big deal, find a way." He opened the door, and then threw the bunch at me.

I stood there stunned, then erupted, dropping the bags on the veranda, and stormed off to the Ford, my mind in black turmoil. I spun the wheels as I reversed out of the driveway and tore off down the street. I just wanted out.

Chapter 20
The Highs and Lows of Love

I DIDN'T even get to the end of the street before I cooled down, realizing I'd been such a dick—again.

I stopped the Ford and turned carefully around, parking back in the driveway. I quickly ran to the little workshop we had at the rear of the house and drilled a hole in my house key so I'd always be able to tell it apart from the many others on the key ring. The confusion I felt when I looked at a heap of keys would always be there, I knew, but Sammy was right: if I always relied on other people for everything, my personal development wouldn't go anywhere.

It was fine to have people at my back like Sammy at home and Mrs. Shields at work, but in the end, I was responsible for me, period.

He'd put the frozen food in the freezer, and satisfied nothing else would spoil, I took his hand and led him into our bedroom, his face still streaked with tears. Words were never enough, I reckoned, but my darling responded. We lay there afterward, all forgiven, and his phone buzzed. It was Isobel, asking for a ride home. The raw ingredients for our dinner still sat on the kitchen table.

I took over and slipped Sammy a fifty to fetch some Chinese takeout, as well as his mother. Isobel knew us so well and never interfered, the soul of discretion, still our greatest supporter.

The next morning was Saturday, and after driving Isobel to work for her weekend classes, I came home to find Sammy flat strap with housework.

So I washed, ironed, and folded, doing my bit until lunchtime.

We sat across the kitchen bench from each other, and the question came as I knew it would, about my overreaction with the bloody door key. To get into the car and risk life and limb the way I did had clearly terrified Sammy, and he had a right to know what was going on in my head.

"You aren't going to like this," I said.

"Try me."

"Well you know Craig and Michelle are back in town."

He nodded silently.

"Well I had a visit from Craig yesterday at work. He looked quite defeated, actually, and even though I was forbidden to make any sort of contact with him, I felt sorry for him."

Sammy didn't interrupt, so I continued.

"Something told me to listen because his body language told me I'd nothing to worry about. Mrs. Shields was about to ring and alert the troops, but I stopped her. Craig didn't even try to gain entry to the office, so I extended my hand and he shook it, sheepishly. I mean, at this stage I was still the bloke whose missus he pinched on her wedding day."

Sammy smiled that beautiful smile of his and my confidence soared.

"I took him over to the lunchroom in the workshop so I could talk to him as privately as possible. I explained that he was running up a dry gully at work, that Mr. Davis had anticipated a legal battle, and that he'd be better off accepting the severance offer, which would include all his super plus a cash settlement."

"What did he say?"

"He actually agreed. He said he was tired at the thought of all the drama, and just to have it resolved meant they could get on with their life and that would be such a relief."

Sammy's eyebrows lifted, wanting more information.

"I asked him how Michelle was going, particularly since her dad died, and he admitted they'd only come home to get married."

The look on Sammy's face probably replicated mine when Craig dropped the bombshell. "He admitted what had started as a casual affair had blossomed, and they fell in love. And I believe them, because I called around and talked to her as well."

At this stage I was shitting myself, because on the face of it, I'd gone behind Sammy's back and I hadn't thought about the consequences, even though my intentions were totally honorable.

He didn't even hesitate. "You still feel guilty because you think you used Michelle, don't you?"

Bingo.

"And yet the opposite is the case."

"That's what she said."

"What about Joanne and the kids?"

"Craig and Joanne are talking again. It appears he did begin paying maintenance after a month or so, and he's been back to see the kids several times."

Sammy smiled gently. "Truth is always a casualty in broken marriages, and Joanne's story's quite different, as you know. The fact is that no one's a winner in that situation."

I agreed with him, although in my case I was a winner, it just took a little time.

"What are you smiling at?" he asked.

"I was just thinking how easy it's been for you and me as a couple, while poor bloody Craig and Michelle are about as popular as a fart in a phone box."

Sammy threw his head back and roared with laughter. "So what's your point?"

"My point is that every couple needs reassurance that they're heading in the right direction at this stage of their life together. Craig and Michelle have sneaked back into town so they can have their family and friends around them on what is to them an important day. Yet not one person has indicated they'll come along. That's not a solid foundation for married life."

I thought he wouldn't understand, but he did. Completely.

We faced a hostile reception with our families, particularly when I first floated the idea, but Sammy pushed them along, and they eventually agreed, even Dad. Michelle was welcomed back into the fold with caution at first, then with affection. Craig was clearly terrified of our potential reaction. Dad took him to one side and convinced him to relax, promising we'd all be there on the day, that the past was exactly that.

Sammy could have been accused of baser motives, but I knew his level of confidence in me had never wavered after I'd proposed in Phuket.

But strangely it was Mum who voiced the obvious. "Don't you lot understand," she yelled across the kitchen table, in a fit of something approaching temper, "this girl needs to be settled and happy so she doesn't come after Jackson ever again. After all, he'll be a married man himself in a few months."

Chapter 21
Mum

IT'S HARD to explain, but there's an old expression, "blood's thicker than water," and that certainly applied to the relationship between my mother and me. Even though she held me at arm's length as a little bloke and was sometimes a little harsh, she was still my mum and I loved her. Dad was always a known quantity, but Mum was all over the place, protective and caring one moment, remote and negative the next.

Dad explained only quite recently that she'd experienced postnatal depression after Travis was born, but she went against medical advice to first have Alison and then me, because they both wanted more kids.

It helped me to understand that I was actually wanted in the first place—a fact I struggled with until I met Isobel and Sammy. Isobel seemingly understood my bewilderment, and she compensated in so many ways. Love came easily for her, and Sammy was just like his mother, showering me with unconditional love.

But subconsciously I still craved attention from Mum, determined not to give up on her. Mum was the person who helped create me, and that genetic pathway would always be there, that special link between a boy and his mother.

Mum was obviously in a vulnerable state of mind when the religious crazies got hold of her, and poor Dad struggled for years to keep them at arm's length. Finally it all came to an end, the collapse of the Church of Abraham happening with lightning speed, due in no small part to the interest of the police in its pastor, the Reverend Clement Spears.

Because the reverend was caught in an inappropriate relationship with a twelve-year-old boy.

Before he could be charged, the reverend hurriedly left for overseas but was apprehended in Auckland and extradited. His career serving God was over, and he'd soon embark on another—serving time as someone's bitch.

In all, Reverend Spears had molested around twenty kids, some as young as eight years old, making Jimmy Swaggart look like a saint.

Clem Spears's teaching had been designed to glorify his religious beliefs by denigrating gay people and stoutly insisting that learning difficulties were the work of the devil.

Hypocrisy had a human face, together with an element of criminality involved. Surprisingly, Mum seemed calm, almost relieved at first, because we kids had never been to the reverend's Sunday school; Dad simply wouldn't allow it.

But it was the lull before the storm, and hell hath no fury like Mum. She pursued the reverend with the same dedication he'd demanded from the pulpit, but the coppers were there first.

And Mum, pissed off, with a damaged ego and a faith in tatters, knew it was decision time. She'd already begun the process of gradually withdrawing from their influence, Dad confirmed. With her kids gone and the house quiet, she'd time to think about the next generation. Despite the hints from Travis and Alison, their kids didn't want to be near Mum—not because she was weird with religion, but because they hardly knew her.

Mum, of her own volition, decided she wanted her grandchildren back. She'd stay home on Sundays, and with Dad's help there were roast dinners and the old house sang along with the sounds of little kids.

Bribery in the form of food had defeated Jesus hands-down, and Mum began smiling again. Dad was delighted, but he and I knew there was one more hurdle Mum had to cross.

Me.

Frankly I didn't think she would ever change her attitude to me, even though my progress through life so far had been stellar with Sammy's help and motivation, plus Isobel's support.

My near marital disaster with Michelle didn't seem to worry her at all; when she was at her most devout she would have demanded I go through with it all, but she was strangely quiet at the time.

Then the scandal broke with the Reverend Spears and his authority base disappeared instantly, reassuring Mum that to move away from the church had been the right decision for her. She decided at last that her family was more important than Jesus and she needed help in this world, not the next.

When we called around a few days later, Dad was at work and Mum was actually preparing dinner, a rarity for her.

But something wasn't right. Her coordination seemed wrong somehow. Sammy noticed as well and sat her down to talk to me as he finished the preparation.

She wanted, she said, to enjoy Sammy and me while she could because that was so important to her, that to see us happy and together was something that nature always intended.

Her change of attitude was welcome, but the suddenness of it all was alarming.

IT WAS just Trav, Ali, and myself with Dad a few nights later; Mum had gone to bed early.

"Mum won't be with us all that much longer," Dad said with a sole tear slowly cascading down his cheek. I grabbed my hanky and wiped it away, then kissed his cheek. Trav and Ali looked slightly uncomfortable, but Dad and I always shared a closeness and our emotions were always nearer the surface.

What you saw was what you got with Dad and me; Trav and Ali were more reserved, like Mum.

"What do you mean, Dad?" Ali asked.

Dad's voice filled with emotion. "Mum has Alzheimer's disease. She was only diagnosed last week, but the experts say she's probably been affected for nearly twelve months, given the advanced nature of some of the symptoms." I nodded, more to myself; this would totally explain Mum's vague behavior, which seemed to be worsening every time we saw her.

"With senior-aged people," Dad continued, "the disease and the patient linger on for years. In Mum's case the prognosis is very grave. As she's only in her fifties, she'll not last more than four to five years."

Denial immediately hit Trav. "So she could go on another twenty years."

"No, Travis, as I've just finished saying, she has maybe four to five years to live, if we're lucky," Dad replied.

I understood perfectly, poor Ali did too; we both cried, and finally the facts hit home to us all.

Mum would be increasingly removed from reality and from us quite swiftly, leaving behind a shell of what she was. Then I turned to Dad.

"She'd like us to get married as soon as possible, wouldn't she?"

"Yes, she specifically mentioned it, so she can enjoy the occasion while she's still able to, and to give you her blessing."

"I won't have any problem with Sammy, he half expected something like this."

Dad smiled, which made him look younger. "Sammy will convince Mum it was all his idea, and she'll believe him. You're marrying the right person this time, Jacko."

Chapter 22
Here We Go Again

MATT WAS doing well, really well. His website business had taken off, with plenty of work locally, so much so he opened a small office and employed a senior lady to coordinate the workload and manage the accounts. He'd been offered more work overseas with the international hotel chain but declined for one reason.

Scott.

Matt's future had finally overtaken him in Phuket, and Scott duly moved south, complete with his old electrician's van, "Scott the Shocker" on the side.

He walked into contract work immediately, and within a few weeks they bought a suburban home with a huge workshop at the rear. Neither of them could stop smiling.

Matt had made the transition from a party-boy lifestyle and a free spirit to a responsible, hardworking member of a strong partnership because he wanted to. A free spirit, now enjoying life like never before.

He and Scott loved each other and worked together, just as we did, and the four of us grew even closer.

A few days after my family meeting, I reminded Matt of his commitment to be my best man—or best person, for Sammy's sake—only it was now less than six weeks away, not four months. Matt was stoked, and Scott kept asking what frock he should wear.

With my family history of "difficult" weddings, no one dared interfere, and Sammy and I were expected to organize the day ourselves. Which we did.

Bringing the timing forward wasn't an issue with my lovely man, but I felt it was time for me to state my case once again.

So we went out for a nice dinner by ourselves, and he understood what I was doing. "Just because we're getting married earlier than planned doesn't diminish what I feel for you," I said.

His eyes misted over, but he listened without interrupting.

"The wedding is still about us," I said. "Having Mum cognizant enough to enjoy the day is important, but it's still our day. I wanted to reassure you that I'm getting married because I want to, not just to please my family."

"I know," he said across the table at our favorite sushi restaurant. "You didn't have to do that, because we're so much on the same page, but I'm glad you did anyway." I raised my eyebrows at him and he laughed, that beautiful musical sound that meant everything was right in our world.

But I still needed to reinforce what was on my mind, and as a dyslexic person, that's sometimes easier said than done.

I couldn't help myself; I had to remind him that it was love that brought us together and love that would keep us that way. We were besotted with each other, we both knew that, but I wondered how many partnerships had failed because the participants neglected to tell each other how they felt. So I told him, quietly and truthfully.

"I wanted to tell you how much I love you, and how our life together is amazing. I'm not perfect, but you forgive all my faults and make me a better person."

Sammy smiled that beautiful smile, holding my hands and speaking into my eyes.

"What you've managed to do since we became a couple is to progressively exceed all the expectations and hopes I held for us as a partnership. But I can't emphasize more that the best is yet to come. You will even surprise yourself and all our family and friends, because I believe you have special abilities that will emerge progressively over time. My rationale? A deep personal bias." He laughed. "And a sense of greatness because you think on a deeper level to ordinary people. Just like Leonardo da Vinci, Albert Einstein, Alexander Graham Bell, Sir Richard Branson, Walt Disney, Jay Leno, Whoopi Goldberg, Nelson Rockefeller, Agatha Christie, Steven Spielberg, Harry Belafonte, Winston Churchill, Richard Strauss, etcetera."

Mrs. Hutton's words had come back to me but I couldn't see how I'd ever be that great at anything, certainly not in that league. But it was enough to make me think. My other half didn't talk bullshit, and if he thought I could achieve something special, then he was probably on the money.

My confidence level had just received another boost; all those years of being told I was useless were now far behind me.

EVERY DAY Sammy attempted to get inside kids' heads and unlock their learning potential, while I was helping out when I could.

In what spare time I had, and sometimes in working hours, thanks to Mr. Davis, who called it "community service," Sammy dragged me into the classroom to illustrate my academic progress over the years.

"Because," he said to the kids, "Jackson is proof of what is possible."

But it was more than that, I proudly told his pupils, because I understood everyone needed inspiration of some sort to drive them along and turn their learning difficulties into opportunities. They had to imagine what they wanted to do with their lives, how they saw themselves in the future. Knowing there was absolutely nothing wrong with their intelligence, just that they were different, and not in a bad way.

"What was your inspiration, Mr. Smith?" a cheeky fourteen-year-old boy asked.

"My teacher," I replied, "the same one you have. If he says you have a future, listen to him because he's always right."

MARGARET REEVE, the vice chancellor of the university, became interested in Sammy's work. She told us that a huge number of Asian students were presenting themselves for tertiary education who couldn't read or write English properly, and she suspected dyslexia and ADHD as the prime culprits. Margaret wanted the education department to extend the Special School to retrain and reskill those kids so they could cope with a university education. With no equivalent facility anywhere in Asia, the Special School catered to families whose kids had gone as far as their local system would allow, some much further than they should.

The university had a small campus in Kuala Lumpur, but most families preferred the learning experience in Australia and the discreet nature of the Special School. Children with learning difficulties, a source of embarrassment in their own country, could be hidden away in Australia.

Nine Malaysian students attended the previous year, and currently there were a further twenty-five who needed specialist coaching before they could take on a degree course. Some of the kids thought Margaret Reeve was a pushover and that their families would buy their degree for them while they had a good time, as in the past. Margaret threatened to send them home again immediately, filling them with fear.

Slowly but surely Sammy began to unlock their mindset with his specially designed courses for adult students, and every single one thrived and developed with lightning speed, attitudes were reversed, and parents were delighted.

But Asian families needed to save face, so the decision was made to shift the Special School to the main campus of the university, where Margaret found a very nice 1980s building in good condition that was currently underutilized.

Sammy was made principal and he had a staff of six. All of them flat-out like lizards drinking, all day every day, using the very latest in teaching aids.

The students ranged from just five or six years right through to early twenties in some cases. The results were stupendous.

The older kids were fascinated by the little ones, and the sense of family, so much part of Asian culture, helped bring the best out in everyone as the Special School became a melting pot of cultures.

All the families at home in Kuala Lumpur, Bangkok, and Jakarta were grateful; their kids were transformed from academic mediocrity to functioning, confident students, a task thought impossible back home, supporting the two billion dollars' worth of business the university attracted annually from Asia.

BUT MARGARET also loved us as a couple.

A high-profile supporter of same-sex marriage, she'd championed the cause when it wasn't fashionable to do so. She actually asked if she could attend our wedding and bring a media contingent with her because she claimed the concept of "education for everyone" needed reinforcing in the community.

Our love affair went viral on social media. People warmed to our story, how important it was to other people out there who were struggling with learning difficulties.

The teacher marrying his former student.

We were seen as education over illiteracy. For years society struggled to help dyslexic people. Our town, through the efforts of many people, became a center of expertise in Australia, and therefore to many families, we represented hope. From the moment we announced the date of our wedding, all hell broke loose; it appeared we'd struck a nerve in the community, pushed along by Margaret Reeve.

We went from a quiet wedding with a few family and friends to a massive community happening, people glued to bloody Facebook for the event.

Chapter 23
The Right Person, the Right Reason, the Right Time

WE FINALLY settled on a female celebrant, after interviewing no less than three. Only one of them offered to write our story, allow us time to approve it, and do a rehearsal so we knew what we were doing on the day.

The venue was easy: the Grand Chapel at the International Centre for Human Partnerships, part of the university. We had a preferred rate anyway, but the ICHP had been founded years prior to support same-sex couples around the world and was a comfortable icon in our town.

Driving a maroon Jaguar on loan from the grateful family of one of Sammy's students, Scott delivered us to the forecourt. He looked resplendent in a new business suit, the high collar not quite hiding the tattoo on his neck.

The numbers and the atmosphere were truly intimidating. Sammy's pupils, their families, and his fellow staff members sat together with Margaret Reeve.

We'd decided to arrive together as a couple; there was no reason for us to ape hetero marriage, and while some people thought parading down the aisle on your big day was desirable, we didn't. Firstly we couldn't define who the bride was, and secondly we thought one person showing off to all and sundry was an insult to the other half of the partnership.

So Matt as best man/person and Dad, who was to give me away (which I thought was still a terrific tradition), would be standing with the celebrant.

And our two mums would also be up there, Isobel to give Sammy away and my mum to be his best person, an amazing turnaround in a relationship that once saw them at opposite ends of the earth.

With all that very ordinary history, Mum and Sammy had grown to love each other. Sammy knew Mum had been driven by the church, yet he respected her for being strong enough to walk away from them and her beliefs in favor of her family. And Sammy was family. Mum adored him primarily because he loved me, and secondly because he made her laugh at a time when she needed all the humor she could possibly get.

Sammy had repaired Mum; where she'd blamed herself for giving me an unnecessarily hard time as a kid, Sammy counseled her and pointed out the new me, with a happy life, a good career—and a rosy future.

Mum's coordination worsened; where she could be unsteady on her feet at times, Sammy would take her hand and walk her as often as he could. They were like two girlfriends together, chattering away, completely relaxed in each other's company. Isobel and I worked harder at home to give him that extra time with Mum, which in turn gave Dad a welcome relief.

WE WALKED in the door and waited as the celebrant started the music on her iPod. She asked everyone to stand, and nearly two hundred pairs of eyes turned to face us. Our hands fell naturally in place as we grinned at each other, the stress at least partially overtaken by excitement.

Our families remembered us as ten-year-olds walking to school hand in hand, and today was just a replay of those events. Only we weren't walking to school anymore, but it did remind us how long we'd been in each other's lives before we got it all together.

Michelle and Craig were there, of course. She looked radiant—most women do when they're pregnant, and she was at the end of her second trimester. They'd actually moved back to town and bought the house next to Joanne and her new husband.

So the adults had grown up and the kids were being raised by the "village."

Chart and Solada, their kids, and all our Muay Thai mates, such an important part of our life together, sat in the next two rows. I choked up a little when I saw Pa and Ma; they'd come all the way from Phuket with several generations of their family, including children and grandchildren. Pa and Ma were such loving and generous people, there was no doubt where the travel fund had emanated from. They waved and smiled, hugely proud of us, and we felt humbled.

The music began to rise in volume as we walked, but my brother and sister, their spouses and children, stood in the aisle and began clapping and cheering like bloody imbeciles.

It was like an anthem; it spread and the roar of approval nearly raised the roof. They all thought we were terrific, and they wanted to tell us so. Not just the things we'd done or were about to do, but what we were about, two guys getting married because we loved each other.

Chapter 24
Life Returns to Normal, Sort Of

AFTER THE wedding Mum's condition worsened quickly. It was as if she'd been mustering all her mental energy for the occasion, and once it was over, she relaxed. Sammy and I were working long hours, so Isobel elected to scale down her course load at TAFE to spend some time with Mum, mainly walking with her, which allowed Sammy to have a breather.

We had one night a week to ourselves—Thursday, for Muay Thai and a meal with Chart and Solada afterward.

But we had a plan: finish the renovations, help settle Isobel into her new quarters, then have our honeymoon in Phuket with our other family. Several months of hard work, without an exact time frame.

Travis and Dad decided to combine their businesses formally, which meant Dad could now semiretire to care for Mum.

WITH MRS. Shields I'd found a new level of confidence, knowing someone was watching my back and had the initiative to get things done and solve problems before they escalated. It allowed me to get out in the field, not to spy on my blokes but to stand alongside them and show an interest in their work.

As the acting operations manager, I now had operational duties involving garbage collection, roadworks, parks and gardens, signage, and general maintenance. A quantum leap in responsibility in a very short period. Effectively the new job specification rocketed me up the organizational tree to where I reported to Mr. Davis, and the other managers had to report through me. But only on a temporary basis.

There were some green eyes too, but after talking it quietly through with Sammy, I had to be inclusive with everyone and not get too upset if someone had the shits with me.

With Mrs. Shields's help, I was able to short-circuit the industrial relations issues and encourage the managers to come directly to me for help. Many of them were older than Dad, but I treated them in the same way I treated Dad and I suddenly had everyone's attention.

I INITIATED the Waste Collection Special Project Committee because I thought the City could do much better than the current system.

It just stared everyone in the face: huge capital outlays for the garbage trucks with their specialist compactor bodies, at least thirty drivers, and five specialist mechanics. Let alone the inventory of spare parts, which was enough to keep NASA in space for ten years.

My business studies at TAFE had helped me rationalize the strategy to outsource waste collection, but I was amazed no one else shared my vision, not even Mr. Davis.

Mr. Davis warned me that the unions would fight any attempt to contract out the garbage collection service. And despite several other cities and municipalities having done exactly that, our CEO and the councilors were nervous about change.

In addition, the level of interest in our work wasn't high, because we were all amateurs with little business expertise and no credentials at all.

When we presented the report to him at our final meeting, he was polite and appreciative, but as yet had no concept of the minute detail of the financial workup we'd done with the help of a local accounting firm. We'd also involved the unions—two committee members were senior officials of the two unions whose members would be impacted by any change in garbage collection methodology and operation.

The next day around midmorning, I had a call from Mr. Davis, and my bloody heart sank, wondering if we'd all made dicks of ourselves. He was polite and supportive as always and told me to expect a visit from Mr. Lowther, Chief Financial Officer.

There was a commotion in Mrs. Shields's area about thirty minutes later, which could be heard from the parts store where I was checking the week's invoices. Shouting.

A small, bald, bespectacled man backed out of the office door with Mrs. Shields looking decidedly territorial and most upset, her normally calm features like a rapidly approaching thunderstorm.

Jeremy Lowther, whose face had turned a dirty white color, backed down the steps as Mrs. Shields reamed him for some indiscretion. I kept out of sight as I heard her using language like "disrespect," "same-sex discrimination," and "make a fucking appointment next time, you asshole," before she slammed the door closed. I stayed hidden as Mr. Lowther sped off in his City vehicle and grinned to myself; he must have really got up Mrs. Shields's nose for her to protect me as she had.

"What on earth's wrong?" Never, ever had I heard her use bad language, apart from a mild "bloody thing" or "bugger it."

Barbara Shields was a lady, but Jeremy Lowther had rudely demanded to know "where was your pansy boss with the disability."

"So I told Lowther to leave," she said, "after he tried to push past me and take over your office."

I couldn't help it; I laughed until my sides ached, and then she joined me. We'd always been a team, but Mr. Lowther didn't understand that. He was an accountant, his friends were numbers, and he was surrounded by dour types just like himself. But he'd made several mistakes, not the least of which involved expressing personal opinions that could get him sacked if I'd decided to complain.

Within minutes I had Mr. Davis on my mobile, also laughing. "I think Jeremy might have upset Barbara," he said. "What do you recommend?"

"Leave him to me," I said. "He's shitty because his department wasn't involved in this project up front. But we both know he would've been impossible to extract information from, and the report would've taken years, not months. I'll ask him to come back here in the morning before Mrs. Shields comes in." Giving myself time to think about what I had to say and to let the dust settle.

I thanked my protector with a hug. She was magnificent in all the tasks she undertook, and she was totally loyal to me. She understood what we'd done through teamwork. Poor Jeremy didn't have a clue.

THE FOLLOWING morning at 7:30 a.m., I was polite and welcoming.

Jeremy Lowther sat quietly across the desk from me, the outburst of the previous day not mentioned. I needed him on my side and another set of eyes to run over the figures we'd prepared as a group. Mr. Davis had read the report overnight and was a convert.

"As your report stands," he said, "I'd like to see it remain intact. I'm amazed how professional and comprehensive it is. In fact it's quite magnificent, congratulations."

But now I needed the City's financial approval, and I smiled at Mr. Lowther, lying my way along, feeding his fucking ego, and probably stroking his small-dick syndrome concurrently. "I didn't bother you with this exercise initially because I understand how busy you are in your department."

He nodded patiently, and I suddenly realized Mr. Davis had probably reamed a new arsehole for him, because he seemed eager to please.

"These are the spreadsheets," I said. "They weren't included with the report because they wouldn't mean anything to nonfinance people," I lied again.

"Who did the workups?"

"Smithers and Crane." I smiled. "We used them because their credentials are impeccable, and they've done work for the City in the past."

"How did you pay them?" he snapped, forgetting his "be nice to Jackson Smith" policy drummed into him by our CEO.

"We funded this through the savings we generated in this department year-to-date, and we're still way under budget."

It was clear our friend needed some reminding of the shaky foundation he'd placed himself on, because at this stage, he still seemed determined to sink the project to satisfy his own ego and his hatred of same-sex-attracted people.

"Not bad for a pansy with a disability," I said to Mr. Lowther, and he paled.

I'd already switched on the recording device Mr. Davis had installed in the office in case poor Craig Murray gave us trouble, which of course he hadn't, but this prick was far more dangerous than Craig could ever have been.

"Mr. Lowther, I know your department will examine this proposition fairly and without bias." I smiled. "And expeditiously."

Shock registered on his face, and something told me our friend was battling his own demons.

"Furthermore, I understand your distaste for my sexuality and my dyslexia would never be a consideration at all in your department's recommendation, so I'm very relaxed about the process." I smiled at him.

"Don't fucking count on it. People like you have no right to be treated the same as decent people. If I can find a hole in this fucking thing, your project is finished before it's started."

I waited until his car had disappeared, then packed the duplicate spreadsheets and a copy of the voice recording, and was in Mr. Davis's office half an hour later. I spent only a few minutes there, returning to my own office and busy schedule.

It was the next day that I learned Mr. Lowther had elected to take early retirement, effective immediately. As he was only in his midfifties, it was *very* early.

Mrs. Shields smiled all day. She didn't say anything; she didn't have to. She'd "backed the right horse," she said mysteriously, and I thought how if you planned for outcomes rather than just allowing them to happen, success usually followed.

MR. DAVIS beamed at me, his excitement palpable.

"The concept isn't new," he said. "Other cities and municipalities have outsourced their waste services, but all of them have resulted in major employment losses for local people and disruption caused by union unrest, trying to protect their members' jobs. Which in turn upsets the ratepayers, the people who employ us and pay our wages. Your point that staff is already at an all-time efficient level means the new operator should take them all on."

"But what's to stop them using their own people?"

"It would simply be a condition contained in the tender document, a condition of us awarding the contract. There would be an annual performance review, and our employees who transferred to their payroll would have similar rights as they do currently. Their employment would be guaranteed for as long as their employer held the contract with the City, which would make everyone try that much harder."

With the help of all the members of the committee, we presented the final document to the councilors at a full meeting. When Finance presented the final costings there was no argument. They were close to our original figures and were signed off in an audit by Smithers and Crane, Accountants.

So it was a go project.

Our legal guy helped me draft the tender, but before it was advertised, the committee called in the four companies, individually, who were likely to bid for the business. As with the entire process, we documented everything: conversations, projections, and every concern that had been raised by all parties. It was impossible for there to have been any misunderstandings; everyone knew where we were going and what we were doing, and more importantly, what outcomes we were all seeking. With committee members, we'd spoken to five other cities and/or municipalities, had long consultations with the unions, and helped finalize a fiscal plan that was bulletproof.

Three months later Kleen-Around Australia won the business, and a further three months later the transition was complete.

I felt like I'd aged ten years. We'd delayed our honeymoon and we were both tired. I was about to close up my office in readiness for nearly three weeks in Phuket when Mr. Davis's car swept into the driveway. He handed me an envelope and suggested I open it.

Council had authorized the position of acting operating manager be upgraded by deleting the word "Acting." Furthermore, Council authorized that the new position be filled by internal promotion rather than being advertised. And the person to be promoted was me.

Leonardo da Vinci, Albert Einstein, Alexander Graham Bell, Sir Richard Branson, Walt Disney, Jay Leno, Whoopi Goldberg, Nelson Rockefeller, Agatha Christie, Steven Spielberg, Harry Belafonte, Winston Churchill, Richard Strauss.

The salary being offered nearly made me faint. It was close to double what I was currently receiving. A City vehicle was part of the new job specification.

I shook my head. "No, that makes me look too much like the big executive. I'd prefer to drive the new shop ute. That way I'm still one of the workers, and they'll tell me what's on their mind."

MUM HELD her own. She didn't recognize us some days, but her overall physical health seemed okay. Good enough for us to have our honeymoon in peace without worrying too much, particularly with Dad and Isobel around her almost full-time.

Chapter 25
Return to Paradise

CHART AND Solada were already in Phuket with their kids, and our other "family" expected us. We called to see Pa and Ma at Phuket Town on the way from the airport and managed to catch up with most of them for an hour or so. But they understood we were really tired and needed to rest. They told us they'd see us in a few days, and we gratefully agreed.

We booked into the same hotel, and while we'd only been there once before, it felt like another home away from home. They remembered us, and even though it was high season, we were upgraded without asking, an extraordinarily generous act. When it was the same room as fourteen months earlier, Pa's hand and his local network of Thai people was obvious.

We slept, ate, swam in the pool, and rested. And just talked to each other, which was lovely. About our progress so far, and our future.

We agreed marriage does change things. We embraced a hetero tradition because there was nothing else more suitable at the time, but it had also embraced us. We felt better because of it, a peacefulness and calm that comes from your other half saying publicly that he loves you more than anyone or anything in the world. That he really thinks that much of you to want to be married at all, because it is a commitment for life. In the process I felt particularly good about myself; it was the best decision I'd ever made. Because we were meant to be and we continued to improve each other.

Nothing really bad had happened since I proposed—a few temper tantrums mainly on my behalf, and very rarely Sammy would spit the dummy, sending Isobel and me into hiding until it was over. I'd always been the one with the short fuse, thanks to my dyslexia. Sammy was slower to anger, but the explosion was nuclear in effect and much worse.

We'd coped beautifully with Mum's illness, supporting her and Dad when they most needed it, although her condition could only get worse, not better.

The wedding was the official high point of our partnership, but we both felt the most tender and meaningful moments were right here in this hotel room, where I'd kissed him for the first time in a less than innocent and very determined manner. Where we began our life as a couple.

Neither of us had a religious bone in our body, but we acknowledged the part in our partnership that Mother Nature continued to play.

"Do you ever miss women?" Sammy asked quite seriously.

My ability to read people worked best with Sammy, and to me it felt quite natural and normal to have such an honest discussion here on our honeymoon. Because everyone needs reassurance, particularly as you plan your life ahead. "I still like watching them." I laughed. "You even pick out the ones with big tits for me to look at."

He laughed, that musical sound like a little waterfall, yet full of confidence and love.

I remembered girls with their softness, their nice perfume and powder, gentle and acquiescent. Sammy was almost in the same category back then, as a young boy before we took on Muay Thai as both sport and exercise.

But that all changed fourteen months ago when I kissed him, and he knew it. He just wanted me to say it again, and that was fair enough.

The fact is Sammy always turned me on, but the grown-up Sammy with the fit and trim body, looking decidedly super masculine, thrilled me. Even with clothes on he made me instantly horny. In the past I'd been in denial, put it down to circumstances, but once I was honest with myself, my libido seemed permanently out of control around him. As now.

I hadn't run off with the first available woman, nor had Sammy ditched me for someone better-looking or smarter, because we loved each other. That's what continued to drive us along, and while we'd never really discussed it, monogamy suited us.

In the meantime, I tried to look nonchalant as my bloke began removing his shorts, undies, and T-shirt, leaving nothing more than a big smile. The hugeness that was Sammy below the belt always fascinated me. It seemed to have a life of its own, swaying from one side to the other as he walked over, and I surrendered without a fight.

AT WORK my star had risen to the point where I'd gone from mower operator to operations manager, with a career paying me a substantial salary, an extraordinary achievement in such a short time frame. My creativity was always strongest around Sammy, but it had accelerated when we became a couple.

In the same period, Sammy had grown the program where his Special School was shepherding kids of all ages through primary, secondary, and now tertiary levels of study. People from overseas visited and studied his teaching methodology, and the pressure had strained the administration. Margaret Reeve had helped with part-time staff so Sammy could keep teaching.

It was only now, on vacation and away from the coalface, that I understood with a degree of shock that I'd also had an effect on Sammy's career.

We were a team, no question about that, but I realized that this was only the beginning. A very good beginning on a sound basis, but Sammy always thought we were headed for something much bigger. I never doubted what he said, as he was usually right about most things, but whatever we achieved in the future would clearly be the result of our teamwork and our love.

ISOBEL'S LITTLE cottage came together beautifully, and the transactions had been finalized. The bank and we owned the big house, and Isobel was debt-free in her little unit at the back.

Nothing had changed, thank heavens; we still walked in and out of both properties without knocking, we'd all seen each other in a state of undress on many occasions, and Isobel had even caught us copulating in the hallway once and simply laughed at us. She was vital to our future existence, and we told her so, but we all knew why we needed to have our own space for the future.

Kids.

Sammy and I'd discussed having a family while we were still young enough to grow up with them ourselves. But surrogacy and legal fees were a huge and nearly insurmountable hurdle with our current financial resources, and there was only a certain amount we could borrow.

We reckoned five years before our first, and we'd have to go without a few things to get there in that time frame. But life was lovely, even with my mum's health issues, and we'd eventually have our kids.

Chapter 26
More Magic in Paradise

WE STROLLED to a bar in Patong Beach, but we'd had dinner first and so weren't in a big drinking mood. The bar was a favorite of ours in the gay area of Patong, quieter and better behaved than Walking Street, which at this time of night was winding up like a giant rubber band.

There was a mixed group, some hetero couples joined in, everyone enjoying a tipple in a very relaxed and convivial atmosphere. Russians, Germans, Brits, Australians, and a few Chinese. Some Americans and Canadians. Several couples with senior-age westerners and their male or female Thai partners, drinks at reasonable prices, and some free snacks supplied by mine host, a lovely English guy.

My phone beeped—a missed call.

I scrolled through recents and Travis's number came up straight away.

Sammy talked animatedly with two German guys so I didn't bother him, because it could only be bad news, probably Mum.

But when Trav answered, he was very upbeat. "You sitting down?" he asked.

"I'm standing up, thank you, having a nice scotch and soda."

"Can you remember your numbers?" Trav asked.

I fished my card out of my wallet and repeated our numbers. It was religion for Sammy and me; we always bought a lottery ticket every Friday for the Saturday night draw and checked our numbers online every Sunday morning.

"And it's draw number 5397," I said with my innards tying themselves in knots and my pulse rate heading toward the stratosphere.

"That's the one. You've got a Tatts card, haven't you?"

"Yes."

"Good," Trav replied. "Then you won't have any trouble claiming your prize. You and your other half have won TattsLotto. Not only do you have the six straight but the two supplementary numbers as a well. This was meant to be. Congratulations, bro."

The bar began to spin. I grabbed a stool for support, sitting my arse down with some force, feeling the blood drain from my face.

Sammy almost leapt over the bar, the two Germans probably wondering what they'd said.

"Jacko, what on earth's wrong?" he asked.

"We need to go back to the hotel, use the free Wi-Fi because I think we've won TattsLotto." Sammy tried to process the information, but I may as well have been speaking Swahili for all it mattered. Being told we'd won the lottery was the last thing either of us expected, so I had to repeat the conversation I'd just had with my brother.

"That was Trav. Not only do we have six straight numbers, but the supps as well. Before we get carried away, I want to check the numbers online to make sure we've got our facts right."

Nearing the hotel, we broke into a run, flying past several staff members, apologizing as we went.

I awoke the laptop from its slumber and stared in wonder at the screen. First division was 4.3 million dollars and there was only one other winning entry. So we would get half.

Then my phone rang again and it was Isobel, asking if the numbers on the notice board in the kitchen were the ones we used in our ticket, and had we bought a ticket before we left home.

Sammy took over and spoke to his mother quietly for a few minutes, and finishing the call turned to me.

I was overwhelmed and didn't know what to do next. My bloody heart was racing as I tried to get my head around our new status. We couldn't pretend our life wouldn't change; money was involved in almost every human decision about anything, both good and bad. It wasn't called the root of all evil for nothing.

So many questions going through my mind all at once, I was hyperventilating and nearly catatonic.

Do we tell anybody about our good fortune? Who do we tell? If we don't tell someone and they hear from another source, what would happen to our friendship? Who do we give gifts to? What do we spend the remainder on?

Do we stop working? Can we afford to? Do we invest it all and pretend it didn't happen? Do we buy a new car? Do we buy a new car for Isobel? Do we buy another house? What will our families expect of us? A lump sum for every niece and nephew?

A shadow fell across the chair, and it was him, of course. He always knew what to do.

It was a wonder Sammy had any reserves left in the "giving tank" inside him, because I felt I must have drained him dry. He'd given generously of himself even before we were a couple, but since that time, he'd given everything he had and more. Nothing was ever too difficult or too much trouble, and in this latest turn our life had taken, he was still there for me.

I could feel myself getting emotional.

"Why don't we sleep on it," he said. "Then in the calm light of day tomorrow we'll know what to do for the best." I nodded in agreement. He was just so sensible, understanding our first responsibility was to maintain and enrich our own partnership before we could help anyone else.

SAMMY ENCOURAGED me to take charge in the bedroom. Even though I preferred bottoming for him, there were times I needed a little role reversal, and this was such a time. Sammy sensed it and took me on the ride of my life.

Exhausted, we fell asleep and were only awoken by the dining room staff who rang, asking what we'd like for breakfast. Ten minutes later they delivered a beautiful spread to the room. I opened the balcony door and the fresh morning air filled the room, the gentle splashing of someone below in the pool the only background noise.

"So what's the first priority?" a coy Sammy enquired as we sipped our coffee and tea.

"Kids, our family, has to be," I said without even thinking about it. "We both want a family so badly, now they can grow up with us instead of us being just another pair of old farts with young kids."

"And then?" he asked.

"We get rid of our debt, pay the house off."

"Then what?"

"We have to share with close family and a few friends."

We put together a list with no disagreement, even the amounts were the same. We rang everyone at home, begged them to stay quiet so we could avoid unwanted notoriety and to save us the distress of saying no to other people.

In our minds we penciled in a sum for our superannuation, which we couldn't touch until retirement, and a huge lump sum that we would invest so one of us could stay home to bring up the kids until they were at least school age.

If Sammy hadn't calmed me down the previous night, we'd still be talking and probably arguing; as it was, the whole process took us just two hours.

So we celebrated again. It was our honeymoon after all.

Chapter 27
In Paradise, the Perfect Solution

MY PHONE chirped again in the late afternoon, Chart and Solada asking if they could come over. We'd trusted them with our news knowing they would only tell essential people, as necessary, like Pa and Ma.

We decided to have an evening meal at Patong's most famous seafood restaurant and our favorite. It looked out across the busy road at the Andaman Sea with the waves gently lapping on the sand. It was early evening and relatively quiet, and so lovely to have the time to focus on our friends. They'd been in our lives since our early school days, and more importantly had been with us every inch of the way since we became a couple. Through them we had gained an extended family, and we'd absorbed much of the culture and mindset of the Thais, who were by and large gentle people, loving and so focused on family issues.

And Thai food was just sensational—Sammy once said lemongrass and coriander turned me on more than he did.

We chose a table near the front of the restaurant and close to the tanks full of fresh fish swimming around and lobsters crawling over each other.

CHART KNEW us both so well, having seen us at our best and worst, both physically and mentally. He looked at me and smiled that handsome smile that no doubt had melted a string of hearts until Solada came along.

"You seem a little thoughtful, Jacko," he said, "but I suppose that's natural in your case. Most people we know, particularly back home in Australia, would be partying all night and throwing their newfound wealth around. Yet you two are composed, quiet, and making plans for the future, which is what we expected."

Sammy and I grinned at each other across the table.

"Yes, I guess we now have to start the process of creating a family," I replied, "but in our case it gets complicated. In Australia surrogacy is available, but the regulations vary widely from state to state. In addition, to find someone who's prepared to carry a child for nothing is almost impossible because we're forbidden to pay anyone a fee. It's called altruistic surrogacy and we think it's hopeless, not practical for us."

"It needn't be so complicated," Solada said. "That's what we came to talk to you about. Thai people have a view of family that is quite different to western societies, but I think you already understand much of that difference through your association with our family. Some of our attitudes are influenced by Buddhism, but mostly it is a Thai attitude, and the Chinese influence through Pa is even more considerate of family needs. The love and respect of each member of the family group for each other is general across Thailand. No one is ever alone, and if a person for some reason has no family, then the community takes care of them. Just another, bigger family."

Chart nodded in agreement and continued.

"Thailand in general does not have the social conservatism of western civilization because we've never been colonized by them. And because of that the influence of the Christian churches has been negligible. That is why your beautiful partnership and marriage is such a natural fit in our family, and why when we say we have no hang-ups, you know what we mean."

Sammy caught my eye and we smiled at their seriousness, but we also found it intelligent and insightful and I said so.

As if on autopilot, Solada took over again. "Chart's uncle is a gay man, living with his partner now for nearly fifty years. They've raised their own family—they adopted two boys and a girl. All now partnered and have families of their own. In my family I have a cousin in very poor circumstances who fell pregnant late in life. Her husband lost his job and they couldn't feed another mouth. So another cousin, a successful architect in Bangkok, a gay man, together with his partner, took the little one and raised him. That happens all the time in Thailand, but no one even thinks to mention it because it's considered a normal event. In other cases, for both gay and straight couples, girls in the family group have been surrogates a number of times, and that's just in our family." She smiled.

The main course arrived and I forgot about everything else. They laughed at me as I inhaled my meal of curried tiger prawns. The meal was so spicy I resorted to copious quantities of cold Singha beer to wash it down and to cool my palate. But it was an amazing feast and I was in foodie heaven. Sammy rubbed my tummy and remarked that maybe we wouldn't need a surrogate.

"WE HAVE a niece from my side of the family," Solada said, "who is twenty-seven years old and has two children of her own. She and her husband moved to Phuket two years ago, but they are really struggling financially. Of course Pa and Ma make sure they have plenty to eat and clothes for the children, but they are just like many other young families here who work in industries connected to tourism. He is a driver and she works in a commercial laundry. We think the money you gave us could be better used to pay her for surrogacy services, because I'm certain she would be grateful and happy to oblige."

"No, under no circumstances. That money is for your own use. I know family need transcends everything in your minds, but you two have given of yourselves so much, too much. Use it to grow the Muay Thai business or just for your own kids' school needs, like laptops or books. We have plenty more where that money came from. Your gesture is appreciated, but we can afford whatever it costs."

I quoted a figure that I knew, after our online inquiries for an organization in California, was the going rate.

India was less expensive but still fraught with red tape.

Solada shook her head. "You could not offer such a figure here. To do that would create a precedent and turn an act of love into a commercial operation. So much money so quickly would draw attention in a bad way to what should be seen as a family affair."

"A payment up front," Chart said, "to get them out of debt, and several smaller payments as the pregnancy progresses, then a final payment when the child is born. How many kids do you want?" Chart asked.

"Two," we said together.

"Pa has suggested you create a fund for the education of Natth and Arisa's children. That fund would be invested, with another family member to cosign when funds are needed," he said. "You see, Natth and Arisa aren't good managers. We will have to help them through this as well as helping you create your family."

So we finally knew their names, and Solada scrolled through her iPhone to show us a picture of them. Late twenties, Natth was quite handsome, but Arisa was beautiful in the way that only Thai women can be, naturally elegant. She wasn't overweight, far from it, but she had the generous natural curves of a young mother.

WE HAD lunch with Chart, Solada, Ma, and Pa the following day in Phuket Town. We'd gone to bed the previous night with our heads spinning, but once again in the hard cold light of morning our thoughts were more rational.

We assumed the medical process had to begin in Australia and discussed ad infinitum suitable females as egg donors. Which went nowhere because there was only one donor on my side of the family— Alison—and none at all on Sammy's side. In the end we accepted Arisa's good medical history and more importantly seemingly uncomplicated genetics and decided she would be the birth mother of our kids. With me the father of the first child, and Sammy the second, at his insistence. We reckoned Eurasian-looking kids would be both beautiful and intelligent, and fit in perfectly in our new modern society in Australia, where by 2050 half the population would be able to trace their ancestry back to Asia anyway.

All our concerns about the attitudes of the Thai Medical Council and the government came flooding out, including laws forbidding commercial surrogacy with farangs.

Pa patiently nodded his head.

"There will be no problem, that legislation is no more. We will have an arrangement, which will be approved by the government. They are mainly concerned about the character and suitability of the people who will be parents. When we tell them you are part of our family there won't be any difficulties, I can assure you. However," Pa said, sternly, "it is important that even within the family group that everyone understands their commitment to each other.

"It will be written down in a document translated from English into Thai so we agree on every detail. Close family needs reassurance, and it is worthwhile doing properly," Pa confirmed. And so there it was, as simple and as easy as that.

On the face of it anyway.

We didn't even concern ourselves too much with the international or even Australian legal ramifications because our baby would be legally ours before we reentered the country. But we knew we had to plan ahead and ensure all Australian legal requirements were in order. Surrogacy had been abused in several countries, taken out of its original context, and couples like ourselves had to sometimes convince governments that we simply wanted a family, like anyone else.

Chapter 28
Natth and Arisa

SOMETHING WASN'T quite right, and doubt crept into Sammy's eyes as well. Arisa was every bit as beautiful as her photograph had suggested, and her lovely personality was a bonus. She had a very dry sense of humor and made fun of all their troubles, but it was clear that her handsome husband was something else.

So after buying them a nice lunch, we cut short our meeting, excusing ourselves and confirming we'd meet again the following day at the same time. Sammy rang Chart, and he agreed that he and Solada should also be there, unannounced.

We wandered back to the hotel, hand in hand, lost in thought.

Arisa was ideal in every way as a surrogate. She seemed placid and easygoing, a happy personality, clearly physically and emotionally healthy.

Natth, on the other hand, couldn't sit still, and he kept glancing away, as if he were looking for someone, or maybe someone was looking for him.

We'd only been back in the room a few minutes and were headed toward bed and a nice matinee when the phone shrilled. We had a visitor at reception, Natth, and could he come to our room. I relayed the request to Sammy who agreed, and within minutes there was a soft tap at the door.

Natth was even more on edge, and I wondered idly if he was on drugs, so I asked him straight out.

"Oh no," he said, "just a little dope if I have a good win."

"Win at what?" Sammy asked.

"Ah, I sometimes bet some money on cards."

So our mate had a gambling problem.

"And you have a little flutter online?" Sammy asked.

"A little, yes, but my credit card not work anymore."

Yes, I thought, *no wonder poor Arisa has to struggle to make ends meet.* "So my guess is you like to go to the boxing and bet."

His glance told us we'd hit the jackpot, even though he clearly hadn't.

"So you owe someone some money and can't pay, and they're looking for you, right?" I asked.

"Yes, I am frightened they will hurt me."

"How much?" Sammy asked.

"Three hundred thousand baht."

I did some quick calculations; it was just under four thousand Australian dollars at the current rate of exchange.

Sammy nodded at the bedroom.

"Can you wait here?" I asked. "We need to talk."

Sammy closed the door and we sat on the bed, whispering to each other.

"This has got under the family guard, but Arisa must know already and keeps forgiving the dickhead."

"Yes, but it has to be resolved because our surrogacy relies on his support. I reckon this money has to be the tip of the iceberg, and if we're seen as the bankers, he'll just keep on gambling in the hope we'll pay off his creditors."

"Yes, I agree, we'll have to find a way to stall him off until we can talk to the family properly, otherwise this whole thing could go off the rails."

"Leave it to me."

We opened the bedroom door and walked into the living area, the smiles on our faces changing to looks of amazement. Seldom had Sammy ever been lost for words and neither had I.

Natth lay along the couch, his head comfortably back on the cushion, one leg along the backrest, the other draped along the floor.

With not a stitch on.

He was well-endowed, and the prime object of interest appeared as hard as a rock. In the best relaxed style of Thai bisexual tradition, Natth was keeping his options open—wide open—as he smiled at us, gently massaging his pride and joy.

"We can work something out?" Natth asked before we could get our vocal chords to work.

"Yes, Natth, but only if you put your clothes back on."

"But I can make love to you both all night, every way. I am Thai stud."

"Natth," I said more severely than I intended to, "put your bloody gear on now or the whole deal is off, the surrogacy, the money, everything."

Natth looked at us in horror, the blood draining from his dark face and his erection at the same time. His eyes flew from Sammy to me and back again, making sure we were both on the same page. His shoulders slumped and he looked a picture of abject misery.

He'd misjudged us and his disrobing had worsened his case, not enhanced it.

Sammy, as usual, took over, knowing exactly what to do.

"You are a very handsome man, Natth," he said, "but we don't need any more sex than we have at the moment. Maybe in a couple of years," winking at me and making Natth feel that his charms were still working and leaving his ego intact.

IT WAS a balancing act that we were involved in, but when in doubt, tell the truth. That's what Dad always said.

So we rang Chart and told him everything, chapter and verse, and made him promise not to embarrass Natth with his attempt to solve all his financial issues with a good old-fashioned Thai fucking. Which he'd hoped would be rewarded by bucketloads of cash.

Instead we wanted to focus on what would settle Natth down and keep him away from gambling. Because the one thing Arisa needed was a stress-free nine months as she carried our baby.

We'd nearly been caught in the "Thai siphon," a determined effort to wring cash out of us by any means available. While Natth's modus operandi was common, we recognized a degree of desperation beyond a few local thugs, looking for their money.

We didn't have long to wait. Pa was told, and early the following morning Natth was summoned to explain. Chart was unusually angry. Natth had married a cousin of his wife, yet now his family had to sort the mess out. He'd also insulted us as Chart and Solada's best friends and benefactors to the family group. Chart had evidently promised Natth a little demonstration of Muay Thai principles unless he cooperated, and he wisely did so.

"There's good news and bad news," Chart told us later. "We now find Natth has outstanding debts in Bangkok, which is why he came here in the first place. Natth's family will help settle those. The good news is that his debts here in Phuket are a third of the figure he gave you. He simply wanted a nice float so he could keep on gambling. We will settle those, and he will pay us back, a little every week. A similar amount will go to his family in Bangkok."

Chart paused, shaken. "I am very sorry, boys. We will work hard and find you another surrogate."

"No." Sammy looked at me for support. We took hold of Chart's hands as a gesture of our intent and friendship. "We think Arisa is ideal. We don't want to change anything. But when we document all of this, we have to make sure Arisa is the only one who can authorize funds. You see, we all thought Arisa was a bad manager, but I reckon she was covering up her husband's mistakes. Natth doesn't deserve her loyalty, but she's a Thai woman, after all, capable, clever, and forgiving, always in the background, always making her husband look good even if he's not."

"What if I were that bad?" Chart asked, his eyebrows arched, a smile on his handsome face.

"Easy. Solada would always forgive you. But don't forget, she's a modern Australian woman now."

"Meaning?"

"Meaning I wouldn't dare upset her in case you lost part of your anatomy."

Chapter 29
Getting the Show on the Road

I E-MAILED work and added another week to my leave after speaking to Mr. Davis. He was one of the people we'd chosen to tell of our lottery win, and he was totally supportive, as expected. A hint of regret came through as well, and I decided to put his mind at rest. "No, I'll still have to work, so you won't need to look for another operations manager." A chuckle sounded in his voice, and relief also, as he switched me through to Mrs. Shields.

She'd also been taken into our confidence, and we'd told her there would be help with her eldest boy's college fees and coaching because he, like me, was dyslexic. Sammy had coached Jonathan at the Special School and we simply wanted him to realize his full potential. Now we were in a position to make sure he did.

No one in my working life had done as much for me as Barbara Shields. She was my backstop, my secretary, and my advisor. She read documents, wrote and sent e-mails, and was an expert on warehousing, plant maintenance, and people management. She understood how my brain worked because her own son faced similar integration problems as he grew up. She'd been in tears ever since we told her what we'd planned to do for Jonathan and, more importantly, her and her husband. They'd never been able to afford a holiday, and we were busily arranging one in Phuket they wouldn't forget.

WE MET with a local solicitor who presented us with a contract, and came away so upset and confused we felt like catching the next plane home. It was the prick's attitude rather than the content of the contract. The location didn't concern us, be it at home or in Thailand. We simply wanted to be treated like customers; this guy used his knowledge of the law to patronize us.

We spoke next to Pa and Chart because he refused point-blank to e-mail the contract to our legal people at home. "Not necessary," he'd said. We made the point that our surrogacy arrangements had to survive both Thai and Australian legal requirements, and we simply wouldn't proceed unless we were convinced that was the case.

We hadn't heard Pa in full flight before, but it was an education. We didn't speak either Chinese or Thai, but it was clear our eightysomething friend hadn't lost the fire in his belly. Chart smiled at the performance, as Pa went up a few octaves and shouted through the phone at the unfortunate bloke. Pa stopped for a moment and looked at me. "E-mail address, Jackson, please?"

"He has it already, Pa," I said.

There was more shouting from Pa as he began scribbling on a piece of paper. "Is this correct?" he asked, and I nodded.

Pa thanked me in his beautifully precise manner and spoke slowly and clearly for a minute or so, finally smashing the handset down. He and Chart exchanged knowing smiles.

"Job done," Chart said. "When can your people get back with any alterations or additions?"

"Two days." I'd already spoken to them.

The laptop chirped at me and there was the contract. I excused myself for a moment as I forwarded it onward. To be sure, I rang our contact, the same guy who'd done all my family's work for years, to tell him to check his e-mails. He confirmed it was there and that he'd left nothing to chance, calling in specialist opinions from a number of sources.

The following morning we flew to Bangkok on the early plane and visited the Australian consulate. The Phuket "honorary" consul was out of town, and Pa didn't know him anyway. In the Bangkok office an attractive and courteous Australian immigration officer, Lucy Brooks, met us. Lucy treated us to morning tea and gave us all the documents we needed for a passport once our child was born, and the procedure to follow. We couldn't believe our ears. It was just so easy and so different from all the horror stories we'd heard from the media over the years.

Lucy assured us we were one couple among many; at least one couple per week accessed consular advice and assistance in Bangkok, and it was increasing. The surrogacy guidelines had been redrawn, previous legislation repealed and for the first time, same-sex couples were now predominant.

THE LAST week rushed up on us. We'd certainly had an unusual honeymoon by any standards. When we left home we didn't expect we'd be two million dollars richer or to be organizing the beginning of our family.

There was only one task remaining, and that was entirely medical: tests and more tests, on me in particular, as I was to be the biological father. According to the experts, Arisa was ovulating and the next few days were critical. So I had to come up with some samples.

"Samples of what?" I stupidly asked Sammy.

"Sperm, you know, Jacko, cum."

Thank goodness I hadn't had an audience other than my other half, I was so embarrassed. Sammy held his sides and I promised retribution if he told anyone.

The clinic was in a plain, nondescript building around the corner from the hospital. They were expecting us; Sammy was shown to a private waiting room while I was ushered into a small room not much larger than a cubicle.

A small container for the sample kept company with a pile of porn magazines on the shelf. Straight porn. This part of the Thai medical profession clearly hadn't adjusted to the realities of the new client base.

"Take your time," the nurse said warmly.

As I turned the pages, it was like reading a history book. Fond memories but no excitement. Not even a twinge. I started to panic because no erection meant no bloody sample. I tried massage, I tried lovely dirty thoughts, nothing.

I threw the door open and hissed at Sammy to join me, much to the consternation of the nurse. I waved her away as I dragged Sammy into the bloody room with me.

It was a little crowded in there, but Sammy kissed me softly and I was like granite instantly. Two minutes later the nurse had a huge bloody sample, and I couldn't wipe the smile off my face. Over the following days, several more samples were taken, and each time Sammy helped me out. Successfully and enjoyably.

We were involved in the conception of our baby in a unique way with the knowledge that the magic was still there for us, more than ever. So our kid would be a fusion of our love.

"A happy beginning," Sammy said, "even better than a happy ending."

Chapter 30
Kate

WE PAID out the mortgage and it was *our* home, an exciting time.

I collected Isobel from TAFE one evening, and sitting under the portico where the Ford usually sat was a brand new small Peugeot. She actually asked who it belonged to. I handed her the keys and said "you."

The process of giving away money was fun, but it had its serious side. Our solicitor insisted all beneficiaries sign a waiver stating any further gifts were totally at our behest and that they had no future claim on us. I felt awful asking Dad to sign it, also Trav and Ali, and apologized, blaming our solicitor, which was true. But they seemed to understand. Dad in particular was actually pleased with the way I'd progressed with my attitude to things financial, reminding me how all those years ago he'd appointed Sammy to be the treasurer when we worked part-time for him. And I wanted to blow everything on one night out.

SAMMY WAS the subject of an article in the local daily press one Saturday. A four-page spread with photographs, in and out of the classroom.

It seemed some seriously wealthy people had kids with learning difficulties whose lives had been transformed because of Sammy's teaching methods and dedication at the Special School, and they wanted him recognized.

The article made sure the community understood that Sammy was a unique resource who should be encouraged, who was already responsible for around two hundred kids going on to continue their education, becoming productive students and future productive members of society, where in the past most had fallen by the wayside in mundane occupations, never realizing their full potential. I was dragged in too; they photographed us on the couch at home in the living room.

Rather than talk about me, I wanted to talk about Sammy as a teacher. That I was his very first pupil, and because of that I'd done so well with my work, and in life generally. And that he continued to inspire me, but that I was naturally biased, because I'd married my teacher and the lessons in life never stopped.

I made the point that the scope of the Special School had been enlarged and extended to include overseas students from Asia, and it had become an annex of the university where funding wasn't quite so problematic.

I also mentioned our first child being due in a few months and how we'd planned for one of us to stay home until our kids were of school age themselves. But the Special School needed Sammy's expertise, and he felt he had to finish building the resource he'd started. He just couldn't walk away from it, and I supported him. He could train teachers to eventually take his place, but that took time, skill, and money, the latter item in short supply as always.

In my case my senior management role meant I had many people relying on my direction, management, and support for essential services that the City provided. The City and the University evidently talked to each other, Mr. Davis and Margaret Reeve.

Between us all a commonsense agreement was reached. We would both be away for at least a month in Thailand when our child was born, on leave of absence. Suddenly at the Special School, a fully staffed crèche was in the advanced planning stages, with the advantage that at least six other parents would use its services. So no one could say Sammy was getting favored treatment.

We thought about it all long and hard and finally agreed that we couldn't stop contributing to the community in either of our paid roles. Interaction between our own child and other kids would hopefully balance the nurturing family environment we had intended to create at home.

So we agreed. The Special School wouldn't miss a beat, Sammy would delegate as much as possible, as I would at the City with Mrs. Shields's help.

Parental leave for us would mean child care some days and turning up at our work regularly, probably giving everyone the shits, but keeping in touch with the priorities.

ARISA FELL pregnant with our child, as planned, probably before we even left the airport to return home.

"Lack of fertility has never been a problem with our family," Solada told us with a smile. We were amazed that paternity testing before birth was available in Thailand, so at three months it was done, and I was certainly the father.

Slowly but surely we seemed to be ticking all the boxes.

But we worried, like most expectant parents. We were uptight about everything, and idly wondered if it would be any easier if we brought her to Australia.

Solada was adamant. "No," she said, "certainly not. That would unleash unnecessary jealousy in the family, and who would look after Arisa's other children? Just leave it alone and you'll be surprised how easily it all comes together. The most important thing is Arisa and the baby are healthy, and everything is going to plan. Do you want to know what sex the child is?"

"No," we said categorically—at this stage we'd had enough medical science to last us a lifetime.

Every Sunday evening we had dinner with Chart and Solada, usually at our place so Isobel caught up with the latest. Once a month the whole family group met up. Travis's and Alison's kids were being brought up by the village, and we wanted ours raised the same way, so we involved everyone up front. Dad's eyes twinkled. "Everyone taking some ownership," he said with a grin, "and most of them potential babysitters."

Quite often we would skype Pa and Ma in Phuket Town, usually with Arisa and Natth in the room. Arisa was clearly blooming, and to our pleasant surprise, Natth seemed really proud of his wife's achievement. So was Pa.

Natth had quietened down because homes didn't run themselves, and with Arisa needing plenty of rest, Natth became quite domesticated. Proudly he told of his breakfast-making expertise, his newfound ability to work the washing machine, and he even did the shopping each week.

"Because Arisa has a very important job to do," he said.

And a well-paid one too, I thought as I smiled at Sammy.

Our main fear was, and always had been, the rejection of our agreement by Arisa.

Even though everything was written into a legal document, the fact was that Arisa was the child's biological mother. And we worried that Arisa wouldn't want to let go, like any mother, literally giving her child to someone else. If that was ever the case, then the resulting disagreement would probably mean we would lose our family in Phuket, damage our relationship with Chart and Solada, and put strain on our own marriage.

WE BOUGHT a new SUV complete with all the stuff to carry a child safely. Then filled the house with baby paraphernalia, every imaginable aid and necessity for raising a child successfully and safely.

We decorated the bedroom next to ours and knocked a doorway through so our kid would be close to us. "A proper nursery," Isobel said. "Turn it back into a bedroom later." I did see the funny side of it—our kid would certainly hate us later on; ready access to their room by their parents would be the last thing on their mind.

And still we worried, not only about our child's custody, as if that wasn't enough, but what if Arisa became ill and our baby were affected? What if all the genetic indicators had been wrong and we ended up with a disabled child? For once Sammy was as bad as I was, as we effectively wound each other up. We almost convinced ourselves we'd taken the wrong path, organizing a private surrogacy instead of using one of the corporate entities where the outcomes were virtually guaranteed.

At work I couldn't concentrate. I apologized to Mrs. Shields and Mr. Davis, both of whom were understanding and amused at the same time, regaling me with their stories of maternity and paternity, which made me feel worse again.

Dad assured me I was right on track to be just like him. He joked that the hospital thought his water had broken, not Mum's, when Trav was born. Both Dad and Isobel were great sounding boards, and both of them spoke to Solada, who assured them everything would be fine.

Sammy and I were reassured in turn. But it didn't help much.

We trusted Solada implicitly, but we were both focused on that final moment when our child was handed to us by Arisa. If that ever happened.

Finally the countdown was in place. Three weeks to the birth, and we arrived in Phuket. Solada traveled with us while Chart stayed at home, looking after their kids and his Muay Thai customers.

Pa and Ma had a meal ready, so we sent the taxi away and relaxed as best we could for a few hours. Solada stayed on while we went straight to our hotel.

Same room again.

We looked at each other and smiled. Here was a chance to relax. The lull before the storm.

After a light dinner, Solada met us and drove us to see Arisa, Natth, and their children. Arisa remained wonderfully well, but she was by now uncomfortable, so close to the main event. Natth was astonishing. He'd put on a little weight but was organized, welcoming, and clearly in charge of the household. Solada smiled at me as if to say "see I told you, nothing to worry about."

I smiled back. Natth had indeed changed his attitude, and I realized suddenly he was our best ally. No baby meant no money, and I was sure Natth wouldn't be impressed if Arisa chucked a wobbly.

Arisa needed to rest, so after half an hour we left them to it. We walked back to the hotel while Solada drove home to Pa and Ma.

We walked everywhere the following day for exercise and even visited the birthing suites in the clinic where it would all take place. We could sleep there as well, so we'd be close to all the action, but neither of us was quite sure if we needed to be there for the main event, maybe afterwards.

I begged Sammy for a seafood meal, and we naturally ended up back at our favorite place. They recognized us and free beers magically appeared, and being me I decided I'd have some more. Quite a few more. We had the most beautiful meal, toured along Walking Street, and went back to the hotel.

We'd come full circle at this place. Best friends became lovers here; years of dodging around the subject, false starts with other people all left behind us. So we consummated our love all over again. We edged each other deliberately, trying to make it last until we were overtaken by nature, and climaxed together.

Some time later a noise broke the silence, and Sammy, always a lighter sleeper than me, leaned over and grabbed my phone—it was Solada. I looked at the bedside clock, which read 1:30 a.m. Arisa's water had broken and they were on their way to the clinic. Two weeks early.

Somehow we threw ourselves under the shower, found clean clothes, and bolted down the street. It was faster to walk or run than to take a taxi. Walking Street was still noisy, but we were on a mission as we ran past some drunken Australian revelers. "Where ya goin'?" one of them yelled. I couldn't get the words out, I was so focused on doing one thing at a time. Like running.

I had the feeling if I told him the truth he wouldn't believe me anyway.

The soft lighting outside the clinic cast shadows across the footpath as we pressed the buzzer in the entrance hall. We were ushered inside and then into the suite after having been suitably gowned, masked, and gloved. We had a view of Arisa that I supposed only a few people had ever seen. She was calm but clearly working hard.

It seemed natural for me to hold one hand and Sammy the other as she pushed. And pushed again.

Ten minutes later she yelled and gave a mighty heave, and a black head appeared. Another minipush and we jumped to one side as the obstetrician delivered a baby girl. Her airway was cleared, and she wailed like a banshee, and the cord was clipped.

Instead of the child being laid on the mother's breast as was usual, Arisa waved her hand in my direction. Our baby was wrapped in a little shawl and handed to me, and I bawled my bloody eyes out as I gazed into the eyes of our daughter. I passed her to Sammy, who looked down at her with such love it was obvious an immediate bond existed between the two.

Together we handed her back to Arisa and almost immediately our little one started feeding noisily.

We named her Katherine Isobel Collins-Smith, but in typical Australian fashion, she would always be called Kate.

Our Kate, nothing could be more perfect, and I suddenly knew all our worries had been groundless.

Sammy and I clung to each other. This would stay with us always. The arrival of your firstborn is without doubt a life-changing event, and we were no exception. We looked at each other and grinned; it was very early in the morning back home in Australia, but after they heard the news, I doubted if anyone would be too upset at being woken.

A new generation had been created, and we knew our life would never be the same again. That is the nature of things.

Chapter 31
Hard Yakka and a Leap up the Ladder

ASK ANY parent if their life changes with an infant in the house, and usually they'll shake their head and smile ruefully because life does take a different direction, and with different priorities.

No longer are you just concerned about the daily running of a household: shopping, cleaning, washing, bloody ironing, gardening, etcetera. Or having a lovely social life: barbeques, a few beers, good times with good friends. Even a career can become secondary, except maybe to generate enough cash to feed and clothe everyone. And to pay all the bills.

It becomes clear to new parents very quickly that their prime responsibility is to lead the way so the little life they've created develops to their full potential and grows up happily in an increasingly competitive world, feeling loved, protected, and nourished, mentally and physically.

Sounds easy, but it's not.

But we were fortunate with Kate. From day one she was the best kid. Other parents looked on in disbelief when we told them she was sleeping the whole night through at four weeks.

That time frame coincided with our homecoming from Phuket. She coped beautifully with the day flight home, sleeping on and off in the little cot provided by the airline. There were some amused glances from passengers, but as we realized later, we were far from the exception these days.

We took turns at changing and feeding her, and she was amazing.

Isobel had set up the nursery for her, and after a feed and yet another crap, our Kate snuggled down, quite happy in her new home.

The following day she burped and farted her way through her formula so well it prompted Dad to say she was just like me. And Sammy agreed.

While I could still be a handful with my bloody tantrums, they were few and far between these days, but Kate seemed to have inherited placid genes from somewhere else, maybe through Arisa's lot. Isobel told us we were quite silly to even consider genetics when the greatest influencer—the environment created by her parents—was now fully operational.

"Your child is simply following the pathway of love and affection you two have created," she said, "within your marriage. She's responding to that already, and remember, bringing up kids is easy if you remember the three rules."

"Three rules?" Sammy asked.

"Example, example, and example." Isobel smiled sweetly. "You set a good example and the kids will follow. I didn't do too badly with you, did I?"

BETWEEN US all, Kate thrived, but parental leave became a joke.

Sammy worked mainly from home during his parental leave, enjoying the time around Kate but also keeping in touch with everything at the Special School. When he did go in, Kate was looked after lovingly in the new crèche.

Some days she came to work with me when I knew I was tied to my desk all day. She gurgled and giggled at me, but she loved Mrs. Shields, who still managed to put in a full day but changed and fed my daughter as well, supervising her in her playpen as Kate entertained any visitors.

Alison took her other days, as did Sally, Trav's wife. But Isobel was always our main backstop, a wonderful grandmother to Kate.

Kate, meanwhile, developed in leaps and bounds.

As our daughter neared twelve months of age, we watched and listened in wonderment as she uttered her first words. "Dad" for me, "Pop" for Sammy, and "Gan" for Granny Isobel. It was already clear that she was a very advanced child for her age, and we knew we'd need roller skates to keep up with her.

And she was Sammy's little girl. Yes of course she loved me, too, but when she saw Sammy she lit up with squeals and giggles. I didn't blame her, he did that to me as well, always had.

IT WAS an early meeting even for me, a command performance in Mr. Davis's office, and even though I was well prepared, I felt half-asleep.

We caught up with all the current issues in about thirty minutes with Sharon, his assistant, taking notes. Something didn't feel right however.

Mr. Davis looked tired lately, and there were dark circles under his eyes. When he asked Sharon to leave us, I was on full alert.

"What's wrong?" I asked in a panic. "You don't look well."

The father figure on the other side of the table smiled at me. "You're spot on, as usual. I could never keep anything away from that bloody sixth sense of yours. I'm okay, but sadly my wife's osteoarthritis has become chronic, and I need to spend significant time on her care most days. Her mobility has worsened to the point where we either hire a full-time carer or I take over, so I'll be taking an early retirement package."

My heart sank to my boots. Mr. Davis had been my greatest advocate, my protector, and my inspiration. Life without him at work would be intolerable, and I could only imagine what sort of yuppie dickhead would take his place. Together we'd done things conventional wisdom thought impossible, including driving down costs at the City without sacking a single employee. We had the ear of the unions and we'd formed a partnership with them, fighting for excellence in the workplace by introducing KPIs—key performance indicators. I'd lost count of the meetings we'd attended where we took councilors into our confidence and sought their support for major projects. Like the waste collection strategy, which they thought couldn't be done. It had been successful beyond our wildest hopes, and the service to ratepayers had actually improved.

He reached for my hand across the table. He'd been like another father to me, a wise and compassionate man from the country who had left preconceived ideology behind him, becoming a brilliant administrator in his own right. Now he was going, and I started to panic again.

"Who do you think you could train up to take your position?" he asked.

Fuck, now I'm going to be flicked at the same time.

"You've hardly heard a word I've said for the last five minutes." He was smiling as he continued. "You need to come up with a recommendation for operations manager so I can train you for my job," he said. "It's all signed off, the council have unanimously agreed not to advertise again, promote from within—much healthier and looks better to the ratepayers. Congratulations, Jackson, you truly deserve it."

I felt light-headed. Not even thirty years of age, and I was being offered, no, *told* I was to become the new CEO of the City with a package worth in the vicinity of $300,000.

Leonardo da Vinci, Albert Einstein, Alexander Graham Bell, Sir Richard Branson, Walt Disney, Jay Leno, Whoopi Goldberg, Nelson Rockefeller, Agatha Christie, Steven Spielberg, Harry Belafonte, Winston Churchill, Richard Strauss.

Chapter 32
Another Happy Beginning

I HAD a degree of guilt about leaving work for a few weeks, particularly only a few months after my appointment as CEO. But there were no outstanding issues, and nothing new that couldn't be handled with a daily conference.

I used Skype to contact Mrs. Shields every day. She'd come with me from Operations to the CEO's office and had transformed the place. Sharon, Mr. Davis's PA, had also decided to retire early, which was probably just as well. Cyclone Barbara was a force on her own, yet she had a persuasive way with her, including with other women, which was unusual. She also thought in a linear fashion like me, and with a dyslexic son of her own, I wasn't surprised.

For Sammy and me, the rest of the world would have to wait because the arrival of our next child quickly became our first priority. And our other family in Phuket were missing us.

I made an executive decision. Leave of absence again.

SAMMY HAD left some samples behind after Kate was born, and by the time we finally returned to Phuket, Arisa was eight months pregnant with our second child.

When we did arrive, Kate charmed everyone. A chubby, contented, happy little kid.

At the hotel she was never alone; the staff "stole" her in her pusher to show her off, particularly at breakfast, and our daughter loved it. She was a little people person, seemingly stimulated by everyone new. We wondered what would be her reaction, if any, to her biological mother, and more importantly, what Arisa's reaction would be to her. We needn't have worried; Arisa and Natth were like an auntie and uncle to her, and Kate seemed to accept them at face value, including Arisa's big tummy.

As Solada explained later, "It was the Thai way, after all."

Pa and Ma were so genuinely pleased to see us, and Kate seemed drawn to them. She talked to them in her language and was quite animated, both of us understanding the ancient in our daughter connecting with the ancient ways of Asia through Pa and Ma.

Arisa was really cool and marvelously healthy, but more importantly, so was Natth.

I'd always looked at people with gambling addictions in a similar light to alcoholics and drug addicts. But Natth, who'd seemed born to gamble, wasn't much interested these days, which puzzled me. He looked and sounded contented, and seemed totally absorbed in their kids and the domestic duties that made their home run along well. He was also doing much better as a driver, always on time, and brought his tips home to Arisa.

Pa had spent a lot of time with Natth. No one was naïve enough to believe he was "cured," but he was obviously trying. Pa persevered, and then came the breakthrough—Pa discovered Natth was a slow learner at school.

His family of wealthy merchants sent him to an English-language school to prepare him for the family business. But Natth bombed out in a big way.

The only thing that stayed with him from that experience was the English language itself—spoken, not written. But his family disowned him because they thought he was an idiot, and pushed his younger brother ahead instead.

Poor Natth had just existed. The normal Thai family structure wasn't there to look after him because his parents thought he was just lazy. Natth clearly wasn't lazy, Natth was dyslexic like me. Only Arisa had saved him from a life much worse.

"I think you boys can help Natth now more so than me," Pa said.

It reminded us that dyslexia is a global learning difficulty. It is present in all races and certainly doesn't recognize borders.

THIS TIME around we were better organized. Naturally.

Anxiety hardly existed—well, just a little because we were expectant fathers again, after all. But the birth of Kate solidified our relationship further with our family in Phuket, and we knew the outcome this time around would be just as perfect as it was with our firstborn. Or we hoped it would, because sometimes even when the cards are stacked in your favor, shit happens.

As if following a script, Arisa started early again, but this time after breakfast just five days later. The hotel's child-minding people were prepared and waiting, and I mentally thanked our lucky stars for the placid nature of our daughter as we set out for the clinic. We knew Kate would be entertaining the staff, not the other way around.

We ran and walked down past Walking Street again. It was 9.30 a.m., yet a few punters bravely ignored the hour. A few tired-looking girls sitting at one of the bars waved at us in a desultory fashion as we sped past, our level of anxiety beginning to exert itself as we mentally prepared ourselves for what lay ahead. It was the same drill as before—gowns, masks, and gloves—and we were allowed inside.

Arisa actually smiled at us this time; she had some time to go.

After it stretched past two hours we began to panic, even though the obstetrician and midwife were calm.

Kate had almost fallen out; this baby hung back.

The obstetrician was reluctant to do any more than "let nature take its course," so we were advised to go for a coffee. They would phone us as she got closer.

We were absolutely shitting ourselves by now, as much for Arisa's sake as the baby's. I nearly scalded my mouth with coffee, and Sammy ran to the toilet and heaved. Finally, after another two hours, they rang. They were going to hurry things along a bit, induce her.

We tore back, not knowing what to think. We were told to wait outside this time, and that just made things worse.

I grabbed Sammy's hand and we wove our fingers together, just fearful of what might happen. Everything seemed so out of our control.

The door opened, and the nice nurse from Kate's birth smiled at us and beckoned us in. She told us that after another copybook pregnancy, the baby had become breech in the last few days since Arisa's last checkup.

Finally they'd managed to turn it—with the baby's help, and a caesarean wasn't necessary, but she was induced to ensure it happened without delay.

Poor Arisa struggled. We alternatively held her hand and mopped her brow as she pushed and bloody pushed.

After a total of six hours' labor, the moment arrived and a head appeared. We stepped to one side, and with a heave she delivered a baby boy. The midwife held him up, cleared his airway, and there was an almighty roar. Clearly there was nothing wrong with his lungs.

She wrapped him in a cloth and handed him to Sammy, who looked at him in wonder, passing him over to me. We were both emotional as we gazed into the face of Maxwell Peter Collins-Smith, our son.

Quickly we handed him back to Arisa, but he didn't want to feed. Just roar his head off.

Arisa expressed some milk from her copious supply and caressed his lips with her milky finger. That was all he needed, and he started feeding with gusto.

Somehow I knew there was going to be a special bond between him and me, in the same way there was a bond between Sammy and Kate. Even though Sammy was his biological parent, I sensed he was going to be a difficult little bastard like me. This was my little boy, a red-faced protesting little brat who pulled a bloody face at me, but I was sure he loved me. Because I loved him.

Chapter 33
The Excitement of the City

WE FINALLY made it home a full month later.

Everything was different to Kate's early weeks. Max was loud, raucous, and demanding. On the flight home, he roared and screamed, and we were the center of attention in the worst possible way. It looked like we were just useless blokes who didn't know how to raise a child, or worse still, that we were being diabolically cruel to a little infant. It was a battle of wills. He was fine while I held him or if Sammy was feeding him, but screamed when we put him down in his little airline cot. In the end it was his sister who sat on Sammy's knee so he could see her and they "talked" to each other. After nearly two hours of wearing himself and us out, he slept.

Life as we knew it would never be quite the same again; our youngest kid would make sure of that.

MRS. SHIELDS asked if she could meet me at home two days before I was due back at work. I was intrigued and concerned at the same time; she clearly wanted to raise some private issues before the spotlight focused on me the following Monday at work.

Kate was ecstatic. She loved Mrs. Shields and gave her a great welcome, squealing with delight as Barbara swung her through the air. Excitedly, Barbara walked over to the crib to inspect the newest member of the family, who scowled at her. Sammy and I held our sides. "Different, isn't he?" she asked, and we nodded in unison. Max had his favorites, and he hadn't yet decided whether he liked Barbara Shields. Being the smart woman she is, rather than make silly baby noises at Max as most people did, she turned away instead and ignored him. There was a roar from Max like a fighter jet and her eyes sparkled.

"Gotcha," she said and went back to the crib, pulling a face at him. I don't know whether six-week-old babies are supposed to recognize facial expressions, but bloody Max did, because I'll swear he did the same to Barbara. She picked him up and nursed him, almost immediately being rewarded by a wet nappy. Sammy changed him, but his eyes never left Mrs. Shields.

"How did you do that?" I asked.

"Experience," she said with a smile. "Same as Jonathan. He had a mind of his own at a very early age."

I nodded, understanding a lot more, and wondered if Max would be dyslexic like Jonathan. Or like me.

Only time would tell, but I swore that both our kids would never be disadvantaged as I was early in my school career. With Sammy teaching and me encouraging, they would probably blitz their way through the academic marshlands and be prime minister or something.

"YOU KNOW the new mayor was elected in your absence," Mrs. Shields said.

I nodded. The City had changed from a system where after councilors were elected, they in turn chose the mayor. The mayor was now elected via the ballot box and by the ratepayers. On the face of it, a more democratic process, but in reality, a minefield of misconceptions.

We sat across the dining room table from each other as she detailed the events, day by day of my absence, particularly since Andrew Fitch had been elected mayor of the City.

"This is only a stepping stone for him, you do realize that."

Mrs. Shields nodded her understanding as I spelled out my information on Dr. Andrew Fitch. "He's a member of the Liberal Party, clearly intent on winning preselection for the seat of Hinchcliffe. The sitting member is due to retire at the next election and Andrew badly needs to raise his profile in the community."

Mrs. Shields agreed.

"Trouble is, Jacko, he's intent on making the news by proving how well he can run the City."

"But that's my job," I said, and she just smiled.

"I know. He refuses to believe the City is as well run as it is. The problem is he has no real background or experience in business. He's been a local GP, and evidently quite a good one, but no real exposure to business management. Discussing the debt to equity ratio of the City is like talking in a foreign language to him. He just doesn't get it. He's also been through every expense report lodged in the last five years and of course can't find anything amiss."

I roared with laughter. The guy was an idiot. Looking for savings in expense reports is small-picture stuff, like a shopkeeper counting the sweets in a lolly jar. But I sensed there was another agenda, and Mrs. Shields agreed.

"Judging by the questions he's been asking, I think he's attempting to make an issue of the wages bill by changing the remuneration structure, salary, entitlements, and superannuation, and to do that he knows he'll have to take on the unions." While the enterprise agreement was enshrined in law, she and I both knew he could cause trouble.

Instantly I knew where this bloke was coming from. "He's trying to impress the party selection panel as an economic guru and a hero for standing up to the unions." A feeling of dread grabbed my gut for the potential instability where industrial harmony and productivity existed.

It was silly old me that saw things, with that ability of many dyslexic people to view things on a different level to ordinary mortals. But I was smart enough to realize I needed people around me like Barbara and Sammy to keep me grounded and to fill in the spaces.

Right now the new mayor hasn't the faintest idea his ambition has well and truly exceeded his ability.

Turning back the industrial relations clock fifty years would achieve nothing, injuring the business reputation of the City and creating unnecessary stress for our loyal, hardworking employees. With Mr. Davis first and then through myself, we'd developed a collaborative management style, and the unions had responded.

A most accommodating and reasonable relationship was the result, where we included the unions in the management group and dealt with problems before they became insurmountable, in the spirit of our enterprise agreement.

Forewarned, I decided I'd go into the office on Saturday. But I made a few phone calls first to prepare.

I was there early, parked in my spot underneath the building, and took the lift to the third floor. As I turned the corner, I froze.

The executive office lights blazed with the rest of the building in relative darkness. On a Saturday morning it was unusual for any lights to be on. Maybe it was cleaners, or even security. Or some bastard trying to rob the bloody place.

Tiptoeing along the hallway, I slipped quietly through the reception area and through the side door, for which I have the only key. There, with his head stuck in my filing system, was the rotund figure of our new mayor.

"Good morning," I said. "Find anything of interest?"

He swung around, just like a kid caught with his hand in the cookie jar. "N-no," he stammered. "I was looking for the forward estimates."

"Expenditure or receivables?"

"Aah, expenditure."

"Well they're certainly not in there. That's all my personal stuff, but I guess you knew that anyway." His eyes took on a calculating expression as if to say "okay, I've been sprung, let's use my authority to talk my way out of it," but it was obvious I had the upper hand as the injured party, and he wisely said nothing. I had the presence of mind to switch on my little recorder, brought with me from the Operations office, which worked beautifully with the acoustics of the executive area.

"Dr. Fitch," I said, "I'm sorry we had to meet this way, which is no doubt embarrassing for you and mystifying for me. While you have authority as the elected mayor of this city to look at whatever you like, it's a shame you had to snoop around like a common criminal looking through my personal files, when if you'd asked to see them, Mrs. Shields would have been happy to provide them in my absence. After clearing the request with me first, of course."

The dickhead looked like he'd been poleaxed.

"Yes, even though I've been on leave of absence I've been in constant touch with the office at least once daily, some days several times. And just to reassure you, I won't be claiming on my expense account this trip because the whole purpose of my travel was of a deeply personal and private nature, the birth of our second child."

The asshole flinched as if I'd struck him physically. The fact that I knew he'd been snooping through expense reports no doubt made him feel even more uncomfortable. But I was smart enough to hold out the olive branch, because I surely didn't need an enemy so close to home.

"Look," I said, "the City has a lot riding on my performance, but there are many things I can help you with if you simply ask for it. Stuff where you can take the initiative and prove to the ratepayers you're earning your salary."

The mayor regarded me with a look of disdain. "The only help I need from you is to rationalize the huge salary that you're paid. The wages bill for the whole organization is scandalous."

The prick sat back with a smile on his face, playing his power games and not in the least bit apologetic for invading my workplace without my permission.

So there it was. Mrs. Shields's gut feeling was correct and the mayor was going to make a hero of himself. Or so he thought.

It was certainly war and I used my iPhone to take several photographs of my visitor, to which he objected.

"I think it's time you left anyway," I said. "I now have evidence of an illegal entry into this area, and my phone has automatically documented the time the picture was taken. It's a great pity you've taken this combative role. We could have worked together for the betterment of the ratepayers, but unfortunately I suspect your modus operandi is more about furthering your future political career than concern for our ratepayers and the community in general. I'll be turning these pictures over to the police and letting them decide if you're to be charged with trespass. Now, as I have a meeting in ten minutes' time, I suggest you leave."

The mayor turned a very deep beetroot color, and I casually wondered what the reading would be if the good doctor took his own blood pressure.

"You can't order me around. You're just another useless, overpaid public servant, and I *am* the mayor of this city."

"Suit yourself, Dr. Fitch, but if you're not out that door in one minute, I'm calling security."

"You'll hear about this, mark my words."

"Yes, I probably will, in court before a magistrate. Wouldn't that look just lovely for the Liberal Party preselection committee? Now piss off, I'm busy."

I was rewarded by the mayor's normally ruddy complexion changing to an ashen gray as he stormed out through reception.

THE EXECUTIVE boardroom was comfortable, quiet, and quite secure.

All the managers attended, and the union reps, twenty of us.

They were ahead of the game, as usual, and guessed what it was all about: the new bloody mayor. Dr. Fitch had visited every single one of them and asked the same questions. All of us in the room were good friends; we'd worked together over the years and appreciated the fact that I was never far away from the coalface. Every week I put on my old duds for a few hours and talked to all our people in the field as they performed the essential tasks that kept the City's heart alive and beating. I still drove mowers now and then and amused the guys and gals as I took over their machines for a few minutes. I also spent time in the garbage trucks with permission of the contractors, and called into the Operations workshops for a yarn with some old mates. The information I received was priceless, as were the shared ideas.

Collaborative management had brought trust, passion for excellence, and loyalty—the very things we needed most to keep the City functioning efficiently and happily into the future.

Sadly, more than ever, the councilors themselves were divided in opinion between the various political parties and independents, and despite me presenting a written report on the City's operations every quarter, the information usually sailed over their heads. Clearly they couldn't be relied on to support us.

I TOLD the guys we should record our meeting, so as not to attract criticism at a later date, and Sallyanne Bulmer volunteered to keep the minutes.

Even as I showed them the microphone of the recording device, they certainly didn't hold back. Jock Fleming, the parks and gardens manager, was forthright as usual. "He's trying to provoke a strike, laddie," he said, "no doubt about it. We simply have to be prepared and not take the bait, even though he's an insult to any thinking person's intelligence."

Information within our ranks and in the community was going to win the day. The mayor had an ally in the managing editor of the local newspaper, but we had access to a free-to-air television channel that dealt with local issues.

I had to protect these people; they didn't deserve to be pilloried because the mayor wanted some political mileage.

I was half listening, half thinking, when it came to me. "Phil," I said to the union guy from Admin, "how far along is the quality assurance program now? We must be close to full accreditation."

"About a week," he answered, and then it seemed to hit him as well.

"Is it possible," I asked, "to do an exercise under the quality umbrella where the process of enterprise bargaining is spelt out?"

"It's already done, Jackson," he said with a grin. "Watch this space. Ours is the only structure linked to key performance indicators, and yet we blitz all municipalities in the state on every cost comparison. Our system is less expensive per hours worked than any similar organization. Our relationship with the unions, no matter how you measure it, is also the best in Victoria. Several cities in mainland China, the United States, the UK, and Europe want to benchmark us as the world's best practice, so if the bloody mayor wants to start a fight, we have all the evidence to the contrary."

I looked around the room and there were broad, knowing smiles everywhere, waiting for my response.

"I don't think we should wait for Dr. Fitch to attack," I said quietly. "I think we should be proactive. Let's face it, if he gets chosen as the next Liberal candidate for Hinchcliffe, our problem will eventually disappear as he'll have to resign to contest the election, correct?"

We knew what had to be done, but we didn't have any time to lose.

Chapter 34
The Politics of It All

WHEN WE were ready, I quietly spoke to each of the councilors in turn, knowing the mayor would hear about it before the sun went down. I told them we all needed some good news, and I was about to provide it for them. That the City was about to be awarded ISO 9001 Quality Assurance, AS 4801 Occupational Health and Safety, and ISO 14001 Environmental Management.

Not only had our accreditation gone without a hitch, it had been completed in record time because we already had written procedures in place and key performance indicators linked to everything we did.

What it did, I emphasized, was to illustrate how well the City was run, and that would have a halo effect on everyone associated with it: councilors, staff, and even ratepayers.

We had one of the budding writers from Admin write a terrific press release, journalists were invited, but my coup d'état was made possible through networking, thanks to Sammy and Margaret Reeve, and the stage was set.

I'd deliberately turned my phone off, and we didn't answer the landline at home the night before because we knew the mayor was furious. He'd screamed and shrieked, threatened people, and yet no one took the slightest notice.

The press conference began in the executive boardroom where Mr. Davis had first told me I was to be the CEO of the City. The press releases were handed out as the journalists arrived, chattering among themselves like parrots.

I knew what I'd done was cheeky but not illegal, and I reasoned that if the mayor could blur the lines between elected representatives and employed staff, then I could do the same. In the meantime the mayor sat there with murder in his eyes, temporarily rendered mute because he'd been set up so beautifully.

We were presented with our accreditation, the flashes from cameras adding to the atmosphere. Then my coup d'état was ushered into the room, the Minister for Local Government, Sheryl Wilson. The mayor looked on astonished as he mentally composed my letter of dismissal.

It was my turn, and I first thanked the loyal, hardworking, and dedicated people from the City who had worked tirelessly toward our formal accreditation. I then stressed that in working through the process, we'd discovered that the cost of all the services provided by the City was less per head of the population than any other municipality in Victoria.

"I know that result is deeply satisfying to our mayor, Dr. Fitch, and councilors," I said, "and that's why they've encouraged us to share these excellent figures with the minister and the general public. In particular it is a great credit to the mayor's continuing leadership that we've been encouraged to continue our pursuit of excellence."

Several of the managers had to lower their heads to control their mirth; others pretended to blow their noses. The councilors sat there as if they'd been poleaxed. They simply didn't have a clue what was happening, except they now looked pretty good in the eyes of the ratepayers who elected them.

I handed over to the minister who commented on our collaborative style of management and the sensible and productive role of the unions, which had clearly contributed to this wonderful result.

The mayor was, by this time, smiling broadly, because for him there was no downside. Someone else had set up his economic credentials for him, and he had the common sense not to antagonize the minister, even though they represented polarized political opposites in views.

And to my delight he simply ignored me at the morning tea afterward, which wasn't unexpected.

Three weeks later he was chosen as the Liberal candidate for the seat of Hinchcliffe, and we hardly saw him. He came and went, signed what he had to sign, and stayed out of trouble, pausing only for photographic opportunities.

Chapter 35
More Bloody Politics

LIFE WAS akin to jumping over a waterfall every day, grabbing at things as we headed downward, eventually hitting the bottom with an armful of what was most precious to us, like each other, the kids, Isobel, Dad, Mum, and all my family—in other words setting priorities and sticking to them.

My career as CEO of the City was exactly what it was—a means toward an end. Yes, I was proud of my achievements, but I regarded that as secondary to raising our kids. Sammy and I planned our workdays; if there was likely to be an extra workload, we tried to start work early—despite my hatred for early mornings—so we could be home for the kids at the normal time in the evenings.

Mum had finally been institutionalized. Green Valley Park was a nursing home close by, and Dad, heartbroken, visited her every day. She'd been a security risk to herself and people around her. The fateful day had been approaching after she'd escaped from the house on two consecutive nights, and the police were called to help. Within the week she was admitted and appeared quite happy there in her own room. The two people she recognized regularly were Dad and Sammy, but sometimes she even stared blankly at them. Travis and Alison were so upset they mostly stayed away, while I went around when I could. Only when I took Kate and Max with me one afternoon did she know who we were. But she was slipping away from us into a world of her own. Sammy coped amazingly with Mum's illness. Obviously the grief of progressively losing contact with a close friend affected him, and we spoke about it regularly so I could be sure he didn't internalize his feelings. The family group grew even closer because of his strength, but he reminded me that the kids and I had to be his first priorities. He loved Mum but urged us all to understand that there was literally nothing more we could do but keep her comfortable.

Isobel filled in Dad's days by giving him a different focus and taking the pressure off herself and Sammy in particular, while reintroducing Dad to Kate and Max.

Dad became a regular part of our family group and would eat with us most nights, walking home afterward just a few minutes around the corner. Isobel had given up teaching at TAFE when we brought Max home—in her typically unselfish manner, she'd just decided her career was less important than ours.

Now she had the time to return to her career, which we encouraged her to do, but she decided only as a relief teacher.

STORM CLOUDS gathered for the Special School.

Sammy and Margaret Reeve had traveled to Canberra to talk to government leaders and came away shaking their heads. Successive right-wing governments had been determined to deregulate the universities in Australia, searching for savings while ignoring the Asian education market and the competitive edge that Australia needed in its own young graduates going forward. Standards in the Australian education system had fallen like a stone, pushing us out of the top twenty nations ranking. And no wonder. Where education should be an investment, it was being progressively regarded as a fiscal liability.

The expansion of the curriculum of the Special School and its relocation to add mature-age local and foreign university students with learning difficulties was, we all thought, a smart move.

Sadly it now appeared to weaken the case because Margaret was asking to increase university infrastructure funding, not decrease it, and even with funding being shared by both state and federal governments, there was never going to be enough money to go around. Then the federal minister, James Craig, took exception to the business model and insisted Victoria fund it in its entirety. Which was a try-on and just bullshit.

Politicians playing with people's lives and the future of our children.

Just a few years ago, a well-known Liberal front-bencher and minister complained about all politicians, but at the time it seemed he was talking mostly about his own lot. Because they hadn't learned the lesson about respect for people, cutting budgets without concern for people and for the social and business repercussions. Once elected they claimed a mandate for everything and set about doing exactly what they wanted to without any further consultation, while the top end of town paid less than 10 percent tax. And the Labor people squabbled over small-picture stuff without any vision for the future, just criticizing the government without offering an alternative. It fucking frustrated me; we needed every kid to realize their full potential if we were going to tread the stage in Southeast Asia and the Pacific region and be properly competitive.

Sammy had moved back to a consultancy position at the Special School, working entirely from home after Max was born. He'd trained some wonderful teachers over time, and he tendered his resignation as principal to a reluctant Margaret Reeve. We decided one of us should be a full-time parent while the other worked; the kids needed us around before school age, not after it, as we seemed to be doing currently. I initially volunteered because I knew Sammy's work was so important, but he was adamant; he felt my full potential hadn't been reached. But he also wanted me to continue as a functioning example to dyslexic students everywhere, and I thought that was fair enough. The house sang along, the kids thrived, and we loved the extra time we spent with each other. The Special School consultancy still involved some serious hours, but working from home brought everything precious together in the one place.

NOTHING PREPARES a parent for illness of their own child. I found emotions so close to the surface that I never knew existed.

When Kate developed a high temperature out of nowhere and we presented ourselves at the emergency department of the university hospital, I knew for the first time in my life the true meaning of terror. That our little girl could be taken from us through illness.

We'd been good loving parents, careful with their health matters, but none of that seemed to matter as the emergency staff and doctors struggled to diagnose her problem.

Her appetite had diminished over the last two days or so, almost imperceptibly, but now after we were asked about it, we agreed. She'd been just a little off her tucker, progressively more so. Fear gripped my guts like a vise. This had come upon us so quickly we had no option but to trust the doctors on duty.

I eventually became tearful and bloody useless. While my other half stayed visibly calm and coherent, I was anything but.

They sent me home in the early evening; Sammy stayed on.

Isobel knitted away quietly half watching television as Max slept on peacefully in the nursery. Isobel and Sammy seemed to cope with all of this stuff, but I simply couldn't.

I remember that moment in time as one where all my personal priorities in life were highlighted in my mind. I'd long since thought my way around religion; Sammy and I had discussed the likelihood of a Supreme Being but decided that without evidence we'd be better off doing our own thing, believing in each other with our families and extended family around us. And that did it for us.

But with Kate so terribly sick in hospital, I envied those who actually believed in all the Christian claptrap. They could probably find solace in prayer and in the hereafter, but I couldn't stand the thought of our lovely Kate going to a horrible place like that.

The next morning I arrived at the hospital almost at daylight with a change of clothes for Sammy, now not required, most relieved to find her temperature had dropped to normal and her condition stabilized.

Her appetite returned with a vengeance; the nurses were both delighted and amused that she devoured two breakfasts, hers and the kid's from the next bed. But her face seemed spotty, and I wondered why.

"Chicken pox," said the resident pediatrician, grimly. "I hope all the adults in your family have had it—not nice in adults at all."

I laughed out loud; everyone except Sammy must have thought me a touch strange.

"It's all right," Sammy said. "My husband thought it may have been something more serious." The pediatrician, Sally Wilcox, an old after-school acquaintance of mine, actually understood my quandary.

"After a while you take it all in your stride, Jacko," she said, "but when it's one of your own, you panic. So don't feel badly about it. You guys are amazing parents, and a bit of overreaction is a good thing."

Sammy and I looked at each other. He seemed to recognize Sally from school, even though her name had changed. "You've done extraordinarily well, Sally," he said. "You're one of the state's best pediatricians, and yet you've stayed close to home."

"I could've gone anywhere, Sammy." She smiled. "But my husband is a local lad and this town is a great place to raise kids." There was no doubt we all remembered our school days and our hormonal urges, but were well-mannered enough to keep that stuff in the past where it belonged.

"But what about you two," she said. "Look at you, our version of royalty!"

We laughed at her, the hand of friendship extended across the years without judgment or recrimination.

"You guys are an inspiration. Everyone knows your story, your success as a couple, and your success as individuals, both in the field of education and local governance. I wish to Christ you'd been involved in medicine, that's all."

With Kate's current state of health now a nonissue, I found my curiosity working overtime. "What do you mean?" I asked. "I thought the new children's hospital in Melbourne was well equipped, and it's only an hour away."

"Yes, but it's already struggling to treat the increasing volume of patients from the new outer suburbs. Despite public subscription it's already overrun, and the facilities aren't capable of sustaining a proper service to the public in the not so distant future. Here, in this place, we're even farther behind, yet the politicians tell us it's not possible to increase beds or equipment." She reeled off a list of equipment needed to run a children's ward with an acceptable treatment regime, and we were gobsmacked.

"Do you mean to say that if either of our kids were admitted for something really serious, you'd struggle to treat them successfully, and airlifting them to Melbourne might be pointless if they were inundated with patients?"

"Precisely."

WE GOT our little girl home but she wouldn't settle. She had the constitution of an ox and a matching energy level that was impossible to contain. Covered with spots, she was everywhere—sooner rather than later Trav's and Ali's kids had chicken pox, and so did Max.

He sulked, but somehow he knew screaming wasn't going to make him better, so he attached himself to me like a limpet and we got through it all.

Eventually the household settled down again, but it seemed to Sammy and me while our blessings were many, there were others in society that weren't so lucky these days.

The "new" Special School was announced, catering for those with intellectual disabilities rather than simple learning difficulties as I'd had. So kids were all lumped in together regardless of IQ—a recipe for academic disaster.

Margaret Reeve told us Canberra had become personal, and she was a marked woman for her lefty views. She reckoned it was the thin end of the wedge: the decision ignored the Asian market and the 13 percent of students affected by dyslexia and related learning difficulties.

AFTER OUR brush with the public hospital system, the comfortable lifestyle we'd enjoyed not worrying about who was paying for what was quickly coming to an end. The federal government in Canberra wanted to blame everyone; their policy was counterproductive and not directed at bringing in new income streams, rather they were focusing on tearing down the overheads as they saw them and preparing us all for financial Armageddon, which was silly. I could see it for what it was: ignorance and the old way of doing things.

Running the country didn't seem all that different to running the affairs of the City; all the players were the same—private enterprise through both big business and smaller operators, the public service, the unions, and the ebb and flow of debt. Oversimplified, but the essentials were still there.

The economies of the Asian nations were growing and developing while we sat on our fat asses and watched, complaining loudly about our comfortable lifestyles going south as our GDP fell like a stone.

Australia sat on Asia's doorstep, perfectly positioned to take advantage of new markets, yet no one wanted to do the work creating new business relationships. Trade missions? None for years, considered old-fashioned.

So we sat around not even knowing what the needs of our neighbors were.

IT BEGAN with a not so innocent comment from Jock Fleming, the parks and gardens manager, when we were inspecting his planting and design plans for the following spring at the Botanic Gardens.

I didn't really have to get down to such fine detail, but Jock was a father figure to me, and I enjoyed him and his passion for gardening and presentation. The gardens were also a wonderful source of revenue from weddings, refinancing Jock's work and even leaving some change over. I admired his plans for spring. Every year he seemed to outdo himself again, and this year was no exception, and I told him so.

He smiled, knowing I genuinely loved his work, but he was also smart enough to read me like very few other people could. Jock understood me like Sammy and Barbara Shields, and was a great strategist. He and I had cooperated closely to neutralize the influence of the mayor, hardly needing to speak to each other. When I came up with the idea, he was already well ahead of me, already on the same wavelength.

So it came as no surprise when he came up with a further suggestion.

"Why don't you stand for the seat of Hinchcliffe in the federal election, laddie?"

"Have you gone totally mad, Jock?" I asked. "I've got some respect for myself and my family. Jesus, politicians have become the lowest form of life in our society. Their performance, through the major parties, is nothing short of disgusting. They've totally lost the plot, there's no vision for the future, no respect for the people they represent, and they struggle from one corruption scandal to another. They make me sick."

Jock waved his hands around like he was conducting an orchestra, wearing his passion for our town and provincial area like a badge of honor.

"There you are. You've just given a string of reasons why a fine young man like you should have a go. Individuals *can* make a difference, laddie. Just look at the leadership and management skills you've brought to the City. We desperately need someone in Hinchcliffe who can take the fight right up to the government, because they're going to ruin our chances of growing this city as it should. It will never reach anywhere near its proper potential with the current policies, if you can call them that."

"But, Jock, I'd have to stand as an independent. The major parties have chosen their candidates, so I'd be wasting my time."

"Then stand as an independent, give your preferences to Labor, and we'll knock the mayor off his perch."

"You're a dreadful man, Jock."

"I've honed me skills working with you, young fella."

Chapter 36
The Proposition

LIKE THE reluctant debutante, Jock dragged me into the fray of a soon-to-be federal election campaign, driven locally by the issues of education and health, impacting on our own little family in no small way. Politics was something I'd never considered as a career, and I agonized over the decision, even though I understood I'd never be elected, standing as an independent candidate. But I understood the ramifications for the mayor and the Liberal Party because my preferences would flow automatically away from them to the Labor Party, and if the numbers were as close as I thought they might be, then the mayor and the Liberals would be in real trouble in what was previously a safe Liberal seat. So on the face of it, my actions seemed a good investment of my time and money.

I still agonized over my actions, but if I thought I was going to walk away from it all, I had another thing coming. Dad, Isobel, Trav, and Ali all thought it was a good idea. But my bloody other half told me it was a *great* idea.

"Jacko, don't focus on the terrible reputations of modern-day politicians. Try to position yourself as a true representative of the public, always with an ear to their needs and wants, just as you do for the ratepayers and the staff at the City. They need someone to listen to their agenda and influence the decision-making process that runs our country."

Sammy was adamant. "If you have a fault, it's that you're so modest—you don't believe in yourself as you should. Remember when I taught you stuff at school and you started getting good marks? This is similar, have a go and you'll be brilliant. I keep telling you, the best is yet to come. You may hate the reputation of politicians, but somewhere in the future you have the ability to change the public perception of politicians anyway."

Hell would freeze over first, I thought to myself.

Sighing inwardly, I went through the formal process of advising the city council of my intention to stand as an independent candidate for the seat of Hinchcliffe. Immediately there was a call from the former mayor for me to resign, as he had done. But in my case the law only required me to stand down at the appropriate time because I was an employee of the City, not an elected officer as the mayor had been.

The shit hit the fan in a big way, and we were months away from an election, which still hadn't been called. The local newspaper, driven by their managing editor, trumpeted their righteous discomfort at my actions, forcing me to release a letter stating the facts. I was careful not to criticize anyone, just state the facts as they stood under law and my desire to continue my work helping to run and provide essential services to our city.

"Your first lesson in political bastardry," Jock Fleming, who had appointed himself as my unofficial campaign manager, said with a laugh.

I SAT in the kitchen, busily feeding the kids while Sammy was shopping for supplies, when the landline shrilled. I answered it absentmindedly; Max was being difficult while Kate just wanted more tucker. What I expected to be another nuisance sales call turned out to be something totally unexpected.

"Oh, is that Mr. Jackson Collins-Smith?" said a cultured but very businesslike voice.

"That's me."

"Mr. Collins-Smith, my name is Patricia Long. I'm the personal assistant to Jason Bellamy, and he'd like a word, if that's convenient."

Sammy walked in the door, loaded with shopping bags. Both kids were now yelling for food or whatever, and my darling just took over, understanding from the look on my face that I was in mental overload.

The Leader of the Federal Opposition was on the line. Jason Bellamy would be our next prime minister, of that I was certain.

If the polls were to be believed, the current government was languishing badly and was falling further behind as time went on, making an earlier election more than possible.

"Oh, hello, it's Jason here, how are you?"

"Well, I'm Jacko, and I'm wonderful, thanks. You blokes seem to be heading in the right direction."

"Yes, we have the advantage of a delinquent government who are imploding on themselves as we speak, but we have a lot of work to do to earn the trust of ordinary Australians. I'm just wondering if you'd be available to have a quiet conversation tomorrow evening. Perhaps we could meet somewhere private?"

"Why don't you come here, at home, as long as you don't mind the tribe gathered around."

His response was warm and positive, he'd love to meet my family, and so it was set for 7:30 the following night.

"That was the Leader of the Federal Labor Party," I said, not quite trusting my own voice, "and he wants to talk to me."

"I'm not surprised," Sammy replied calmly. "The word around the traps is that Gerry Sullivan has been caught with underage girls from our old high school, doing the nasty in a local motel, so I think he's trying to recruit you."

I stared at my other half. How he ever knew all this stuff when the information had clearly passed me by made me feel quite inadequate—but not in a bad way.

"Well I didn't have the faintest idea," I said.

"I know. You always look at the good side in people. I'm just a good listener, as you know. Now's your opportunity, darling," Sammy said. "He'll ask you to join the Labor Party, and then stand for Hinchcliffe as the endorsed Labor candidate."

My mouth went dry and my head spun. If that was the case, then I would go from playing numbers games to the real world of politics.

Sammy suggested I ring Jock Fleming, who roared with laughter.

"Aye, laddie, that's what he's on about. I've been told to keep me mouth closed, and that's been difficult as you can imagine."

JASON BELLAMY was in his early fifties with sandy, receding hair and an affable grin. I was immediately drawn to him. There was no doubt he was a people person; his body language invited you into his world.

He shook hands with Isobel, and then Dad. Then I introduced Sammy and his face lit up, grasping both hands and kissing Sammy on the cheek. It was clear none of this was planned—that was just the way this bloke was—and I had to admit he had my attention immediately.

Kate ran over as fast as her legs would carry her, and Max, unusually, held out his arms to be picked up. My son, the ultimate judge of character!

As usual it was Sammy who pressed all the right buttons.

"Jacko, why don't you take Jason into the study? At least you'll have some peace there." I nodded, and Sammy turned to our guest. "Jason, you're staying for a meal, right?"

"Well, that's very kind, but—"

"And you have a driver out there. We'll make sure he's fed as well."

"I'll fix that," Dad said. "Can't have people sitting around waiting outside, it's not our way."

Team Collins-Smith had taken over, but Jason Bellamy demonstrated his natural good manners, recognizing he'd better go with the flow.

"Roast lamb," Sammy said with that beautiful smile of his. "Could you handle that?"

"Wonderful."

I trusted very few people in the world instinctively, and certainly no one at first meeting. But this bloke was different. He was quite unique; he originally came from a small-business background. His current business as a convention organizer had grown exponentially and was now one of the top three in Australia, specializing in creating conventions, mainly for Asian companies, the business now run by other senior directors.

He'd always been a worker and entered politics because he felt Australia and Australians had lost touch with the basics. That we'd spoiled our children by simply trying to give them something better, only to find they were reluctant to put the hours in and work hard for a living, as he'd done.

That excellence of endeavor was frowned on by many young people, and a pleasant social life seemed far more important.

"Similar," he said, "to the mature societies of the western world, particularly the United States and Europe."

I understood what he was saying. "But why the Labor Party?"

"Because the Liberal Party has moved so far to the right, and I believe their social extremism is potentially dangerous. It reminds me of the Midwest of the United States, where the God-botherers place their mantle of religious reasoning over every piece of legislation they bring. Plus they seem to think the end of the world is Darwin Harbour, and that we should honor Queen and country. The Poms are good blokes, but they're in so much economic trouble themselves, they couldn't help us even if they wanted to. Frankly the sooner we can become a republic, the happier I'll be because our love of British royalty has the capacity to confuse Asia and Asians.

"I want to focus on our place in Asia as a priority," he said, "retaining our unique character, but recognizing our economic future lies in *integration* with Asia."

"You're not in bloody Parliament now," I teased him and he laughed at me.

"Sorry, I get carried away because it's all so obvious."

"Well I happen to agree with every word," I said, filling him in on our experiences with the university and our efforts trying to attract students from Asia. He nodded, and I realized he already knew a great deal about me. Given the problem with the now-previous candidate, he'd be insane not to check out the potential replacement.

"I suppose you've checked me out thoroughly, then." I grinned. "Did they tell you I was an axe murderer, kleptomaniac, and a sexual predator?"

"They told me what I needed to know, and I apologize for the intrusion, no wonder your interest in education and Asian affairs is so well honed. You've turned your dyslexia into a positive in your life, and one only has to look at your kids to know you understand Asia better than most people. So are you going to join the team and try to win Hinchcliffe for us?"

"No."

His jaw dropped, and I knew I had *his* attention. His lip even quivered a bit, and I thought, *Jesus, he's a crier like me.*

"There's absolutely no point me joining the Labor Party and being chosen as the new candidate, because as leader, you could never give me what I want."

"Try me."

"If Labor wins the election, and *if*—and I stress *if*—I was to stand as a candidate and won Hinchcliffe, then I'd want to be in the cabinet, as Minister for Education and Training, so I can fix the system that very nearly overlooked me."

"Done," Jason said, surprisingly without hesitation. "What a bloody bitch you are. I'd hate to have you on the other side of politics."

He held out his hand, but it wasn't enough, and I found myself being cuddled by the Honorable Leader of the Federal Opposition.

We laughed at his use of language, and he explained with a smile.

"I grew up a bi man. Oh, I played both sides of the fence when I was young and enjoyed it all so much. But I met Jenny, and we clicked, just like you and Sammy. It's clear you guys are also a great team, and that gives me even more confidence in your ability. The reason we're where we are is that both of us understand there are no great individuals in this world, just great partnerships."

Chapter 37
On the Hustings

I FOUND it amazing to attend my first branch meeting of the Labor Party and to find so many of the blokes I knew and worked with over the years were already members. Like Matt and Scott, for Christ's sake, and so many employees of the City.

When the vote was put to the meeting that their latest member be endorsed as the candidate for Hinchcliffe, there was a roar of approval and not one dissenter.

Jock Fleming was now in an official capacity as campaign manager with Matt and Scott assisting.

Sammy was there and happily took on the role as advertising coordinator and treasurer; Isobel and Dad stayed in the background because someone needed to look after our kids.

Six weeks later the prime minister called the election, so we knew where we had to aim and how long we had to hold everyone's attention to get our message across.

The former mayor made it clear that it was war, and for the first time in all of this process, I felt the full force of his vindictiveness and even hatred.

Dr. Fitch had gunned up the local press again, posing for photographs with his wife and children, looking every bit the well-educated, caring, and very heterosexual candidate.

Some of the article was so personal and so pointedly critical of me that Jock wanted to slap an injunction on the good doctor and his mate the managing editor. Our team were horrified, but I wasn't so worried.

We regrouped back at our headquarters the next night and I made my point.

"I don't want to antagonize him any further," I said. "Why allow ourselves to enter into a discussion about personal issues? I've every right to feel proud of my husband and family, but by verging on discriminatory remarks, I reckon he's dug a hole he'll never climb out of."

Sammy sat there with a huge grin, and the others looked thoughtful.

"We need to talk about *policy*," I said, "the things that concern the voters of this electorate, not personal things because they mean nothing at a time like this. Besides, everyone has known for years that Sammy and I are a couple. The mere fact that he opens his campaign discussing such things means he and the Liberal Party don't have much to talk about. They're already in defensive mode."

As with all campaigns, the national media circus was already up and running, from breakfast television shows to the ABC *Q&A* program on Monday evenings. The current prime minister was wailing about the deficit and how Labor was intent on squandering the public purse, "propping up useless institutions and running the nation into more debt. There are no easy solutions," he said. "We have to trim our sails to survive as a nation."

Perfect, I thought to myself, *the battle lines have been drawn*, as Jason Bellamy came on the line.

"Hello, bitch," he said cheerily. "The media whores can't work us out. They think we're not bothering with a launch at all now, but I've just spoken to Margaret Reeve at the university and I think I've made her day."

Like me, he wanted to keep his powder dry until the last four weeks of the campaign. Labor was still ahead, the Liberals had delivered their manifesto, and now the media was guessing where and when the Labor launch would happen.

THE LIGHTS dimmed in the big hall at the university.

Jason and Jenny Bellamy walked on hand in hand, and we walked on behind them.

For the first time since the campaign began, I felt just a little nervous, but Sammy *bloody well knew*. He ran his hand up my lower spine, and I thought to myself, *Jesus, I can see the press reports tomorrow: the candidate spoke very well, his erection at the election was outstanding.*

Jason spoke. I'd been allowed to critique his speech so I knew the content.

He began by saying how pleased he was to have our national launch here, in a Liberal stronghold, hoping it would soon become a Labor-held seat. And that was the last time he referred to the Liberal Party.

He spelled out detailed plans for growing the GDP of Australia by closer economic cooperation with Asia, that the process of integration with Asia was already underway, laying out the Labor plan to become part of ASEAN as soon as possible, and as soon as we were invited, spelling out the member nations—Brunei, Cambodia, Indonesia, Laos, Malaysia, Myanmar, Philippines, Singapore, Thailand, and Vietnam.

The brows furrowed on some of the older punters, and shock registered on the faces of others. Jason had been correct; this campaign was going to be about reeducation and realignment of attitudes, and we all knew how negatively Asia was viewed by parts of the electorate.

The Liberals pumped fear into the hearts of the voters in the past by stopping boats full of Middle Eastern refugees headed our way, but Asian people were still seen as the tribal hordes, come to take over our country. The Yellow Peril.

Jason's strategy was a clear one, however: maintain our living standards where possible, while selectively increasing our spending on education and health. Run the economy at a deficit, all the time working toward growing the Australian economy.

"Joining the Association of Southeast Asian Nations would only be the beginning," he said. "The Labor Party has been discussing our national case with this group of nations, where the current government has given up. There is a long way to go, but with goodwill and bipartisan support, I believe our membership is closer than it ever has been at any point in history."

Then Jason ramped it up, his voice rising.

"Another reason I'm glad to be here is that this university has been an example of initiative and foresight, selling education services to almost all Asian countries, earning in excess of two billion dollars annually for the Australian economy."

Margaret Reeve beamed back from the front row.

"That association has been strengthened by the university's *comprehensive* services on offer to all the community, including the client families from Asia"—which was a nice way of saying the Special School had created extra business by its very existence.

Then Jason went on to spell out the assistance package conditionally available to organizations, both public and private, who actively went after business from Asia.

"I'm pleased to say the university already qualifies for that package, as does the university hospital, which is reinvesting in new technology enhancing treatment options for Australians but also attracting patients from several large Asian centers, particularly the ASEAN countries."

What a bloody beauty.

The seat of Hinchcliffe, through some smart local people, would be receiving government assistance of the right kind for the right reasons, generating employment and growing the local economy. Which would be nearly enough to create a 5 percent swing against the government alone and give me a running chance of taking the seat.

Jason was smart. This was the central part of his strategy; the individual portfolios would now be covered separately in the days leading up to the election. His message was clear and a simple one, and the government would immediately begin burning the midnight oil to discredit it.

But now it was my turn. Jason personally introduced me and spoke about my career and collaborative management style, which had transformed the city council in a very short time frame.

As I stepped up to the podium with my sheet of prompts, I felt humble. I could see it all so clearly; I knew what had to be done, and now I had to get off my bum, with Jason's support, and make it happen.

Yes, it was the party faithful and family supporters gathered together, but what happened next was extraordinary. Every bastard stood up and started wildly applauding!

I realized it wasn't just for me and beckoned a reluctant Sammy over, and the noise increased. Sammy kissed me on the cheek and sat down again next to a visibly moved Jenny Bellamy, and I began.

I told them our story and reinforced our vision for a smarter, kinder Australia, better connected with Asia, but a country where no matter how poor one's family circumstances, access to a good education was a right, not a privilege.

And for people like me, skilled teaching services would be available for everyone so people could grow and realize their full potential, so up to 13 percent of the population had the opportunity to be as productive as possible. Where instead of winding back support for the working people of Australia, we were intent on at least maintaining, and in some areas increasing, funding for education and health.

"But I want to warn everyone," I said, "we don't want to overpromise," and Jason gave me a sharp look. "This won't happen overnight. Our new interface with Asia is a long-term strategy, and we have to stick at it to make it happen. Once we were an economy driven only by primary production, then came the mining boom, and then when demand for iron ore slowed, we became a pauper state again.

"This election does concern every Australian. We all have joint responsibility for growing the economy, as Jason has so eloquently demonstrated. To sit on our arses and do nothing is not an option. Here in Hinchcliffe we have a marvelous opportunity to grow. We already have at least two federal grants, and private enterprise only has to come up with sensible propositions to be on the way to selling some of the unique goods and services we produce in this area to the buyers in Asia.

"Roll on election night, and let's get the show on the road. Thank you."

AGAIN THERE was pandemonium. It hadn't gone unnoticed that Jason, Jenny, Sammy, and I were already a team, but I felt rather than knew there were some green eyes around on our side of politics.

The rabid Catholics with their anti-same-sex attitudes, the entrenched union leaders who thought they were already home and hosed. The shadow ministry in the front row of the hall looked decidedly pissed off at the young bloke on the stage, not even an MP as yet, all close and comfy with their leader.

I was under absolutely no illusions at all that if I did make it to Canberra as a member of the new government, or even in opposition, I would face the most bitter protection of hard-won privileges from the union-driven left wing of the Labor Party. As well as the church-driven hatred of same-sex couples.

And I wondered what would happen if all the stars aligned and I ended up as a minister in a new government.

Chapter 38
The Campaign

As EXPECTED, the former mayor rushed in where angels feared to tread. There didn't seem to be any plan to his campaign, which I found surprising, knowing the powerful Liberal Party "machine."

It was some time later that we heard Dr. Fitch refused to follow advice and decided to do his own thing.

He ignored the power of social media, refusing to allow his people to put up a special page on Facebook. Our campaign, by comparison, featured active participation through Facebook, and the hits were astronomical.

Then he plowed money into free-to-air television at huge expense, and we guessed he'd blown nearly 50 percent of his budget on that alone. It was targeted strangely, probably based on cost; much of his advertising seemed to run outside of peak viewing times, so he was consistently missing his main audience.

Our campaign decided to focus heavily on social media. It was low or no cost, but reached a huge section of the younger voters. The decision was made *not* to telephone people or to go door knocking; it was too intrusive, and the risk of upsetting voters and turning them off instead of enlisting their votes was real.

Instead high visibility at shopping centers with our volunteers working around the clock seemed more effective, and several information booths in key positions around town were set up.

A print campaign with heavy loading became the central part of the advertising. Even the managing editor wasn't silly enough to knock back the revenue, and Sammy made sure the placements were correct. A deal was done with the free press: if they'd print and insert our flyers every week, we'd deliver them to every letterbox in town for no cost.

Discipline was important. All questions from the public were referred to me so a consistent voice was maintained.

Above all, I insisted that criticism of the performance of the government and any of their policies was off the agenda. Everyone thought I'd gone mad, but I reasoned that politicians squabbling with each other was such a huge turnoff in any electorate that it seemed smart to take the high ground and show some leadership.

Jason Bellamy visited on three occasions and, despite alarm from the national executive, refused to interfere with our strategy. He was so impressed that with several weeks to go, he amended the tonality of the national campaign to follow the example of Hinchcliffe.

No comment on the former government's lack of performance, no comment on their policies. Just a hard sell on what the Labor Party was prepared to do, and more importantly, *why* we had to do it. We spoke about a vision for the future, and were careful, bloody careful about promises, even though our opponents talked about fiscal responsibility with one hand and showered various schemes with cash on the other.

Essentially we had copied the Liberal's fiscal policies without their cruelty, maintaining education, health, and social security while boldly engaging Asia with a long-term view of growing the economy.

I was invited to debate Dr. Fitch at a public meeting, but I declined. Immediately I was called "spineless, gutless, a yellowbelly, and a piss-poor debater, frightened of being shown up for inexperience."

We focused on our central story, and with about ten days to go, I started answering some intelligent questions from members of the public.

My team could feel it too: the tide was turning in our favor. People started shaking hands with our volunteers and our phones rang nonstop with sensible questions.

After a slow start, the Liberals closed the gap nationally, and the media had it as anybody's election, so we used what funds we had to "own" the local paper. The ex-mayor plowed on, and to our delight his campaign started coming apart at the seams. His mate the managing editor had a change of heart, and actually wrote an editorial supporting us. Sammy cut it out and had it laminated for posterity.

ELECTION NIGHT arrived. Sammy and I decided to have an early dinner at home with the kids, Isobel, and Dad. We'd hardly finished when Trav, Ali, and their families arrived, complete with babysitters. We adults piled into our vehicles and arrived at the tally room just after the polls closed at 6:00 p.m. Our scrutineers were ready, with Jock Fleming leading our group. I smiled to myself; no bastard would get under his guard. He'd make sure we contested every vote where the intention to support us was clear.

Dr. Fitch was also in the tally room. I went over and shook hands, which didn't go down very well at all.

"May the best man win," I said.

"You haven't got a chance, you prick. I'm going to teach you a lesson. People like you are out of your depth. You need to leave parliamentary representation to decent, professional, educated people. I hope you don't try to go back to your job at the city council, because I intend to bring pressure to bear to have you removed."

It was then I actually felt sorry for the poor man. I smelled some alcohol on his breath, but he was clearly delusional, and I worried about his state of mind.

One look at his wife, a lovely lady by all accounts, confirmed she too was concerned. She stood at the back of the room looking terrified. While her husband was ranting at someone else, I went over and quietly spoke to her, offering her assistance in case things didn't go the way her husband hoped. She thanked me profusely. If the good doctor did make it to Canberra, he'd be a liability there as well; he was a sick man.

The early count from booths in the town's wealthiest suburb went against us, but only slightly, and Fitch could be heard laughing uproariously. The next boxes came in from the eastern suburbs and the results were dramatic. We won every booth with a good margin, and the doctor fell silent. The most conservative part of the seat was a smaller regional town at the southern end of the electorate, dominated by the farming community. We won almost every booth there, the first time Labor had ever done so, and the die was cast. It was the beginning of the end for Fitch and the Liberals.

By 9:00 p.m. the result was clear: over 65 percent of the votes had been counted, and even if we'd lost all the remaining booths, Dr. Fitch and the Liberal Party still couldn't catch us. We'd captured one of the prize blue-ribbon Liberal seats, with a swing toward us, at this stage, of 10.5 percent. I walked over to the microphone provided, hand in hand with Sammy, and claimed victory for the Labor Party. Concurrently in Canberra, the prime minister conceded defeat and wished Jason Bellamy well.

Sammy and I were interviewed on a video link to the central tally room, being asked all sorts of silly questions. But it was the private call from Jason Bellamy that really mattered. "You're still a bitch," he said, "but a bloody beautiful one, what a result." He then burst into tears and Jenny took over.

"Thank you so much, Jacko," she said. "Your victory has been the most special to him. He's never trusted anyone as much as you, he's just so delighted."

Jason and Jenny Bellamy came into focus shortly afterward as he officially claimed victory. His tone was positive, but not patronizing. He promised we'd govern for all Australians, whether they'd voted for us or not, and would actively seek bipartisan support for many of the issues facing our nation.

A terrible scream of rage emanated from our tally room as Dr. Fitch was half carried, half dragged from the building. I recognized one of his former colleagues from the clinic and pulled him over, explaining what I thought was his problem, and he nodded seriously.

"Please don't leave him to his own devices. He needs supervision. His wife is frightened he'll harm himself," I said. He clearly understood Fitch's problem, but he looked at me in a new light.

"You're a good man, Jackson," he said. "I'll make sure he's supervised through all of this. By the way, I voted for you."

I HAD to act quickly, and act now.

Together, Sammy and I with Jock, Matt, and Scott, rounded up all of our team and corralled them in a spot just outside the tally room. I noticed a few stubbies of beer had already appeared in some of our team's hands and knew I wasn't a moment too soon.

"Look," I said, "now we have the real test ahead of us." Everyone stared at me as if I'd lost my marbles.

"Your hard work and dedication over the last few months has been exemplary, and it shows if we work as a team what can happen—we can literally achieve the impossible." There were smiles everywhere again as they all relaxed.

"But now we're in government, and the positions are reversed. It's human nature to chop the tall poppies down, and guys, we're the tall poppies now. Please don't do anything tonight during or after the celebration that will reflect badly on us as a group and allow our opposition to discredit us. Don't drive your cars if you've had anything to drink at all. It's easy to make a miscalculation. You guys achieved so much. Please, please don't deal yourselves short by hurting yourself or other people, because I'll need you to do exactly the same job at the next election." There were nods and an understanding of where I was coming from.

I could see the bloody headlines: Labor Party thugs in jail for drunk driving and creating a public nuisance.

"One more thing," I said, smiling at them all. "As you all know, we've won a resounding national victory and created an unprecedented upset of huge proportions here in Hinchcliffe. We did that job by refusing to engage in the tactics of smear, innuendo, and criticizing our opponents. Jason Bellamy saw the early results here and asked every electorate in the nation to do the same thing, focus on our policies and leave the criticism and personalities out of it. It's worked, but that's not the end, it's only the beginning. Please remember that the public have understood that for the first time in living memory, some of Australia's politicians have appeared to be almost human." The stubbies were put down and our team listened.

"The last thing we need to do is to gloat over our opponents. That would undo the good impression we've made with the public. We're also going to need the goodwill of the Liberal Party to get the sales job done in Asia." I paused as their eyes glazed over and grinned at their tired but eager faces.

"I know better than most people that Dr. Fitch has been a prick ever since he entered public life as the mayor of the city. There's a reason for that behavior, because he's a very sick man. Right now my guess is that he'll be institutionalized until his mental health issues are stabilized. You can be sure the Liberals won't make the same mistake in the future, so his career in politics is over."

Sammy, Dad, Isobel, and all our family had joined the group and gave me the signal.

"How would you guys like to go to a party?" I asked.

There were relieved cheers. "That bloody Jacko isn't a bad bloke after all" was going through their minds. So a few beers, a glass of wine or two, and a really nice barbecue was ahead, in a now much calmer atmosphere, so we could all enjoy ourselves.

When Sammy did the wrap-up of campaign expenses next week with the executive of the local branch, it would show a healthy balance that would go back into consolidated revenue instead of paying for entertainment.

Instead Sammy and I were funding the celebration. It wasn't every day I was elected the honorable member for Hinchcliffe, but I didn't want anyone to accuse us of plundering the party purse before we even got started.

Leonardo da Vinci, Albert Einstein, Alexander Graham Bell, Sir Richard Branson, Walt Disney, Jay Leno, Whoopi Goldberg, Nelson Rockefeller, Agatha Christie, Steven Spielberg, Harry Belafonte, Winston Churchill, Richard Strauss.

Chapter 39
Canberra

NEVER DID I ever expect Canberra to be what it was. Yes, obviously a city built for politics, not necessarily politicians.

Away from the eyes of home and their electorates, politicians resembled a collection of wild animals housed in a setting in itself inhospitable, hot in summer, freezing cold in winter, a showplace for a system of government that I reckoned was failing the Australian people anyway.

The old hands seemed to revel in the lifestyle. They owned the members' bar like a prized possession: it was theirs and no one was going to take it from them. Many were there until closing, went home, and did it all again the next day. The loneliness of the long-distance politician.

Feeling lonely was quite foreign for me, and it was horrible, understanding fully the old hands who sought company where they could. Sammy and I had hardly ever been apart, and it hurt. We'd discussed the new lifestyle and thought we'd adapt well, but frankly we hadn't done so. We phoned each other several times every day, and I tried to speak to the kids before bed at night.

I'd rented a small apartment nearby, and went home one night to find a beautiful warm body in bed, waiting for me with a big smile on his face and an even bigger friend under the covers. "What would have happened if I'd brought a bedmate home?" I asked.

He looked directly at me, with not even a hint of a smile. "Then you'd deliver your maiden speech sounding like one, with a high-pitched squeaky voice."

All wasn't well in my world, however.

There were around seventy sitting days for the year, split up into three sessions: autumn, winter, and spring, the latter the longest session and sometimes running into December.

I knew my best work performances were when Sammy was close by—not that I needed to discuss affairs of state with him, but he helped me decipher documents and all sorts of stuff, putting his spin on it. That set my brain into overdrive, and I always found myself instantly creative.

I'd previously explained my situation to Jason, and he authorized me to pull whatever resources I needed from the public service. The people I interviewed as my assistant were almost all hopeless. They simply didn't understand my requirements and looked at me as if I was retarded, which did nothing for my level of comfort and confidence.

Eventually I chose a woman about my age, Tracy Phillips. She wasn't perfect, but she seemed to understand the brief better than most, although I spent the best part of a working day explaining, in great detail, how the mind of a dyslexic person worked. Why it was difficult for me to read and absorb some material, and how she would have to use the ATM for me when I needed cash. The fog seemed to clear a little when she realized I wasn't mentally deficient, quite the opposite. It was frustrating because I had another group of the public service running the portfolio of Education and Training, where I'd be spending much of my time, and I knew I'd have to make my special needs known all over again.

I toyed with the idea of bringing Sammy and the kids up here for the parliamentary sessions, but he was now a full-time parent and overseeing the electorate office concurrently. Thanks to Isobel and Dad, he found time to appear overnight when I least expected it and that helped, because the next morning he was able to unscramble a lot of stuff for me.

As I expected, to come through the ranks as a novice and be rewarded as Minister for Education was never going to go down well with my own party room. The atmosphere in our first caucus meeting turned icy cool toward me; it was like a group of generals gathered around, carving up the spoils of victory. The problem was that they saw me as a foot soldier who had been elevated without even going to war.

But all that changed when Jason entered the room.

They stood and applauded; he was the miracle worker who had returned them from the political wilderness to power again, a charismatic, even visionary leader. But if they thought it was going to be business as usual, they had another thing coming.

He was like a football coach, giving them a bloody good pep talk.

Some realized the party was already headed in a new direction, and their faces mirrored the excitement of the challenge ahead. Others, particularly the older traditionalists, clearly resented being instructed on party policy but knew they had no option but to go with the flow, lest they be seen to be expendable by the public at the next election. Because there was just a chance this crazy strategy of the new prime minister would actually work.

Ministers were elected and endorsed by the caucus, the link between the new cabinet and the backbenchers. It was clear deals had already been done between the various factions, and in my case, a deal done by Jason, which he expected to be upheld. It was, and I was duly endorsed. The chill finally started to thaw; we had a cuppa afterward and I got to meet my fellow soon-to-be ministers and other caucus and cabinet members.

The deputy prime minister was Phillip Gregson, an older man but very much a progressive, someone I sensed had been a mentor to Jason. A kindly soul, he offered to take me under his wing, to spend time with me, and "fill in the blanks." And there were plenty of those.

Angela Chan, a brilliant academic turned politician, had a wife and two kids. She was the new Minister for Health and decided to adopt me. A great person and someone who didn't suffer fools gladly. She'd already been in a stoush with the old guard who were scandalized by same-sex partnerships, and told them in her inimitable way "to fuck off, grow up, and get with it." To have someone else in cabinet who was part of a same-sex partnership was "just heaven," she said, and I knew I had a mate for the rest of my political life and beyond.

The swearing-in by the governor-general was due to happen at Yarralumla that afternoon, and our families would be there to witness the event.

I actually felt a little nervous, but both Phillip Gregson and Angela Chan were there to help settle the butterflies, and I was amazed how quickly and how unselfishly those two senior ministers had sprung to my aid.

The day simply got better. Dad, Isobel, Trav, Ali, and their partners and kids were all there, so were Matt and Scott, Jock and Mrs. Fleming, and Mrs. Shields and Ted, her husband. Then our other family emerged from around the corner of the old building. Chart and Solada, walking slowly with two tiny but unmistakable figures in wheelchairs, Pa and Ma.

SAMMY LOOKED breathtaking.

He'd invested in a magnificent midblue suit, perfectly cut, with a navy-and-gold tie to set it off. Max was trying to adjust to my frequent absences and dropped his bottom lip just for effect. But he couldn't conceal his delight at seeing me; he held his arms out and I picked him up as he made it perfectly clear everyone else should piss off because his dad was there. My not-so-little boy was by now a one-person promotional team for me, much to the amusement of the other guests and my fellow cabinet members. Then it was Kate's turn and she neatly elbowed her brother out of the way.

Jason and Jenny came over and made a huge fuss over Sammy. It was clear he was a favorite and met with scowls from some of the other wives and partners. Immediately I knew what I had to do.

We gathered the kids up and walked around the entire cabinet.

I enjoyed the looks of amazement from some of them, nothing like dispelling old mindsets. We looked just like "normal" people according to the astonished wife of one of the devoutly Catholic members from the western suburbs of Sydney. Just to rub salt into the wounds, Angela and her wife, Christina, also circulated with their two little boys, Jason grinning broadly at our public relations campaign.

"God, you were made for politics, bitch," he said under his breath. "You've got those old cunts eating out of your hand."

NOTHING REALLY prepares a newbie for the House of Representatives, with all the pomp and pageantry that the Westminster system demands.

A total waste of time, I thought. The ceremonial bullshit added little to the day, similar to the swearing-in ceremony. Still clinging to the past and British colonialism, by the time we'd dispensed with the unnecessary rubbish, we could have put in motion legislation that had the propensity to change lives. This was supposed to be the people's house, not something with a rarefied atmosphere, bogged down in tradition and formality, and I found it depressing.

Ceremony certainly has its place, but something uplifting that had the ability to focus on an exciting future, not mired in the past with outdated stuff and with the politics of class structure. After the swearing-in, it was just hard yakka.

Outside sitting days I was flying around the country, talking to state ministers for education, inspecting schools, reading spreadsheets, planning, planning, planning for the future, trying to make sure no kids were left behind.

In between I had visits from the private school associations, wondering what the future held for them, losing students because the previous government had made university education so expensive parents couldn't afford both.

So the government school system was becoming overloaded to buggery.

BUT I was deeply aware of the very personal commitment I had to the voters of Hinchcliffe. We appointed Peter Prentice, an arts postgraduate and favorite of Margaret Reeve, to run the electorate office, and he was sensational. Peter thought ahead, studying the progress of legislation as it went through the House and finally the Senate, e-mailing me with questions to preempt questions from the public. He knew probably more about legislation than I did, and the office sang along, allowing Sammy to focus on the kids and running our home.

But one piece of legislation was particularly poignant for Hinchcliffe and for me. The Education Equal Opportunity Act. It delivered a major promise from the election: mandatory assessments were written into procedures for all kids from preschool onward to identify those with learning difficulties.

Retraining of teachers to ensure those kids developed to their full potential as early as possible within the school cycle, so their integration into the general education system was seamless.

But the real victory was the recognition of the Special School, where profoundly dyslexic people like me could receive one-on-one coaching that the school system simply couldn't provide. A facility with accommodation where kids from around Australia could live and study. And more importantly, provide a discreet safe haven for those students from Asia that required specialist assistance before progressing with their tertiary studies.

MARGARET REEVE, Peter from our electorate office, and a few other notables from the town wanted to make a big deal out of the reopening of the Special School, but I thought long and hard about how we should do it.

The school was too important to the community and to the nation to be lost again through bloody-minded politics. It was also the place where Sammy first wove his magic with kids desperate to embrace literacy and become productive members of society, and in that respect it had become an icon.

I spoke to Jason and he agreed with my strategy.

Three weeks later, Jason and Jenny, Paul Sinclair, the new Leader of the Opposition, and William Hogan, the Shadow Education Minister, all fronted up for the official opening ceremony, as did the State Minister and her Opposition counterpart. I had my series of prompt notes to refer to and kept it short and sweet, reminding everyone that for the first time since Gough Whitlam became prime minister of Australia in 1972, equality of opportunity in regard to education was now back on the agenda. And even though I'd quoted E.G. Whitlam, this was a genuine attempt to place the Special School above politics, and I thanked Paul Sinclair and William Hogan for their attendance and support.

Margaret Reeve read out a message of congratulations from the prime minister of Malaysia, congratulating the university for also creating equality of opportunity in language through the Special School, and suddenly we had everyone's attention.

The sunshine reflected off the new paintwork as the keynote speaker came forward and took my place at the podium. He was clear, eloquent, and convincing.

He was already well-known in Canberra, and the senior figures from both sides adored him. He told our story all over again and reminded everyone the reason for today's ceremony was because he was able to unlock the intellect of his star pupil, who had not only become his husband, but an ambassador for a kinder and smarter Australia.

Sammy turned, and together with Margaret Reeve, used a gigantic pair of garden shears to cut the ribbon, declaring the Special School "open for business forever."

Chapter 40
The Wheel Turns

WE WERE into our second year in office, and while I'd adapted to the routine of living in Canberra, living at home, and traveling all over the place, I still wasn't happy. I missed the kids, I missed Dad and Isobel, and all the friends who'd stuck with us through thick and thin, including Matt and Scott and Chart and Solada.

But I missed Sammy so much.

I actually cried myself to sleep some nights, and that's not normal behavior for a thirtysomething man. Or was it? Sammy was my whole life, and I was his, but with kids approaching school age, our options were limited.

All in the name of service to the public, service above self.

It was the autumn session of Parliament, and we'd been working long hours massaging the education numbers in readiness for the budget presentation by the treasurer. We'd run a new broom over Education, not making many friends but managing to reduce staff with voluntary early retirement and redundancies, and the thing now looked quite sustainable.

It had been a long day and I felt sorry for my assistant, Tracy. She wasn't the brightest bulb in the chandelier, but she was a good worker, being saved by her persistence and long hours that eventually got the job done.

With some basic coaching, she vaguely understood the role of supporting a dyslexic person, but I knew my efficiency was being impaired.

She didn't fully understand that I wouldn't type e-mails and risk spelling mistakes, so I dictated them. As a result, e-mails would bank up when I needed them sent immediately.

Reading *War and Peace* at school was a walk in the park when compared to absorbing transcripts of draft legislation or discussion papers; her comprehension of that sort of stuff was zero, and that was on a good day. So I'd run along the corridor to Angela Chan, who could decipher everything in a flash and thought nothing of it. But it was a less than perfect scenario, and it pissed me off no end. Living at

home and working at the City I'd been spoiled with Mrs. Shields and
Sammy accessible at all times, and it had made such a difference. I was
determined to find a way around the problem but was aware I had to set
an example of good government with sensible overheads, and having
specialist assistance in my office would only draw criticism from the
Opposition. So I had to suck it up and I hated it.

IT GREW quite late, and I thought I should do the gentlemanly thing
and offer to buy Tracy dinner as I knew she lived alone. She accepted
graciously, and twenty minutes later we were seated at Julio's in Kingston,
a place popular with politicians but not overwhelmed by them. It was
slightly upmarket Italian cuisine, which was still good value with the
emphasis on quality, and with magnificent fresh salads.

Julio was a charming middle-aged Spanish gentleman, always
making me feel welcome and at home in his restaurant. Julio loved
Sammy and me, and always asked after him. He smiled warmly at Tracy
when I introduced her, but she didn't seem on the same wavelength, and
I just wondered what was going through her mind as Julio raised one
eyebrow a little artistically.

In the past Tracy had always avoided discussion on family. She
was single, and I'd steered away from those subjects, leaving the door
open if she wanted to volunteer that type of information, because it was
her business.

Tonight she seemed to brighten up and began an amusing tirade
on former boyfriends as we waited for our meals. I'd ordered a nice
sauvignon blanc, which she seemed to enjoy, although it was disappearing
rather quickly.

Our main course arrived, and as usual I bolted into it, my appetite
rampant.

Julio served penne pasta with a truly amazing marinara sauce, a
delicious filling meal on a quite cool April evening in Canberra, and I
thoroughly enjoyed it. Tracy ordered another bottle and was drinking
away in a most dedicated fashion before I realized there was a problem—a
personality change, brought on by drinking to excess.

Around the time my brain kicked in, so did her hand, which reached
under the table and grabbed my penis. With my cock in one hand and a

glass of grog in the other, she was nothing like the almost mousy PA I was used to.

Instead she assumed the role of predator as I swept her hand away, almost falling over as I made a beeline for the men's room, hard as a rock, leaving her smirking at the table, calling the shots, or so she thought.

Of course I was horny. I missed Sammy in every way possible, and despite several invitations from both males and females, I'd never strayed, and that wasn't going to change now. I slammed the door of the men's room, pulling my phone out of my pocket, intent on speaking to the only person who made sense to me at a time like this, when the bloody thing rang—and it was him.

THE MENTAL telepathy that has always existed between us kicked in. I knew whatever he had to say to me was a lot more important that what was on my mind. And I was right.

"Darling, I'm afraid I have bad news."

My bloody heart nearly leapt out of my chest as I hung on his every word.

"It's your mum. She had a massive stroke about an hour ago, and she passed away shortly afterward."

I felt guilty immediately; my first thought had been something was wrong with one of the kids, but I was actually relieved that it was Mum. I confessed to Sammy and he counseled me, telling me that was a natural reaction, which in hindsight was correct.

"She'd been having little ministrokes, as you know," he said, "but this was major. It was like it's time to go. She wouldn't have known anything," Sammy said. "Nature telling us all we'd suffered enough, particularly your poor dad."

I nodded through a few tears. I knew Dad would be devastated; down through the years and through all of Mum's difficulties he'd been devoted to her, and loved her equally through good and bad times. No one could have done more. I spoke to him quietly. "Darling, can I ring you back, please? In a few minutes, I'll have the flight number for you. I have to handle something first."

My dinner guest. She was by now beyond comprehension of any sort, but I tried to communicate.

"Tracy, I'm afraid my husband just phoned to say my mother has passed away, so I won't be around Canberra for a few days." Her look of disbelief and disappointment suggested she may turn nasty at any moment but before she had a chance to cause a scene, Julio had her on her feet, handbag and coat collected, and magically there was a taxi waiting outside. She said not a word; the taxi drove off, and I thanked Julio profusely.

"She is well-known," Julio said, "a serial alcoholic who preys on unsuspecting men, regardless of sexuality." Julio's expression softened, and he took both my hands. "I am so sorry for your loss," he said. "You should not have to endure rudeness at a time of such sadness."

He opened a door I hadn't noticed before and ushered me inside. "I know you will be busy now with all the arrangements you must make both in Canberra and at home, but Tony and I would love to spend just a few minutes with you." It was Julio's private dining room, and there was another smaller serving of pasta with crusty bread and a beautiful big glass of red beside it. I studied Tony, a swarthy-looking late-twenties waiter who had just removed his apron before sitting down with Julio and me. The light bulb in my silly head lit up and I laughed; Julio had entrusted me with his most intimate secret as they sat across from me holding hands.

Out of sadness and strife had come some wonderful new friends and a determination on my part to set myself up properly in Canberra so I could deal with this politics business with all my resources around me.

Chapter 41
"The moving finger writes;
and, having writ, moves on"

WE DECIDED on a private funeral, just family with a few friends who had known Mum over the years, and held in the sunny chapel at the crematorium.

We were fortunate to know what was coming at us; the old celebrant had visited the night before and read the ceremony through. He told us bluntly that no one could do anything more to help Mum, but he was trying to help us move through it all and get on with our lives. So we had our own private little service around the kitchen table where we kids had grown up.

He spoke about the web of personal relationships that holds all families together and how important they are for the ongoing stability and future of the family group. How it was love that held those relationships in place.

My brother and sister looked troubled. Hunched forward over the table, their body language spelled out the sadness of the early days, when Mum herself was a child at the hands of the church, and I in particular had such a difficult time at school.

The next day was easier than we imagined, it certainly helped that our formal grieving process had begun the night before with the celebrant.

Sammy took over at the podium to deliver the family statement. I couldn't. Neither could my brother or sister.

He spoke beautifully and directly, reminding everyone "how each of us made a contribution to her life in our own individual way."

Suddenly I understood what he was doing. Trav and Ali didn't visit much when Mum went to Green Valley Park because it upset them and their kids.

"It didn't matter if we had the ability to be with her once a day, once a week, or whatever. At some level she knew you were always thinking of her, and that's all that mattered."

Trav and Ali sat upright in their seats, lifting their heads, their shoulders relaxed, the tension draining away.

They'd been carrying that burden of unnecessary guilt around for years, and Sammy had lifted it in a few minutes.

Sammy also reminded us how Mum had worked it all through, deliberately walking away from religion and reconnecting with her family, particularly her grandchildren, before the dreadful disease had taken over and progressively destroyed her mind. And how she and Sammy became friends in the process, so poignant and so loving when she was best person for Sammy at our wedding.

So if anyone should be grieving, it was Sammy. I looked into Dad's bright eyes as he nodded at the message and understood.

I'D BEEN granted a pair to attend the funeral, but I was needed back in Canberra as soon as possible. The whole lot could wait, I decided, so I could spend some time with Sammy and the kids, and I booked my flight late the following afternoon.

Dad decided to stay over for a few days. Isobel fussed around him like an old hen, and Dad loved it, quietly allowing the positive experiences to wash over him as he entered the next phase of his life.

After dinner we put the kids to bed, then excused ourselves, heading for an early night. Sammy never failed in his magic; I was as hard as a rock in seconds, and we made love with a torrential urgency.

In hindsight I shouldn't have been surprised that Sammy was on exactly the same wavelength as me, but I lay there with my mouth open as Sammy detailed The Plan. He'd worked it all through, because to function properly as a couple and a family, we needed more time together. I didn't need to tell him that. He'd done the arithmetic, studied prices, and decided we'd probably buy something in Canberra rather than rent. Because it made better long-term business sense.

"What do you mean long-term?" I asked. "I could lose Hinchcliffe at the next election."

"You'll be there as long as you have the desire to serve the people of this electorate," he said, spooning me. "You don't understand, Jacko, the feeling around the traps is amazing. Your star is ever upward here. They see you as a humble, hardworking, but effective person. You're their darling!"

"I only have one darling," I said, and Sammy smiled that smile that always set my heart aflutter. He kissed me passionately and the covers went flying, and we were into it again. I just hoped the kids were tired out so we wouldn't wake them, because I felt quite uninhibited. If they asked what was going on I'd tell them Dad and Pop were loving each other; nothing like the truth—and Kate would have a lovely story for show-and-tell at kinder.

THE NEXT morning we sat around the breakfast table, Dad and Isobel listening with smiles on their faces, already ahead of us. Sammy had his bag packed, his seat booked, and Dad was thrust into kinder duty with Kate.

Isobel was already trying to distract Max, who wanted to come with us.

His bottom lip started to quiver, then I caught his gaze. He was older now, and he was so intelligent he remembered what worked and what didn't. He realized it was a hopeless task to keep me at home where he wanted me, but perhaps if he was a good kid I might stay a little longer.

So I took my time and sat down with both of them and tried to explain what was going on, and how their little lives would change. They both worked it out, and for the first time as a family, the little bugger didn't sulk. Dad and Pop were buying another house so we could be together—every night.

The look he gave us as we kissed them good-bye was priceless— like "get on with it, and get the show on the road."

We laughed all the way to Canberra, about how our little boy could wind us around his very small finger. But Sammy reminded me that Max seemed to have a sense of direction of where we all should be going. We thought we'd imagined it at first, but as he grew older he continued to surprise us. "It has to be genetics," I said, and my other half pretended he didn't understand.

"Max is pure Samuel John Collins-Smith." I laughed. "He just imitates you."

Sammy had the graciousness to blush as we deplaned in Canberra.

Within thirty minutes we arrived back at the apartment. I went to the office to find Tracy was on sick leave, then straight into the House where Jason gave me a sympathetic smile as I took my seat.

It took me two days of careful negotiation to have Tracy transferred to Agriculture; I'd forgiven her, but I couldn't rely on her.

Not only was she slow, but I didn't need a drunk unloading her mouth in public. Trust was implicit in this job. Many confidential things moved around before the legislative process even began, and sadly she'd demonstrated she couldn't be trusted.

Sammy helped me—he actually took over for a while on a part-time basis, and only when we convinced the union he wasn't being paid for his work did they relent. Then I had another battle on my hands. It was unheard of to bring in someone from outside the public service and just plant them into the system with all the benefits that "suitably qualified" officers had earned with many years of service. When I pointed out my chosen appointee had already spent half a lifetime in local government and with superior qualifications, their arguments were fucked. I wasn't popular; I was offside with the union and I was a Labor politician, supposed to be supporting the workers. I had to pull the only card remaining, which I hated doing. I told them outright I needed much better support than they could offer me—not a worker who got pissed, couldn't keep her mouth shut, or keep her hands to herself.

Three months later Barbara Shields walked into the office, and I unashamedly wept with joy. No one I'd ever worked with knew me better and understood the issues a dyslexic person coped with each day. She also had vision, perseverance, and critically, could handle people better than anyone I knew. Her kids were grown-up and her husband, Ted, had been retrenched with a payout, so he was a big part of the decision to move.

The day Mrs. Shields started work, we signed the papers and bought the Canberra house, a brick veneer place in Ainslie about thirty years old, with five bedrooms in good condition. A few maintenance jobs needed to be done, and Dad couldn't wait to get at them.

Sammy was over the moon and it showed. His smile grew broader by the minute when he discovered a kinder at the end of the road, a bus stop within walking distance, and a big shopping center a short drive away.

"We're so lucky, darls," he said. "This is perfect. We'll even have a spare bedroom."

I tried adding them up: the master for us, one each for Kate and Max, one each for Dad and Isobel, who were moving with us, now part of Team Collins-Smith. Five bedrooms, no spare bedroom.

Sammy beamed at me, and finally the penny dropped. Stupid, stupid, dull me. My father and Sammy's mother had given each other love and support as life threw every imaginable bit of shit at them down through the years, and now they'd found love together.

Yes, a spare bedroom, how lovely.

Chapter 42
Achieving the Impossible:
Happy Families in Canberra

IT ACTUALLY worked better than I'd dreamed. We had two complete sets of clothing and toiletries, so our trips back and forth meant we carried almost no luggage.

I finally had a proper life in Canberra. Jason and Jenny, always close, had now become great mates, as had Lucas and Oliver, their teenage sons, and were regular visitors at our Canberra house.

Every visit meant a security presence. They tactfully stayed out of sight but were well fed, keeping our egalitarian reputation intact. It was obvious over time that our family members had become Lucas and Oliver's extended family—their grandparents weren't around any longer, and both Jason and Jenny were only children, so the kids had no cousins.

Lucas, an outgoing college boy, a confident, good-looking young bloke, had a string of girls in his shadow. Quieter, smaller, and a little more introverted than his brother, Oliver had a wicked sense of humor. They loved the laid-back atmosphere at our place that was impossible to find at the Lodge and sometimes stayed over in the spare bedroom. Lucas and Dad spent time together, Lucas learning to work with his hands. Dad had him painting, plastering, even making cabinets, while Oliver stayed close to Isobel and Sammy, learning to cook. With their sons "in touch with the basics," Jason and Jenny continued to be amazed at their industrious natures, which they'd never seen before. Other kids their age were just so bored—Lucas and Oliver gave everyone around them the opposite impression, Isobel watching with amusement as first Lucas then Oliver turned their phones off, because they wanted to spend some time with their greatest fans—Kate and Max.

If the "First Family" was coming for dinner, it was always an early meal because Lucas and Oliver wanted to catch up with the kids before their bedtime. I had to pinch myself at the little tableau, Lucas reading stories to the kids and Oliver acting them out, but Jason was far from the average father. He and Jenny had become parents later in life and were the least judgmental people I knew. Other kids may have been playing sports, perhaps clubbing at weekends, yet these kids were just so happy catching up on life's simple pleasures at their own pace.

ISOBEL AND Dad continued to thrive, and while we gave them every opportunity to do their own thing, they enjoyed being part of our family structure, and we were grateful for it. We never underestimated our good fortune. With me keeping parliamentary hours and Sammy providing backup, sometimes both of us were out of the house for the entire day. Isobel and Dad cared for the kids in our absence, taking them to and from kinder, feeding them, nurturing them, and as a result, Kate and Max's education continued twenty-four hours a day.

I thought how appropriate it was, our family had become just like a Chinese family, the kids growing up with their grandparents in the same dwelling.

When the kids were tiny, we worried about leaving them in day care centers and promised ourselves—and the kids—that one parent would be around 24-7. But we both agreed this arrangement was helping the kids grow up with another dimension to their upbringing, and more importantly we told their grandparents how much we appreciated their loving participation.

Sammy continued to be sought after for his expertise in remedial education. At least once a month he flew home to be a guest lecturer for Margaret Reeve at Henry University, then the Australian National University in Canberra sought him out for a similar role.

Three separate not-for-profit organizations, one in Melbourne and two in Sydney, all related to the LGBTI movement, appointed him to their boards of management, and that required extra time and dedication on his part.

We'd all moved on from my mother's passing extraordinarily well, and thanks to Isobel, Dad hadn't imploded as we thought he may have done. Instead Dad acknowledged the gentle and loving atmosphere Isobel had created around him, and when nature took its course, it was the most beautiful thing.

My father and Sammy's mother were simply besotted with each other, gently reaching out across the years of their association and joining together seamlessly into an extraordinary partnership. My father grew younger, his worry lines seemed to disappear, and likewise Isobel, always worried about other people, just blossomed, finally able to treat herself to some personal peace and happiness. So it wasn't such a surprise when they announced at breakfast one morning they'd decided to get married, and in the little garden in the Canberra house that Dad had resurrected. Something terribly simple and low-key with just family attending, and a light lunch afterward.

A month later we all stood in a semicircle as the celebrant who had conducted my mother's funeral spoke of the healing process and the majesty of the human spirit, and none of us disagreed.

The prime minister was there with his family. My brother, sister, and their families had booked a local hotel for the weekend. Plus Matt and Scott with their kids, and Chart and Solada. Barbara and Ted Shields, and many of the prime minister's security people who knew Dad and Isobel so well because they usually fed them.

What began as a low-key gathering grew to nearly forty people, and we all had a blast.

Lucas Bellamy was Dad's best man, Oliver was Isobel's best person, and Sammy and I witnessed the documents.

There were tears as the celebrant presented the latest married couple in the Australian Capital Territory, and a surprise because the guests of honor had decided to use our names: Peter and Isobel Collins-Smith.

Chapter 43
Off and Running

THE SPRING session over and Christmas only a few weeks away, we became part of the mass exodus from Canberra as politicians returned home.

Peter and I toured every corner of my electorate for two weeks, our fifth such journey since my election as the member for Hinchcliffe.

I made myself available to listen to problems and help where I could, meeting in libraries, schools, and coffee shops. Sammy joined us where possible, and finally I had to admit to him the extraordinarily positive feeling and feedback that now existed, his assessment accurate, as usual. In the most conservative heartland of the electorate, the smaller regional center where I'd created history by winning almost every booth, I could do no wrong. I'd been in my old working duds, touring from farm to farm because dairying was the biggest earner here and farmers were naturally interested in their future. The questions were thoughtful and intelligent as I plowed my way through mud and cow shit, standing alongside people and just listening.

Every person I spoke to had a basic understanding of what our prime minister was attempting to do. There was no doubt Jason communicated the agenda well, but people were toey; they wanted to know when their back pocket was going to be improved, "like what's in it for me, forget the big picture stuff, *when* are you going to put more money in *my* pocket?"

The best news I could give them was the domestic economy had improved slightly so we could maintain the education, health, and social security settings. But I was honest and told them the long-term future of our country was still very nebulous. We'd redoubled our efforts in Asia, and investors visited in droves, looking at everything from real estate to airlines, but very few wanted to invest in manufacturing or primary produce. A strange situation because cost of manufacture in Australia shouldn't concern the growing nouveau riche of Asia, given their sudden wealth and our close location.

"You can stay as long as you want as member for Hinchcliffe," Jock Fleming said to me afterward, "because you're hardworking, humble, and smart. But if the government doesn't show some progress by the end of their second term, we're all fucked, no more second chances."

WITH THE election due midyear, some encouraging economic indicators appeared as the autumn session got underway. The balance of trade figures showed marked improvement, and that was all Jason needed.

The next day he visited the governor-general and we readied ourselves to hit the campaign trail once again.

When Jason returned from Yarralumla, I was summoned to his office. I was ushered in, the door closed, and the prime minister gave me his usual welcome. Not the standard greeting for his ministers, but then I clearly wasn't usual or standard, so I cuddled him back.

There are some things a dyslexic person can visualize particularly in the future, but other obvious things in the present often go unnoticed. So I sat there as Jason told me that as Phillip Gregson had decided to retire and wouldn't seek reelection, Jason wanted me to become deputy leader and deputy prime minister in the new government if we were reelected, in addition to the Education portfolio.

My head spun as Jason laughed at me, assuring me he'd already done the numbers and I would have a clear margin in caucus, despite the "gang of fifteen" from the right wing of the parliamentary party who opposed everything progressive, including the newbie who seemed a carbon copy of the prime minister, with the same crazy ideas about embracing Asia and Asians. I knew I was hated by them; they were mostly middle-aged Catholics who hated gays, Asians, and anything out of the ordinary. They also clung to the monarchy like leeches and organized themselves into their own factional group but were clearly outnumbered and looking more irrelevant than ever.

"Don't look so surprised," Jason said. "Politics is like shooting snakes. A leader needs someone to keep the reptiles under control on one hand and who won't plug him in the back with the other. How could I possibly choose anyone else?"

Leonardo da Vinci, Albert Einstein, Alexander Graham Bell, Sir Richard Branson, Walt Disney, Jay Leno, Whoopi Goldberg, Nelson Rockefeller, Agatha Christie, Steven Spielberg, Harry Belafonte, Winston Churchill, Richard Strauss.

I thanked him and accepted the promotion, because our teamwork was undeniable, and regardless of my relative inexperience, I knew I'd quickly grow into the role. We read each other's minds miles ahead of the action, sharing a common purpose and strategy, and I felt excited for the future.

Jason had taken a huge risk with the first election, but the electorate sought change from the previous poorly performing government, and we were duly elected with a comfortable majority. This time they would not only judge our progress toward our stated goals, but what was in it for them—the feedback from Hinchcliffe was exactly what the focus groups were saying around the country.

In our favor was the fact we'd delivered on every election promise made and had, we'd hoped, demonstrated we were more interested in running the nation than trying to score political points by running down the Opposition. In fact we tried for good reason to approach everything we did in the Asia Plan with bipartisan support, for the long-term sake of the strategy and the nation.

The opinion polls favored us, but not by any huge margin, so it was anybody's election as it had been nearly four years previously.

This time, however, for our own party there were some mandatory guidelines and discipline on election strategy and the national campaign, and the gang of fifteen didn't like it. Jason reminded them they'd been banished to the political wilderness until he came along, but their conservatism ran deep; in fact both Jason and I found it easier to talk to some members of the Opposition—they were more progressive than this lot.

In the final caucus of this parliament, Jason got tough, offering to accept their resignations from the party if they didn't throw their energy behind party policy and the campaign. Instantly their faces gave them away, smugness replaced by concern. This wasn't a pep talk from our rather gentle leader, but a serious offer to fuck off and be replaced by someone else. Just to ensure there were no misunderstandings, Jason and I had some informal discussions with each of them, one at a time, in Jason's office.

They were like naughty schoolchildren, but they knew Jason's authority embraced all the factions, and he'd have no compunction having them disendorsed as Labor candidates even at this late stage. If not this election, then certainly the next, and that was a risk they simply couldn't take.

At last we seemed to have some consensus, but not before time, and I mentally filed away some of the looks of hatred in my direction as they left the room after their lecture.

By the time Sammy and I returned home to Hinchcliffe, Peter had the campaign off and running.

But the first thing I did was to ring my Liberal opponent, Alicia Bennett, which seemed to catch her off guard. Using the pause in conversation, I invited her for coffee, and after some hesitation she agreed to meet me just after lunch at a little-known restaurant in a back lane in the city center.

Peter had done some research on her background, so I was well informed. A little older than me, early forties, Alicia owned a successful real estate business. She'd never married but lived with her partner, John, in the town's oldest and most posh suburb. She liked nice cars and drove a very new-looking BMW with her personalized number plates. She belonged to several service clubs, including Rotary, and had been president of the Chamber of Commerce.

I made sure I arrived early, but she came earlier and sat there with a smirk, a natural tactician. I ordered her choice of coffee and a nice slice of cake in a gentlemanly fashion, and that seemed to break down whatever barriers she'd erected around herself.

"Go on," I said, "this is for you. It's only fattening if you eat the whole sponge."

She laughed; we seemed to have common ground in a shared sense of humor, so I continued. "I wanted to talk about the campaign, because it's important to me that we both present ourselves and our policies to the electors of Hinchcliffe without descending into personal attacks and character assassination." She gave me a hard, calculating look, not willing to trust me in any way, rather naturally, because I stood between herself and a seat in the House of Representatives.

I sought to explain myself more fully. "Last election I was up against poor Dr. Fitch, and I never want to see that sort of stuff ever again. The guy attacked me personally; as it turned out he had severe mental health issues, but sadly it lowered the tone of the campaign, and in the end did more than anything to lose the seat of Hinchcliffe for you guys."

Her eyes narrowed and she slammed her now empty latte glass on the table, because clearly Dr. Fitch was still involved in politics at the local level. She shouted, causing some other patrons to turn and stare. "Dear Andrew suffered through the most despicable campaign I've ever seen," she said. "You caused a fine man to have a breakdown, an educated gentleman who would have been such an asset to this community and who would have maintained a proper sense of decorum in Canberra, rather than you big-noting yourself with a pack of union thugs."

All I could think about was backing out gracefully before she became really wound up. There was no point in talking further; she'd listened to the wrong advice and was intent on running an old-fashioned, patronizing campaign that used smear tactics and personal innuendo instead of policies.

A crowd had begun gathering outside as the noise of her shouting attracted their attention. I paid for the coffee, apologized to the barista, waved to Ms. Bennett, and left rather quickly. I didn't know whether to feel elated or just sad because our opposition appeared set to make the same mistakes as the last election. If she followed through with that approach, she'd alienate herself further from the voters, and while it gave me an advantage, it upset me that the voters of Hinchcliffe would think politicians hadn't made any progress in nearly three years—that all politicians were scum.

We didn't have long to wait. She was interviewed on national radio and went on the attack immediately.

"Mr. Collins-Smith is weak and ineffective," she ranted, taking my words totally out of context. "His party is born of the union movement, and they're all thugs and criminals. Why elect people like that to Parliament?"

It was ridiculous and childish as she went on and on about affiliations and personalities, without one policy statement. When the host of the ABC morning program went after her, she told him he'd have to wait for the policies, that the official launch of her party would see Paul Sinclair roll out "some of the old Liberal magic," and she wouldn't comment until then.

The guy gave up and chopped her off, ending the interview.

My phone rang and it was the anchorman himself, Bryan Friedman. I liked him because he was maximum substance and minimum bullshit, a man with a towering intellect and a reputation for going straight for the jugular if someone's attitude didn't suit him. Over the years he'd attacked church leaders who tried to cover up child abuse, shonky employers who short-paid immigrants, and criticized environmental banditry with unlicensed rubbish disposal, to name just a few of his pet hates.

"Why would someone standing in a provincial seat want to talk on a metropolitan-based program?" I asked him.

"She told me she had information that everyone in Hinchcliffe should know before the campaign began in earnest, but as you probably heard, she just wanted to attack you personally and the unions, in that order. I'm duty bound to offer you the right of reply, just don't arrive without your policy manifesto, Jacko."

My phone screamed at me later that day, and it was him again. "How would you like to join me tomorrow as cohost?" he asked. "I've just had a cancelation and, as you're coming in anyway, why not stay a little longer? We'd be finished at twelve noon."

"Okay, but can I bring Sammy with me?"

"Oh your husband, he's so interesting in his own right, so I've gone from rags to riches. We'll have two cohosts."

I smiled to myself; if Bryan Friedman was going to attack me, Sammy would be there to give me some breathing space and some time to think. A magnificent distraction.

MODERN, STATE-OF-THE-ART broadcasting technology surrounded us, but because Sammy and I were there together, it didn't feel intimidating.

From the outset, Bryan's charming nature welcomed us. He'd clearly done his research but was cautious as he led into the initial on-air discussion. It was one thing to interview yet another politician, ream them out for poor performance, heap shit on their policies, and entertain the listeners with a show of verbal fisticuffs. But Sammy wasn't a politician, and he wasn't fair game, and Bryan circled us like a fox around the henhouse, waiting for the opportunity to pounce, which didn't eventuate. Sammy and I hadn't even spoken about how we would handle the interview, but we just fell into step together as he began speaking.

Sammy had that air about him, friendly, approachable, and sincere, but it was obvious when we were together that it was a team. Team Collins-Smith.

And while Bryan Friedman had a reputation for destroying those who were pretentious and downright evil, he was just putty in Sammy's hands.

The conversation went back and forth about Sammy's teaching methods, and then settled on dyslexia—my dyslexia. We both sensed Bryan wasn't doing anything else but leading into my favorite topic, when he asked me what had been my most notable achievement during my time in office.

"The Education Equal Opportunity Act, of course," I replied, pleased he was giving us great air time and even greater publicity, "because it restates the case for education across the board, even though it centers on helping those with learning difficulties make something of their life, developing to their full potential."

"As you have."

"Thanks, but I was lucky. I married the teacher, so my education never stops."

Bryan chuckled, then turned the discussion briefly to our kids, Dad and Isobel, and from an interview that we thought would be probing and insightful, the great Bryan Friedman suddenly went all hearts and flowers on us.

It was done so well, we relaxed in his company and talked honestly about our life together and what we hoped for the future.

There was some talk-back, and he cleverly weeded out a few homophobic comments by advising those callers they were verging on breaking the law and then cutting them off. His producer began waving madly from the control room because the system neared meltdown—so he "parked" one of the guests on the program and let Sammy and me just talk to the callers.

One of the first was Des, a dairy farmer who was a member of the NCP but a favorite contact of mine. We seemed to speak the same language, slopping around in mud and cow shit under the shadow of the Simpson Ranges. We found common ground because we both worried about the future for our kids. "Is there any good news, Jacko?" he asked.

"I can't say at the moment, but I'm hoping I'll have something for the campaign launch next Wednesday."

"You wouldn't hold out on me, would you, Jacko?" he asked.

"I promise you'll be the first to know as soon as I know."

"Good, I'll see you there."

Bryan looked at me, raising one eyebrow; a National Country Party supporter at a Labor campaign launch would normally be ostracized by his NCP mates, but times had changed.

Sammy scribbled a line on a scrap of paper to explain: *Dairy farmers down there are dependent on foreign investment to reopen the local butter factory, negotiations still in progress.*

"So your campaign launch is in a country hall this time?" he asked.

"Last time it was at the university as we needed to highlight the inequalities of the education system. This time it's where it is because a whole community down there is struggling along, just keeping their heads above water and trying to build a future for their families. I hope to have Ron Hoy with me, the agriculture minister. He's been working on something that could have huge importance for the area."

Our talk-back was interrupted by a news bulletin, then one of Bryan's guests, a well-known artist in ceramics who had some beautiful stuff, and we began asking questions about both the process of manufacture and marketing, which would have been riveting stuff under normal circumstances, but it didn't turn the listeners on. Bryan's producer was giving us the signal once more, so talk-back took over. I apologized to the ceramics man, but he seemed to be enjoying himself, even asking questions not about policy, but about us.

I caught Sammy's eye and he nodded, understanding where all this was going but relaxed, the type of questions and the upbeat tone of the whole thing in surprisingly good taste. They wanted to know why we had two houses, and I answered, telling them life without Sammy, even for a few days, wasn't a life—we missed each other too much. And yes, my father and Sammy's mother had married after enduring years of my birth mother's illness. Yes, Sammy was a guest lecturer at colleges in Canberra and at home, as well as running a household, raising our kids with the help of our parents, and supporting me most days in my parliamentary office.

Then a lady asked me how Sammy and I met, and Sammy took over.

Sammy described our lifelong friendship and almost everything in between, not the sort of subject normally the material of the national broadcaster's morning show.

The very next caller identified himself as another dairy farmer, but this time it wasn't about farming. "I'm a grandfather," he said, "and because people are human, they tend to lose sight of their priorities. We worry about good and bad seasons, whether we can sell our milk, and yes, I'm a neighbor of Des Nightingale, and I too worry about the future for the generations of my family who've decided to soldier on as farmers.

But the physical and emotional health of your nearest and dearest has to be the true priority of any family.

"I had a lovely gay brother who was a great farmer, a wonderful human being, but the expectations of the community wore him down while he was still a young man, and he took his own life. I promised myself I would never allow this to happen in my family circle ever again, and so we've taken a leadership role in this community ever since on that very subject. And it's just as well, because as of a few days ago, my second grandson has come out, so we are fortunate to have two lovely gay men in our family. When I hear the member for Hinchcliffe and his husband on radio talking about a life that is full of love and promise, it makes me proud to be Australian and proud to have such a representative in Canberra. To speak so openly and lovingly about your marriage and each other sets a great example to all our society, and I want you to know that everyone of voting age in our family will be casting their vote in your favor. Thank you and good morning to you both."

Bryan Friedman's eyes misted over, and I was flabbergasted that we could have had such an influence in such a conservative heartland for the reasons given. Sammy took my hand and I couldn't speak, I was so overwhelmed by the human kindness of it all. It was right on news time and twelve noon. As Bryan wound the program up, the afternoon host tried to persuade us to return for his program, but we shook our heads; we were mentally exhausted.

Outside the studio Bryan smiled at us tentatively and invited us to lunch "for a debrief," which Sammy accepted on our behalf. Our commitments for the afternoon could be put back until the following day, as Bryan led us to a lovely Asian restaurant just a short walk away.

Chapter 44
In the Thick of It

THE MORNING show had fabulous reach into the electorate, particularly the dairy farmers in the southern part of Hinchcliffe, who had the radio stuck on the national broadcasting station during morning milking and cleanup in their cowsheds. But what Ms. Bennett had hoped would influence voters up front in her campaign seemed to have the opposite effect, judging by the feedback we'd had. Her disrespect and her old-fashioned, aggressive political stance pissed people off. But in our case, as a result of Bryan Friedman's management of talk-back radio, Sammy and I had bared everything personal that seemed to unlock any mystery around us. We came out of the radio program as being an astonishingly normal couple, not shy about our feelings for each other, and very up-front about our family and our history together.

But more importantly, I wanted to talk about our future because what we wanted in simple terms was pretty much what other couples wanted.

The morning after the radio program, I listened to the bloke on air who I now classed as a friend—not a place I should be, according to some of my colleagues, who refused to allow journalists to get any closer than the other side of the table. But I sensed Bryan would never let us down, and Sammy agreed; life was too short if we couldn't make friends on the way through.

"Well," he said, "after yesterday I could be excused for feeling somewhat deflated because the hundreds of text messages and telephone calls simply underlined what was probably, for me anyway, the most enjoyable day's work I've ever put in. So I have succumbed to the 'day after' syndrome. If the honorable member for Hinchcliffe is listening, could I also say that you are a better pourer of wine than you are a drinker? However I suspect your head would also be somewhat heavier than normal this morning, which serves you right because when I surfaced at 4:00 a.m., I can tell you I wished I was somewhere else. Seriously, however, I suspect this station has never had a talk-back segment like that in its long history. It did what the media is supposed to do: it joined people together, vast numbers of people in discussion and enjoyment. Management will probably offer the member for Hinchcliffe and his husband a contract at my expense. I think it was worth every minute, because it was radio at its very best. But while today is a touch ordinary by comparison, I've managed to persuade yesterday's guests to return a few days before we go to vote, not necessarily for any major policy statements but for some great entertainment. We'll keep you informed and confirm when the Collins-Smith family have a few hours to indulge us again."

THIS TIME Jason decided to have the national launch within a week of announcing the campaign, and he decided on Sydney, in a large old suburban town hall in his own seat. I had to attend as deputy leader and education minister, as did the entire cabinet and their partners. There were filthy looks again as Jason insisted Sammy and I join him and Jenny onstage, and I was well aware that while I had the numbers as deputy, I was tolerated only because Jason wanted me there. Jason, as Mr. Magic, provided their meal ticket, and they would demonstrate absolute loyalty while he was around. If we lost the election and returned to the political wilderness, Jason and I would disappear from executive positions, of that I was sure. I'd only had one term as a politician, but the realities of political life were firmly embedded in my brain—produce or piss off.

I studied the audience carefully, as Jason had asked. Many of the attendees, mainly unionists and party faithful, sat talking, but a few well-known business people, including bankers, industrialists, and media moguls in attendance meant they were at least listening to us. The element of surprise stayed with us since the previous election—we had a merchant-based strategy, which, if successful, could bring consistently good returns to the top end of town, and it appeared to be working, albeit slowly at first. This was New Labor, Jason told them, and in the same breath warned employers, investors, and the media they shared responsibility for the vulnerable and the poor. "Making embarrassing margins out of health and education services is all over," he said. He next announced a national first home buyers' allowance that addressed home affordability aimed at middle Australia, but quadrupled when applied to regional areas, encouraging decentralization.

There were more funds for education and health, but more about maintaining what we'd already put in place. Age pensions were to be permanently indexed after successive governments had tinkered with them, and superannuation contributions got a small tax benefit.

Then Jason put policies behind him and spoke of respect for people.

The top end of town sat there stunned, as did many of the hierarchy of the party, probably hoping our mild, moderate leader would launch into a headlong attack of the Opposition and their policies. It didn't happen.

Instead he embarrassed me by telling everyone how it was a rookie politician standing for Parliament for the first time who reminded him and the national executive how politicians were perceived by the general public.

How the very last thing they needed to hear was an argument, in parliament or out of it. A healthy policy debate, yes, deliberate character assassination, a resounding no.

"Yes," Jason continued, "we understand that our performance over the last three years will be scrutinized by the people who put us in power, and that the famous hip-pocket nerve may drive people's decisions. But the economy *is* improving, and we're beginning to hand back the rewards to the people who need them the most. So we ask Australians to be patient and share with us the responsibility of growing our economy until it can sustain itself once more. Thank you and good afternoon."

There was polite applause, hardly American presidential style, but it was befitting the somewhat homely, no-nonsense image Jason had created around himself, and supported by me. We knew by the focus groups held all over the country that our style was appreciated, and so was our apparent honesty, a rarity in modern-day politics.

BACK IN Hinchcliffe I had a welcome phone call and an invitation for not just coffee but for morning tea at her home from Alicia Bennett, my opposition.

Her face fell as I knocked on the door with Sammy by my side. What she had planned I didn't know, but away from the public eye there are always CCTV cameras just waiting for a silly sap like me to be compromised. I'd been embarrassed once before, learning my lesson in the process, and it wouldn't happen again. "I'd hoped John would be here," I said, rubbing salt into the wound, and she had the decency to blush while Sammy smiled sweetly.

She was well fucked without a man in sight and she knew it.

"I wanted to apologize," she said, and I knew at least in that regard she was genuine. "I assumed that your Mr. Nice Guy strategy was just another politician's punch line, and I was terribly wrong. In fact I think my reaction to it has already cost me any chance of winning the seat. Your interview with Bryan Friedman was awesome." She poured nice coffee while she spoke, her voice softer this time, her manner quite the opposite to her outburst of a few days ago in the city.

"I also took your remarks about Dr. Fitch personally," she said. "Several of us in the party have been concerned because he has mood swings, good some days and off the planet the next, and I guess one would have to judge his real ability somewhere in between. But he continues to excel as a general practitioner. He has the largest private practice in town."

"No," snapped Sammy, quite forcefully, "his ability is flawed because of mental illness. Andrew Fitch will destroy anything and everything he lays his hands on because he's a schizophrenic, probably not even on medication. What I think is verging on criminal behavior is that the man has been allowed to continue practicing medicine. We had no idea that was the case. If you consider yourself a friend of his, you should stop him practicing before he kills someone."

"Oh no, I don't think he's that bad."

"Fine, let's not argue about it, but four years ago Jacko made sure the poor guy was having treatment from one of his colleagues who understood his mental health problems, and we thought he was doing something about it."

She shrugged her shoulders, and I caught Sammy's eye. He was absolutely correct, the guy was dangerous, and I made a note to have a chat to Angela Chan as Minister for Health as a matter of urgency. The Medical Board would have to be involved; this was much too much.

"What I can't get my head around is why Hinchcliffe, a safe, blue-ribbon Liberal Party seat has now drifted away to your party," she said. "It can't be just poor Andrew Fitch alone, surely."

She caught the look in my eye. "Oh I'm silly for asking you that question. Clearly you wouldn't want to give away Labor Party secrets just like that."

Sammy's eyes twinkled, and I took the hint; our morning tea was nearly over.

"Alicia, it's primarily the reason for which I first contacted you. If you treat the voters like human beings and listen to what their needs and wants are *and show them respect*, rather than trotting out *your* agenda, you might earn the right to represent them again. The voters of this electorate are heartily sick and tired of listening to politicians attacking each other's reputations rather than providing worthwhile alternative policies. Remember, Alicia, that's why nature gives us two ears and only one mouth, so we listen twice as much as we speak. Now if you'll excuse us, we've an important meeting to attend. Thank you so much for the coffee."

Alicia Bennett stood there with her mouth hanging open, but I didn't feel the slightest bit sorry for her. The only thing I regretted was that the voters of Hinchcliffe would have to put up with her old-fashioned and disrespectful attitude.

Sammy spotted a camera up on the picture rail as we walked past, and we waved cheerily at it as we got on with our day.

AT EXACTLY noon the following day, I stepped up to the microphone in the little country hall. The meeting was deliberately held at that time so my dairy-farming friends could attend, in between morning and afternoon milking. I'd rung Des Nightingale the night before as promised, and he was sitting, beaming, in the front row.

Beside me on the stage sat Ron Hoy, the agriculture minister. He had the national agriculture package to launch with something for all farmers. So I introduced him and Ron began.

A small, precise man from a Chinese immigrant family and a farmer himself, his unique qualifications and experience allowed him to say it the way it was. He thanked me for being his backstop and his negotiation partner in what was, he said, "The best possible outcome for this area and its hardworking and dedicated farmers."

Ron announced how the old butter factory on the edge of town would be reborn as a manufacturing entity. That a cartel of Asian buyers had bought the freehold and had committed to spend millions to bring it up to its full potential, manufacturing butter, cheese, yoghurt, and dried milk product. Chinese money underwrote the finance, and Shanghai would absorb much of the volume product. But a significant amount was intended for the ASEAN countries as well, and if the project was successful, then it would be rolled out further.

"If anyone has poddy calves at the sale tomorrow, I strongly suggest you pull all the heifers out," he said. No one had ever spoken their language in this context before, and Ron had their undivided attention. "This deal is set in concrete," he said, "and work will start on the plant next Monday. Orders have already been placed for new processing machinery, and much of that will arrive in six months from now. What you have to do is to breed, breed, breed." There were big smiles at what could have been a double entendre anywhere else, but it made perfect sense here in the bush.

"We think you will need to double your milk production to satisfy demand for this first stage of investment. After we've built up a reputation for reliable and consistent supply, there's no telling where this could end up. Now it's your turn to put your investment dollars into more stock and particularly your own milking sheds and pasture improvement, so you can run and milk the number of cows necessary to become reliable suppliers. But yes, this is a happy day here in Hinchcliffe, because the dairy industry now has a future. It's certainly not all my doing, because your local member has helped drive this project with his Asian contacts and his refusal to say no.

"I might add that the initial interest came through his husband, thanks to his association with the Special School and the university. There's no doubt this one project will have a profound and lasting effect as we seek to grow the Australian economy. It won't happen immediately, it'll take time, but if we all work together, it will happen."

The speeches and presentations took only thirty-five minutes, probably a world record for a political rally, but Jock Fleming noted that it was the first time such a meeting had been held by the Labor Party in this part of Hinchcliffe, and was delighted by the positive feel in the old hall.

We were packing up our gear when Des Nightingale rushed up, and to our amazement demanded we all stay for lunch. We agreed, knowing there would be many questions on such an important day for the district, but intrigued that such a level of organization could happen in such a short time frame.

I'd phoned Des at eight o'clock the night before, yet the local Country Women's Association looked like they'd been planning the event for months. They'd certainly catered for country appetites as massive amounts of sandwiches, homemade pies, and pasties kept on emerging from the kitchen, followed by puddings, fruit salad, and more. I watched fascinated as two big Italian coffee machines hissed and snorted away; it seemed only a short time ago in the City's workshops that instant coffee was all the rage, quick and easy, but hardly as healthy as good coffee, *proper coffee*. I looked around and Peter smiled at me. "The ladies understood you hated instant coffee, so at their expense they hired these from a local restaurant, plus two baristas."

"Just so I could have a decent cup of coffee?"

"Yes, they reckon you're worth it, but this is a much more sophisticated little society than people give it credit for." Peter pointed to a line of people waiting for their flat whites, cappuccinos, and long blacks.

I felt very humble. Sammy came with me as we walked into the kitchen, making sure I spoke to everyone, a handshake here, a kiss on the cheek there, and I really began to enjoy myself. If this was politics at the grassroots level, then I was at home, with the workers, the dignity of labor.

Des Nightingale tapped me on the shoulder and introduced his neighbor Gus Evans. Gus identified himself as the caller on Bryan Friedman's show, and he wanted to introduce us to his family. About forty people waited to meet us from the Evans family, and they were all beautiful—male, female, young, middle-aged, or elderly, just a good-looking, happy group. Again we did the rounds, shaking hands, and finally were introduced to the two out and proud grandsons, who were probably embarrassed as hell in front of their siblings and cousins. Outwardly, like Sammy and me and most other same-sex-attracted people, they were indistinguishable from those around them.

The boys, Trevor and Harry, were first cousins. Trevor had a steady boyfriend, Jamie, whom he proudly introduced to us as the family looked on with knowing smiles. Poor bloody Harry just stood there, blushing, probably feeling like shit as he appeared odd man out.

Suddenly I had an idea and consulted Sammy, who smiled and nodded. I completed the first section of the old four-minute mile as I ran out to our car, where Justin, our driver, was checking his e-mails, looking thoroughly bored with himself. "Sorry, mate," I said, "I must apologize, we always feed our drivers along with ourselves, so come on inside."

"Oh no, Mr. Collins-Smith, I couldn't do that."

"Justin, what part didn't you understand? I saw you up the back, then you piss off back to the bloody car. Didn't you like the meeting?"

"Oh yes, sir, I did. My family are farmers only an hour away from here. Dad will vote Labor for the first time because your rural policies are spot on. Actually I voted for you at the last election because I just admire you and your husband so much."

I smiled at the bloke. He was every bit of twenty-four or so, dark hair with even features, perfectly groomed, well spoken, with a lovely gentle nature. Someone at the Commonwealth garage had clearly matched him up with Sammy and me.

"I'm truly sorry, Justin, but I've neglected you badly and I apologize. Firstly our drivers always eat with us. There's no master–servant relationship here. We'd be honored to have your company wherever we are."

I then took a deep breath and jumped in. "Secondly someone as handsome, thoughtful, and gentle as you is most probably same-sex attracted, am I right?"

I breathed in; this could go very badly if we'd been wrong.

A nod and a brilliant smile rewarded me, albeit with a blush of temporary embarrassment.

"Fine," I said, "follow me. We'll grab you something to eat, and there's someone inside who we think you should meet. Oh, by the way," I took his arm and steered him inside, "I must compliment you on your lovely manners."

He smiled his rather infectious smile as we walked over to Sammy, who was in animated conversation with the Evans family. I winked at Sammy and he took over. "Justin, thank you for joining us. Come and meet the Evans mob."

We watched on as Justin was introduced to all the family members one by one, all genuinely welcoming, particularly when Gus Evans discovered he knew Justin's father—the bush telegraph would be soon running hot.

Then he got to Harry, and Mother Nature did her handiwork. The first time it was Matt and Scott; this time it was Harry and Justin who lit up the room around them.

Sammy and I grinned at each other. It had been a long shot, but there was magic in the air as Harry and Justin sat down with a plate of sandwiches between them and exchanged phone numbers.

Chapter 45
Once More unto the Breach, Dear Friends

WE WORKED bloody hard, repeating all the activity from the previous election and taking nothing for granted. Again the university in our town became the next venue for another public meeting where I went through all the major policies point by point. Not just for Hinchcliffe, but nationally.

We did our show-and-tell sessions outside supermarkets, staying far enough away from the entrance so as not to raise the hackles of some senior shoppers who simply wanted to buy their groceries and not be accosted by political messages. Surprisingly however, we were inundated by questions at a very early part of the campaign, and they were intelligent queries, which indicated they'd understood what we were trying to achieve. Most of them centered around the time frame of when things would improve. While Australians hadn't been struggling in poverty, they knew that we'd kept the purse strings tightly reined in, that there were no luxuries or new projects that required external funding on the horizon. They wanted to know how long it would be before we could hold our heads up as a nation and look toward a sustainable future.

Jason and I spoke every day. The country was in caretaker mode effectively under our control; wages had to be paid, hospitals and schools had to keep functioning, and there was always something that needed attention, albeit briefly.

I told Jason, if he had a moment, to listen to the morning program on the national broadcaster in Melbourne. We compared notes over stuff I knew I'd be asked about, but with nearly four weeks of heavy campaigning, it was relatively easy to keep our message consistent. Alicia Bennett had been offered the right of reply but declined, choosing to spend her remaining time with her team, telephoning everyone in the electorate. Sammy agreed with me that most people would be heartily sick and tired of politics by now, and a telephone call from Alicia would be the last thing anyone would need to hear.

Which frankly worried me because it meant the voters of Hinchcliffe would judge all politicians as a result, not just Alicia and the Liberals.

The Greens had become a resurgent force as an alternative party, and while their numbers were small, I feared disenchantment with the main parties generally would increase their share of the vote, just something else to chip away at my margin. Nothing was guaranteed in politics, but I'd given everything its best shot possible. Now it was up to the people.

BUT FOR now we sat with Bryan Friedman in the studio as he swung through the introductions and a background of his two cohosts, Sammy and me.

"Before anyone accuses me of political bias, can I say that Jackson's opponent in his electorate of Hinchcliffe has declined her right of reply, as has the Greens candidate, which suits me fine because my cohosts are usually bent on having a good time anyway."

Bryan put some music on, and I began to feel some trepidation as it played out, the time advancing steadily toward answering questions. Sammy's hand slipped over and squeezed mine, and Bryan smiled at us.

"So, Jackson," he began rather gently, "the driving force for you entering politics was a very piecemeal and nepotistic education system, which didn't cater for pupils as you once were, in the public education system and a sufferer of dyslexia, correct?"

It's a story that most back home knew by now, but taking a deep breath, I started again for a new audience.

Bryan took calls. I knew he wanted to talk education and compare me to the late Gough Whitlam on education, but I sensed there was another agenda out there. As it turned out, there were several, and after a music break Bryan took calls again; this time he threw it open to any subject and the hip-pocket nerve took over.

By now, with the campaign nearly over, I knew we were on notice with the public. Caller after caller echoed the sentiment of "what's in it for me, what about me," and it went on and on. Healthcare costs, education costs, the price of fuel, stamp duty on real estate—a state issue—and a myriad of items important to individuals. I answered them all and was honest. No, I didn't know when things would improve, but the basics of life were still in place and everyone should feel that the worst was over. That we'd poured what funds were available into the Australian embassies in each of the ASEAN countries, encouraging trade like never before.

The positive support had been too good to be true, because the next caller fixed all of those perceptions. Bryan wrinkled his brow and was about to cut him off, but I held my hand up.

"Dr. Fitch, how lovely to hear from you," I said, and Sammy's face mirrored his distaste.

"I wanted you to be the first to know," he said, "'Australia for Australians' will be marching in every capital city on Saturday. Just think how interesting that will make the Election Day for you."

"Dr. Fitch, we live in a democracy, and if you wish to demonstrate your views on any subject, at any time, you're welcome to do so, provided you do so in a lawful fashion."

There was a cackle as he continued, Bryan's hand over the cutoff button. I held my hand up again.

"Your stupid policy of getting cozy with the Asians will ruin this nation. Australia was settled by the English and that's the way it must stay. It's unacceptable to have these people infiltrating our society. Not only does it diminish Anglo-Saxon and Celtic bloodlines, but it's a massive security risk."

Bryan Friedman shook his head, mortified by his outburst and plainly upset by the blatantly racist overtones.

I outlined the facts as gently as possible. "Dr. Fitch, I wouldn't dignify your words by a response, except to say that by maybe as early as 2040, 50 percent of this country's population will be able to trace their genetics back to Asia anyway. So you can march up and down, scream out your message of hatred, but intelligent Australians will understand why we're accelerating the process of assimilation with Asia. But all of that aside, Dr. Fitch, we're very concerned about your personal mental state, and your fitness to practice medicine in particular. We want to save you from yourself and protect the public." Bryan Friedman cut him off, as Sammy shook his head, his body language telling me not to take him too lightly—he reckoned Andrew Fitch was dangerous enough to be locked up, but I felt he was so sick nobody would take any notice of him.

In fact he'd done a great job for us because there was an avalanche of calls from people horrified at his extremist views.

JASON INVITED me to join him in Canberra, but I preferred to be in Hinchcliffe with my workers, my family, and more importantly, the voters who until now had given me the honor of representing them.

Alicia Bennett was already there, so I walked over and wished her well. In a friendly, almost apologetic mindset she wished me luck also. Regardless of the result for either of us, Andrew Fitch was nowhere to be seen and I breathed a sigh of relief. This election the kids were old enough to be included, and Max was fascinated, asking questions about everything, while Kate was the new, "almost grown-up" little girl, suddenly demure and even shy, hanging on to Sammy's coat. She still had "a little pain in the tummy," however, which she felt could only be cured by an ice cream, so Isobel and Dad were pressed into service. Max overheard and decided his sister couldn't possibly enjoy something he didn't, so he stormed off after them.

Sammy turned to me. "Come over here," he said, leading me toward Matt and Scott. They gathered around as Sammy kissed me discreetly yet so passionately I was hard as a rock instantly. "Win, lose, or draw, I'm so proud of you, and there's a special reward tonight, if you care to take up the offer?"

"I care, but what happens if the Liberals wipe the floor with me?"

"Ah, you'll need consolation, so I'll feed you in between consoling you."

"You've got a deal."

MATT, SCOTT, Jock Fleming, Peter Prentice, and the whole campaign team stayed upbeat about my chances. I'd lectured them over the last few weeks about being publicly overconfident because I saw that as arrogant and disrespectful of voters. I reminded them that if I was reelected I was still the servant of the electorate, and that was important to me.

The Liberals lost Hinchcliffe because of their arrogance and their refusal to listen to the ordinary people who put their faith in them as their representatives, and I wasn't about to make the same mistake.

The first figures were posted and something was up, they were from Newhampton, the most affluent suburb in this provincial town of ours. With old money everywhere and the most expensive real estate, they even seemed to speak with a posh accent and were so up themselves it was painful. For those of us that disliked pretentious behavior, it was hard to pay them much attention as a group and as a suburb because it was such a right-wing bastion.

Yet as the figures flew up on the board, a swing toward us took everyone by surprise. Last election I'd polled around 15 percent of the vote in Newhampton, mainly I reasoned from the few wealthy academics that lived there. But while it was still early, this time around I seemed to have in excess of 80 percent of the votes counted, an extraordinary result so far.

Then the first figures from the southern part of Hinchcliffe came in. Des Nightingale and Gus Evans were clearly men of their word as the Labor Party recorded an astonishing 90 percent of the primary votes, almost a mathematical impossibility.

And so on it rolled, the result building all the while to the point it was clear I'd been reelected with a massively increased majority.

I tried to contain my excitement. Tempered by my own edict of respect for the voters I politely claimed victory on behalf of the Labor Party. I thanked my team profusely for their professional expertise and dedication, and my family for tolerating the lifestyle and the sheer hard work necessary to put us in the position we found ourselves.

Then Jock Fleming took over as we joined the national television network. Jock's Scottish accent always grew broader when he was excited, and tonight wasn't any different. But then, ever the statistician, Jock claimed that when the numbers were finalized, it would show the seat of Hinchcliffe was won by the largest margin ever between the two major parties in any seat in Australian political history.

Just then my phone buzzed; Jason could barely speak.

"What an amazing result, but stay on the line. I want you to share in this. We're going to claim victory nationally. Not a bad result for a pair of old sheilas, is it?"

Chapter 46
The Turning Point

WE'D LOST a few seats but picked up others in areas we didn't expect.

By some miracle our five losses were all from the gang of fifteen, which were now effectively a gang of ten. So the new makeup of caucus was quite different to the previous parliament, a more relaxed and talented group with the inclusion of some new blood.

I was busy; the duties of deputy leader were many and varied, but as minister of education I was blessed. We'd taken the hard decisions in the previous parliament, and the department was busily running the new programs we'd instigated with only cursory input from myself.

Jason and I, together with Angela Chan, who was now Minister for Foreign Affairs and Trade, had several trips to Asian countries, particularly the ASEAN group where we thought the most potential existed for growth. Angela, as a third-generation Australian-Chinese, an obvious choice for the job, underscored our desire to be taken seriously and to grow our presence in Asia.

Then we visited Singapore for the annual APEC meeting, but it frustrated the hell out of Jason and me. The Asia-Pacific Economic Cooperation group was founded in 1989 as a forum for trade, and its twenty-one member economies were all Pacific Rim countries. But the presence of the larger western nations such as the United States, Canada, and Russia meant a high degree of reticence from some of our key Asian neighbors from the ASEAN group.

They put up a wall of politeness and asked to study everything, stalling any effective decision-making process.

Chile and Peru were already trading strongly with some of the markets to which we needed access, which I found even more upsetting, successive Australian governments having neglected the opportunities because they were too comfortable and couldn't be bothered. Too wealthy, too lazy, and quite racist.

So we made separate contacts with each of the ASEAN countries attending and were headed home an hour after the closing ceremony.

THE FOLLOWING weekend we decided to have a party—with Barbara Shields's birthday as a wonderful excuse, and we all needed a chance to relax.

Sammy's essentially calm nature and delegation skills impressed me as always. I've never known anyone who could do so many things at once and still smile about it all. He enlisted Oliver Bellamy's help, and together with Isobel, they created a beautiful buffet dinner that would've done a five-star restaurant proud. Lucas Bellamy volunteered as barman, while Jason, myself, and Jenny looked on, feeling a little useless.

Winter in Canberra meant white frosts in the mornings, which sometimes took hours to melt. Around midafternoon the cold atmosphere reinstated itself and Dad lit the big open fire in the lounge room, warming the house. Max and Kate shadowed me. When I was away they were well behaved for Sammy, but when I walked in again they wouldn't let me out of their sight for hours. Jason reckoned I had my own security service with the kids because they watched me so closely. He may have been prime minister, but it was I that had their attention.

Jason was just himself, one of the few people in the world who was so easy to read. There was never a hidden agenda, as was the way with many politicians—one of the many reasons he was so admired.

Ted Shields walked in with the guest of honor on his arm and someone we'd not seen for ages—Jonathan, their lovely son. He and I had always connected because of our dyslexia and the rather public face I'd put to it over several years now. It turned out to be a double celebration, as Jonathan had just accepted an offer to take up a post in the history department of the Australian National University and had decided to live with his parents in the interim. Just a little older than Lucas and Oliver, he connected with them instantly. They were all on the same page together as they chattered away like a mother's meeting, making Jenny smile.

"Jacko," she said, "thanks."

"What for?"

"You and Sammy have given our kids a normal family life. They're better prepared and more resourceful than when we met just five years ago."

As if on cue, Kate and Max slid off my knee to allow themselves to be led away by Lucas and Oliver. Even though they were older now, the kids wouldn't sleep unless Lucas read them a story and Oliver acted out the words. Sammy fed them and they toured all the guests, kissing everyone good night. Jason loved it all; he cuddled the kids and got sloppy kisses in return, Jenny's eyes sparkling as Lucas roped Jonathan into the performance upstairs.

I'd been in the middle of a pleasant dream, and woke, staring in the half-light at the wallpaper above the picture rail in our bedroom. The strident screaming sound that coaxed me awake came from the bedside table, where my phone always sat, a prerequisite of being deputy leader.

Suddenly the lights went on, and Sammy and I rolled over each other as I grabbed it.

I answered, looking at the clock radio, which registered 3:59 a.m. Jenny spoke quietly on the other end. Knowing full well she'd never ring at this hour unless it was an emergency, I was immediately on alert.

"It's Jason," she said with a sob in her voice. "He's been taken to the intensive care unit at the National Capital Private Hospital."

"What happened?" I asked, my sleep-deprived brain still catching up with the facts.

"We went to bed soon after we returned from your place, but he was restless. I woke up and I knew there was something wrong. I couldn't wake him. The ambulance people were here in a few minutes. I'm leaving now."

"Okay, I'll meet you there. Sammy will go straight to the Lodge and stay with the boys."

Sammy nodded as we flew around, dressing ourselves and trying to think of a million things at once. Sammy grabbed the old Ford, which we'd brought up from home, and drove off; five minutes later a Commonwealth car pulled up at the door for me.

I hadn't much time to think except that perhaps this could go very badly for Jason; having become unconscious while asleep and evidently showing no signs of coming to could only mean something deeply traumatic.

I ran in through the side door and was directed to the ICU. Jenny stood up as I appeared, and flew into my arms, her face full of worry.

"It's not good, Jacko," she said. "The diagnosis isn't complete, but they seem to think it's a brain aneurysm."

I knew immediately there was no hope, and I'm sure Jenny did also, but neither of us wanted to say it out loud.

The senior resident appeared and asked if we'd join him in the interview room adjacent to the ICU.

"Mrs. Bellamy," he said, "sadly your husband is being kept alive only by life support. It was indeed a massive brain aneurysm so profound that he'll just gently fade away once everything is turned off. I'm deeply sorry."

I looked at Jenny, who nodded and thanked him, a picture of composure.

"I'd like the boys here when that happens, together with Sammy of course," she said, looking at me. I nodded my agreement and called Sammy. I explained what had happened and he, like Jenny, was totally under control, knowing he had to help two teenagers through the worst thing that they'd ever cope with in their young lives. I handed the phone to Jenny who spoke to each of them in turn. Fifteen minutes later they walked into the ICU, both boys distraught, so we all sat down and the resident went through the scenario, including causation, and the fact there were almost a zero chance of any sort of recovery, certainly none with any quality of life.

Holding Oliver's hand, Lucas spoke through his tears. "Doctor, is this a hereditary ailment, and if so, what are the chances that my brother and me could be affected the same way, later in our lives?"

"Your mum tells me there is absolutely no one in the family tree that she knows of who has been taken by an aneurysm. Yes, the genetics can be passed down, but simple regular medical checks are the best way to avoid a tragedy like this. Your dad has average blood pressure according to his records, didn't smoke, and exercised every day. So this has come out of the blue, as sometimes it does. Unless you were specifically looking for this, there would be no way of telling what was ahead. I'm very sorry, boys, but does that answer your question?"

Lucas nodded and looked stricken, probably feeling guilty for asking while their father lay a few meters away clinging to life.

Sammy jumped in as I cuddled Lucas and Oliver just wept on.

"Boys," Sammy said, "knowledge makes us strong. Without knowledge we can do nothing. You care about your brother so much, Lucas, and you couldn't bear the thought of Oliver ever going through something like this. Your dad would be so proud of you."

We all had a bloody good cry, and then made our way into the ward to a bed in the corner, surrounded by a thick curtain. We gathered around him and each of us had a hand or finger to hang on to as the machines were stopped and Jason Bellamy passed peacefully away.

We kissed Jason good-bye and left the room, Sammy suggesting Jenny and the boys come to our house so they wouldn't be bothered by a rapacious press contingent.

Chapter 47
To Hell in a Handbasket

LIKE ANYONE responsible for anything, I had to get on with it.

Australia had to be seen as in control of its day-to-day business, despite the death of its elected leader.

Mrs. Shields arrived at the office within half an hour of my phone call, and Dad dropped in a suit and toiletries so I could shower and change, while Isobel and Sammy cared for Jenny and the kids.

The press clamored for a statement; the ambulance had been spotted leaving the Lodge in the early hours, but unbelievably they hadn't connected it with Jason. Someone spread the rumor that it was a member of staff and they believed their own bullshit for once. The hospital wouldn't comment, naturally, so for the next few minutes it gave me some breathing space.

I called an emergency caucus meeting for 9:00 a.m. sharp, and they were all there. It wouldn't be a secret much longer; some members were like leaking sieves—despite being threatened they couldn't stop babbling news to the press.

"Ladies and gentlemen," I began, "I'm deeply saddened to advise that the prime minister passed away at approximately five o'clock this morning at the National Capital Private Hospital. Cause of death was a brain aneurysm, which occurred earlier in his sleep. Sammy and I were present with his family when life support was removed. I have extended the deepest condolences of the parliamentary party and cabinet to Jenny Bellamy and her sons, Lucas and Oliver.

"Are there any questions?"

There were several, and I explained the nature of the condition and its relative rarity. That Jason and his family had been with us for a meal only a few hours before and all seemed well, no sign of any symptoms, as is often the case with an aneurysm.

"As we all know," I continued, "it's our duty as a government to be decisive and to spell out a clear future direction, acknowledging this awful tragedy but demonstrating leadership and concern for the future, at home and abroad. I believe Jason would expect nothing less."

The people in front of me struggled, trying to cope with the loss of their leader and focus on what they knew they must do.

"I understand how you must all feel," I said, "and because I've had a little more time to digest the facts, it's probably easier for me. If you feel you need counseling, don't hesitate to ask. It's really important that when this dreadful time has passed, we'll all be able to stand up and move on with our lives. Something as devastating as this puts a very human face on politics. We're all human beings, and we're all in this together."

"Thank you, Jacko, that helps me feel a little better," Ron Hoy said with feeling.

"Yes, Jacko, thanks so much," several others said, echoing Ron's words.

"You all know what must be done now," I said, and some looked mystified.

"We have to elect a new leader, and that person has to be sworn in as soon as possible."

My fellow ministers sat in the front row with puzzled looks on their faces, and it was Angela Chan who no doubt verbalized everyone's thoughts.

"Jacko," she said, "there doesn't need to be a ballot for leader because under the party's constitution the deputy automatically takes over, both the party leadership and the office of prime minister."

"Thanks, I know and appreciate that, Ange, but I want to offer everyone here today the opportunity of electing someone they want, rather than me just stepping into the breach because I'm deputy."

There was a chuckle from further along, and Simon Hansen, the party whip, stood up. "Jacko, I'd like to nominate you as the new leader."

"Seconded," said Angela Chan.

"Are there any other nominations?" Simon yelled.

Silence fell as Simon turned to me.

"Jacko, Jason made you deputy because he knew his legislative program would be safe in your hands, and he also knew you brought something special to the office. Your leadership and respect for your fellow members of caucus is acknowledged, and Jason would be proud of you, as we all are. There being no further nominations, I declare the honorable member for Hinchcliffe as Leader of the Parliamentary Labor Party."

In a show of support, everyone stood and applauded, to my deep embarrassment, but I had my answer. Some of them would probably hate me down the track, but I'd given them the opportunity to piss me off and they'd given me their support in return.

FLAGS FLEW at half-mast across the nation as, together with my new cabinet, I was sworn in as prime minister of Australia. While my appointment was a stopgap measure, I became the youngest prime minister in Australian political history; Chris Watson in 1904 was the previous youngest, at thirty-seven years old. I was thirty-six, and I was shitting myself.

It gave me no sense of achievement that I now occupied the highest office in the land by default; one of my closest mates had passed away and I had to step into his shoes. My friendship with Jason had thrived in spite of the adversity and strife that surrounds politicians on a daily basis.

But again, true friendship was entirely reciprocal, and I found myself doing what I knew so vividly that Jason would want me to do. Get on with it, bitch.

Angela Chan became my deputy as well as continuing in Foreign Affairs and Trade, Ron Hoy stayed in Agriculture, and Edward (Eddie) Chi, a middle-aged Chinese-Australian merchant banker, became treasurer. Grace Anderson, a fortysomething university lecturer, newly elected, was given Education. There were some minor reshuffles, but essentially the team was very close to the one we started out with Jason just a short time ago.

I CALLED in to the Lodge on the way back to catch up with Jenny and the kids. She was still shell-shocked but had her secretary and Sammy with her while the boys looked on.

I listened as she tried to verbalize what she wanted for Jason's farewell. The words of the old celebrant from my mother's funeral returned: *"healing, moving on, and celebrating the past while looking to the future."*

Jenny and I discussed what was on my mind, and we made a date for the following morning to finalize the funeral details.

I called David Canning, the celebrant. He understood the task and promised he'd be in Canberra in a few hours. Accommodation was to be at our place; he could use Sammy's office.

This time Jenny was by herself, looking out the big windows into the garden. She turned to me and thanked me for helping.

"As soon as this is over, I'll get packed and get out of the Lodge so you, Sammy, and the family can move in."

"No."

"Jacko, I can't stay here. It's the official residence of the prime minister, and I have no place here now."

"In the first place, you can stay here as long as you wish. There's no hurry. Secondly we'd like to swap houses, you have ours and we'll have yours."

"But I have to move back to Sydney now, and try to restart life again. I have so much to do, the boys' education is so important."

"Precisely. That's one of the reasons you should stay in Canberra, so their studies aren't interrupted. The other reason I'd like you to stay in Canberra is as the new member for Keating."

She looked shocked, but I could see she was thinking.

"What a marvelous thing to do for Jason's memory," I said, "and what a wonderful example to set for the children. You would carry the family name on into politics and serve the people of Keating with distinction and compassion. I've decided I should address the nation tomorrow night, after we finalize the funeral details with yourself and the boys. I'd love to announce your candidature for Keating at the same time. That would help everyone move on as we should do."

For the first time since this tragedy befell us, Jenny smiled. "You wouldn't put the pressure on me, now, would you, Jacko?"

I felt I'd somehow betrayed her and Jason's memory, despite the now broad smile, but she put me at ease immediately.

"I actually think that is the most beautiful, loving, and even sensible thought, and it comes at a time when I thought my brain had atrophied in the last two days. I promise I'll think about it overnight and of course consult the boys."

Her brow furrowed as she caught up with some of the new practicalities of life she would have to face if she went ahead. "You said we could swap houses—the boys and me move into your lovely home after you move to the Lodge. I'm not sure if I could afford it, to be honest."

"The rent would be one dollar per annum, so we have a legal agreement to protect us in terms of accident, etcetera. That's it. You forget I wouldn't be here if Jason hadn't persuaded me to become a politician. This is my way of saying thanks to Jason and yourself."

"You want to thank us for making you into a politician," she said. "That's like whip me harder. I like it."

She laughed at her own joke, and then burst into tears. I held her and let her cry herself out. "That's good, sweetheart. You've been holding that in."

"Thanks, Jacko, but it's human kindness on your part that's helping the boys and me take the next steps. The friendship of you and your family has become such a big part of our lives, so much I really don't know what I'd do without you."

BACK IN my office, a surprise visitor was waiting, the Leader of the Opposition, Paul Sinclair. He strode over and engulfed me in a hug.

"How are you holding up, Jacko?" he asked. "I know how close you were with Jason. This must be awful for you."

Paul Sinclair and I hadn't been exactly close over the years, but he'd taken an interest in the Education portfolio and had surprised me by attending the reopening of the Special School, at my invitation. We'd spoken when we needed to; he seemed much more approachable than his predecessor, Graham White, who'd resigned after Jason defeated them so convincingly at that election.

A big man, tall, with fair hair in his early fifties and with a no-nonsense attitude, Paul reminded me of Pooh Bear, big and cuddly. We'd already agreed some time ago that neither could suffer fools gladly, and he hadn't disappointed me over the years because we always knew what was on each other's mind. This time I saw a different Paul; politics were clearly the last thing on his mind, focused on a personal level—me.

Mrs. Shields brought some cool drinks without me asking. She always read my mind and read situations better than anyone I knew, as Paul and I settled down in the small lounge area in my office.

I briefed him fully on what had happened, with a brief synopsis of the funeral arrangements and the huge communication task ahead.

"I want to do a fireside chat tomorrow night, so everyone knows what's ahead, because it's important both here and overseas that everyone understands Australia and Australians are back in business, that despite this tragedy, life must move on. Jason would expect that much of me."

I suddenly dropped my head into my hands, and the tears flowed; the more I tried to stop, the more upset I became. I began by apologizing and the next moment the big bear of a man was beside me on the couch, talking quietly to me. "Jacko, don't be so hard on yourself. You've been running on empty since this all happened. You need to get home to Sammy and your family as soon as possible."

I nodded and thanked him for his understanding, but the big fellow had a deeper message.

"In the past when a deputy has taken over for any reason, this bloody place," he said, meaning the House of Representatives and the Senate, "smells blood, and they come after the poor bloody new leader. I'm here to tell you that's not so in your case, Jacko, certainly not from our side of the house. It's early in this new parliament, and the legislative program put in place with Jason as leader hasn't had a chance to be properly debated. The public would be appalled if we tried to block that legislation for no other reason than there's a new leader at the helm. Besides, from our side of the house, even the rabid right-wingers reckon you're a great bloke. Some of the old-timers even say you've done more than anyone to improve the public perception of politicians since they've been in parliament, and as a matter of fact, I agree with them. So you have our support, Jacko, and good luck."

He stood and we shook hands. "I'll have a copy of my fireside chat I'd like you to approve before I go live. Can we meet back here at say 3:00 p.m. tomorrow?"

"But I don't need to see that. It's the government's business, not the Opposition."

"Paul," I said, "it's very much a joint effort. You've extended the hand of friendship, and we'll return it. This will have a tremendous effect with our Asian neighbors if we show solidarity at such a terrible time."

"MY FELLOW Australians," I began, "by now you would be aware of the passing of Prime Minister Jason Bellamy in the early hours of Monday morning at the National Capital Private Hospital. Cause of death was a brain aneurysm, which occurred earlier in his sleep. It goes without saying that this is a terrible tragedy. This type of illness is almost impossible to detect, and while it is sometimes genetically passed on, there was no evidence of this anywhere in his family.

"The government and the nation extend to his wife, Jennifer, and his two sons, Lucas and Oliver, our heartfelt condolences. Their pain is our pain.

"Yesterday, as deputy leader I called a meeting of the Australian Labor Party Caucus, where I called for a vote for the leadership of the party. There were no other nominations and consequently I was elected leader, and later in the day we met with the governor-general, where I was sworn in as prime minister. A new cabinet with minor changes was also sworn in.

"The Leader of the Opposition and I have met, and we are in total agreement that parliamentary business should proceed as normal in both Houses, given this tragedy has occurred so early in the term of office of this government. This government will run its full term, bringing forward the raft of legislation Prime Minister Bellamy took to the Australian people for their approval such a short time ago.

"Ladies and gentlemen, Jason Bellamy's family have declined a state funeral with their thanks, but have decided he should be farewelled in the first instance among the people and by the electorate that he represented for many years, at the Highridge Community Centre, where the Labor Party launch was held only a few months ago. Timing is next Monday, July 19, at 1:30 p.m.

"The public is therefore most welcome to join the Bellamy family in this most open and wonderful manner to say good-bye to Jason. For those unable to be there in person, all television and radio networks will be broadcasting from twelve noon onward.

"My fellow Australians, when we lose someone close to us, the grieving process varies from person to person, and if we think about it, that's quite normal, because we're all human beings and the one thing that binds humanity together is that we're all different.

"But more importantly when we look back with fondness on someone's life, we should also prepare ourselves to look forward with anticipation and even excitement, because that's exactly what Jason would have wanted.

"Jason has gone. We can't bring him back, so let's prepare ourselves for the task ahead, as his widow, Jennifer, has done.

"At my request she has agreed to set such an example to the nation by contesting the by-election for her late husband's seat of Keating, a loving and practical way of remembering Jason Bellamy.

"Thank you and good evening."

Chapter 48
Striding Out into the Future

THE OLD celebrant did his profession proud, the funeral becoming a joyful event. With all the electronic media present, millions of Australians felt better about events that should have been tragic, but that now somehow filled us with hope, his words helping us heal.

After much discussion, we decided to bring Kate and Max with us. Their questions about Jason were such that we decided to spend a lot of time with them because the issues were so important. We explained how the cycle of life could be cut short, why they wouldn't be seeing Jason anymore, hopefully giving our little people some closure.

The secondary purpose was to keep Lucas and Oliver occupied, and Jenny understood. Lucas and Oliver behaved like two little fathers, concerned for Kate and Max in return while Jonathan Shields was also there concerned for everyone, as was his nature. Sammy squeezed my hand and pointed proudly to our kids, growing up so well and so intelligently.

At the function afterward, I shook hands with many more foreign dignitaries than at the APEC meeting. Every one of the ten ASEAN countries were represented, and I thought how proud Jason would have been at their attendance, a fact that wasn't lost on Paul Sinclair either.

Isobel and Dad noticed Jenny wasn't doing so well, and we all made our excuses and left. I'd used a RAAF 737 to get us here along with Jenny and her kids. If ever there was a legitimate use of VIP aircraft, this was it, and Paul Sinclair agreed. I invited him and Joan, his wife, to join us for the flight back to Fairbairn Air Force base at Canberra. I introduced him to the rest of our family, including the kids, and he was astonished at their maturity.

I pointed to Dad and Isobel as a major reason and he understood.

We thought Joan Sinclair lovely. A kind, natural person who had the basics of life firmly in place and made sure her husband kept his feet firmly on the ground and his head out of the clouds, rather like Sammy had done with me. What had begun as a tragedy had spawned an unusual friendship between the leaders of the two major parties, and I encouraged it.

I knew what had to be done, and this was the only way to do it, to honor Jason's memory and to push through his legislative package. But as a nation, I could see we needed to change the way we did things. I sensed a strong, sensible, and compassionate leader in Paul Sinclair, and I knew we'd not get an opportunity like this for some time.

"YOU'RE MAD, Jacko. You can't do that," Paul Sinclair said. "You're such a breath of fresh air in this place with all the get up and go of a young bloke, but what you're asking us to do is to ignore the basics of the Westminster system of government."

"What's wrong with that?" I'd chosen Julio's in Kingston for a quiet dinner and discussion in Julio and Tony's private dining room because I knew I could trust our hosts implicitly. And it also helped that their food and wine were beautiful. Paul instantly picked them as a couple, and I laughed at him; the big bear was just so aware of what was going on around him. "I didn't know this place existed," he said, "particularly one run by a lovely couple such as yourselves."

Julio laughed and placed his arm around Tony, fully aware of the implications of what he was about to say. "Mr. Sinclair, we were below the radar until Jackson became deputy prime minister, and then we thought, this is Australia, both of us are now citizens, and Jacko and Sammy are up there showing everyone what a same-sex couple can achieve, so next month we are getting married."

I jumped to my feet, as did Paul. We were both softies and tonight was a reason to celebrate. We had a beautiful meal with countless glasses of red, but I'd put the germ of an idea into Paul's head.

"This idea of yours might just work, but you're a cunning prick. If we agree to this, then this will cement you guys in place for years to come."

"You forget one thing." I tried desperately to string the words together after far too much red. "The fact is we have probably more dickheads on our side of politics than you do. We have to sell the bill of goods to their subzero intelligence, so they may have a chance of winning their seats back at the next election. Because if this goes ahead, it will be the first time the public has an opportunity to elect the most suitable person for the seat rather than just voting along party lines. Different concept, isn't it?"

By this time we were past reason, and we entered dangerous territory after yet more red wine. When we were poured out of the restaurant by Julio and Tony, we wouldn't have known whether we were punched, bored, reamed, or drilled. We were just well pissed, but I thought it was productive, as Paul said the next meeting was on his account, same venue in a week's time.

THE JOINT Party Room concept happened as the result of much hard work by Paul and myself, but not without dramatics on both sides. My cabinet colleagues stood behind me 100 percent and helped me sell the sizzle to the caucus. Immediately an outcry erupted, even calls for me to stand down and create a spill of positions.

So I waited for my time and pounced again, just when they thought I'd forgotten all about the JPR. "I'm told the other side have approved the concept—" I smiled. "—with a ninety-day trial period, and for your information they had an identical presentation. Looks like the Liberal Party are way ahead of us this time. Sorry people, but sadly we're very slow to change, what a shame."

I tried to move the discussion on, but the new member for Keating got to her feet. If anyone thought Jenny Bellamy to be a pushover, they were sadly mistaken. The fire in her eyes telegraphed the fact she was clearly on a mission.

"What a lot of arseholes you are," she shouted, walking to the front of the room, tall, beautifully dressed, and with striking dark silver hair. "That applies to all of you. Those of you who voted against this measure are the lowest of the low, but those of you who sat on their arses and allowed the remainder to get away with it are just as bad. Look at you, what a splendid group of idiots. My late husband would be horrified to listen to the drivel and the lack of support you've offered our new leader at this important time. Jason was a fervent believer in the very same measures Jacko is trying to introduce. They discussed it, but he passed away before it could be implemented. He watched Jacko's first election campaign, and the message to the Australian people was so consistent and sensible, he adopted that same approach—don't argue and debate your opponents, but know your own strategy and policies backwards and sell them to the electorate. Because the electorate is why we're here, or had you forgotten that? Here you are wanting and wishing to turn the clock back again, going back to the traditional Labor roots of church and unionism, and try to govern by pissing on the opposition. What imbecilic attitudes, what stupidity in this enlightened day and age. The benefits of a Joint Party Room are many, not the least of which is that the squabbling, the name-calling, the character assassination of the past will disappear from view, and we might even appear almost normal people in the eyes of the public. Thrash out legislation in private, then bring it to the parliament to be rubber-stamped, a simple, smart process. Common sense. You guys must take ownership of this. It's your future, the future of the parliament, and the future of the nation. With respect I suggest we take another vote before we commit political suicide."

I thanked everyone and asked Mrs. Shields to send a text to Paul Sinclair.

All go here the plan worked better than expected. The new member for Keating excelled herself. Time for you to turn up the wick over there, tell them the ALP is leaving them behind if they don't participate. Tell them they'll look like idiots if they don't support the principle. If necessary I'll send the member for Keating over to assist—Jacko

THE INAUGURAL meeting of the Joint Party Room happened a few days later. It was decided we should have a Moderator rather than a Speaker, so Paul Sinclair nominated Jenny Bellamy, and I seconded her.

The big room we had was quite suitable with its own catering, well removed from the daily business of government so there was no pressure other than to consider what was coming down the track in proposed legislation.

Jenny addressed them. "Don't hold back, any of you. If this was the House of Representatives, you'd be grandstanding, looking for a television camera. Here you won't find one, so you can insult who you like, how you like, until I tell you to shut up because you're wasting time. The various government ministers who'll be introducing draft legislation and discussion papers will need to be on their game more than ever. They need to know their stuff, own their material, and not to throw a hissy fit if we pick holes in it. This will be the very first time that Opposition members have been exposed to this stuff at the very same time as government members, so think about that for a moment. The myriad of standing committees, joint committees, and Senate inquiries will continue as usual, the only difference is that they will report to the JPR first.

"The prime minister has also advised the resources of the Department of the Prime Minister and Cabinet are being directed to this group. Naturally this is highly confidential material, so we don't need it out there in the arms of the media until we're all happy with it, if at all. It goes without saying that for the first time in Australian parliamentary history, Opposition members are being offered a chance to properly participate in the process of government. Over time the prime minister and the Leader of the Opposition have built a trust between them that has allowed this project to proceed. They in turn have an expectation of all members to deny the media access to details of our deliberations. To do otherwise would allow sometimes-sensitive material into the public domain, where they put their spin on it and circumvent the proper process of government. Let me speak plainly," she said, and there was a grin from Paul Sinclair, who was delighted that in her new incarnation she seldom did anything else. "Those of you who feel you simply must bleat it all out to the journos for a nice dinner and a roll in the hay with whomever, think again, because if I catch you at it, I promise your career as a politician is over. Do you understand me?"

"What about stuff we object to on grounds of ideology, stuff we'd never agree to in a blue fit?" asked Robert Walls, a Liberal from Queensland.

Jenny deflected the question to me and I was truthful. "There'll be stuff we'd never agree on, but at least you'll have the opportunity to discuss it and listen to our reasons for introducing it, and to have your say based on party lines. Knowledge is power, all the cards are on the table, so let's see if we can do something that no other western democracy has ever done."

Paul grinned at me across the room as Jenny urged everyone to get comfortable and "sit where you like."

I watched, fascinated, as everyone fanned out, with some government and opposition members sitting next to each other and actually *talking to each other*.

We reviewed first the Dairy Industry Appropriation Bill brought forward by Ron Hoy. Ron was excited and it showed; he described how we'd been working with the Asian conglomerate that purchased the old butter factory in Hinchcliffe long before Jason had passed away. Jenny's eyes flickered down, but she straightened her gaze again.

Ron realized he'd probably hit a nerve, but it was Jenny who comforted him and drew the admiration of the room.

"That's all right, Ron, go for it. He'd be so proud of this moment."

Ron brought everyone up to speed, how the project was already underway, and how the factory would soon be in limited production. But for the project to be completely successful into the future, it required ongoing investment by the local farmers in terms of stock, plant, and equipment. Ron's bill proposed 1 percent interest loans for those farmers through the Development Bank.

"Communists!" roared Robert Walls from Queensland. "We have a perfectly satisfactory private enterprise banking system. Why can't they be involved and save unnecessary government expenditure at a time like this?"

"Oh, they are involved," Ron replied through his teeth, "at anywhere between 15 and 35 percent. The essence of this deal is to grow the resources quickly, so the factory's production will be able to meet demand on time in this new Asian market. If we guarantee these loans, we'll be assured that we'll meet that time frame. The commercial banks aren't interested in that concept, only profit, so we simply must step up to this proposition as a government or lose the opportunity that Jason, Jacko, and I negotiated."

After discussion, good manners and common sense prevailed, and Robert Walls backed down. Ron successfully used a prodigious grasp of the facts to win his argument in record time.

Ron was nothing if not organized. Eddie Chi, the treasurer, then gave a timeline of how farmers could claim their entitlement, and everyone in the room looked on at the detail.

Done deal.

Chapter 49
The JPR in Action

THE JPR was a runaway success, but not strictly for the reasons we'd originally planned. Many members from the major parties actually became *friends*, and unusual alliances and joint interests sprang up. It became quite usual to see members and families from opposing viewpoints and party policy socializing together. The minor parties were asked to join; they were hesitant initially, but when they understood the benefits, they were quickly onside. Senators were also encouraged to be part of the JPR; while we had a workable majority in the house of review, it helped that they could prepare for what would be coming at them. We subsequently broke every record for legislation in time elapsed from introduction, second readings and review, and finally signing into law by the governor-general.

The press was puzzled and tried their best to create a furor and a scandal where there was nothing but hard work and good fellowship. Vindictively they sought out opinion from members but were amazed when none of their normal "leaking sieves" would comment. One of Australia's most decorated journalists who claimed to have the ear of everyone who was anyone wrote a syndicated review entitled "IS THIS THE END OF DEMOCRACY?" which contained some serious inaccuracies and outright lies. We all declined to be interviewed. Paul Sinclair, myself, Jye Chandler, the Leader of the Greens, the Speaker of the House of Representatives, the president of the Senate, and Jenny Bellamy as Moderator of the Joint Party Room all signed a document demanding a retraction from the publisher to be printed immediately.

The publisher, hoping for an even better story, listened to his journalist, who insisted we were operating illegally, and refused. The following day a summons was delivered to the publisher in Sydney by a well-known firm of barristers on behalf of the Commonwealth of Australia. A retraction was printed twice because the first one was inaccurate, the journalist sacked on the spot.

I'd done several little fireside chats since Jason had passed away, just so the public knew what was happening with the issues that we took to the election when he was prime minister. I also gave an update on the economy every quarter. The chats were expensive but a great way to communicate, and the Opposition were always offered equal time, which they'd declined until now.

This time I invited Paul and Jye to join me as we told the story of the Joint Party Room and what a resounding success it had been in just a few months. How as a nation we'd reduced the number of parliamentary sitting days, how we'd pushed through draft legislation, considered discussion papers, and cut the red tape accordingly. Paul and Jye supported me and confirmed the reason journalists couldn't find a bad story was that there was only good news. All members of parliament fully endorsed the process and enjoyed coming to work—"working for Australia and Australians," Paul said, and Jye agreed.

"What's more," Paul thundered, "the concept of the JPR has actually strengthened the democratic process, not detracted from it."

Jye, bearded and dressed like a forester, but a former QC with a razor-like intellect, then shyly told the public how we'd been forced to pull the publisher into gear and confirmed the Commonwealth bore no costs whatsoever in the exercise.

The three of us then flew to Melbourne the next morning to be on Bryan Friedman's program, and as expected we got great publicity for the JPR.

Bryan was excited beyond belief. "Jacko, this is the greatest thing to happen to Australian politics since Federation. Congratulations."

"Don't thank me—thank our fellow members of parliament and their leaders, because this is collaborative management, and it simply wouldn't work if we didn't have the full support of all parties, literally."

BARBARA SHIELDS became chief of staff, as well as running my own office directly. She worked extraordinarily long hours but thrived on it, with Ted as her "home husband," happily retired and supporting his wife in their new home in Canberra.

She buzzed me and said I had a handsome visitor, and yes, he'd been cleared by security, and did I have a few minutes to spare?

The door opened and in walked Lucas Bellamy. He'd grown even more like Jason, so much so it was even painful—it was just like a younger version of his father in the room.

"Uncle Jacko," he said, and we hugged each other.

I indicated the lounge area, and we sat down with a cool drink from Mrs. Shields, who raised her eyebrows and smiled.

"I told you your visitor was handsome. I was right, wasn't I?"

"Well, you've always had good taste. You know how I like my blokes."

Lucas rewarded me with a blush, and I thought to myself that I needed Sammy here right now, because even though I'd been a surrogate father to Jenny's kids, I never had to discuss the birds and the bees with them, and this certainly seemed to be heading in that direction.

The door closed and Lucas relaxed. *Funny*, I thought, *he and Oliver always loved Barbara, yet today he seems embarrassed in front of her.*

"Uncle Jacko, can I ask you a few very personal questions?"

The pleading look in his eyes said something was going on in this young man's life, and I put him at ease.

"Your dad didn't give us enduring power of attorney for nothing. I'm sure he knew you could ask me anything. Besides, you and I could have been brothers. We're only a few years apart."

I moved over to the big comfy couch beside him and held his hand.

"When you and Uncle Sammy got together, I thought I heard you say you were, umm, straight by orientation."

"Yes, that's correct."

"Are you still that way now?"

I didn't hesitate. "Technically I suppose that's true, but when you fall in love with someone, all bets are off. When I realized I was in love with Uncle Sammy, my desire and my interest in anyone else just disappeared. Something told me I'd never get another opportunity to be with the one person who completed me like he does, and when he got me between the sheets I was gone, fascinated. He was and is the most physically attractive person I'd ever been intimate with."

Lucas grinned broadly, and I thought maybe I'd been too explicit. Then he grew emotional. "That's me exactly," he said. "I knew I was right all along. I should trust my own judgment, shouldn't I?

"It's Jonathan," he said. "All this time now and I can't get him out of my mind. We talk all the time, every day, we go out together, but we're both frightened of the elephant in the room—my sexuality. I mean, I've had chicks crawling over me for years, but there was always something missing, if you know what I mean."

"I do know what you mean, but you love him, don't you?"

"Oh yes."

"Then why don't you tell him so?"

"How did you convince Uncle Sammy that you were fair dinkum, you know, that you wouldn't run off with a lady?"

"I asked him to marry me ten days later."

"No wonder you're prime minister."

I laughed out loud. Genetics were working overtime; he sounded just like his father, but there was no point telling Lucas that Jason had been bisexual before meeting Jenny. No point at all, because Mother Nature was about to have another run in the lower paddock anyway, and it looked like it was all headed in the right direction.

Mrs. Shields smirked at me as I went off to a late meeting, but I wasn't commenting. She was just like Sammy in her ability to read people, and I'll bet she knew of the attraction between Lucas and Jonathan before they did.

THE BIG car whispered through the gates at the Lodge and swept up to the main entrance. Security shadowed us these days, and I'd been lectured on countless occasions to understand the issues involved—that when you become the leader of the nation, the loonies are never far away.

I loved nothing better than to hang out with the garden staff at the Lodge. They had old, dilapidated mowers and garden-care gear, so I helped organize some machinery more appropriate to the task. They were all lovely people, and the feedback they gave me on how the country was running was invaluable. Likewise I had a turn around the grounds on a new Indian ride-on mower around Parliament House. It was clearly superior to anything I'd ever seen, so the operator suggested I go for another spin, and soon there was a crowd watching and laughing at Jacko the gardener, down to the basics and seriously enjoying this early part of the day. I walked around the staff and shook hands in the same manner I did with the cleaning staff in the big building behind me. Normal practice for me until I had a tap on the shoulder from a security guy.

"Sir," he said, pleading with me, "you would have been a sitting target for a sniper," probably trying to scare me, which he succeeded in doing.

Sammy finally cracked it, and I decided I'd better listen to a formal security briefing "or progress through life alone."

Charlie Lim and his group were attached to me for the length of my tenure as prime minister. The fact that I was a fill-in made his task even more difficult because there were always those out there who reckoned I didn't deserve to have the job.

If they only knew, I thought. *I didn't ask for this. I'm just trying my best to do what my mate would have wanted and to give the public good value as their representative.*

So I listened, and the facts were disturbing. Uncovering terrorist threats remained a concern, a few a year—even some greenies so obsessed with protecting the environment they were prepared to use violence to make their point.

Australia for Australians was still making a lot of noise about Asian immigration, but thankfully there was no sign of Andrew Fitch. I hoped he'd been taking his medication and was no longer a risk to the public. At least I knew his license to practice medicine had been withdrawn permanently, which was a relief.

"But they still strike a chord with the public," Charlie said, "and that's extremely worrying."

Charlie came from a Chinese family who had been in Australia from the Gold Rush days, and while the Lim surname had survived, the genetics had been changed forever by intermarriage with Anglo-Saxon and Anglo-Celtic bloodlines. But he was upset at the ignorance and the persistent message that was being sprouted mainly through social media that Australia was in the process of being taken over by Asia. That our country was doomed, people would arrive here in boats and take our property over.

I rang Angela Chan immediately and asked if she'd call the cabinet together, requesting Charlie to put together a presentation on his security feedback for the following day.

Together with Angela we activated focus groups in the major capital cities and some regional centers to ascertain just how entrenched the anti-Asian sentiment was in the community.

THE FOLLOWING morning I read a précis of the morning news in old-fashioned newspapers. Mrs. Shields organized coffee and asked if she could join me. "Of course," I replied, and she drew a chair up alongside my desk. It was a moment I knew I'd always remember, because she knew I'd been asked for advice and it had borne fruit.

"Page fifty-eight," she said.

I turned the page, and there in all its glory in a double column was the announcement:

"It is with pleasure that Edward and Barbara Shields announce the engagement of their youngest son, Jonathan, to Lucas, eldest son of Jennifer and the late Jason Bellamy, and brother to Oliver. Their joy is our joy."

We hugged each other. We all needed a lift, and I thought how if ever there was a match made in a perfect place, this was it. Jonathan had actually phoned me the previous afternoon and asked my permission to marry Lucas. Because, as he said, I'd taken over fatherly duties since Jason had passed on, and he felt he should show some manners and ask my permission!

My private line buzzed; Sammy had found the announcement. "Jacko, I just talked to Jenny. This is the best news ever. Jason would be so proud." Unusually there was a sniffle at the other end, and I began to worry. "It's all right, darling," he assured me. "When I see lovely things like this happen, it reminds me of when we first got together in Patong. I love you, Jacko."

"I love you too." I sniffed back, feeling a wave of nostalgia sweep over me. I said good-bye and asked Barbara to order some flowers for him. Bugger it, what price a romance like ours? What a lucky man I am.

It was a sitting day in the House and I stood, seeking leave from the speaker to make a special statement to the House. The Speaker, Joe Green, nodded and I continued, "Thank you, Mr. Speaker.

"Mr. Speaker, seldom has the parliament experienced a period of such tragedy with the death of our former prime minister just over a year ago. Yet, Mr. Speaker, this morning's papers carry news of a different kind, announcing the engagement of the Member for Keating's eldest son, Lucas Bellamy, to Jonathan Shields, youngest son of my chief of staff, Barbara Shields.

"Mr. Speaker, as custodians of this place with all its inherent responsibilities, we sometimes forget we are all human beings, and we all need some good news occasionally, such as this, to brighten our day.

"Mr. Speaker, I wish to move a motion of congratulations to the member for Keating and the Shields family on this most joyous occasion. Jonathan and Lucas are fine young men. They are already great contributors to our society, but as a partnership I believe the best is yet to come.

"Thank you, Mr. Speaker."

"Hear, hear" rang out, and Jenny smiled back at me as members from both sides voiced their approval.

What a way to start a day.

Chapter 50
Asia, Here We Come

THE SECURITY briefing got underway as Charlie Lim traced the history of the outpouring of what amounted to hysterical, ill-informed bullshit from clearly dangerous people. Australia for Australians would prefer we establish links with European countries and governments "to keep the fucking chinks, slant-eyes, and mongrels out of Australia, cancel all Asian immigration, and let decent white people in."

Yes, I thought bitterly, *let the Europeans in with no money, nothing to offer, just like their governments. None of them would work in a blue fit, just hang around on the dole long enough to qualify for an aged pension and then sit on their arses forever.*

"They miss the point altogether," I said. "We don't need or want to increase immigration further. We need to open up trade with developing Asian countries before the business slips elsewhere. And attempting to trade with Europe is pointless. There's no money, honey, so we'd be in worse trouble than most of Europe in no time. Asia is a gold mine, particularly the ASEAN countries, because their economies are smaller and we can target their needs as they grow with our limited resources, just as we did with the butter factory in Hinchcliffe."

The outcome of the focus groups wouldn't be known for a further ten days, after which we'd take all the information to the Joint Party Room.

We briefed Paul Sinclair who was onside immediately, and we waited.

THE FOCUS groups by design included all parts of society, trying to quantify just how many Australians were anti-Asia/Asian people. When we designed the survey, we had a specific question linking Australia's economic future with Asia: "How important do you think future trade relations are with Asia?"

That particular question came back with an average 90 percent positive response. Bingo.

But the other 10 percent were loud, raucous, full of bias, and the violent language was frightening.

At the Joint Party Room, we tabled the security messages from Charlie Lim, then followed up with the focus material. I'd briefed Jenny the previous day and was interested what the JPR would have to say about it.

They found consensus in just a few minutes.

A working group of six, including two former advertising executives, came back with a costed advertising campaign some three days later. Properly targeted it would have a launch on national television, then slip away to a maintenance level in newspapers, magazines, and social media for a year or so.

Eddie Chi "found" some funds he'd squirreled away, but we were still talking around nearly one hundred million dollars as a cost, just to minimize the influence and hatred of the Australia for Australians organization, which Charlie Lim now suspected was being funded by some Eastern European drug cartels.

We couldn't justify the cost, even though the economy was now running at 3.2 percent growth and rising steadily. "Democracies must allow their citizens to have diverse views, indeed any views at all, provided they're legal," I told the JPR.

"Even if those views could potentially damage our reputation and economic future?" asked Andy Garcia, the Liberal Member for Cosgrove in Tasmania.

"Indeed," I said, "we must be consistent with democratic principles. But what if I told you that there's another project Paul Sinclair and I have been working on."

All eyes turned to me, and Paul nodded, agreeing that I should spill the beans.

"We plan to create a traveling show," I said, "Australia on the wing, as it were. An airborne trade mission cum diplomatic group visiting each of the ASEAN nations, one by one. We'd need two RAAF 737s plus a Hercules aircraft with mobile displays representing what we have to offer as a nation. We've done a lot of research, and Eddie Chi should have the numbers soon. The Department of Finance is burning the midnight oil.

"I think it would be perfectly acceptable if we ran that television campaign before our mission took off—then it has a legitimate business purpose and no one could argue otherwise."

Just twenty-four hours later, Eddie and the Department of Finance came up with a figure: 250 million dollars. We'd use the Christmas break to get the job done. The Joint Party Room was enthusiastic. I couldn't believe my ears as they approved the exercise without any dissent whatsoever. They trusted Eddie, but he'd grappled with many unknowns in the costings and warned them it could be more. They all laughed at him and said his pockets were so deep, even he didn't know what was in them.

Bullshit, I thought. *Eddie would never give me a costing that wouldn't stand scrutiny.*

So I dragged Paul Sinclair to yet another fireside chat, and we told the Australian people what we intended to do and why. We also explained the advertising campaign and how we needed to be united as a nation to make the hard work of our trade mission and foreign affairs project work in our favor and why. And how much it would cost, stressing this wasn't just a junket. That many parliamentarians were heading off on this project immediately post-Christmas, investing their personal time and energy just to sell Australia to the ASEAN countries instead of enjoying their annual leave with their families.

Bryan Friedman picked us up again, and we worked solidly in radio and television for several days around the nation until we were sure there was nothing more we could do to inform the Australian people.

Angela Chan as Foreign Minister and Minister for Foreign Affairs and Trade drove her department mercilessly. Mrs. Shields and the Department of the Prime Minister and Cabinet also had a hand in the project, but typically no one complained because our team had already "sold the sizzle" and "there wasn't a single sick day anywhere," Angela told me proudly.

Chapter 51
Brunei, Laos, Cambodia, Vietnam, Myanmar

ON A warm late-December morning we gathered for photographs at the Fairbairn Air Force base. We'd decided to invite the press along to cover the long weeks ahead. There were ten journalists and a film crew with the ability to broadcast live back home. I specifically asked the air crews be part of the group photograph and watched amused as the mouth of one of the journos dropped open. *Too much democracy for him*, I thought, *but he'd better get used to it; without these guys to keep us in the air the whole project would come to a halt*, and I told everyone so.

We were a team. Team Australia.

As we were guests in these foreign countries, we were all expected to observe the traditions and culture of that country, particularly as we were representing our own country. That applied to everyone, including the journalists and public servants who were with us on our working holiday.

Sammy was with me as my husband; that was made very clear to the countries we were about to visit. Through the Special School he'd met many families across the ASEAN nations, and I knew there wouldn't be a problem, quite the opposite. I asked Paul Sinclair to bring Joan along also. She and Sammy were great mates, and it completed the balance for us as we fronted up together, representing both sides of the political spectrum in Australia. It had been one of the Liberal Party's more infamous gaffes some years prior that legalization of same-sex marriage should never happen in Australia because it would be offensive to our Asian neighbors and injure our trading relationships. Well, here we were some years later, Paul Sinclair embarrassed at such inanity as I reminded him how it used to be.

We decided to tackle the smallest country first, Brunei.

A tiny but important Muslim nation, very traditional in their social views but also very wealthy per capita, with less than 500,000 population. One of the journalists took bets we'd be thrown out within hours, but he hadn't counted on an already warm relationship with Australia culminating in a free-trade agreement, and the reputation of one person in particular—Samuel Collins-Smith. Margaret Reeve had introduced several students to Sammy at the Special School, and my darling was a legend in Brunei. As he was throughout much of Asia.

The journo, an anchorman with a television network, watched on as we were honored at a state banquet—a very dry affair, naturally, and everything we had to show them from Australia was taken on board and considered. The Sultan of Brunei, also the prime minister, loved his apples. Particularly Red Delicious apples. Could we set up a reliable Australian supplier, and he would cancel the supplier from California in due course? A small done deal.

Three of Sammy's former students, all of them now successful in business in the capital Bandar Seri Begawan, were at our dinner with the Sultan. All spoke perfect English, and all had mastered their learning difficulties. At that stage I had no idea that one of the three was a close relative of the Sultan's family, but Sammy clearly did.

The cameras rolled as the Sultan presented Sammy with the Brunei Meritorious Service Medal, and we were off to a flying bloody start.

The following day as we prepared to leave, there was enough interest in Australia as a supplier to keep a team busy for weeks. We had to be thorough, we had to answer every question, and this was from the smallest country in ASEAN. I worried that our resources wouldn't cope, so Angela requested more of her department to return early from annual leave.

Our media contingent flew on ahead for filming as we rolled into Laos.

Laos, as well as Cambodia, had been recipients of foreign aid packages from Australia for some time, and we were clearly trying to keep on giving with one hand while trying to sell stuff with the other. They were small but growing economies, with Vietnam more populous, robust, and developed.

I knew it would happen eventually, but it was Angela who burst into our hotel room with a red face to confirm she'd been offered a huge "commission" to get a deal done. The reality of doing business in parts of Asia hit home. The question was, how should we handle it?

Angela, even with her Chinese heritage and deep understanding of how business had been transacted for centuries in Asia, was furious, and we agreed that we would never enter into a deal where personal reward was a feature. The Australian taxpayer would be right to throw us out on the street at the next election—or before.

I called Paul, and we agreed the only thing we could do was to walk away, ensuring no one lost face. We quietly gave our reasons discreetly to the office of the president, and our aircraft were prepared for takeoff.

Our media contingent was intrigued but had the good sense to understand the diplomatic issues and were as quiet as church mice.

We arrived at Wattay International Airport and were about to be transferred to our aircraft when a flustered, red-faced official asked to see us privately. We found a quiet lounge where the official apologized on behalf of the Lao government and asked would we reconsider the "unfortunate oversight" of their foreign minister and minister for trade, who had a bad migraine.

"No," I said.

Angela, Eddie Chi, and Paul Sinclair looked at me aghast.

"We have given your country so much in foreign aid over the years, yet a member of your government wants to steal from the hand that has tried to feed it," I explained.

"Please wait," the official pleaded.

I knew our abrupt departure would be very bad publicity for Laos; we had them on the back foot, and I wasn't letting them off the hook.

"The president has asked that if we suspend the minister due to ill health so he no longer takes part in these discussions, would that be acceptable?"

"No," I replied.

The official looked terrified; Angela, Eddie, and Paul tried to keep straight faces and were almost successful.

"The only condition I would accept is that the minister retires permanently and is never again in a position where he can influence trade between our two nations," I shouted, and the official fled out of the room.

Within minutes we had a positive answer, and we returned to our hotel.

We had long-term commitments from both Laos and Cambodia to buy Australian preserved fruit in cans in ever-increasing quantities. In return we were prepared to subsidize various education and health services, with an end date and a dollar amount that made Eddie Chi smile for the first time since we left home.

Ron Hoy was ecstatic; presiding over a primary production-led recovery at home, but we needed some investors to put their hands in their pockets and gun up some mothballed canneries back home in the Goulburn Valley. Paul looked pensive and asked if he could help.

Within two days we had a commitment from an Australian company from the top end of town, previously mainly a mining company, looking to diversify. With watertight contracts they were enthusiastic, price was almost secondary to supply as long as they weren't too greedy. We flew into Phnom Penh, the capital of Cambodia, where we signed the deal.

Cambodia's tourism industry was a mainstay of their domestic economy, and their prime minister insisted we visit Siem Reap, the town servicing the famous Angkor Archaeological Park containing the magnificent remains of the different capitals of the Khmer Empire. We knew this would produce absolutely no business for us whatsoever, but to refuse would be undiplomatic and undo all the effort to get us this far.

It was worth it, to drive around a corner and come face-to-face with Angkor Wat, sitting across its moat, its stonework reflecting in the water, an experience I'll not forget in a hurry. Even the dozens of camera-wielding tourists chattering away couldn't detract from the majesty of the place, and we all felt humble in its presence.

I suddenly realized this was the face of Cambodia their government wanted us to see for our future relationship, trying desperately to put the Khmer Rouge genocide of the late 1970s behind them. Hundreds of thousands lost their lives in that conflict, and as horrible as it was, we all had to move on. I told the prime minister we understood, and the curtain of reserve lifted immediately.

On our return to Phnom Penh, Sammy and I were ushered into an audience with the king, a figurehead of the Cambodian constitution but an important point of reference and a stabilizing influence in the region, similar to the Thai Royal Family.

We greeted him with a wai. He was a small, nimble man in late middle age, a legacy of a lifetime spent in dance. A humble, intelligent fellow with a quiet sense of humor who congratulated us for being so brave. Many years ago he'd publicly come out in favor of same-sex marriage before it was fashionable to do so. He told us we were living evidence that the world was repairing itself, and for any help we needed in our trade mission to simply ask.

Vietnam, Laos, and Cambodia all had water and hydroelectric projects centered around the giant Mekong River, good for their local economies, bad for the thousands of families who had derived a living from fishing the river for centuries, and who would now be struggling to survive. And cheap, fresh local fish would almost cease to exist.

We convinced the three nations to trial aquaculture. The fingerlings would be supplied from Australia, and we would pay 25 percent of the start-up cost for the first farm. It was good business because we already had the infrastructure in place to supply the product.

Another done deal.

In Vietnam we were greeted cordially by the president and cabinet, the aquaculture deal already creating a positive tone.

I couldn't help but ponder on the history our nations had shared since the Vietnam War, with a large, vibrant Vietnamese community at home and Vietnam itself hosting thousands of Australian tourists every year. How quickly time and goodwill had healed the scars of war.

It was here I had my first argument with Paul Sinclair because all the Vietnamese could talk about was renewable energy and wind farms.

They needed wind turbines, lots of them, and I knew we had three manufacturers back home who worked well together and who could resurrect substantial production capacity with short notice.

The global debate on climate change had progressed to the point where there was no debate. We had to look after our environment or pay the price, ruining the planet for our kids' future. Vietnam had thousands of wind turbines and wanted more. Paul's party had legislated some years ago to guarantee a twenty-five-year lease on certain coal mines that were exporting into Asia, and we wanted to sell wind turbines, reducing Asia's reliance on imported, nonrenewable energy such as coal. I also wanted to create a substantial tax break back in Australia to reward those industries using renewable energy rather than penalizing those who used nonrenewables.

Paul exploded. "You can't do that! I knew all of this was too good to be true. We have signed contracts with these people. You can't run around like a bloody lefty just to please all of the people all of the time. We have to honor those agreements."

"Not at the expense of the environmental health of our nation. I'm seriously thinking of tearing those contracts up. It's social and economic vandalism to continue with those particular mines in the light of international climate agreements. In any case we have the biggest deal of a lifetime here producing wind turbines, not just for Vietnam but most of ASEAN as well."

Paul stormed out of the room.

We had a brilliant deal within our grasp that required us to gun up the renewable energy sector at home where Blind Freddy could see there was unparalleled growth. If that upset the miners, then so be it. They could get fucked.

We went on to Myanmar and in Yangon met the now retired Aung San Suu Kyi, the heroine of Myanmar.

She was charming, intelligent, and resourceful. I commented on her ability to think her way around situations and find a solution.

She'd heard of the near fiasco in Laos and laughed, congratulating me on my stand, and confirmed what we'd all thought, that the siphoning has to stop somewhere. We were introduced to the new prime minister, also a very beautiful lady who had an economics degree and, just like her mentor, refused to take no for an answer.

Not unexpectedly it was the first country visited where we gave more than we received. Eddie Chi was very optimistic, Angela Chan even more so. We had to invest in Myanmar's infrastructure so their economy could grow, and after several years of stable government, we would get a return down the track.

As planned I sent everyone home for a ten-day break while Sammy and I flew by a commercial flight to Bangkok and on to Phuket, where Dad, Isobel, and the kids were waiting.

Chapter 52
A Little Break in Paradise

TO SAY we got a great welcome from our kids was an understatement; Kate and Max were just so excited. Seldom had both of us been missing together for so long; Max clung to me for hours and Kate did the same to Sammy. They were also happy to be back in this exotic part of the world where they rather naturally felt so much at home.

Chart and Solada had arrived a few days ago. Their presence calmed us, and we felt happier. It was also a little emotional for us—our last visit to Phuket was brief for Pa and Ma's funeral. They'd passed away within twelve hours of each other and had loved us unconditionally, making us part of their family, even more so when our kids came along.

I found it difficult to express to other Australians the closeness Sammy and I felt for Thailand and the Thai-Chinese community, but one only had to look at our children with their Eurasian features to understand. Perhaps they would understand more so if they could see inside our hearts. We would go and light a candle for Pa and Ma in due course. They were still around us here; we could feel them.

We were back at our normal hotel, where not that many years ago Sammy and I had started our life together as a couple.

But not in our old room. "Too hard to secure," Charlie Lim said, so we had to go to the bloody top floor where we had almost a small house to ourselves. Sammy and I on one side, the kids' rooms in the middle, Dad and Isobel on the other end with interconnecting doors. With Charlie and his mob all around us. And Barbara and Ted Shields opposite, just to make sure I wasn't slacking.

After the kids were satisfied we'd be there in the morning, we put them to bed, telling them stories about our travels, with a few harmless embellishments to impress Max, and watched lovingly as their eyelids drooped and they slipped into the land of Nod.

Dad and Isobel understood, as they always did, and pointed to our room, knowing we needed some Jacko and Sammy time. We relaxed, knowing the kids would be watched over all night.

Surprisingly, nothing much had changed physically with either of us over the years, as we ate well and made time for exercise. But Sammy still managed to press all my buttons at once. We showered together, and he slipped inside me. We then took it to the big bed and did it all again.

"It's not the same room but it's even more romantic," Sammy said and I felt my heart do somersaults.

"I love you so much, darling," I replied, "perhaps even more so." We kissed for hours before I sat on him again and we climaxed together once more. We slept deeply, the work of the previous weeks tiring enough, but our lovemaking more effective than any sleeping pill.

THE FOLLOWING morning the doorbell rang and it was Charlie.

"Sorry to interrupt, boss," he said.

"You're not sorry. You enjoy it."

There was a snigger behind him.

"There's a bloke here who wants to see you, but he wants to know if he needs a crash helmet or a parachute."

Sammy had just surfaced also, and we looked at each other. It could only be one person.

"Tell him he may need both if he's going to be a bloody bitch about it," I said, my memory of that day in this hotel forever in my head, as Matt flew in the door and launched himself at me, closely followed by Scott who was playing—in his own words—the Good Shepherd with their now five kids.

Max was a light sleeper, so he was there next, Kate stomping out not awake but pleased to see her "other cousins."

Our visitors made enough noise to wake the dead, but it was part of home that Sammy and I missed. This was only the second time we'd seen their latest additions: twin boys, Craig and Peter, naughty little two-year-olds with masses of freckles and plenty of attitude. They hadn't meant to extend their family, but the Department of Human Services had contacted them soon after the parents had died of a drug overdose. What was comforting was that Matt and Scott were first choice because of their amazing parenting skills, and within months they had formally adopted them.

Dad and Isobel struggled out, and Sammy quietly ordered breakfast.

I was happy. On holiday in a place we loved, surrounded by kids and good people, including Matt, who after all this time was still my best and most loyal mate.

After a very rocky start, he'd pushed Sammy and me together and got my stupid head right. Then at the same time as we became a couple, so did he and Scott. Scott the Shocker, the crazy electrician, a wonderful husband and parent, and the pair of them hard workers and the guts of the Hinchcliffe electoral campaigns.

I summoned the entire mob, including Barbara and Ted and the security guys, and we tucked into breakfast. Charlie wanted someone on the lookout, but I persuaded him that a hungry security officer may be more of a threat than a well-fed terrorist, so he locked the fire doors and we had a feast.

As PLANNED, the size of our party increased on the final leg of the ASEAN traveling show, when Kate, Max, Dad, and Isobel joined us. I'd sought advice from the Department of Finance long before we left and made a substantial contribution to their airfares and accommodation, so I wouldn't be accused of rorting the system, which I told an amused Paul Sinclair.

"Jacko, you're the first prime minister in Australian history to lead such a mission to Asia. There really is no precedent for what you're doing, and frankly you shouldn't be paying anything. Your kids are little ambassadors in their own right, and Peter and Isobel are their carers while you and Sammy are working."

"Paul, can I ask you something in total privacy?"

"Fire away," the big fellow said.

"Do you think I'm shamelessly using our kids to advance our chances in Asia because they have Eurasian looks?"

"What does Sammy say?"

"He says it will be wonderful for their education, something they will remember all their lives, and demonstrates that if you work together as a family, anything is possible."

"Couldn't have put it better myself. Do you feel better now?"

I grinned at him. He really was a good bloke, probably closer to me than his own shadow cabinet. I'd been watching him as he began to enjoy himself on this mission, his sometimes remote, even shy attitude, which I attributed to his private school education, seemed to be melting away as he stood alongside me making contact with people of all social statuses and all nationalities.

Our Minister for Industry and Science, David Carlisle, had joined us, and asked if his opposition shadow minister, Owen Fry, could also come along. Hopefully we'd all be talking about a resurgence of industry back home over the next decade after years of decline, and it was important we presented a united front, both major Australian political parties, a true, bipartisan effort looking to the future, agreeing on policy as we went.

At home the papers and television were full of our exploits. There were even maps of our flight path and our planned itineraries in each country. Australia watching us, a little bemused, I think, that politicians could actually achieve something, but hopefully understanding we were carrying out our election promises, everything costed and delivered via our fireside chats.

Chapter 53
Indonesia and Malaysia

WE LANDED at Surabaya with its modern airport, Indonesia's second-largest city. An important port, home to shipbuilding and much of the Indonesian Navy, it was the foundation stone of the modern Indonesia because it was here in 1945 when the now infamous Battle of Surabaya was fought.

I glanced out the window, and sure enough the Australian media contingent was in place, cameras rolling as we gently slid to a stop.

The door slid along and out, and the gangway wheeled into place as Sammy and I with Kate, Max, Dad, and Isobel, followed by Paul and Joan, then our ministerial colleagues made our way down the gangway. We used the wai as a gesture of respect, as did all our party including the kids, and I shook hands with the new Indonesian president. A handsome man in his very late fifties, he wore the national ceremonial dress of Java, the sarong with a little velvet hat, the peci that caught Max's imagination, and I thought, *Jesus he's going to ask a question or fifteen*, but he didn't.

"Kiddie Diplomacy" was on the lips of the media, I could tell, but everyone at this stage was well mannered and well behaved. The president and I stood side by side as our national anthems played, and then I was asked to inspect a guard of honor. I winked surreptitiously at Sammy, who knew Max wanted to look at all the guns but stayed where he'd been told like an angel, smiling sweetly at those around him. Kate was enthralled at all the dresses; the president's wife was especially colorful and Kate couldn't tear her eyes away.

Clearly in a break with protocol, she quietly moved over to my family, and in perfect English relaxed everyone, taking Kate's hand and pointing to the huge, fake ring Sammy had bought her in Patong a few days ago. Kate chatted away, and everyone laughed and smiled as the president and I completed the inspection.

Then it was into a motorcade that drove through manicured lawns and gardens, reminding me of the drive from Singapore's Changi Airport.

We arrived at the Surabaya Memorial where a huge crowd gathered. Charlie Lim was strangely calm, knowing the Indonesian police were in total control. "There'll be no nasty surprises here," he said. "I trust their ability completely."

That's what I was on about, too—trust—as Sammy and I laid a wreath in memory of all those who had died at the Battle of Surabaya in the pursuit of freedom.

Sammy stepped back to our family as I mounted the podium and addressed the Indonesian nation. I began by thanking the president and his family for their courtesy and interest as I attempted to build trust, tolerance, and understanding in the relationship between our nations.

"The reason I stand here at Surabaya is to apologize to the Indonesian people for the part played by the Allies under the British in 1945 after the defeat of the Japanese. It has never been said before, but at that time Australia remained under colonial direction and we were unwittingly part of a military operation that was responsible for bloodshed and the loss of lives on both sides as the Allies tried to reinstate the Dutch as rulers. For our part in that conflict, on behalf of Australia and Australians, I humbly apologize to the Indonesian people.

"Thankfully subsequent events here and in Jakarta culminated in the creation of the Republic of Indonesia. I feel it necessary, Mr. President," I said, "to return to those events so we can begin again. Indonesia is Australia's closest neighbor, a democratic republic and with a population of two hundred and fifty million people. We have a checkered past relationship with differences of opinion on many subjects. This is healthy.

"But it is not healthy to be so close geographically and yet be so remote in our hearts. Many of our past disagreements occurred simply because we didn't bother to learn about each other; our differing ethnicities and our backgrounds were major factors in our remoteness.

"While Australia was originally settled by the British, by 2050, 50 percent of all Australians will be able to trace their genetic roots back to Asia, and that can only be a good thing. Because now more than ever, we are part of Asia and we are your brothers and sisters. Brothers and sisters look after each other, we care about each other, we help each other through good times and bad times. I want today to be marked as the day when our nations decided to stand together and to be friends forever.

You have our promise we will value our relationship above all things, because we are family together. Thank you."

The Indonesian president, normally a reserved man from a less than demonstrative society, applauded loudly, and the crowd caught on. Then the president hugged me and kissed me on either cheek as a gesture of friendship. I thanked him and gave him a wai as he took my place on the podium. He spoke of the many months of dialogue instigated by us, which had culminated in our visit. He announced an immediate relaxation of visas for Australian citizens: sixty days for tourists and unlimited for people doing business with simple and straightforward conditions.

He went on to comment about the changed political atmosphere in Australia, how the tragedy of Jason Bellamy's passing had actually accelerated his most fervent wish of closer integration with Asia.

"However," he said, "it is through the new prime minster, Mr. Collins-Smith, that a system now exists in Australia where the opposition parties have been invited to participate in the process of government. This is an especially important factor because even if governments change, our relationship doesn't change. The relationship between our two countries is a joint responsibility of the two major parties, and so we also welcome the Leader of the Opposition in Australia, Mr. Sinclair."

There was a polite smattering of applause for Paul, who bowed deeply to the president.

"This means that all of Australia's elected representatives are involved at the outset, and it underscores the importance Australia places on the beginning of this new partnership with the Republic of Indonesia. Welcome to Indonesia!

"I agree with Mr. Collins-Smith, we are brothers and sisters. May our family be a happy one where we are honest and forthright with each other as we look forward to a bright future together."

WE WERE nearly a week in Indonesia. In Jakarta we saw how the government was tackling traffic congestion in probably the worst-affected city in the world. I now understood why we made the trip to our hotel by helicopter.

"Does Australia build trains?" the president asked.

"We build them for our own requirements, and each of the states have different rolling stock. I think we have the expertise but probably not the volume," I said, looking to David Carlisle for help.

"We're building a double-decker carriage a week currently, but I think there would be extra capacity if the manufacturer ran two shifts. That would nearly double the volume. How many do you think you would need?"

"Five hundred in three years, all electrified and double-decker, please."

"Let me get back to you, sir."

The president smiled, nodded, and we moved on to other subjects.

Paul Sinclair looked shocked. If the numbers came to be, that one deal would have a profound effect on our economy, investment, jobs, and financial security for hundreds of Australians.

On the day before we left to fly to Malaysia, we signed a Memorandum of Understanding with the president and his transport minister. If the financials were acceptable, the Australian and Indonesian governments would create a joint venture company to oversee the manufacture of railway carriages almost identical in specification to our New South Wales product.

Paul Sinclair shook his head, bewildered. "Congratulations, Jacko, but how in Christ's name did you do that?"

"We didn't even ask for the order, did we? What we did was to get off our fat arses and create a relationship. The Indonesians are our family, and we're theirs now. This is the first meaningful dialogue we've had with Indonesia since the days of Paul Keating. They aren't concerned about cost so much as timing. They need new trains yesterday. Here we are a few days away by cargo ship with a facility already in production. I think previous governments of both persuasions should hang their collective heads in shame."

We flew into Kuala Lumpur, and the Malaysians were determined, it appeared, to outdo the Indonesian welcome. Which was not unexpected, given Sammy's reputation in Malaysia, the strength of which seemed to surprise those traveling with us, particularly the Liberals.

I reminded Paul what his previous leader and their education minister had done to the Special School, and how they'd nearly pissed away two billion dollars' worth of business at Henry University alone.

Paul was curious, not quite understanding why the Special School was so important to the Malays, even though he was present at the opening.

"Paul, you've seen me struggling with stuff on a daily basis, and you know I had learning difficulties at school."

He looked at me sorrowfully, shaking his head, and murmured, "Dyslexia."

"Correct, but in Asia, particularly in some Muslim nations, it can be seen as a sign of weakness and very damaging to a family's reputation, particularly if they are part of the government. The prime minister's son was so affected, he tried to buy his degree, but Margaret Reeve threatened to throw him out. So Sammy took him on as a student and he was brilliant. Within a few months, the young bloke's life was turned around, and he's now a most successful architect here in Kuala Lumpur. There were several others from high-ranking members of the UMNO Party, which controls Malaysia, and Sammy turned them all around using language education, especially written English, as a reason for them attending the Special School. Saving face is everything in Asia."

"How did you guys figure all this out?" Paul asked.

"We listen closely to what the market requires. It's a good habit."

Margaret Reeve had flown up to meet us, and the Malaysian prime minister and I officially opened a new wing at the Henry University campus in Kuala Lumpur. Ironically its customers were mainly Malaysian and Singaporean Chinese, the Malays preferring "the whole Australian experience."

There was a lot of back slapping without much substance; I didn't mind as long as we kept the education business humming along.

Indonesia understood the reasons Paul Sinclair was a big part of our epic Asian journey, but his presence clearly puzzled the Malaysians because of their rather arbitrary attitude toward their main opposition party.

I'd invited Paul and Joan along to share a sushi dinner with Margaret Reeve in Kuala Lumpur. Margaret was quite comfortable playing both sides of the political street, but as time progressed, it was obvious she enjoyed their company, as we did.

She frequently visited KL, and she was a great listener with an astute feel for Malaysian personalities and politics.

"Jacko," she said, "something's eating you. Spit it out."

"I just have this feeling there's something the prime minister wants to talk about, but he seems to be dithering," I said.

"I'm not surprised after what you did to the Laotians," she said. "The family companies are everywhere and into everything, but he's not silly enough to offer you baksheesh. In fact he's quite a nice fellow."

Suddenly the penny dropped. Whatever business was done by Australian companies as a result of our desire to integrate further with Asia, their Malaysian counterparts would very likely have a member of the Malaysian parliament on the board of directors. So far as I knew, disclosure of financial interests wasn't necessary in Malaysian politics.

So while we sought to cover our own arses in Australia as politicians through proper disclosure and rightly so, the Malaysian people may well be outraged that Australian companies were dealing with the very people they voted in or out of office.

Tricky stuff, but there was no question how we should position ourselves as a nation in our future dealings. With a heavy heart, I asked for a private meeting with the prime minister.

WE MET at his home office, a quiet and peaceful area looking out over some well-ordered gardens. A younger man than his predecessors, the prime minister was somewhat of an academic, which under normal circumstances would have made me feel a little self-conscious, with just a simple business degree. But it was clear my host was well informed about everything, including the very different political environment back in Australia.

"I was surprised," he said, "that a prime minister would be personally leading a trade mission, and to have such a good grasp of international business."

Then he went on about Sammy and how he and his family would be forever in his debt, allowing his son to reach his full potential and even beyond.

"As you have, Mr. Collins-Smith—I trust you were also a good student for Mr. Sammy."

I laughed and nodded; the prime minister was indeed well informed.

"Your stewardship of Australia since the death of your previous prime minster is the talk of Asia," he said. "Many of our neighbors and ourselves have studied the changes you have brought to your country, and we can see friendly faces turned towards Asia on a consistent basis and that is most encouraging. But it is your domestic partnership and your children that have broken down barriers, particularly in those nations with a Muslim majority. We will always be slower to embrace social change, but contrary to expectation, we *are* capable of change," he said and actually smiled at me.

"You represent a new normal," he said. "We hear no criticism from your country. It is just a given that two men can produce and raise wonderful children together, and it is quite coincidental that one of you happens to be the nation's leader, and a most successful one at that. You may be surprised to know that ASEAN as a group need Australia as much as you need us, going forward. So you are quickly becoming *our* new normal."

The prime minister paused, as if deciding to confide in me further. He was normally quite reticent, and I was surprised he'd been so frank thus far. With the third-largest economy in Asia and a growth rate of 5 percent annually, it dawned on me that he was the unofficial spokesman for ASEAN. But there was something else.

"My wife and I have been blessed," he said. "We have four children. The eldest, as you know, is now designing skyscrapers for the KL skyline, thanks to Mr. Sammy. Then we have two girls. The first is married, a journalist, and she and her husband have given us our first grandchildren. The next girl is a university lecturer, also making a difference, educating young people in the sciences. And then there is our baby boy. He is just twenty-one years old. Always a brilliant mind but troubled until quite recently. We worried about him constantly, but my wife and I made sure he knew we would never judge him, no matter what. It was a news story of your impending trip to the ASEAN countries with a photograph of you and your family that encouraged him to tell his mother and me that he is a gay man. Finally we understood why he'd spent such a troubled time as a teenager, but we assured him it was all over now. Together we would make sure he would have a happy life, just like his siblings."

The prime minister dabbed his eyes with a handkerchief and apologized, admitting they could have lost their child to suicide, such was his mental state.

"You see our families' lives are intertwined now on two levels. You have directly or indirectly affected the lives of two of our children."

"Thank you for entrusting me with that information. I feel very privileged," I replied. "Will we have an opportunity to meet your family?"

"Jusuf would be so excited. Can you join us here for dinner tonight?"

I GUESSED very few people from a western nation had ever, through personal circumstances, been invited into the epicenter of Malaysian politics as we had. There was trust on both sides, given and received, and finally we got to the reason I'd called the meeting.

"The history of our economic dealings has not been without some notoriety," I began, careful not to accuse any individual.

"Ah, my uncle and the Australian banknote contract."

"Precisely, and there have been many complaints since. So much so, my government is concerned that dealings with Malaysian companies in the future could be jeopardized. My government's dealings, whether undertaken directly or indirectly, must be transparent. Australian taxpayers rightly expect everything we'd helped organize would never be mired in corruption or have any hint of impropriety whatsoever."

"I understand," he said. "We must ensure every politician discloses his or her financial connections. We have such a register, but it was never updated and largely ignored until some months ago. We must understand that international business will not continue to grow for this country if we give companies any reason at all to doubt the integrity and honesty of the political system. It is in Malaysia's interests to keep these details updated, open, and transparent. I have faced severe opposition, even personal criticism from some of my ministers, when I proposed these changes, but I went ahead anyway. It helped that I had the ear of some useful press contacts who were prepared to publish the names of those who refused to cooperate."

The prime minister chuckled at the expression on my face as I contemplated his courage in the face of old guard of the UMNO Party.

"I survived because we couldn't continue to live in the past, and the party finally understood that. I updated all my details first to set the example, and they followed like sheep. But I knew there were some holding back a substantial part of their details and named them in Parliament. Then I threatened to add fines to the package and even suspend or sack them from Parliament unless they complied. Like you, Mr. Collins-Smith, I don't suffer fools gladly, so I actually gave one of my ministers responsibility in his portfolio to ensure the Disclosure Statement Register is maintained with correct details. Now the question is, under those conditions, can we continue to do business together?"

Chapter 54
Singapore

SINGAPORE WAS all business. As expected.

I reminded the current prime minister that the founder and first prime minister of modern-day Singapore, the late Lee Kuan Yew, had described Australians as "the white trash of Asia."

"He was correct back then," I told the current prime minister, "but we've changed a lot." I certainly held his undivided attention.

One of the new breed, and a wealthy businessman in his own right, the young prime minister represented part of the "renewal" of Singapore, as the old guard voluntarily retired to make way for them. As with all Chinese, he was inscrutable, but there was an excitement just under the surface linked to a gung ho attitude not so very different to mine. Every so often it would bubble up as he described some new project or strategy that had the potential to fire up their economy again. The growth in Singapore's economy had plateaued some years ago. It was by now a mature economy literally restricted by the small size of the place, but he insisted it wasn't over yet—not by a long shot.

He was my age, late thirties, and he didn't appear to be married. The Department of Foreign Affairs and Trade had no further information on him at all, which was unusual. Highly unusual in this most family-oriented of nations. My mind flicked back to the welcome ceremony at the airport the previous day; his eyes had lingered on Sammy and the kids, and I'd put it down to curiosity. After all, I was the first leader of a country in a same-sex marriage to visit Singapore in an official capacity.

He was also an exceedingly handsome man, tall for a Chinese man, and slim, very gym-fit, and perhaps gay, I finally decided, but how could I raise the subject discreetly?

The following evening we were due to jointly host a dinner with Australian and Singaporean business people, but tonight we were free and I hoped he was also. "We would love to meet your partner," I said, fishing for information, and his face registered slight amusement. I'd pushed the envelope, but he wouldn't comment except to smile graciously and nod. "I would enjoy a pleasant, quiet meal with friends. I will bring my personal assistant."

To my surprise we didn't even leave our hotel. Charlie Lim had the night off, and we were whisked upstairs to a private dining room with a stunning view of the lights of Singapore.

We'd hardly walked in the room when a door opened noiselessly and the prime minister walked in, followed closely by a slightly younger and stunning-looking man of Indian extraction.

"Ah, Mr. Collins-Smith, welcome. Please, I'm James, or Jimmy, as he calls me," the prime minister announced, pointing to his PA.

"And I'm Sanjay," his companion replied with a huge smile revealing beautiful white teeth, a contrast to his dark skin.

"And this is Sammy, and I'm Jacko. This is a lovely room."

"Yes, we can relax and be ourselves, for once the walls don't have ears."

Our host beckoned us toward a well-stocked bar in the corner and took our drink orders. I thought him quite democratic, serving his assistant before himself.

A beautifully arranged self-service buffet dinner sat on a big table at the other end of the room, the staff long gone. Sammy smiled as I tucked into the fresh seafood and our host noticed. "You enjoy our food, Jacko."

"He has a healthy appetite and loves any seafood. If you need his attention, just feed him beforehand and he'll do anything."

The prime minister's eyes sparkled. "Ah, I will remember that."

The view was quite beautiful, and Sammy slipped his hand over my leg. I hoped I didn't have to stand up too soon because I could have given an illustrated lecture on how to pitch a tent.

It was Sammy who rushed in where angels feared to tread, and I felt uneasy. "You guys are a couple, aren't you?"

The prime minister smiled and nodded while his PA looked stricken.

He rubbed Sanjay's hand and calmed him. "I hardly think our visitors would give you away, darling," he said with a smile, and I thought, *How good is this? Old "Uncle" Lee would turn in his grave if he knew Singapore had a gay prime minister.*

For the first time since we left home, I felt a little overwhelmed.

Across the table sat one of the most influential men in the world, a dynamic, handsome bloke with his stunning boyfriend, looking all domestic and relaxed, while his partner still looked terrified.

"How long have you been together?" Sammy asked.

Sanjay appeared tentative but answered the question. "We have known each other almost all our lives. We went to school together."

Sammy and I looked at each other; we had, after all, some common ground.

"Then we went to university in Australia," Jimmy interrupted gently. "We shared an apartment together, and he got drunk one night."

"I did not."

"Yes you did, and you propositioned me."

"Well you didn't put up any resistance."

"Of course not. I thought I planned it well."

We laughed at them. They were like playful teenagers, but they'd trusted us with information that could have ramifications for Jimmy as prime minister, and I assured them both their secret was safe with us.

Sammy smiled but didn't say much as we helped ourselves to a sumptuous meal and just a few glasses of Australian wine.

We found them delightful people. They had a sense of fun and were easy to be with, but I thought with sadness how restricted their life must be, how living in the shadows hadn't allowed their relationship to flourish like ours.

It was Sammy who voiced those concerns, and for once in my life I wished he'd bloody shut up.

"I feel so sad that something as lovely as your partnership must be hidden from sight. It must make life so difficult."

Jimmy sighed and nodded, but Sanjay looked terrified again.

"It's not the job, so much as your families, isn't it?" Sammy asked, hitting the target head-on as usual.

"Well my family are aware," Jimmy said. "My father and I disagreed over my lifestyle, but before he passed away, he forgave me. He realized I was born this way, there was no choice involved. He was such an intelligent man. He also instructed my mother, sister, and two brothers to accord me the proper respect that is due to the head of the family. Yes, I know I also outrank everyone in Singapore, don't I? But there is now open discussion in my family on the subject, which is rare among Chinese people."

"My family must never know!" Sanjay almost shouted out the words, the distress clearly written on his face.

"Fuck your family," Sammy responded.

Jesus, I thought, *this could turn back Singaporean/Australian relations to Uncle Lee's day*, but strangely enough the prime minister smiled broadly.

"Your family don't pay your bills," roared Sammy. "You're a smart, educated man with a divine partner who cares about you, and you don't want your family's tender sensibilities offended? It's your life, yours and Jimmy's together, not theirs, so why let them interfere? Sometimes I think we're frightened of fear itself. Here we are well into the twenty-first century, and you and Jimmy together could set a magnificent example to young Asians everywhere by being proud of who you are, not ashamed because you have nothing to be ashamed of."

"But I love my family. If I tell them, I know I will lose them forever."

"Sanjay," Sammy snapped in a threatening voice, and I moved to stop him but Jimmy passed his fingers over his lips, suggesting I shut up and let Sammy continue.

Sammy reached across the table and took Sanjay's hands in his, an action that seemed to calm him. "Sanjay, do you love Jimmy?"

"Oh yes, I always have."

"Just like Jackson and me." The use of my full name warned me not to interrupt him. "So your family are Hindu, correct?"

"Yes, they are."

"So have they ever tried to marry you off to a woman, an arranged marriage?"

"Oh no, they would never do that."

"Well what are you worried about, for goodness' sake, get Jimmy to propose to you, then drag him home and say guess what, folks, I'm getting married, to the prime minister!"

Sanjay smiled in spite of himself. "Oh they know Jimmy. They are so proud of him, he is like another son to them, but you forget, Sammy, we cannot get married in Singapore."

"But you can in Australia."

Jimmy's face lit up with sheer delight while Sanjay, rendered speechless with a look of wonder written all over him, tried to digest the information.

Sammy pounced, the element of surprise fresh. "Get married in Canberra by a celebrant. Invite both families to attend. Eventually introduce retrospective legislation in Singapore to recognize same-sex marriages carried out in other countries. Give it time to sink in, then bring forward the full same-sex marriage package for other Singaporean couples, because by then you two would have shown by example, simple."

But my darling had another card up his sleeve, and I thought, *Well, I'll just follow along and see what happens.*

We slipped down to our level where the Australian contingent had taken over the entire floor, and we walked into our suite. Isobel and Dad were just putting the kids to bed as Sammy proudly introduced first his mother and then my father, explaining they were just dirty old senior-aged people who liked a romp in the hay. I thought the humor would be lost on our guests, but both of them laughed at Sammy—by now they expected him to entertain them.

Kate and Max shared a bedroom at this hotel and it was story-telling time. Sanjay's face lit up as he sat down on Kate's bed and told of baby elephants and magic wizards, while Jimmy scratched his head and told of Doctor Dog and the Golden Beetle.

Within minutes both of them were sound asleep, Sanjay looking wistful as he kissed both our kids on the forehead, neither waking from their slumber. "They are beautiful, Jimmy," he said, and I thought the prime minister had something in his eye, producing a handkerchief and vigorously blowing his nose.

We all sat with Dad and Isobel, who were peppered with questions, particularly about our early life together. They excused themselves after half an hour or so and left. I noticed Sanjay had a less defeated look about him, even confidence, and Jimmy certainly had a spring in his step that wasn't there before.

OUR FIRST official duty of the day was at the Kranji War Memorial where Jimmy and I stood side by side at a service to commemorate the fallen in the Second World War. Dad was there also; we had several relatives who didn't make it home, and after the short service, I asked to speak to the gathered media.

"Nothing can turn back the hands of time," I said. "This is one of the saddest sights any person can see, row upon row of graves, filled with young people who died before their time in the service of their countries. These cemeteries are dotted all around Asia. They are the most poignant reminder of humanity at its least human. We will never forget them, but we should also remember the reasons they were pressed into the service of their country.

"Down through history it has almost always been countries acting alone in the search of power and wealth that have been the instigators of international armed conflict. Or terror organizations driven by militant religious fervor.

"If we in Asia work together to build strong economies, we stand united for the future. Nothing like strong economies with all of us sharing in the good times and the bad, but all of us working together. That's the strongest deterrent against those who would seek to divide and conquer."

WE TOURED the Port of Singapore and marveled at its automated organization, then the petroleum refineries, an unlikely industry for a nation without any oil resources of its own, but running consistently second to the United States in terms of global volume. Then to a huge building site where the columns of steel and concrete reached for the sky.

Jimmy insisted we inspect the living quarters of the migrant workforce, portable air-conditioned two-story buildings nearby and on-site. He and I had agreed on this part of the script, and I let him have the floor, so handsome and so articulate, wearing a bright gold hard hat with the words "The Boss" emblazoned on the front—even the Australian businessmen were quiet and well behaved for once. Jimmy explained that in order for Singapore to grow and develop, they needed a permanent migrant workforce because there simply weren't enough locals to do the work involved. He explained how there were strict rules and regulations that employers had to observe, standards of accommodation, food, and wages. Most of the workers were from Bangladesh, Myanmar, India, and the Philippines. "So we license those people," he said, "and after five years if they work hard and stay out of trouble, we allow them to become citizens of Singapore. So our labor and immigration policy are one and the same."

I was busy, as usual, talking to the workers, even shoveling some wet cement and getting in the way, and, as expected, there was huge respect for Jimmy in the feedback from the workers. "Jesus," one of our businessmen said, "he really knows his stuff, doesn't he? Anyone would think he owns the place."

"He does," I said, reminding a rather shocked Aussie of the gold-colored hard hat. "This is one of his companies. He's so proud of it. He has an economics degree, but he spent quite some time alongside the migrant workers when he was just a kid, and eventually bought the company—pretty smart, isn't he?"

THE OFFICIAL dinner that evening, a lavish buffet, underscored the importance both governments placed on our visit. Another thirty or so Australian business people flew in especially for the occasion. Our stalls were set up at one end of the huge room looking resplendent, the weeks of setting up and tearing them down again covered up by some clever repair work and some paint by one of our team. I found her and thanked her for her attention to detail, telling her that of all the countries we'd visited, presentation was everything in this place, and I appreciated her help. "Team Australia, boss, remember?" She smiled and gave me a high five.

Sammy and I circulated around the Australians present, including a good number of expats living in Singapore, because every bit of networking helped. The questions were coming thick and fast, and on one subject in particular—migrant workers. "Why did you show us all that stuff this morning, Jacko?" one of them asked. "We'd never get away with it in Australia—the unions would never allow it to happen, haw, haw, haw," he said, braying like a lovesick donkey.

"Well for your information, Joe, the ACTU have already agreed to it."

The purple face of our captain of industry registered shock.

I waved over a journalist who'd been shadowing us, and together with Paul Sinclair, I gave everyone both barrels at once.

"The Joint Party Room some months ago discussed the very real possibility that if we stimulated our economy, even mildly, that several industries would never find the labor required to grow as quickly as they needed from local sources. That is particularly obvious in the hospitality industry right now, and if the situation is allowed to worsen, we will damage our international reputation and stunt the growth of tourism. Legislation is currently being drafted. It will go to the Joint Party Room first, then to the parliament to be ratified in the autumn session. The rules will be similar to Singapore: migrant workers will enjoy the same wages and conditions as Australian workers currently, and after a qualifying period, they will be encouraged to apply for Australian citizenship. Preference will be given to the ASEAN countries."

There was a flurry of questions, and I began to walk away, but Puce Face ran after me. "You can't do that. No one's ever been able to do that before."

"Joe, what part don't you understand? The train has left the station, and it will happen. It's common sense and everyone has agreed. What I'm more interested in is you, Joe. What are you doing to upgrade your airport, your restaurant franchise, and your three hotels to make them ready to do some extra business? Team Australia, Joe, remember?"

Jimmy and I stood quite proudly together as we each addressed the assembled dignitaries. We admitted we'd found much common ground together, and Jimmy gave me a surreptitious wink from an otherwise impassive face. Then he got smartly to the point where he directed Singaporean businesses to give preference to Australian suppliers where possible in the spirit of the free-trade agreement already in place for some years. "I think Uncle Lee would be well pleased," he said quietly as we shook hands for the media.

THE FINAL day was a rest day. We took the kids, Dad, and Isobel to the Singapore Zoo for breakfast, and then on to the prime minister's residence for lunch.

For once both Sammy and I were totally unprepared for what happened.

The families of the prime minister and his assistant surrounded us, Straits-born Chinese and Indian people, but all proudly Singaporean, the harmony of it all so noticeable.

Alison Green from the Australian Embassy stepped forward. I remembered her from somewhere, but she was all business today. The

Notice of Intended Marriage was duly signed by Jimmy and Sanjay, and witnessed by Jimmy's mother and Sanjay's father. We checked the date in our diary in about six weeks and agreed the weather should be perfect for an outdoor wedding at the Lodge.

Chapter 55
The Philippines

ALL ALONG I'd been worried about the Philippines. As with all the ASEAN countries, there had been a thorough briefing and our stated expectations of our visit made very clear. After all, Australia had been a good neighbor, and the Philippines had enjoyed Australian foreign aid continuously for a very long period.

Trade and diplomatic relations with the Philippines, as with most of Asia, had been a ministerial responsibility for years. This time it was my job to connect at a leadership level and talk business, remind them what Australia had to sell, but above all find out what they needed to buy.

The official welcome at the airport, in polite but subdued fashion worried me a little. The morning after, I was still uneasy. Something in their attitude wasn't quite right, and I couldn't put my finger on it.

Sammy was supervising Kate and Max with their homeschooling, and Joan was shopping with Isobel and a long-suffering Dad.

As planned Angela, Eddie, David Carlisle, and I represented the government, while Paul and Owen Fry the Opposition. We were waiting in a boardroom for the president to arrive when I quietly voiced my concerns to Angela.

"Jacko," she said, "remember they're a Christian country. That's what's different here. They're holier than thou, they don't appreciate our sexuality one little bit, even though there are more openly gay people per capita here than the rest of Asia put together."

I nodded and smiled. Yes, it hadn't escaped my attention; it was just so unusual for anyone to be even slightly homophobic in Asia, when the prevailing mood these days was of good manners and a desire to understand differences rather than magnify them.

"The Pope was here only a few weeks ago," Angela whispered. "That sends them back to their worry beads for a while."

I nearly choked on my coffee as the president walked in preceded by armed bodyguards. "We come in peace," I said to Angela, and she bit her lip.

I began by introducing Paul and Owen as members of the Opposition, the background to their presence through the Joint Party Room, and the long-term strategy we were promoting as a nation with both major political parties represented on this visit.

The president, a tall, thin man with a close-cropped dark but graying beard, nodded, spoke to an aide beside him, and made notes. Ferdinand Lopez had the Spanish name without the manners, reminding me of Fidel Castro as a young man. He wouldn't speak to me directly, only through one of his aides, and after my response he made notes. *What a silly cunt*, I thought.

We waded through the agenda; it was enforced politeness without enthusiasm, and I became frustrated because we were getting nowhere. At morning tea I pulled Angela and Eddie into a huddle, and we agreed on a strategy to get their attention. When we resumed, Eddie Chi, as Australian treasurer, took over.

"There will be no further foreign aid from Australia until further notice," he said. "We have a much smaller taxpayer base than the Philippines, and whilst we recognize this is a developing nation, we simply have to justify every cent we invest in other nations, disaster relief being the exception." The president sat bolt upright as if someone had run an electric current up his arsehole. Paul Sinclair studied the table in front of him, and unlike Eddie the smiling assassin, we kept straight faces.

No doubt the president heard every word without assistance from his hirelings; he was so shocked he even forgot to take notes.

"Mr. Lopez," Eddie continued, turning the knife now he'd stuck it in, "our contingent needs to focus on the reasons for which we came here, to talk trade and focus on profitable business opportunities that will benefit both our nations. We want to understand what goods and services the Philippines may need in the future, and if any of our products match those needs. That is why we both should focus on the Australian exhibition this evening at the Makati Conference Center and allow our business people to have meaningful discussions. Our prime minister and deputy now have pressing business elsewhere, and they ask if you would please excuse them."

I stood up, bowed to the president, and quickly left the room. Paul told me afterward the president was ashen-faced with rage. The aides clearly knew what was coming at them.

Angela and I walked into our suite. We actually did have some executive duties and talked them through online with Mrs. Shields, as Sammy and the kids joined us for lunch. "Hell hath no fury like a PM scorned," Angela said, and we told Sammy what we'd done.

My other half held his sides; the thought of me being a bitch had him in stitches. "I have taught you something after all," Sammy said. "That's exactly the way to handle that type of rudeness, just rise above it."

We were enjoying our sandwiches when the doorbell buzzed. Charlie Lim stood there with one of President Lopez's aides to see me.

"Come in," I said, as the young man hesitated at the door.

"Oh, I'm so sorry, sir. My name is Miguel and I have a message from President Lopez, but I am interrupting your meal."

"Come and join us, there's plenty."

I introduced Miguel to Sammy and the kids as he handed me an envelope. I opened it quickly—an invitation to dinner that evening.

The kid looked miserable, and Kate got out of her chair and gave him a sloppy kiss on the cheek. "You look sad, and Dad and Pop say we must make people happy. Are you better now?"

"Much better, thank you. You have very nice manners."

"When I grow up, will you marry me?"

He laughed with the fun of it all and relaxed at last, enjoying a big plate of sandwiches and fruit, patting his tummy afterward. "Thank you so much, sir. Are Australian prime ministers always so informal?" he asked politely.

"Less formal than your boss," I said.

Miguel smiled. "Yes, but he is also very, very shy, sir. It is all an act."

I marveled at the loyalty the young fellow had for his employer and the trust he had accorded us; our Miguel was both intelligent and resourceful.

"My reply to his invitation for dinner is negative, I'm afraid, because our family always eats together in the evenings. If, however, there was some way my husband and children could be included, and if it were an hour earlier so your girlfriend, Kate, and her brother, Max, could be in bed by a reasonable hour, then that would be more convenient. But I imagine that wouldn't be possible."

To my surprise, Miguel giggled. "Oh he will erupt, sir, but please don't plan other arrangements?"

He shook hands with Sammy and Max, and kissed Kate on the cheek, finally turning to me. "Thank you for lunch, sir. Keep up the good work."

IN A short but exciting drive to dinner, Max enjoyed the flashing lights and sirens of the surrounding motorcycles as we proceeded to Malacañan Palace at 6:30 p.m. Normally official guests of the government stayed at Malacañan, the official residence of the President; instead we were in a very nice hotel a short distance away because there were so many of us and we needed to be together. I think that gave President Lopez the shits as well, but that couldn't be helped. Regardless of religious affiliation, I expected the president to recognize all legitimate and lawful Australian lifestyles, and I wouldn't allow him to intimidate us as a same-sex family.

My feelings had changed from initial concern to stubbornness, and I wasn't surprised that Paul Sinclair supported me unreservedly.

"Don't you dare back down, Jacko," he said. "Your family is so beautiful, and you've done everything right as a leader. If old Loopy Lopez can't take the heat in the kitchen, well fuck her, dear. She'll soon be history with an attitude like that."

"God, you're gay," I said, laughing at him. "Are you trying to tell me something?"

"Yes, you're such a bitch at heart, and I love it. When you walked out on old Loopy Lou, I thought here we go, our first fatality of the trip, he's going to cark it at the boardroom table."

As we drove toward the entrance, a small army stood to attention and "Advance Australia Fair" rang out. Impressive, unnecessary, but a desperate gesture from a leader who felt challenged by events.

The car door opened and a crisp salute cut the warm evening air.

We waited until the music finished and walked toward the front door. Immediately it swung open and the president appeared with a rather nice-looking woman at his side.

"Welcome," he said. "This is my wife, Raina."

"And you've already met my husband, Sammy, but not our children. This is Kate and this is Max."

Without training, both our kids responded as if they were adults, shaking hands and smiling as they'd always done. What we'd initiated, Isobel and Dad had reinforced—not bad for a nearly ten-year-old and an eight-year-old with the social skills of kids twice their age. We felt such pride in them; they'd thrived with Dad and Isobel helping, and charmed everyone around them in a very adult world. Sometimes I wondered if they were too sophisticated, but Dad and Isobel assured us they were still kids, beautiful kids, and totally grounded, "as expected."

A pretty woman in her fifties, Raina couldn't tear her eyes away from the kids, and her husband looked at them in frank amazement. Sammy and I smiled at each other; this reaction wasn't uncommon in some countries, usually the Christian ones. The word pictures built up by the Vatican had probably painted our type of family unit as work of the Devil himself, ugly deformed creatures with two heads, scaly skin, pimples, halitosis, and warts.

Instead we were depressingly ordinary—a nice, normal family—and poor old Ferdinand was having trouble coping with the facts of life. Unlike Raina, who seemed to come alive, focusing on our kids and that "they were so beautiful." She wasn't shy, had wonderful English, and a natural warmth that drew Kate and Max into conversation.

We had drinks at a bar in the corner of their private dining room, a smartly dressed barman taking our orders, including very clear and polite requests from Kate and Max. Old Ferdinand began to unwind, his body like a huge spring uncoiling, and he actually smiled at something Kate said.

The wine was an Australian merlot, and I thanked him for his thoughtfulness, suggesting he try another with me, which led to yet another.

Raina looked sharply at him, and we moved to the table. If he was feeling as mellow as I was, this could only enhance international relations. The first course was already on the table as he rose to his feet just a touch unsteadily to say grace. We'd instructed the kids in this Christian ritual, and of course there had been questions. Many questions, which we answered truthfully as the kids deserved. Much of it revolved around their response—*amen* was not expected, we told them, just to bow our heads or maybe just avert their eyes as the words were said, and to look "thankful."

"Why?" asked Max.

"That's to thank God for the meal."

"But you and Poppy give us the meal, not God" was the intelligent reply.

Sammy took over, much to my relief, because there's nothing more grueling than an eight-year-old searching for the truth.

"Sweethearts," he said, "I know this is confusing for you, but it's another foreign country and because we're their guests, we have to respect their rules. Do you remember what respect means?"

They both nodded in unison, and so we had a trial run-through.

I watched them now, as Ferdinand offered thanks. My eight-year-old son turned and winked at me before lowering his head, and I thought I'd lose it on the spot.

The food was distinctively Australian in its content and presentation. Rich, rare beef, crisp roasted vegetables, and fresh greens and beautiful gravy, and the kids had second helpings while Ferdinand and I chugged down another merlot.

Then there were sweets on a trolley, and in a stage whisper Kate asked if we needed to say it again before we had those. Sammy smirked, and I thought to myself I was beyond caring, as was my mate Ferdi.

Kate decided to be sociable and circulate, and somehow she was sitting on our host's knee having an engaging conversation. She told him his hairy face was lovely, but she couldn't marry him because he was already married. He nodded and smiled, agreeing that Aunt Raina might not be very impressed.

"But," my daughter said, "I might marry Miguel when I grow up."

"I see," said the president.

"But I don't know, because I think Miguel likes boys better than girls. What do you think, Uncle Ferdi?"

"But even if Miguel likes boys, you'd still like him?"

"Oh yes, but Miguel would want to marry a boy and that's okay."

Sammy and I looked at our firstborn; to have that sort of perception at that tender age was remarkable, even if she'd outed poor Miguel to his boss.

My head hurt like a bastard, and I had an hour to eat breakfast, shower, change, and try to undo the hangover that threatened to slow my day down to walking pace. Or maybe to a crawl. I waited for Ferdinand; we planned to inspect an aquaculture farm with potential Australian investors. Then we had a lunch with the Chamber of Commerce, where I had a keynote address to make.

Fuck, I thought, *I hope the team's ready*, as I dialed up Angela, Eddie, and David for a quick get-together to compare notes.

"Boss, you look like shit," Eddie said.

"Thanks, that's exactly how I feel."

Angela just gave me a knowing look. "Don't tell me you got on the jungle juice with old Ferdi."

I nodded, my head hurting as Sammy handed me more Panadol.

"But we certainly don't have a problem with lifestyle acceptance any more—my family fixed that. Ferdi is actually a really nice man, so shy and very naïve but very genuine. It's safe to say that we're good mates and it's full speed ahead. He promised me he'd move mountains to make sure we have maximum impact in what we do."

David Carlisle looked at me. "You're a genius, Jacko. I thought we were going to fly out of this place with our tails between our legs, achieving absolutely nothing, but your new mate has indeed been moving mountains overnight. There's even a trade delegation on its way from Mindanao, and we've never even spoken to them before on account of the security issues."

"Don't thank me," I said. "Thank our kids—they saved the day."

I hadn't even spoken to them this morning, so I left the room, returning a few minutes later followed by Sammy, who smiled.

"So did Daddy reward them?" Angela asked.

Sammy slipped his hand over mine. "Oh their requests are simple. Our son wants a Jaguar for his birthday, and Kate, well she's easily pleased. She just wants an Order of Australia, as soon as possible, please."

We stayed ten days, a day longer than planned, but the itinerary had some wriggle room. The amount of business interest we'd unlocked was staggering, and the team needed to process information requests so the follow-up was thorough and efficient. No use promoting new business if we couldn't service the inquiries properly.

But there was another reason, because Ferdinand Lopez was on a mission of another kind. "Before you leave I want you to meet someone," he said. "The Archbishop of Manila."

My eyes must have nearly popped out of my head, but he held up his hand.

"I want all of you there, please. Sammy, the children, and your parents, plus Miguel and his partner. Raina and I will have all of our family there as well for support."

My mate Ferdi. We'd spent every spare moment together because he had questions, which I'd answered as best I could with Sammy helping. He'd been nothing if not thorough, also listening to feedback from Dad and Isobel.

Then he picked Miguel's brains, who showed him evidence of the many thousands of young gay people on Filipino websites all looking for love, desperate to make their mark in the world but knowing they would have to continue to live in the shadows.

His eminence had been eager to accept the invitation to afternoon tea—any opportunity to be included as part of an international function highlighting the importance of the church in the Philippines' way of life.

A Filipino, he was a rather rotund and bespectacled fellow, with a seemingly cheerful disposition. Dressed in his full regalia with purple sash and gold trimmings everywhere, he was reintroduced to the Lopez family, then to the guest of honor—me.

"Eminence, this is my good friend, the prime minister of Australia, Jackson Collins-Smith." I showed no deference, just a pleasant smile and a firm handshake. "And this is his husband, Samuel Collins-Smith, and their children, Katherine and Maxwell."

I heard Isobel snort; the kids' full names were never used except on documents and it sounded funny. The kids were impressive however: they didn't giggle or fidget. They knew Team Australia was on show and they somehow knew they had to be good for the man they called Uncle Ferdi.

Then it was Dad and Isobel's turn, and his eminence had, as expected, some difficulty working out their relationship, making a prick of himself by asking about Mum's passing instead of just moving on. I winked at Dad and he calmed down, but I felt for him. The absence of common sense in the clergy at the expense of self-opinionated dogma was typical of their lack of life experience, and we'd all trained ourselves to move on in such circumstances. But it still hurt, and I promised myself some Dad time as soon as we were out of here.

But this was clearly the president's show, as the archbishop was beginning to recognize, his eyes flickering toward the entrance as if planning a sudden departure. The president stopped opposite easily the most handsome person in the room and turned to the archbishop. "You have met my personal assistant in the past," he said with a smile, and the archbishop nodded at Miguel as if he were a piece of shit. "He has been promoted to the post of principal private secretary to myself. With the promotion comes many executive responsibilities should I become suddenly ill or temporarily incapacitated. Miguel has demonstrated enormous loyalty and resourcefulness, and I am most proud of him. He will carry out his new duties with distinction, of that I am certain."

The archbishop inclined his head to show he understood, and was about to move on when Ferdinand put out his hand.

"Eminence," he said, "there is someone else of equal importance you haven't met. This is John Paul Ramos, Miguel's partner. He is fluent in English, German, French, Spanish, Italian, and Mandarin. Tagalog is his born language, but he is familiar with all the dialects of our country. He has been in the service of the government for some time and is also a much valued and loyal employee."

I suddenly recognized the somewhat shy fellow who had been interpreting in Cebuano for the group from Mindanao, and Miguel smiled at me, nodding. The guy was a linguistic freak; his brain must have had so many compartments with different languages going on in each consecutively.

But it was also clear he loved Miguel as their hands reached for each other, showing no fear in the presence of the archbishop.

"Your eminence," Ferdinand continued, "in our country we have an estimated 12 percent of our population who are same-sex attracted, just like Miguel and John Paul. But their partnership has remained hidden because we have made them feel ashamed of who they are. Quite soon our government will act so couples such as

Miguel and John Paul are treated equally in our society. Our friends from Australia have enjoyed such freedom for many years and now marry and raise children together, beautiful children," he said, looking at Kate and Max.

"This way, eminence," Ferdinand commanded, steering him toward the afternoon tea table, laden with every imaginable delicacy guaranteed to increase weight by simply looking at it. I watched the archbishop smile for the first time that afternoon, delicious free food, and he tucked into a huge plate, the greedy bastard. He obviously thought his little lesson on same-sex relationships was over, his shoulders relaxed as he munched his way through his tucker. But it wasn't to be because the president was overheard to give him both barrels.

"I know you feel strongly about the separation of church and state, and I will never interfere in your business as long as you stay out of mine."

Fuck. I wouldn't have missed this for quids, I thought.

"For years the church here has preached against homosexuality, which has caused much hardship, sadness, and tragedy. A sizeable segment of our population has been enslaved because of those rigid views, yet other Catholic societies such as Argentina, Brazil, even Ireland, have embraced same-sex marriage, their societies have been liberated and they have become more productive as a result. It is too much to expect you to preach in favor of this issue, but let me tell you that if I hear of one service that denigrates same-sex partnerships and gay people generally, you are all in big trouble. I will have an ear in every Catholic church in the Philippines."

The archbishop was having trouble breathing, let alone speaking. I strained to hear what he said to our mate Ferdi, but it wasn't very nice. But I did hear what President Lopez said in return, very clearly.

"Don't even think about crying to the Vatican, because I've already spoken to your boss. He is a most progressive man and a realist. His policy is to live and let live, which I find admirable. But he did say that if I found myself in difficulties over this issue and you found it all too hard to be nice and neutral, then he'd give you a well-deserved rest and find someone else to replace you. Another piece of fruitcake, eminence?"

The Archbishop of Manila strode from the room, belching, bellowing for his car and driver. Ferdinand looked sweetly at me and smiled.

"That went well, don't you think, Jacko?" he asked. "But I think we need a glass of red to cleanse our palates."

Chapter 56
Thailand

I'D TOLD the press to expect something spectacular at Suvarnabhumi Airport in Bangkok, so they went on ahead. Then I suggested to the aircraft crew that they make an announcement to passengers just after we landed and before the event so no one shit themselves.

It was like coming home—to our other home.

On Australian breakfast television, our two 737s followed by the Hercules taxied along the runway together in a line as a fleet of fire trucks fired water over us in a welcome archway.

The kids were beyond excited, running from one set of windows to another, watching the display. The pictures were also beamed to the other ASEAN nations at my request; I wanted everyone to join in our sense of achievement as we rolled into our final destination before heading home.

We planned for three venues in Thailand, so there was still a hard slog ahead.

Our Bangkok visit entailed largely ceremonial reasons, and within minutes of deplaning we were on our way to Chitralada Palace, the private residence of the Thai Royal Family. The family connection with Phuket went back generations, to the very first Chinese shop houses in Phuket Town.

Meeting this person at Pa and Ma's funeral we realized the links to Pa and Ma's family were stronger than ever. Pa was so proud of us. He and Ma had been twice to Australia, first to our wedding, and then to my swearing-in as Australian Minister for Education. Sammy and I were regarded as equal members of Pa and Ma's family; we reminded them of Pa's brother, his partner, and their family, and it was clearly important to Pa that we succeeded.

Pa told his connections to watch me—that I'd be prime minister one day and I'd probably need help. Little did I know I'd be PM by default and heading up a traveling circus touring around Asia.

We had a pleasant two hours or so, and the children were reportedly angels once again on a tour of the Chitralada Palace School, initially set up to educate members of the Royal Family, but now the most exclusive school in Thailand, with a strictly limited enrollment.

Our itinerary had already been submitted and we were given a list of names. We had morning tea, with a discussion on regional rather than world affairs and realized we had full and unconditional approval. Our progress and achievements to date on our tour of the ASEAN countries were clearly understood, which we found extraordinary.

THE NEXT day our traveling show arrived at Rayong, the epicenter of the Thai motor manufacturing and assembly operations. A huge undertaking representing Japanese, American, European, and Chinese conglomerates, almost all joint ventures with Thai companies. Ranked number twelve in the world by annual volume, it was already a customer of Australia. These operations were price driven and highly competitive, all separate businesses striving for volume and profit, exporting vehicles all over the world, including to Australia.

So we were under no illusions; we would fly the flag and engage at a diplomatic as well as trade level, and then move on.

After a welcome speech from the Thai prime minister, I gave it my best in a short address, outlining our strategy for the future to integrate with Asia, particularly the ASEAN countries, which I felt we'd ignored. I got some curious stares from the General Motors and Ford representatives who seemed dismissive, even patronizing.

I'd just stepped down and felt a tug at my sleeve; a small Thai man introduced himself. I recognized one of the names on the list from Bangkok. He pointed to a small office at the convention center, and I motioned Angela, Eddie, and David to join me.

"Would there be any Australian companies interested in a joint venture producing automotive air conditioners for several of the Japanese manufacturers here?" he asked. A Thai group wanted offshore production as a backup in times of sudden increases in sales volume. There were at least two manufacturers in Australia, one Japanese, one German, and I hoped they had excess capacity. Fortuitously one of the manufacturers was with our group; he was doing nicely so far, having sold domestic refrigerators to Cambodia and Vietnam.

The following day a Memorandum of Understanding was signed, and everything fell into place. Paul Sinclair shook his head in disbelief; I had to tell him it was called relationship marketing. Which it was, several hundred years in the making.

Chiang Mai was just like our hometown, only bigger. A rural city, second only to Bangkok in population, it had been overrun by tourists and retired expats, one of the casualties of that influx being the leather industry. Beautiful handmade stuff with undeniable quality, but more expensive than the cheaper souvenirs that the new wave of visitors preferred. It was time to give something back, I told our contact there, and we all agreed. One of our business people opened up what we hoped would be a permanent supply line into the major top-end retailers in Australia, as well as the volume retailers, because the value of the product was obvious.

Sammy and I decided to give the kids a treat, riding elephants up in the hills. Isobel and Dad elected to have a rest, but Paul and Joan Sinclair enthusiastically accepted our invitation. Kate and Max were fascinated; this was their first experience of these beautiful creatures in the flesh. They were helped onto the howdah by a Thai teenager who laughed at their expressions.

"Show-and-tell at school next term will be different." Sammy laughed.

I pulled him to one side and whispered hoarsely in his ear, "That trunk reminds me of you," and he had the decency to blush.

Paul read my mind if not my lips, and laughed at us, then suggested Joan, Sammy, and Kate ride on the first animal while he was the "captain" on the second, with Max and me.

We strode away in a rolling motion through the jungle. Kate waved to us. Max was too busy hanging on to notice. We crossed the narrow river and Max relaxed; I could see him taking in everything. Our animal stopped at a platform high up in a tree where a Thai family waited with elephant treats for sale.

"Dad," Max said, scandalized, "we already paid, why do we have to pay again?"

Good question, I thought, but Paul couldn't resist the opportunity for a good stir.

"At least someone in the family has a proper fiscal strategy."

We noticed the hordes of tourists increasing through the morning and Paul wondered out loud if camels could ever be a similar draw card.

"In Australia," I said.

"No, here."

"But they're a desert climate type of animal, aren't they?"

"Camels thrive in the tropics as well, particularly in Africa." He'd been talking to a friend in the Northern Territory who farmed camels. "No reason at all why they wouldn't do well here."

Paul located the owner of the elephant park and innocently asked if he'd ever contemplated camel rides and trekking for tourists.

With our contact translating, the owner admitted he had a large tract of wilderness closer to town that would be ideal for such a venture, but he couldn't get camels from the Middle Eastern countries.

"How many would you like?" Paul asked, and I laughed at him, so enthusiastic like a big kid, and also surprised when the operator said "around fifty."

WE ARRIVED at Phuket airport as darkness fell, the absence of a twilight reminding us we were traveling in the tropics. We'd almost booked out the hotel; anyone fronting up to reception next morning was greeted with "Welcome to Australia House." There were quite a few Aussies already there on holiday, and I caused Charlie to crack the shits because I wanted to eat breakfast downstairs with everyone else. So did all the family, so the six of us had our own table with Charlie's blokes at the doors, the same restaurant where, at an outside table, a spaced-out zombie had walloped me, and Sammy had given him a good swinging kick in the nuts. It seemed like a lifetime but it was only about eleven years ago. Where he called me darling and his boyfriend in the one breath for the first time and I felt about eight feet tall. I looked over and he knew what I was thinking. Nothing much had changed; we read each other's minds even better today than we ever did.

I wandered around the tables. It *was* Australia House—at almost every table the athletic singlets, shorts, and flip-flops were in evidence, but it was the accents and the laid-back attitudes that gave them away.

I wondered what I was going to hear and braced myself for criticism. But it was all good, typically laconic comments instead of outright praise. "How much did you blokes pay the television channels? You've been on every morning," one bloke asked.

"Nothing," I said. "I used your money instead." There was a deafening silence, and then the laughter started. The poor bloke must have felt like shit, so I got him a proper coffee and he thanked me.

"You fellas are the first lot of politicians we've ever seen do what they said at the election, and you've done it. That's really, really cool. Even the Liberals seem to be doing better, and they're in opposition."

Other people came up to us, apologizing for interrupting our meal, but we actually enjoyed it. The kids were front and center of everyone's attention but were voraciously attacking their food. Dad and Isobel were just themselves, and I marveled at their dedication to us. So I told everyone who asked that Australia wouldn't run properly without our parents, and they had put in more hours than anyone else through the last few weeks, allowing Sammy and me to get on with it. The crowd had grown to about fifty and the smartphones were everywhere, recording every bloody word I said, but I didn't mind. These people were my masters, I was the servant, not the other way around.

Suddenly I had an idea. "What are you blokes doing tonight?" I asked the front row.

"Probably getting pissed."

"Before you get pissed, why don't you lob over to Phuket Town? I'm addressing the local Chamber of Commerce, and you can see firsthand how we're selling Australia, and how we find out what they need to buy from us in return. And for your information, this is where Sammy and I finally got it all together, where Kate and Max's birth mother lives, and our adopted Thai family have been for many generations. So you can understand how important this place is to us and currently to Australia while I'm still PM."

There was general consensus, a nodding of heads, and I thought a clear understanding of where I was coming from. Most of them were young people and they seemed to acknowledge how important Asia was to our future as a nation, and that pleased all of us, particularly Sammy. I watched with pride as Sammy spoke to them, asking them questions, and finally, what did Asia mean to them. One of the kids at the rear of the group yelled out very clearly, "Waddya mean part of Asia? *We are Asia.*"

THE HUGE portable tent seemed to go on forever, spanning an enormous distance on a vacant block of ground on the edge of Phuket Town quite near Naka weekend market.

The two remaining names on the contact list from Chitralada Palace were naturally from Chart's family, and everything they had done had Pa's touch about it. The preciseness, the guest list, the family itself; everything had a magic about it, but it was our night, this night, and as we arrived and began shaking hands and kissing cheeks, it echoed our engagement party over a decade ago. Chart and Solada had flown in again, and this time I was prepared. They'd sacrificed so much over the years just to be where we were, and I hoped I had the solution. They'd been part of our lives since we were teenagers and had given us far more than they had ever received. We owed them big-time. They always believed in Sammy and me, long before we realized we loved each other.

During the afternoon I'd spoken to Chart and told him what was on my mind. He asked, naturally, if he could talk to Solada about it, and I suggested if he went ahead without her permission, he was a braver man than I was.

There had been a restructure in Angela's department, and the job specification called for someone fluent in written and spoken Thai language, able to commute back and forth between Bangkok and Canberra. Someone with contacts at the highest levels within the Thai government and who could maintain and manage the impetus we'd generated with the tour.

Chart and Solada met me at the edge of the stage. No words were spoken, but it was certainly a "yes." Angela walked over and shook their hands, as did Paul Sinclair. I made it clear to Paul this wasn't just a job for the boys, but the position had gone to someone with all the credentials to do the job efficiently and well. I hadn't followed departmental guidelines and the position hadn't been advertised, but the minister in consultation with me had made the appointment. Paul was kind enough to countersign the papers because he guessed who the principal contact was and realized who had been helping us to yet another successful result.

I looked out across the crowd in front of me, and many of the young people from the breakfast room at the hotel that morning were present.

They were at the back, all nicely dressed, and it looked like social media was working well, because their numbers had increased to probably two hundred people.

Right at the front was my own family. We'd told the kids they could have an early night, but they rebelled. Sammy and I, Isobel, and Dad, and our Thai family surrounded them. Even Natth and Arisa were there, proud of the kids and the road we'd traveled together.

This was our swan song. The displays would be broken down tomorrow; this was the end of our tour, right where my life began in earnest just over a decade ago.

I told the Chamber of Commerce that we in Australia had been mentally and physically lazy over the years, that we'd expected the business to walk in our door, when we should have been chasing it. That for years we'd arrogantly thought of ourselves as colonials, part of the elite, when in fact it was integration with Asia that would bring us prosperity, not relationships with western countries.

BUT IT was the young Australians at the rear of the gathering that made me feel homesick. They were magnificent—raucous, loud but proud. Proud of me, too, as they began bloody chanting "Jacko, Jacko, Jacko," and as Sammy stepped up beside me I wondered how long this would last, because Jesus, I finally got to enjoy this job.

Chapter 57
Home

WHEN WE touched down at Fairbairn Air Force base, the aircraft had covered just under thirty-four thousand kilometers in eight weeks. We were spent, all of us, but a sense of quiet optimism existed among all the group—politicians, public servants, business people, and air crew. We knew we'd done our best, and I told them so as we held a debrief in the Joint Party Room two days later, where Paul Sinclair held up a copy of the *Sydney Morning Herald*. There was a rather fetching cartoon occupying the whole front page, which was so obviously me, complete with Aussie slouch hat, a row of corks to keep the flies away, and my trusty briefcase with Australian goodies popping out of the top. The headline read "JACKO THE TRAVELING SALESMAN," and as Paul held it up the Joint Party Room gave me three bloody cheers, led by Paul and Angela.

I looked at them stupidly, but as Eddie Chi explained to me later, this had never been done before; the concept of a prime minister, cap in hand, looking for business was extraordinary. Some results were apparent already, most were midterm, and some were in the future. But I agreed with Eddie, what really counted was that we'd got off our arses and done it, making an indelible impression on our neighbors.

I was adamant that having made these initial contacts, we had to maintain them—no more long silences. I'd impressed on the ASEAN group that friendship was a two-way street, and we had to keep talking to each other in a disciplined and organized manner, not just when we were doing business with each other.

Angela had already come up with a complete restructure of DFAT—Department of Foreign Affairs and Trade. Simplified and quite dynamic, it had one person at each embassy in each ASEAN country responsible for our ongoing relationship and reporting directly to her, as well as each ambassador. Chart was the first such appointment.

THE MIGRANT Workers Bill went back to the Joint Party Room for some amendments, and to my dismay, there was a shit fight from my own party, despite long and protracted discussions and agreement with the peak union group months ago. So I called a caucus meeting and told them what I planned to do. Unless we had full agreement and voted along the party line, I would have another fireside chat with the nation, name those who were holding up the progress of this important bill, and then announce a snap election.

"You can't do that. That only happens to break a deadlock on supply and fiscal matters," one of the hysterical backbenchers shouted.

"As I've attempted to explain on many occasions," I said patiently, "and all of you were sitting in the Joint Party Room when this legislation was tabled, we are the Land of the Long Weekend. Much of our workforce are just as hardworking and diligent as they ever were. But in those industries where evening and weekend workers are required, such as hospitality, the operators can't get anywhere near enough employees because everyone values their leisure time more, particularly at weekends. The team that has just returned from Asia are all of one voice. We knew this was coming and we planned for it. So did you, because you sat there and said nothing. Now you tell me it's against core socialist values to bring in overseas workers to do the work that our people either can't or won't do. In most cases we simply don't have the *numbers* to get the job done anyway, so you are causing a deadlock in government, and I won't hesitate to bring on an election at a moment's notice. Have a lovely afternoon, I'm going to write my speech."

I turned and walked out of the room, and according to Angela and Jenny, it was pandemonium. Two hours later the leader of the gang of ten, Bernie Fitzgerald, was ushered into my office where he presented an amendment to the proposed legislation that would have made the process so difficult for employers to hire overseas staff, it would render the legislation useless.

"Mrs. Shields," I asked, "could you kindly bring in my television speech for tomorrow night?"

"Certainly, Prime Minister." She passed over the double-spaced notes.

"Just in case you think I'm bluffing, there's the speech, with your name at the top of the list. You'd better check the other names to make sure I've got them right. I wouldn't want to accuse innocent people of the sort of treachery you cunts are perpetuating."

"You can't be serious, you're a maniac. If you went to the people on that basis, you'd lose ten seats."

"But I'd clean up Parliament and start again. We'll win a few more seats anyway, but I'd consider a coalition with the Greens to make up the numbers. At least they'd be more trustworthy than what I've got now."

He glared at me as I laid it on the line.

"You have less than twenty-four hours. We have to book the media no later than 11:00 a.m., so I'll call a caucus meeting for ten o'clock in the morning."

Bernie turned on his heel without a word and literally ran out of the room.

I picked up the phone and spoke to the branches in four states, to people I *could* trust.

Caucus endorsed the legislation the next morning. It went to the House as the first piece of business as the autumn session began. After the second reading, it passed to the Senate and had Royal Assent a few days later. But the dream run for me was over, and I reckoned the next few months would see an upheaval of mammoth proportions as I struggled with the gang of ten.

BUT GLOOM and doom weren't allowed to intrude on the official visit of the prime minister of Singapore and his partner. Jimmy and Sanjay alighted from their special Singapore Airlines flight in Canberra together with nearly fifty family members, the first time the airline had flown directly into Canberra, albeit on a chartered flight.

The Prime Minister's Department had organized all the logistics. It was important for many reasons that this visit demonstrated the new level of respect both countries had for each other since our recent visit to Singapore.

The Singaporean and Australian national anthems played as our flags were raised side by side, and in deference to Singapore's pacifist attitude to defense, there was no guard of honor, just some nice music from the RAAF band as we walked to the cars.

Jimmy and Sanjay were staying with us at the Lodge, and the families were at a nice hotel in town with good security and free transport.

"My family will still complain," Sanjay said with a sigh. "They wanted to be here with us, but I told them to mind their manners. My father can be a pain. He gets upset when his kids appear to have more than he does." Sanjay smiled at us both. "But at least they came along, including my ever-complaining siblings who were hoping I'd stay single forever so I'd look after our parents in their old age. Now they have to share the task."

It was very low-key for a few days in the preparations for the wedding. There was a rehearsal; the female celebrant was highly organized and well prepared. The media kept a respectful distance for once. The tradeoff was that I'd asked Jimmy to address the Parliament the following week, and they could have access to him at the Press Club lunch the following Friday.

The ceremony was low-key with a few Australian dignitaries, including the governor-general and our mates Paul and Joan Sinclair. For most Australians this was situation normal, but for the Singaporean family members it clearly held huge importance as they followed every word of the ceremony.

When Jimmy and Sanjay faced each other to repeat their vows, they lit up everything around them, and Sammy grabbed my hand, forcing me to forget all the ugliness we'd seen recently and reminding me of what was truly important in this world of ours, the love of one human being for another.

THE UGLINESS didn't take long to reassert itself.

It was a joint sitting of the House of Representatives and the Senate that Jimmy was to address, and some of the gang of ten decided they were going to boycott it, Bernie Fitzgerald venting it all to the press.

He didn't think the address was necessary. Singapore wasn't important to Australia anyway, and the fact our Migrant Workers Bill was modeled on Singapore showed how much the prime minister was out of touch with ordinary Australians. In a separate aside to an eager journalist, he said, "the prime minister of Singapore is just another fuckin' poofter anyway."

Suddenly we'd regressed back to old-style politics. What was alarming was that the Liberal Party were all behaving like ladies and gentlemen while my own party were like undisciplined wild animals.

I called a quick caucus meeting and laid down the law: attend the joint sitting or face the consequences. In the end they were all there, not quite certain of what I had in mind in the way of consequences but,

I judged, some were already feeling Bernie Fitzgerald's outburst was intemperate and perhaps ill-advised.

Jimmy was magnificent. His speech undid all of Bernie Fitzgerald's criticism as he outlined the increasing level of business between our countries and the importance of Australia to the ASEAN group.

He praised our concept of the Joint Party Room and our policy of inclusion, ensuring consistent foreign affairs and trade policies in the years to come, regardless of which party was in power.

He also thanked Australia and Australians for their good wishes on the occasion of his marriage, the courtesy and deep understanding on such an important day, something that he and Sanjay would always remember.

"Hear, hear" rang out as the combined Houses rose and warmly applauded him. Bernie Fitzgerald's face registered a mixture of anger and self-doubt. He was uncertain of himself as members around him ignored him, and I wondered how much time I had. This prick had been totally disloyal, and a leopard never changes its spots.

WE HAD one more important task, and that was another wedding, Lucas Bellamy and Jonathan Shields's, also to be held in the garden at the Lodge.

This was much bigger. Around two hundred people, including my brother, sister, and their families, and everyone who knew the Shields family from our hometown.

Together with Jenny I had the honor of giving Lucas in marriage to Jonathan. We all glanced at each other in unspoken communication, because somehow we expected Jason to walk out of the shrubbery.

My attention was drawn back to reality by the celebrant who repeated the giving question, prompting Jenny and me to respond together as we'd rehearsed. We all missed him so much, and yet he was here, all around us as the ceremony proceeded.

None of us felt the slightest bit sad. If anything we felt uplifted and proud of what we'd all achieved since he left us. "He was here, wasn't he, Uncle Jacko?" Lucas stood in front of me, hand in hand with his new husband, the certainty of his convictions reflected in his smile.

I embraced Lucas, and Jonathan joined in for a cuddle. "He certainly was here and I'm not surprised. Neither is your mum. The feeling is still so strong, as if he's transmitting a message, if that doesn't sound off the wall."

Lucas dragged Jonathan closer. "I agree. I have this feeling of warmth, he seemed so pleased with us, and so happy. Did he have a message for you, Uncle Jacko?"

Lucas represented the innocence and wisdom of youth combined, looking forward with hope but prepared for bastardry. "Yes, if there's a message from your dad, it's 'fix the mess the country's in, bitch.'"

The boys laughed, then Lucas smiled his smile of youthful wisdom and whispered, "Dad and I both thought Oliver was gay, but he's got this lovely little woman, and they're so happy."

"And look at you two, confounded the experts, didn't you? You've been given the gift of love. Don't forget to give it a good feed and look after it every day of your life. Uncle Sammy and I are always in your corner if you need us, and that includes funds if you run short as you start your life together."

Jonathan took over. "I think you've done enough already; trade facilitator attached to the embassy in Singapore is a wonderful start for Luc, and I've got a teaching job—my own little Special School in Singapore. But we worry that it may be seen as jobs for the boys."

"Don't worry. You've earned that posting because you guys had better qualifications than all the other applicants. These appointments focus very much on the partnerships of our people in the diplomatic service, and we know your combined resources will be a stunning success. You, Lucas babes, have your mother's tenacity and loyalty, and your late father's work ethic. Jonno, you have a good serve of your mother's brilliant organizational ability and your dad's persistence. So am I worried about jobs for the boys? Hardly. I wish we could replicate you twenty times over. Just don't try too much too quickly, sweethearts, nothing is more important than your partnership. Just keep on loving each other the way you do today, and Uncle Sammy and I will be proud of you. By the way, there was another factor in your appointment."

They looked at me like two lovesick puppies.

"The prime minister of Singapore thought your presence in Singapore an undeniable asset to his plans to introduce same-sex legislation, and he specifically asked if we could help the appointment process along. I told him we didn't have to, you already had the job."

Chapter 58
Treachery

PETER WILLIAMS, the attorney general, waited for me in my office the morning after the Bellamy-Shields wedding and he was perplexed. "Something's not quite right, Jacko," he said. "I just have a feeling there's something really underhand going on. Fitzgerald and his mob are just so smug, all full of smiles, and they're hardly mixing with the other members at all, so I've cast the net wide, as it were, to see if we can catch any little fish."

Just then his phone rang; he apologized but held up his hand, signifying he'd struck pay dirt. He dropped his phone on the desk and shook his head.

"A new political party has just been registered with the Electoral Commission called the Socialist People's Party. They've complied with all the criteria, and they're ready to go. It has to be Fitzgerald and his mob. Christ, Jacko, they must have been at this for months. While you've been traipsing around Asia, working your butt off, these bastards have been signing up enough members of the public to create their own party."

I must have looked stunned, but if I was honest with myself, the signs had been there all along, even back in Jason's time as prime minister.

A courier dropped a printout on Mrs. Shields's desk, and Peter grabbed it. "Look," he said, ticking the names off until he reached ten, "they're all here, the bastards.

"I don't want to upset you further, Jacko, but I recognize some of those other names from Charlie Lim's security briefing on those crazies from Australia for Australians—what lovely bedfellows they'd make."

"Let's give every indication that it's business as usual and hope we can buy some time."

Somehow we ran under the radar so successfully that we were undetected, a great tribute to the state branches who understood the issues completely.

If this news broke, we'd be on the back foot and would never recover, but if we demonstrated decisiveness and a plan for the future, we might stand a chance of survival. Even though I'd called Bernie Fitzgerald's bluff twice in the last few weeks, he controlled ten Labor seats, and if he won them all, we'd probably need a coalition to survive.

I called a caucus meeting for Friday morning, and an hour earlier I came clean with the cabinet, laying out the game plan going forward. Simon Hansen, the party whip, couldn't wipe the smile from his face.

"Well at least someone's having a nice day," I said with a grin back at him.

He looked down for a moment, and I knew every member of cabinet was on the same wavelength.

"Jacko, it will be a pleasure to see this lot go. They've been such a pack of negative, nasty bastards for so long, it will be a relief to get rid of them. And knowing you, it will all be achieved in a most creative manner. This, in the end, will go well for us, because I think you've educated the public so well they will see through them. But I know I speak for us all here, we're behind you 100 percent. You've turned the party into a vibrant modern force in politics, and our enemies hate that. Rip into 'em. And of course there's plenty of press coverage, I hope?"

"Thank you guys, and yes, Simon, there's some wonderful people from the press just around the corner in the hallway waiting."

I ENLISTED Simon Hansen's help to guard the doorway because he could at least identify every one of the ten. By sheer luck Bernie Fitzgerald was the first to arrive and tried to push past Simon with the television cameras waiting. "Sorry, this is a private function."

"Get out of me fuckin' way, Hansen."

"I repeat, this is a private function, and unless you're a member of the Labor Party, you are not allowed inside."

"I am a fuckin' member."

"No, sir, your membership was canceled yesterday."

The screaming, ranting, raging Bernie Fitzgerald was on national television as the remainder of his group arrived and were in turn denied access. Charlie Lim's men were everywhere, big burly blokes just doing their job, with a group of Australian Federal Police standing by. The noise was deafening, the response from the media perfect as they recorded the ugliness. I rang Paul Sinclair first and then Jye Chandler, who were grateful I'd included them in the loop so early.

I SAT in the governor-general's reception room and handed him the document requesting dissolution of the parliament. I'd decided some time ago I didn't like this prick very much. An ex-Army man, he was clearly socially conservative, and for that reason alone I didn't trust him. I'd watched him at Jimmy and Sanjay's wedding, and the expression on his face and that of his horsey wife was of sheer discomfort and displeasure.

"Oh, I think you're taking the only avenue possible, Mr. Collins-Smith. We can't have this sort of business going on, and it's not at all parliamentary."

I'd had enough. "Don't patronize me."

The GG sat bolt upright, as if he'd copped a rocket up his clacker.

"There is no question of supply being threatened, and we have several months of our term to run. This has been my decision in consultation with cabinet and the Leader of the Opposition. I don't need advice from you or anyone else on this matter. Just ensure you don't exceed your authority. I've discussed your stance on several subjects with Mr. Sinclair, and that has been communicated to the Palace, a true exercise in bipartisanship."

The GG went pale, I noted with satisfaction. For the Leader of the Opposition and myself to put together a memo to the Palace was probably unheard of in Commonwealth history, except perhaps for the sacking of the Whitlam government in 1975.

"How dare you," he snapped. "I've carried out my duties to the letter."

"That you have," I said. "It's your other duties that concern us, like your semisecret association with Australia for Australians. Their behavior is verging on sedition and you're almost an office bearer."

"I suppose you want me to resign."

"No, it's much safer to have you here where we can keep an eye on you. Oh, and don't try anything stupid. There's been a twenty-four-hours-a-day, seven-days-a-week watch on you for some time, and that will continue. Good morning."

As THE campaign was already underway, there was no way I could expect the taxpayer to foot the bill for my final fireside chat, but the national executive stepped up to it without a murmur. "Better advertising than a month of print media," the national president said, "and your audience awaits you."

I began my presentation by laying out my reasons for going early, and my desire to make clear decisions without pressure from the press. By now it was common knowledge around the world that I had a revolt on my hands, and that was the way I presented it. Part of my own party who were making plans to split off separately and who had close links with an organization that was verging on the illegal.

"And while we must always honor free speech and free thinking as part of the democratic process, in a political party, loyalty and the desire to operate as a cohesive group must override everything else. This particular group of ten members have been afforded the freedom of caucus and the freedom of the Joint Party Room to express their views, yet they've chosen to express those views outside of those forums, without giving their colleagues the benefit of debate, but instead taking those views directly to the press. They leave me no alternative but to call a general election. The names of these members and the electorates are as follows."

I read the names out dispassionately, and when I finished, I made the comment that there wasn't one female among them.

"If there had been, then maybe we wouldn't be involved in this exercise at this time, instead allowing Parliament to run its full term. Sadly the whole exercise has lowered the tone once more of Australian politics. Now we are criticizing a few of our own party members who would try to bring down the government because our previously agreed agenda doesn't suit them. In all cases those members have been suspended from the Labor Party and their membership revoked. We will stand candidates of high quality to replace these people. We'll simply be asking you to vote for the Labor Party as usual, not the Socialist People's Party, as this group calls itself."

I asked the public to remember the highlights of the past two and a half years; how as a nation we'd grieved together after Jason Bellamy died, but we'd picked ourselves up and got on with the job as he would have expected. And how, with the cooperation of all political parties, we reinvented the parliamentary system with the Joint Party Room, which had delivered stable and efficient government like never before. And then, with bipartisan support, how we toured the ASEAN nations, making invaluable contacts and showcasing Australian trade into the future.

I LEFT the parliamentary studio and was driven straight to the Lodge where Sammy, the kids, Dad, and Isobel were waiting, together with Craig Watkins, the campaign director.

Charlie Lim followed me in. My phone was ringing its head off, so I forwarded it on to Mrs. Shields. Charlie looked on with approval; for once he was nearly guaranteed of my 100 percent attention. The kids were sent to ready themselves for bed, but Charlie wanted all the adults in the dining room, for reasons best known to himself.

"You will recall," Charlie said, totally without humor, "some months ago when we forced you to sit down in this very room and listen to a briefing. I said to you there was a worrying societal trend across the country, and we actually briefed cabinet and the Joint Party Room on the ramifications of that trend before we toured Asia."

We all nodded.

"Well the risk is now real, Jacko, that someone will try to take a potshot at you, during or even after the election campaign. You see, the Socialist People's Party see themselves as born to rule. They're very poor losers. They see anyone in their way as quite expendable. I warn you, they would rather murder you than even fight an election campaign. To them it's a means towards an end."

Dad and Isobel were horrified, but Sammy was resolute, and Craig must have wondered what sort of a campaign he'd have to run if I were to be kept behind a bulletproof shield.

Sadly it wasn't new to Sammy and me. While my family were hearing about this threat for the first time, we'd discussed at length the issues involved and agreed I should continue on.

Charlie was always serious—it was his job—and he tended to exaggerate the dangers so we'd listen to him. "As we expected, they've informally joined forces with Australia for Australians, which just makes a bad scenario worse. This mob is predictable because their only policies are all negative, anti-Asia and Asian, anti–black people, anti-same-sex couples, anything that's not white Anglo-Saxon/Celtic, but unfortunately their methods are anything but predictable, and there are some big names involved, as you know." I thought of the slimy governor-general.

"At the moment we can keep the lid on the pricks. We think there are about three thousand scattered around the country. The real danger is if they try to have a rally or a convention, then I'd be asking the Army for help.

"Jacko, you've always been such a man of the people, which is admirable in a politician, but we look around and suddenly you're on a ride-on mower, a garbage truck, or just talking away to the workers. You have to moderate this part of your behavior and understand that these loonies hate you and see you as the enemy within. You tick all the boxes for them. I don't want to be the one to deliver you home to Sammy in a body bag just because you wouldn't do as you were told by me or by Sammy. I think Sammy made the point last time, you were to listen to me 'or progress through life alone.'"

I put my head down as I suddenly realized how vulnerable we were, just because we were running for public office. Dad crystalized everything for me again when he asked ever so gently, "Mate, do you want to give it away, and just keep you and your family safe?"

"No," Sammy interrupted. "The bastards aren't going to get away with this. We're going to win this election." And for the first time that night, Craig Watkins smiled.

I would do as Charlie told me and stay safe, but we were going to run it up to them.

Chapter 59
The War of Words

IT BEGAN like an avalanche; the language and the mindset of the Socialist People's Party sounded like a throwback to the attitudes of yesteryear, and the press loved it, allowing the verbiage to pour unchecked across the nation's dailies and on electronic media alike. The public must have been aghast at the noisy headlines, the personal attacks, and the thinly veiled hints of violence. In the space of a few days, it was clear this election wasn't going to be about policies, but about politicians who hated more than they loved. The only policies the SPP had to talk about were all negative: anti-Asia, including jobs for Australians; anti-Asians; anti-same-sex people and couples. Every time the same-sex discussion was raised, Australians were turned off in droves, and it showed immediately in the polls. But for some subliminal reason, anti-Asian historically had traction with some people, and we knew we had to find a way around it. We knew from our research that it had been a myth perpetrated by former Liberal leaders who won elections based on fear of "the yellow hordes" flooding the nation in their war canoes, which was bullshit because the overwhelming number of refugees were from the Middle East.

But the Migrant Workers Act wasn't helping that argument, even though I'd already explained to the nation the reasons we needed them as the economy grew. But there was a silver lining: the Liberal Party was in absolute agreement with us on all the Asian issues, as were the Greens, so the SPP had isolated themselves on the most strident of their policies.

WE DECIDED to dive in at the deep end—in the seat of Arrowsmith, west of Brisbane, and currently occupied by none other than Bernie Fitzgerald himself. It was traditionally Labor, but the voter profile was changing with a lot of self-employed people and white-collar workers supplementing the blue-collar brigade, so I hoped fervently that it would help us.

As we arrived my worst fears were realized with a good-sized crowd waiting for us outside. There was shouting, a few placards, but not all were derogatory, which gave me some hope. Sammy noticed as well. There was one huge sign that said Welcome Jacko and Sammy, and we relaxed a little; clearly that meant we were appreciated as a couple and our policies weren't on the nose with everyone, despite Bernie trying to make this the "heartland of hatred."

"Charlie's Angels," as we christened them—our security guys— cleared the way as we made our way inside, rotten eggs flying through the air, missing their target, but we didn't miss the silent stares from around twenty thugs gathered near the front door, obviously put there to intimidate.

What happened next was something I'll always remember, all of my political life. It taught me to have more confidence in myself, to listen more closely to Sammy, who was always able to read public sentiment faster and more accurately than most opinion polls. He'd had his ear to the ground and most of it was positive. "You underestimate the feeling of affection the public have for you. No one else has that combination of image and trust," he said, "but there will be obvious questions to answer."

We walked in and my first impression was how many people were packed into the auditorium. There was standing room only, unusual for a public meeting these days. We were asked to pause inside the doorway, and then the president of the Queensland Branch roared out, "Ladies and gentlemen, the Labor candidate for the seat of Arrowsmith, Mr. Ben Cashion."

There was polite clapping as our new candidate walked onstage, a handsome heterosexual father of two, with his own accountancy firm. Very high profile and from a traditional Labor family, he'd been shocked at Bernie Fitzgerald's actions and put his hand up the moment nominations were called. Ben's wife was from Malaysia, and they traveled back there regularly to keep in touch with her family. His interface and experience with Asia were unmatched in the electorate.

"And now, ladies and gentlemen, the man of the moment, our prime minister, Jackson Collins-Smith."

All eyes turned toward us, and even the elderly and infirm struggled to their feet as the electorate of Arrowsmith gave us a rousing Labor welcome. They continued to applaud; there were handshakes, pats on the back, kisses on the cheek, and it took us nearly ten minutes to reach the stage, where I finally shook Ben's hand.

I spoke first, followed by Ben, but I sensed a restless mood in the audience and asked the MC if I could have the microphone again.

"I know there are questions about our performance you'd like answered, so I'm at your service to hopefully put your mind at rest that Australia is progressing in the right direction."

"Why are you so close to the Liberal Party?" one old stalwart asked.

"It might appear we are, but I can assure you we have never deviated past the central policy guidelines of the annual conference. Yes, we're closer to the people in the Liberal Party and the National Country Party than before, but our policies remain our own. We created the Joint Party Room to clean up Parliament, and it has. All the bullshit and the fighting goes on in there instead of dragging down the dignity of the House of Representatives, but I can assure you we fight hard for every piece of business that goes through.

"Paul Sinclair is a good bloke, and ever since the death of our former prime minister, he's been really supportive of me and our legislative program, which Jason Bellamy originally put in place. I asked him to be part of the recent trade mission to the ASEAN countries because it showed our Asian neighbors we were serious and looking to the future when the cycle will inevitably turn and perhaps our political opponents will be in government. So it was an Australian delegation, not a political one. Does that answer your question?"

"Yes, thank you so much, I understand, and good luck."

"Why give our kids' jobs away to Asian people?" A woman, very senior in years, snapped the question at me and I recognized Cheryl Chambers, a former member of the New Zealand Parliament, who had ridden the anti-Asian ticket all those years ago. Her racist comments failed to get anyone on either side of the Tasman Sea to take her seriously for many years—until now, with the advent of the SPP and Australia for Australians.

"Cheryl," I said, "how lovely to see you again. I would've been disappointed if you hadn't shown up the moment we started talking about Asia." The crowd chuckled, but she wasn't amused. She sat at the end of the fourth row from the front, and the media were just meters away, all nicely prearranged so she got maximum exposure.

Two of us can play at this game went through my mind as our crew pushed closer to get us in shot. "Fancy you joining a meeting of the party faithful, I thought the Labor Party was beneath your dignity. You must have really wanted to listen to our policies. Can we interest you in a membership?"

She took the bait immediately, and so here I was, the prime minister of Australia, sworn to pacifist politics, in the middle of a slanging match with a harridan from the past, smoked out of her snake hole with an opportunity to vent her pet hatred of Asia and Asian people. I should've guessed she'd be involved; the profile of the SPP and Australia for Australians suited her perfectly.

Sammy nodded, which meant "go ahead," and Craig just looked terrified. I was over it. I hated the position I'd been placed in, and I hated the way the Labor Party had been treated by a group of villains from within. The media were there anyway, and I hoped I'd get a fair run. I knew I could make or break the campaign by taking old Cheryl on, but I was tired and I'd had enough lies, exaggerations, and bullshit to last me a lifetime.

"You bring in this Migrant Workers Act and my kids can't get a job."

"Your kids must be late forties or fifties now, Cheryl, and they still can't get a job? Come on, love, I don't reckon they want to work."

The crowd warmed up. Cheryl's kids would indeed be bludgers if they still didn't have a job.

"I still say you shouldn't bring in one Asian person if there's a single Australian out of work."

"I agree, Cheryl, but we have hotels and resorts all over the country desperate for night and weekend staff in all departments, and our kids refuse to work those hours even with double time on weekends and holidays. So they're now able to bring in workers from Asia in anticipation of a high level of interest in tourism since our recent trip there and pay them equivalent wages. We also have vast amounts of primary produce to harvest, crops like stone fruit that can only be harvested by hand. Farmers have found it impossible to get labor in the bush, when we've generated some useful extra volume with our trade delegation. If we get the orders, we must deliver. We won't get the same opportunities again."

"What a waste of taxpayers' money that was, flying all over the place, all show and no go."

"Well, Cheryl, sweetheart, I'm pleased to advise we've actually done some deals that no one thought we had a chance at. It was simply a case of asking for the order. Next week I hope the treasurer will announce an improved rate of growth in the economy with a corresponding fall in the unemployment rate as a direct result of our focus on the ASEAN nations."

Cheryl was clearly rattled. For every accusation, I had a commonsense and factual answer, so she descended into the gutter, confirming her time was well past and certainly wasn't an asset to either the SPP or Australia for Australians.

"Well I think it's dreadful, you dragging your homosexual lifestyle all over the place. Australia needs some nice normal people to run the country, not faggots like you."

"I hesitate to dignify your remarks by responding to them, except to say that several people quite close to you would be horrified at your remarks."

"Yes, but they're not running the country."

The room fell quiet as I smiled benignly at dear old Cheryl.

"But surely that's the point, Cheryl. Australians couldn't care less about people's lifestyles, and if anyone wishes to become prime minister they could do so, even without your permission." The crowd giggled as Cheryl's face turned a nasty purple color.

"I repeat, Australia remains the land of opportunity. I was born dyslexic and was struggling until I met my then future husband. I've managed to rise to the top job in this country by being part of a wonderful partnership, and until now not one person has brought that aspect of my life into question, and neither should they. Thank you, ladies and gentlemen, for your kind attention and your support. I would be grateful if you would throw your support behind Ben Cashion as the endorsed Labor candidate."

I reached for Sammy's hand as we stepped down from the stage, smiling briefly at Cheryl Chambers as the crowd jumped to their feet, generous in their applause, which roared in our ears as we made our way to the door. Charlie's Angels seemed more relaxed leaving compared to our arrival. Outside, the egg throwers and placard wavers had dispersed, the television cameras recording every positive moment.

At home that night in our electorate of Hinchcliffe, we watched the television news as Cheryl Chambers destroyed her remaining credibility and severely damaged the electoral chances of the SPP.

The exchange between Cheryl and me not only truthfully answered the major questions about our performance but also undermined the rationale of Bernie Fitzgerald and his treacherous mates.

The footage was so good that our advertising agency spliced most of it into the commercial at the center of the campaign, and Craig Watkins had a permanent smile on his face.

We visited the other nine seats as a priority, then the further twenty seats around the country that had SPP candidates standing.

Then we crisscrossed our way around the country, making sure we covered all the important seats where we had a chance of knocking off the Liberals or the National Country Party or simply had to defend what we already had.

It was halfway through the campaign when my phone shrilled. "How're you going, bitch face?" Paul Sinclair yelled, as I held the offending instrument as far away as possible. "Make sure you have tomorrow's papers, all of 'em," he said, then hung up.

Typical Paul, I thought. He reminded me of Jason so much at times, particularly when he called me a bitch. But he was an enduring friend, a kind, thoughtful, and loyal bloke, who just happened to head up our parliamentary opposition in coalition with the National Country Party. He admitted one drunken night when we were discussing the formation of the Joint Party Room that the Coalition was an uneasy alliance, even tenuous, and the more the Labor Party took the initiative in Asia with primary produce, the unhappier the NCP had become.

"The Game Gets Interesting" roared the headline in Melbourne's volume daily paper. But the headline "Liberals' Preferences Go to Labor" got my attention. The national executive of the Liberal Party had given us their preferences in all seats where the Socialist People's Party had candidates. The NCP had gone in the opposite direction, which wasn't surprising.

And Jye Chandler had simply directed the Greens' preferences to us in every seat around Australia.

It was the best news we'd had since the launch, and I rang Paul to thank him, and Jye soon after. Our preferential system of voting ensures that the candidate who is most preferred or least disliked will win. Clearly the Liberals wanted the Socialist People's Party eliminated.

They handed us a powerful extra margin in those seats held by the gang of ten, and we wondered if this was enough to push us over the line nationally.

A PICKET line appeared outside our home the next day. If it had been the Lodge, then that would be not unexpected, or even our Canberra house, if we'd been living there. But outside our own home where we'd grown up together, where Sammy and I had spent the most pivotal years of our life together, where we'd brought our kids home as babies, where we'd all felt safe and nurtured.

And yet here were these horrible people, filled with hate, protesting that I didn't somehow fit the mold of a working man, which was wrong, insulting, and hurtful.

It was Sammy, as usual, who got my head right. I marveled at his strength and loyalty under pressure and his focus on priorities. After explaining to the kids in straightforward, adult language what the picket line was about, we had an early night—a near impossibility during an election campaign. Sammy wanted to talk in bed. "You should be really proud of yourself, Jacko."

"Why? With Australian workers parked on our doorstep, I feel like a traitor to the cause."

"They're there because you've been effective in your communication. The Socialist People's Party don't have an answer to your policies, hence the poor workers displaced by your policies, looking for sympathy."

I listened and racked my brains, but I couldn't find a solution.

My other half smiled in the half-light. "They probably parked their Mercedes and BMWs in the next street, poor things. Let's give them a nice brekky in the morning."

I really thought Sammy had lost it, but when the kids, Dad, Isobel, Sammy, and I carried out plates of bacon, eggs, toast, and cups of coffee, we got a chance to talk to them.

They were amazed as my family sat down on the footpath with them and we enjoyed breakfast together, giving me a chance to spell out our policies again.

A media contingent arrived, and we tried to disappear discreetly, but the protesters wanted us to stay. We had some lovely footage, and we became the victims, much to the annoyance of the SPP.

It became too close to call again; the opinion polls had the Liberals ahead one day, us the next. There were all sorts of models created using the influence of the SPP, and that just complicated the central issue. Who did Australians want in their government? A coalition of Labor and the Greens, or even a coalition of ourselves and the Liberals. And the Nationals seemed to wax and wane daily. What was clear was that the Nationals' vote was going to be well down, voters seemingly deserting them. In an extraordinary piece of electoral history, National Country Party voters appeared to be leaving their own party and voting for us, simply because we'd got off our arses and created markets for primary produce in the ASEAN countries.

We had a few days to go when Eddie Chi rang me. It wasn't like Eddie to display emotion because of his Chinese background, but he was stuttering with excitement. "Boss," he yelled, "the last quarter figures are in. The economy grew by 6.5 percent, annualized that will bring us up to 4.5 percent! Next quarter I predict will be even higher, and the best news of all, unemployment has gone back to 3.5 percent, even with the Migrant Workers Act in force."

The final part of the puzzle was in place, our management of the economy was now unquestioned, and Craig Watkins reacted swiftly. He threw Eddie and me into a television commercial with some simple charts, and it was on air the next day with a heavy frequency. A press release hit even earlier and made the early editions of papers around the country, and I finally relaxed. We'd done the best we could.

Chapter 60
Triumph

I REFUSED to go to Canberra for the result. I overrode the objections; it may have been traditional, but in this era of electronic wizardry, I felt I could be just as effective at home in my own electorate. I felt at home here, and a little guilty also, that my duties as prime minister had kept me away from Hinchcliffe much more than I cared to be. It was important to recognize the several thousand people who had voted for me, as well as Peter Prentice, Jock Fleming, Matt and Scott, and the campaign team who worked tirelessly through two parliamentary terms and three election campaigns. The national broadcaster with Bryan Friedman as lead commentator had decided that they'd set up a national television link on election night from Hinchcliffe, and that suited us fine. After the treachery of national politics, I needed all the good mates around me I could find.

SAMMY AND I arrived quite early with our family. Most of the campaign team was already in place, with Jock Fleming challenging the doubtful votes at the top of his voice. Bryan Friedman made the transition from radio to television seamlessly, and we submitted to some basic makeup, much to the amusement of our daughter and son.

Ninety minutes after the polls closed, I claimed victory in Hinchcliffe with a slightly improved majority apparent in the counting so far. Sammy and I walked over to Bryan Friedman, and I spoke on national television.

"This is the sweetest victory of all, not because we trounced the other parties, but because the people of Hinchcliffe have given me their trust in three consecutive elections. I apologize for my long absences in Canberra and overseas, but as you know, I've been quite busy. I've tried to compensate for those long absences with regular visits from my staff, so hopefully you don't feel neglected. You've handed me a magnificent victory in Hinchcliffe, and I assure you that isn't taken lightly. I remain at your service, and I thank you. May I also thank our campaign team for their untiring efforts, and my family, particularly Sammy for his unselfish support and love."

But it wasn't the case elsewhere in the nation as the eastern states' figures came up on the screen linked to the national figures. Then two hours in, we waited with bated breath as the seats of the gang of ten flashed up on the screen. The first was Arrowsmith, Bernie Fitzgerald's seat, where we'd clearly won on first preferences, not needing the assistance of the Liberals or the Greens. It wasn't so easy in some of the other seats, but we steadily overhauled the SPP as the night wore on.

It was nearly 10:00 p.m. when the game suddenly changed.

Four NCP seats fell to us in a row: one in Victoria, one in New South Wales, and two in Queensland. Then the outlook brightened in the seats we already held, thanks to the preferences from the Greens, and by 10:15 p.m. I knew we'd won.

I rang Angela, and she agreed we could form a government with a majority of at least six seats. Then Paul Sinclair rang and conceded defeat; he wished me luck and confirmed what we already knew, voters had savaged the SPP. Only one seat was in doubt. The Liberals had held their own, as had the Greens, and our increased margin had come at the expense of the Nationals, an extraordinary achievement.

Bryan Friedman beckoned us over. I took Sammy's hand and we made our way to the broadcast podium, with the nation looking on.

"My fellow Australians, I've just spoken to my friend Paul Sinclair, the Leader of the Federal Opposition. He conceded defeat and wished us well in our new term in office. The support of the Liberal Party in directing preferences to us over the Socialist People's Party is pivotal to our success and is evidence of the improved working relationship between all parties.

"But I wish to thank the rank and file of the Australian Labor Party for standing by us and rejecting the extreme politics of hatred and division. I thank the other factions within the parliamentary party, who ignored the approaches of the SPP and created history, joining together with unaligned members in a show of strength, demonstrating to the public we were worthy of being elected because we cared more for stable and productive governance than just fighting among ourselves. That we'd listened to the people who had elected us."

After the broadcast closed for the night, I pulled Bryan to one side for a serious one-on-one. We'd spoken regularly and in confidence over the preceding months on a what-if scenario if we were elected. Cabinet were in agreement, if a little on their guard with his sharp tongue! When I confirmed he could transfer his superannuation, that we would help with moving expenses, and then casually mentioned a salary figure, he didn't hesitate.

He didn't wait for the salary; he was instantly enthusiastic and committed as my PPS—principal press secretary—working next to Barbara Shields. He was a great bloke, he'd been a practicing solicitor early in his career, and a successful journalist in his own right. He'd make a wonderful resource, but above all he understood Sammy and me as a couple. After the confrontation with Cheryl Chambers during the campaign, Sammy and I had talked at length. We realized there were still young same-sex-attracted people in our society subject to homophobic abuse, and Bryan would make sure no opportunity was missed to promote Australian family values like never before, including eradication of domestic violence and homophobia from our vocabulary.

DAD AND Isobel had taken the kids home as soon as I claimed victory, and after circulating at the party for an hour or so, we were told to leave by Matt and Scott. Because we looked like we felt: totally spent, both of us emotionally and physically drained.

Tomorrow I had to be back in Canberra, the cabinet had to be finalized, and we had to be sworn in later in the week. I sighed, and Sammy arched one eyebrow as he always did. "Once I was the most forgiving of all people," I said, "but if political life has taught me anything, it's to watch those who let you down, because a leopard never changes its bloody spots and they'll do it again."

"Darls, I agree, politics is an unforgiving profession for those that expect everyone to be trustworthy and reliable, so your heightened sense of awareness is not a character flaw on your behalf, but an appropriate response to bastardry."

We sat in the dining room at home, enjoying a hot chocolate before bed. He took my hand and kissed my fingers, something he knew both calmed and excited me, if that was possible. I certainly knew its effect in my case.

"You're also the most modest of all people, and the voters love that in you. You're never boastful, yet you've achieved more than most people in their lifetime. You took over after poor Jason died, ran the country, led a trade expedition to Asia, fought off a challenge from within the party, and you've just led the Labor Party to victory, so you're finally prime minister in your own right. How about going easy on yourself for a change? Just for tonight reflect on where we began and where we are now: Leonardo da Vinci, Albert Einstein, Alexander Graham Bell, Sir Richard Branson, Walt Disney, Jay Leno, Whoopi Goldberg, Nelson Rockefeller, Agatha Christie, Steven Spielberg, Harry Belafonte, Winston Churchill, Richard Strauss."

I'd been yabbering those names parrot fashion since I was ten years old, and we both knew them by heart. Every day I was reminded of my dyslexia with some difficulty or other, but because of Sammy, Barbara Shields, Dad, and Isobel, and several other people, including most of the cabinet, I was able to continue doing what I did best.

But I took Sammy's point. I was too critical of myself sometimes, focusing on my weaknesses instead of my strengths.

We'd showered and were in our own bed in our real home, the same bed in which we spent every night of our early life together, and suddenly I wasn't tired anymore as his hand found what he was looking for.

Chapter 61
Everything Old Is New Again

I AWOKE the next morning to a knock on the door as Dad threw the Sunday papers on the bed. Sammy for once slept on, no doubt the exertion of the night before demanding a little more time in the land of Nod. I reflected on how hard he'd worked. My timetable was regularly eclipsed by his activities: he was a board member on three not-for-profit organizations, plus he was still a guest lecturer at two universities specializing in remedial education.

Yet he was there for the kids when I couldn't be, and I remained in awe of his organization and dedication to our little family. It wouldn't be long, I thought, before the door would burst open and two kids would be on our bed, neither of them with any hang-ups over half or completely naked parents. They just loved us unreservedly.

I glanced down at the headlines. Where else in the world would there be such an unpretentious society as Australia, where the prime minister was known best by his nickname?

"Jacko!" simply said the Melbourne paper; another said "Jacko By a Country Mile" referring to the decimation of the Nationals. Yet another said "Jacko Election Triumph" and another, "Jacko Sweeps Clean" and "SPP Routed, Jacko Wins."

But there was a piece by Bryan Friedman on page three in the Melbourne paper in his final piece as a freelance journalist and clearly warming up for his role as principal press secretary. He reminded Australians enjoying their morning coffee that while policies and leadership were important in the historic victory of the previous day, there was another factor: a successful partnership between two people, Jacko and Sammy Collins-Smith. He discussed the abuse leveled at us by Cheryl Chambers and the thinly veiled insults from Australia for Australians and the Socialist People's Party in particular, which had the opposite effect in the ballot box than they intended.

And on it went. Sammy's eyelids fluttered and he smiled at the headlines, but spent a little more time on page three.

I slipped into the en suite, then walked back to the bed, locking the door on the way, and deposited the newspapers on the floor. "Priorities," I said, throwing the covers off and demonstrating my feelings for the person I loved more than life itself.

A few hours later, we were back in Canberra and the meetings began. I had to finalize the cabinet but I wanted consensus from the inner cabinet.

Angela would continue as deputy prime minister and foreign minister, but with a trade minister reporting to her and focusing on our emerging markets in the ASEAN group. Eddie Chi would continue as treasurer, Ron Hoy in Agriculture, David Carlisle in Industry and Science, Grace Anderson in Education and Training, and Peter Williams as attorney general.

These were my trusted colleagues. They'd stood by me and the government through triumph and tragedy, and I thanked them for it. We'd worked together so closely over the years, there were no secrets, no hidden agendas, and no factional fighting, unique in the Westminster system. Beginning with Jason Bellamy, ministers were appointed on ability, not because they belonged to a factional group, and the poll result proved that factions working together was an election-winning strategy.

I asked for a reshuffle of the inner cabinet itself, shifting things around, transferring responsibilities to allow for the creation of a new portfolio without increasing the overall numbers. The new position was special minister of state—responsible for our input into the Joint Party Room. Jenny Bellamy was the obvious choice; her natural expertise as Moderator was a prime reason for the early success of the JPR. None of us ever dreamed Jenny was so strong-willed, disciplined, and downright aggressive when she had to be.

Angela wanted Ben Cashion, the new member for Arrowsmith, as her assistant and trade minister, and we agreed—his knowledge of Asia was an asset.

Next was Simon Hansen, the party whip, who I wanted as cabinet secretary, and once again there was universal agreement.

Finally we adjourned for an hour so I could make calls and confirm we had acceptance of all the positions.

PETER WILLIAMS and I sat together facing our colleagues, who looked puzzled, and I didn't blame them. This should have been the high point of their political careers, yet Peter and I faced them looking quite solemn.

I asked Peter to present the facts, and he did so with legal precision.

"We have a governor-general who has broken every rule in the book and created a legal precedent. There is irrefutable evidence that he's been involved with Australia for Australians ever since its inception, yet he never declared his involvement prior to accepting his appointment. Moreover he's been increasingly active and very careless publicly about his opinions regarding the bona fides of the organization. Australia for Australians is about to be declared a terrorist organization, and therefore his continuance as our head of state is probably unlawful, unconstitutional, and certainly undesirable. The boss and the Leader of the Opposition advised Buckingham Palace in a joint communication before the election that his tenure should be canceled, but agreed to delay his removal because such an action may have been destabilizing for all the wrong reasons at such a pivotal time."

The looks on my colleagues' faces underscored the seriousness of the situation. "He resigned, effective yesterday, but before he did so he appointed the chief justice as his deputy to officiate at the swearing-in, at my request."

"Makes you wonder why we need a GG at all, doesn't it?" As my deputy, Angela was the only other person in the loop.

Peter Williams handed everyone present copies of a file on our dear GG, put together by the Federal Police.

"The bastard." Eddie Chi, mortified at the information in front of him, gave vent to his feelings, and the others were similarly shocked.

The details were concise. General Austin Hay, retired Governor-General of Australia, had maintained his local network of allies as well as his international military contacts around the world after his retirement from the Army and his appointment as governor-general. He had no time for weakness in any form, and he wanted to see his country strong militarily, remain part of the British Commonwealth, and totally independent of Asia. Furthermore he wanted a strong Christian government demonstrating Christian values, free of "lefties, parasites, and homosexuals, which had the capacity to weaken the gene pool going forward."

The hundreds of e-mails were damning. General Hay, as with many criminals before him, had a righteous view on life strengthened by his former rank in the Army and his belief in Christ, so he viewed his activities as not only legal but necessary for the betterment of the nation. So he'd become less than discreet—quite careless, in fact—allowing his views to occasionally be reported in the press, albeit a sanitized version, which initially spiked Charlie Lim's interest, leading to an investigation by the Federal Police. Hay's understanding of and deep involvement with Australia for Australians was frightening; he was advising them how to set up the organization on a paramilitary model. The next step would be to supply them with arms.

"As you can see, while our dear friend was quite delusional, he's caused us some embarrassment overseas in the United Kingdom in particular, and to a lesser extent in the United States. What we have, however, is a list of people we can round up and prosecute from Australia for Australians, plus people from our own defense forces, and a further group who we are turning over to other countries involved to allow them to deal with them as they see fit."

"What are we going to do with the arsehole?" Ron Hoy asked through his teeth.

"I honestly don't know at this stage because as these prosecutions proceed, he'll be involved in each one of them, if not personally, then through his e-mails as evidence. I feel for the public. They have a right to expect that an elected government should be able to proceed with what they were elected to do, without the distraction of idiots playing toy soldiers."

Angela spoke with force and feeling. "Jacko, you've done everything right, and if this issue is handled correctly, this could and should be seen as a positive for us. You're in the process of clearing out the rot in the ship's bloody timbers as we're setting sail for another three years. Captains have to ensure the fucking ship doesn't sink before it leaves shore, for Christ's sake, so stop worrying. Is this bastard secure?"

Peter Williams's eyes sparkled at Angela's analogies.

"Yes, as first mate you can set sail," he said with a laugh. "He's under house arrest in Melbourne."

"Good," said Angela. "Jacko, why don't you give the facts to Bryan Friedman? Now he's principal press secretary, he'll know exactly how to handle it, with our approval of course."

Chapter 62
Setting Sail

CHIEF JUSTICE Samesh Banerjee officiated at the swearing-in, his presence alone demonstrating the progressive integration of Australia into the Asian landscape. But anyone was preferable to the former incumbent. From the outset I'd refused point-blank to have Hay anywhere near the process, and as the evidence built against him, I was relieved I'd been decisive.

I'd spoken to Paul Sinclair on the matter every day since I realized Australia had a problem—a criminal governor-general—and Paul had been totally supportive, even though it had been his party who had appointed General Hay in the first place. We'd written the letter to Buckingham Palace together, united in our concern, advising caution until we had all the facts at our disposal. The tempting, easy way out would have allowed him to continue as governor-general, invent a mystery "illness," and have him graciously retire from public life, never to be seen again, which in Hay's case would be unlikely.

The bastard was a criminal, and I was determined to bring him to justice, even if the whole horrible episode tainted the victory of the new government. We had to act quickly because his absence from the swearing-in ceremony would be immediately noticed. We worked at it for hours, trying to devise a strategy, but none worked. Paul Sinclair had been invited and Jye Chandler, as well as the inner cabinet.

Bryan Friedman sat impassively at the end of the table, absorbing all the comments and ideas. He looked at us all and suddenly banged his knuckles on the timber surface for attention. "Listen," he said in his steady, modulated voice, which often sent shivers up the spine of his interviewees. "It doesn't matter how you package it, it's still shit. You can wrap it up in fancy paper to make it look better, but it still stinks. Sooner or later it gets stuck under your fingernails if you try to manipulate it. There is a very wise man called Peter Collins-Smith, Jacko's lovely Dad, who once said to me, 'when in trouble, tell the truth,' and that's what I propose we do. The public have come to expect that of you, Jacko, and you won't have any trouble if you stick to the facts. I'll prepare a very comprehensive press release for your approval, which I suggest is distributed to your ASEAN countries first as a matter of courtesy, then of course the remainder of the western nations, and Europe, and South America. The only reason this hasn't become news already is because feral investigative journalists don't exist at the moment out of respect for you, Jacko."

I nodded at Bryan. There were smiles all around the table.

I had to stand firm and see justice done. I'd expected it of our Asian neighbors, and now it was our turn to be open and transparent about what we did. There was no doubt the ASEAN countries would approve. General Hay was lucky the offences were committed in Australia; some of our ASEAN mates wouldn't think twice about applying the death penalty.

"On the issue of timing," I said, "I want to call a special meeting of the Joint Party Room first, then make my public announcement a few minutes later." Paul and Jye nodded in agreement, and, I thought, appreciation.

BRYAN FRIEDMAN'S judgment was correct, but the facts clearly shocked the nation and overseas. We'd been a very laid-back society until the Islamist fundamentalists tried to wreak havoc and fear only a few years ago, warning us that our geographic location couldn't save us from terrorist violence and tragedy. As a nation we'd worked our way through that dark chapter in our lives, rebuilding and repairing with the help of all ethnicities and the leadership of the Muslim faith. But to have an Anglo-Saxon ex-Army general, whose family lineage could be traced back to the First Fleet, accused of plotting to overthrow the elected government of the day was hard to believe.

With coaching from Bryan and Sammy, I went on national television again, not the normal fireside chat but an information-sharing session with the public.

I told the truth, but stressed I couldn't go into detail lest my comments were construed as prejudicial to the impending legal action.

I explained that nearly sixty people had been detained as a consequence of monitoring General Hay's e-mails, that Australia for Australians had now been formally declared a terrorist organization, but there was absolutely no cause for concern; we'd nipped it all in the bud, rendering the organization powerless.

I ALLOWED myself to relax a little and focus on government, which seemed logical, regardless of the extraordinary circumstances in which we found ourselves with the scandal of the governor-general. There was a raft of legislation that the Joint Party Room needed to consider, as well as reports from no less than five separate house committees, which had been in progress well before the election. It was hard work, but also therapeutic as Jenny magically guided us through. She encouraged the new members, welding everyone together into a united working group. Members were cheerful again, the halls of government were full of good manners and quite a few smiles, the old hands confident in the results the JPR produced, and the newbies amazed at the courteous and efficient process.

We made sure a light lunch was served every day the JPR was in session, which was an opportunity for Paul, Jye, and me to circulate around the new members. Only one refused to mix, and after only two sessions of the JPR he stayed away—Steven Edwards, the sole representative of the Socialist People's Party. There was no umbrage shown to Mr. Edwards, but I had to admit there was no warmth either. He was an echo of the past, part of parliamentary history we all preferred to forget, and yet here he was, reminding us how easily our country could have slipped into anarchy.

ECHOES INDEED, as a few nights later, I slumbered on.

It had been a night like this when my phone had rung and Jason had died. The bloody number was only to be used in a national emergency, so my heart leapt about in my chest as Sammy passed it over. "Charlie," he said, as I grunted into the thing.

"Sorry to be a nuisance, boss," the voice said.

"You're not bloody sorry at all. You love waking me up," I said, making light of it, and it seemed to work, judging by the chuckle at the other end. "What's the problem?" I asked.

"The GG has topped himself, blew his brains out with his Army-issue revolver."

Suddenly I was wide-awake. "How the fuck did that happen? House arrest in my mind still means prison, albeit with a few privileges. How the fuck did he get his hands on a gun?"

"Sorry, boss, but it appears he had it hidden in a lead-lined wall cavity all along. We went through the place like a fine-tooth comb initially, but nothing showed up. The gun was there, loaded ready for an occasion such as this. Sorry, but it's done."

"Where's his wife?"

"We allowed her to leave yesterday because she's not of any interest to us. She went to her sister."

"So Hay told her to leave."

"Yes, it looks that way."

I rang Angela straight away, who organized the inner cabinet plus Bryan Friedman. I rang Paul Sinclair and Jye Chandler, and a few hours later we all met. I needed to share the responsibility of this new calamity with a group whose common sense was both obvious and welcomed, because I didn't have the faintest idea how to handle it.

I briefed everyone and sat back, allowing the conversation to flow over me.

It was Bryan who brought us all down to earth, as usual.

"We won't have much time and very little flexibility because ever since the GG has been under house arrest, there's been a news team hanging around the house. You should call a news conference, Jacko, and just tell 'em the truth, as you always do. You probably feel pissed off that you've missed the opportunity to bring this bloke to justice after his disloyalty, and dare I suggest, his homophobia, yet you feel sad that a human being has lost their life on a fool's errand, correct?"

I sat upright and nodded. Governor-General Hay had represented everything in a person I disliked, yet he was dead, and that was a tragedy, a consequence of my actions, however well-intentioned and necessary.

Chapter 63
At Last, Something To Smile At

WE'D JUST passed the three-month mark as a new government and things settled down. Chief Justice Samesh Banerjee had been appointed governor-general at our recommendation, and the executive level of government just flowed along. We looked across at the opposition benches with a sense of relief. The whole shitty episode could have made Australia look like a third-world country, but because Parliament stood behind us, together with the leadership of Paul Sinclair and Jye Chandler, we emerged, instead, as a decisive and modern administration.

Considering government agencies had been involved, we'd acted with lightning speed, prosecuting the fifty-eight people Governor-General Hay had implicated in his activities. Nowhere did a plan emerge; Australia for Australians didn't have the capacity to do what Hay wanted, so we'd stopped the bullshit in its tracks. Only Hay had a plan, which thanks to our prompt action before the election, never reached implementation. But the AFP warned us privately that while the threat was contained, it wasn't over, far from it.

I WAS deep in thought as I made my way past Mrs. Shields's office when she called out. "Pardon." I looked up and she took my hand, snapping me out of my trance. "You have a visitor," her facial expression remained neutral, "Steven Edwards, the Socialist People's Party."

I motioned him inside and offered him coffee, but he shook his head, so I closed the door for privacy but left the intercom open. I'd become paranoid about "private" meetings and made sure I had a record of what was said.

"I want to rejoin."

I'd been preoccupied all afternoon with the forthcoming budget, Eddie Chi had put several propositions to us, and Steven's request just slipped through to the keeper. "Sorry, what did you say again?" I asked.

"I want to rejoin the Labor Party."

"You have to be joking, what brought you to that decision?"

"It's a solitary existence here. I tried your Joint Party Room, and while no one objected to my presence, the welcome mat was hardly put out either."

"What do you expect?"

He just stared at me, and despite the bitter recent history that brought him here, I felt a little sorry for him. No remorse, just sorry because he had no political future, and what was worse, he was persona non grata both in the eyes of the Australian public and politicians of all persuasions.

Trying to muster as much kindness as possible, I laid out the facts. "Steven, it would never be my decision to readmit you to the party. First the national executive and then caucus, as you know, and hell would freeze over before that happened. I think you're here to explore your options, right?"

The poor bastard just nodded; life ahead would be miserable even on a good day.

"Why don't you retire and simply vacate the public limelight? It'd be easier."

"I couldn't draw my parliamentary pension until the end of this term."

"There are special arrangements available to me at my discretion, if a member should retire early through health issues, and I'm being totally truthful when I suggest your mental state would deteriorate within the current parliament, correct?"

He shrugged, but he agreed he should resign; ill health would be the reason. He turned to leave and smiled briefly. "For the record I was the least enthusiastic of the SPP, but what really horrified me was the connection with General Hay."

My head snapped up, and I realized he was serious.

"There were discussions, but Hay was a madman, and very careless. He gave us a list of names, which I'll pass on to you as a parting gift. And thanks for getting me out from under, I appreciate it."

THERE WOULD be a by-election, of course, and even though Steven Edwards had won the seat, it was only by a handful of votes. The electorate was originally old Labor, blue collar in the extreme, but as with many other seats, the demographics were in a state of flux, changing all the while. Our previous candidate didn't offer himself up for preselection again, having the dubious honor of losing to the only successful SPP candidate. The branch asked me to participate in the selection process this time because they had it so wrong on the previous occasion.

"We think you'll like our choice this time," the branch president had said. "The State guys have approved also, but he's *very* different."

Sammy and I flew to Sydney. The rank-and-file membership always made Sammy welcome, a given that our partnership contributed to the party's electoral success, particularly at the previous election.

Just as Jason had done with me some years ago, we found ourselves invited to the proposed candidate's home, Frank Gill.

The front door flew open, and a stressed-looking guy stood there, late forties, suit pants, nice shoes, shirt neck open, tie undone. His face lit up and he smiled, holding out his hand. "Tom Tyrone. Welcome to the madhouse, come on in." We walked through a spacious dining room to the kitchen, where four people seemed to be in mortal combat.

Suddenly it all stopped, and they turned to look at us, laughing their heads off. "Sorry," said the adult in charge, "we just cremated the spuds. You'll stay for a meal, won't you? It's not all burnt offerings."

We nodded our thanks as they introduced themselves, Frank first, and their three teenage kids in turn: Alicia, nineteen, and twins Ben and Jacqui, eighteen.

Clearly this was a family who very much worked as a team, yet they were hardly in the poorhouse. Tom was a Toyota dealer, a highly successful and smart operator, while Frank's little florist shop now took up most of a city block and wholesaled flowers all over Australia and into Asia. Under the surface lurked something else. Something the parliament had needed for a long time—a sense of humor—and I felt Frank wouldn't disappoint me. Over a wonderful meal, surrounded by his family, he relaxed further, and *at last*, I thought, *here's the real Frank.*

"We're all mad, like a room full of drag queens looking for a pair of pants. It's always like this when we're all together. Alicia is already in her second year of nursing and living in at the hospital, and it's college for the twins next year. So the kids are growing up, and if I survive the branch selection process, plus your look-over, then allow the electorate to make up their mind, we'll take Ben and Jacqui with us and enroll them in a Canberra college."

"What's a look-over?" I stirred, and Frank didn't disappoint.

"Better to be looked over than to be overlooked, pet. Do I pass muster?"

"Of course you do."

Tom smiled indulgently and kissed Frank. "Now stop worrying, and try to enjoy yourself, you spend all of your life worrying about other people. My wife died just after the twins were born," Tom explained. "I was trying to raise babies, run a dealership, and pay the bills. It was full-on, and a month later there were still flowers arriving for Rosemary. Guess who the florist was, doing his own deliveries that day, and was appalled at the way the kids were being looked after? I had a full-time housekeeper, but she was useless. When I arrived home this place looked amazing. Frank had decided to clean it and then feed Alicia and the twins because they were hungry. We'd never met before, but I just knew he was the right person in the right place at the right time. Frank offered to move in, take care of the kids for nothing. All I had to do was pay the bills and keep out of the way.

"And that was it. The house was spotless, the kids thrived, and there was always a meal for us. Somehow he ran his own business and took us on at the same time. He must have been working eighty-hour weeks. I was fascinated, not just by his work ethic but by *him*. I was a tired-out, run-down, highly stressed widower, and if anyone had suggested I had a gay bone in my body, I would have laughed at them. But Frank made me feel good again, made sure I ate properly and had early nights, and looked after me. Love is a funny thing. I finally knew I just couldn't go on through life without him, and I reasoned that if it was meant to be, the bedroom thing would look after itself, and it certainly did."

Their children were gathered around, smiling and nodding their heads very seriously, not taking the piss out of their parents, and totally supportive. They had really only known Frank and Tom as parents; their birth mother was only a memory to Alicia, but she was adamant. "They tried to explain the new sleeping arrangements to me," she said. "I was so little, but I remember I was absolutely delighted. To me that meant everything was forever. I woke up in the morning and there was Frank feeding us all and organizing everything. I still choke up when I see Dad and Frank kiss each other. That means so much to us kids. It's our family, full of love. None of us have ever heard them have one single disagreement. We reckon we're so lucky."

THE BY-ELECTION was over in a flash. We spent a minimal amount in advertising, but Frank and Tom tipped in some funds of their own, just to remind the electorate of their local credentials, and that it was Labor they were voting for and not the SPP. The news had spread that the SPP were on the nose, just as the late GG and Australia for Australians were. The oldies and the traditional Labor supporters rallied and gave the "gay Labor bloke" their vote without a second thought.

Frank came home with an increased majority, an unheard-of feat in a by-election, and we welcomed him and his family to Canberra.

I wondered what caucus would make of Frank, and I didn't have long to wait.

There were huge smiles from the members. Frank was evidence of the now total demise of the SPP; it wasn't because we had another vote to rely on, it was a mental and physical relief for us all as a government to be finally surrounded by friendly and loyal faces.

But it was in the Joint Party Room where Frank was a sensation. The JPR was beginning to wear a bit thin at the edges, so polite at times it was like a well-mannered afternoon tea party. Paul Sinclair and I were amused at the creature we'd created; the passion that once rocked parliament wasn't replicated in the JPR, even if the legislation was. The atmosphere remained businesslike, which we'd hoped for, but because of its success it was also moribund, devoid of color. Humor was an essential part of our business, and it seemed it had gone the same way. Even the Nationals were less inclined to argue their case, which was a shame because they still represented much of rural Australia, and in our pursuit of trade in Asia, we were depending on investment in the bush.

I didn't brief Frank in any way, just told him to be himself, which I thought should be enough to liven the place up a bit. He arrived wearing a Quentin Crisp-like scarf wound theatrically around his neck and shoulders and was dressed beautifully, a notch above the casual dress code of the JPR.

I introduced the new member for Western Hills, and a smattering of applause greeted him. Jenny directed him to a seat where he made himself comfortable, surrounded by members of all party persuasions.

"I liked your maiden speech in the House," one of the Nationals remarked, which was meant genuinely but sounded just a touch condescending.

"Well thank you so much," Frank replied, "but it's been a long time since maidenhood meant anything at our house, and probably yours as well."

A ripple of laughter echoed around the room, and members sat up in their seats, aware the atmosphere of congeniality now had an edge to it.

Jenny Bellamy moved on to the first piece of business, a Senate committee report proposing to simplify application for youth unemployment benefits in remote areas, and a review of the level of assistance. The report had been in circulation for two weeks, and I was amazed that Frank had not only read it but knew a lot about the subject.

"I'd like the minister to examine this report with urgency," Frank said, "because there's a need out there that simply can't be ignored. Not all of us are lucky. Sometimes it takes more than luck and hard work to survive and prosper. The worst aspect is that kids in remote areas can't afford to leave home and find a job somewhere else, so they get in with the wrong crowd and cost the community even more. I'd like to see subsidized accommodation in regional centers as part of the package. At first glance it seems expensive, but when you look at the numbers involved, it becomes a case of not if, but when we should do it. And we shouldn't forget many of these areas are likely to have Asian immigrant families in the future that we're duty bound to care for."

"Here we go again, using public money to prop up the great unwashed," roared a Liberal back bencher from Western Australia.

"Why don't you save your criticisms for the bill when it arrives here," said Jenny. "I thought the new member for Western Hills summarized the report most succinctly."

"He needs some real-life experience first."

The room fell silent.

Frank's business, at last count, employed nearly two hundred people and turned over one hundred and twenty million dollars annually. It had been leased out so Frank, in his own words, could "put something back into society."

"It's simply a case of mind over matter." Frank smiled sweetly.

"Huh" came from his detractor.

"I don't mind, and you don't matter."

Jenny dropped her head into her hands and snorted, and the Joint Party Room rang with laughter. Across the room Paul Sinclair nearly wet himself, and Jye Chandler held his sides. The Honorable Member for East Swan, Glen Southey, blushed crimson, but then laughed at himself. He walked over, smiling, and shook Frank's hand but fell short of an apology—it was after all the Joint Party Room. He'd badly underestimated Frank but still didn't realize the full extent of his miscalculation. Frank smiled at him as he returned to his seat, rather like an eagle watching a field mouse, patiently watching and waiting.

"My mother always told me to be wary of men from the West," Frank called out to Mr. Southey's retreating back.

Glen Southey was a male whore, never married, mainly heterosexual, but his real weakness was never understanding how the forces of nature could cloud his judgment. All he could think of was his next conquest, and Frank was a good-looking guy. Surely a bit of harmless flirting wouldn't hurt, even if it was in the semipublic domain of the Joint Party Room.

"Your mother was right, but I'd be so gentle with you."

I knew what was coming next, not the exact words, but something close.

Frank's voice was steady, his demeanor not at all malicious, but the meaning of his words were crystal clear.

"I wouldn't do you for practice. I need nourishment, not punishment."

Chapter 64
A Sense of Foreboding

THE FEEDBACK from the ASEAN countries was magic. Every day there seemed to be a new development, and I was swept along in it, as were those of us who had participated. Something as simple as a trade mission had worked, and we appeared to have struck a chord everywhere we went. Now they wanted to visit us, and it was the turn of the Philippines—Ferdinand and Raina Lopez with their entourage were due in less than two weeks.

Kate and Max were ecstatic, looking forward to the visit. They were growing up so quickly, their minds racing ahead of their physicality. They actually enjoyed the company of adults, particularly Ferdinand and Raina; there was a bond in place there that Kate and Max had already forged without our help. Ferdinand reminded me it was Kate, in a few well-chosen words, who forced us adults to focus on the basics of life and brought our two nations closer together.

The Lopez itinerary included Sydney, Melbourne, and Canberra, and they had a traveling circus similar to ours. Trade missions had a two-way benefit, and we were mindful of the fact. Angela, Paul, and I gathered together our old gang, plus a few more captains of industry, to ensure we didn't miss any opportunities.

The plan was to have an official welcome and trade fair in Sydney, then replicate the exhibition in Melbourne, followed by Ferdinand addressing a joint sitting of the Australian Parliament in Canberra.

While in Canberra they would stay with us at the Lodge, and we'd planned some private touring with them afterward, showing them the sights, in this, their first visit to Australia.

Charlie complained he hadn't enough time to pull the security together, but that was Charlie. If he was complaining, it meant he was right on it and things were going as planned. But he shook his finger at me; he didn't like the idea of visiting places like the Gold Coast, the Blue Mountains, and perhaps Uluru with our visitors where it was difficult, if not impossible, to guarantee safety for all concerned.

But Charlie insisted there was another element to the security task on this occasion. He was genuinely worried, and his mates at the AFP were also concerned, telegraphing what they saw as yet another iteration of Australia for Australians simply known as Australia First. Like the original group, they weren't a threat to law and order unless the various groups joined together and made a national statement, and they could do that in either Sydney, Melbourne, or Canberra.

Not for the first time, I felt betrayed by my own country. I accepted the fact that everyone was entitled to their own point of view in the most simplistic sense, but it made me sad to think anyone could hurt someone, even kill them, because they didn't agree with their point of view.

Charlie was able to quantify it. There were around two hundred of these people spread around the country, but the one thing that united them and brought them together was their hatred of Asia and Asians.

So our dear friends Ferdinand and Raina could be targeted, as I would, Charlie reminded me, because I was seen as the archenemy, the nation's leader who had driven us closer to Asia. If they could stop me and take out an Asian leader at the same time, they felt they were true Australians.

Sick cunts.

We told our visitors what was involved, but there was no way they would cancel. They too had similar issues at home, and these were the risks we all took as part of the job.

I'D ALWAYS had that ability to think on a different plane to nondyslexic people, and with that ability came a sixth sense that telegraphed a change of circumstances up ahead. And this was such a time, except a real feeling of dread would sometimes overtake me, rather like depression, "the black dog on my shoulder," as Winston Churchill put it so succinctly. Thinking back over my life, I'd had similar feelings before my mother died, then Jason, but it was never bad enough where I felt I needed help, as in counseling.

It was just part of me and who I am.

I shared my discomfort with Sammy, and as usual he made me feel better by talking it all through, using our common sense and not taking risks of any sort. But we kept it to ourselves; no point worrying family or friends about something that was impossible to explain. As an educator

Sammy didn't feel surprised by my sixth sense, I'd always been able to see things the way I did, and it didn't alarm him.

But I seemed to have reached part of my life where reflecting on what I've achieved is the last thing I need to do, and I worry about this book. It feels to me as if I'm blowing my own bags too much. I know it's a good story, and Sammy assures me it will help inspire those people like myself, but it's all about me, where in fact it should be at least 50 percent Sammy, maybe even 75 percent.

It's always been Sammy. It took a lot of intestinal fortitude on my behalf to take the final step and claim him as my own, but when I did, it was the most natural and beautiful thing in my life. I knew instantly what I wanted and I wasn't about to let him get away again ever, so ten days later I proposed.

The moment Sammy and I began living together, my career at the City began to change for the better, but when we became a couple, my career flourished. Sammy completes me; I can't function properly without him, but I do accept that he feels similarly about me.

So while I feel embarrassed at all the attention, I remain a total romantic because I recognize it's been our love for each other that's driven this show along. Sammy's devotion and management has turned me from a kid with severe learning problems into an adult high achiever.

I'm so looking forward to Ferdinand and Raina's visit, but some days I can't shake the blackness that seems to envelop me. This time the feeling is quite intense; I *feel* rather than know that something could happen. Some days I'm reduced to tears, worrying about the kids and Dad and Isobel. Worse still, I worry about Sammy. If something happened to him, I'd find it hard to continue on, the entire family would. We finally consulted our GP and both came up with perfectly clean bills of health, scoring higher than average in all facets for men's health in our age group.

Chapter 65
Tragedy, Written by Sammy Collins-Smith

THIS MANUSCRIPT has been sitting in the same drawer for over two years. I've tried to ignore it, even contemplated throwing it out, yet I know I have to go on and complete it. The day my life changed forever sticks in my mind as if it had just happened, the tragedy of it all still haunts me and probably always will.

The Philippines state visit had gone well. Sydney was a sellout for the welcome, and there was sustained interest in their products and services. Melbourne was even more positive, and I remember as a side benefit they bought a heap of wind turbines from us.

Next it was Canberra's turn to welcome the Lopez entourage and Ferdinand's planned address to Parliament. They were transferred to the Lodge directly from the airport, and we welcomed them into what had become our home.

At the official reception, I'd detected a note of urgency in Charlie Lim's body language, and I remember him wagging his finger at Jacko in the corner of the room. I invited myself over and was included in the conversation, or rather the lecture, that Charlie gave us. It appeared that his worst fears were in the process of materializing, that several hundred Australia First members were in the process of converging on Canberra from around Australia, protesting at the visit of the "slant-eyes and the poofter prime minister who invited them." Police tried to limit their numbers, but it was like an invasion, and it was impossible to identify who wanted to cause trouble and who was innocently going about their business.

Charlie was very specific. They were in the process of setting up temporary fencing to put some distance between us and our visitors, and the protesters, and we were not, under any circumstances, to go anywhere closer than fifty meters to the fences. The Army had been called in and snipers would be high up on rooftops out of sight of the public but watching every movement of the crowd.

We had several personnel movements where we would be exposed; the main one being at the Australian War Memorial on our way back to the Lodge, after the joint sitting of parliament and Ferdinand's address. Ferdinand was determined to lay a wreath there. We realized the United States' presence in the Philippines was continuing to wind back, and he was looking for friends.

We'd just moved outside, Ferdinand and Raina were already in their car, when the fence nearest to us collapsed and a wall of people ran at us.

A glint of sunlight bounced off something and I threw myself on top of Jacko. A shot broke through the cries and Jacko twitched beneath me. Blood fanned out on the concrete, and the pattern of it held my fascination before pain slammed into my body a moment later, and I fainted.

Chapter 66
A Life Well Lived,
Written by Sammy Collins-Smith

JACKO'S TIME as prime minister was spectacular for many reasons, but it had its foundation back in his period working for the City, firstly on the mowing gang, then as operations manager, and finally as CEO. Jacko was always hands-on; he didn't sit behind a desk all day every day. He was out talking to the workers with his collaborative management style, and it was a habit that he never lost. Consequently he knew what was going on before anyone else, and it gave him precious time to fix a problem, real or imagined, before it became insurmountable. He also spent an inordinate amount of time talking to the "customers"—the ratepayers at the City—because they were his employers, and that was replicated when he was elected the member for Hinchcliffe, always consulting the people who elected him because they were his "employers" also. That was at the heart of Jacko's customer focus, and I think the major reason he became a much loved and respected person in Australian public life. Nothing was too difficult when it came to his customers, and that's why he became probably the most televised Australian leader in history. His fireside chats were the product of a brilliant mind that acknowledged the ongoing place he felt the electors had in any government.

He felt strongly that an election only signaled the people's choice for a government for the next three years. If there was something specific that wasn't the subject of an election issue, he went on telly and told everyone what he proposed doing and why. Never once was there a single objection; the fact he'd consulted and informed everyone was good enough.

At first his thinking was criticized as being simplistic, unsophisticated, even childlike. The Joint Party Room concept was laughed at initially, but Jacko was smart enough to sell it to Paul Sinclair and the Coalition first, followed by the Greens. The concept took hold and transformed parliament. Politicians weren't openly criticizing each other anymore because there were no votes in that sort of behavior, the press despairing because there were no headlines in people being civil to each other.

But both politicians and the public warmed to the idea, and it worked.

Then he decided we'd have a trade mission to the ASEAN countries, which followed months of careful planning and consultation with the member nations. Once they became accustomed to the Australian prime minister arriving on their doorstep with a briefcase trying to sell them something, they became as enthusiastic as Jacko was. Again such a simple strategy, and to this day it's still working so well, quietly growing the Australian economy through a variety of exports no one thought had any potential.

Jacko understood it wasn't just about trade or dollars. It was about relationships with our lovely neighbors—whenever we talked to them, we were usually flooded with new business.

JACKO MANAGED his dyslexia. It wasn't allowed to intrude on his life, and in fact, as I pointed out to dozens of my students, Jacko was born with the special qualities of some dyslexic people, thinking on a different level to most of the population. The lesson was if they sought assistance as Jacko had, and identified their strengths as well as their weaknesses, then anything was possible.

He was brilliant at delegating of course, and he would frequently point to Barbara Shields's initial appointment as the turning point in his political career, and I'd have to agree with him. But he had other good people around him as well, particularly Angela. Angela Chan was now prime minister, and I couldn't think of anyone more deserving and more competent. Even before Jacko became prime minister, she was interpreting documents and backing up Barbara in her role, while still managing to look after her own portfolio of Health. She was the perfect deputy, a kind, loyal person who guarded Jacko's back like no other.

But because Jacko saw dyslexia as an opportunity, he was honest with everyone around him, particularly cabinet members, and they helped him as well. I smiled to myself many times on tour around the ASEAN countries as Eddie Chi, Angela, or even Paul Sinclair discreetly translated something for him. It was situation normal, and not one person was concerned about it.

Jacko had everyone on the same team—another magical ability, building and running a team, and part of his magic was to also draw in the opposition parties and place them firmly at his back.

In hindsight their reaction wasn't surprising, but Jacko was lucky to have Paul Sinclair on his side and he knew it. The JPR wouldn't have happened under normal circumstances, but Jacko realized Paul was a good thinker, a man who put the country ahead of partisan politics, as did Jye Chandler from the Greens, and, unbelievably, Henry Purcell from the Nationals.

ONE WOULD have thought that a person of his intelligence would comprehend feedback from the very people he was always so concerned about.

He had no idea that the Australian public idolized him. To them he was more than the working bloke that had made the journey from a council mower to the highest office in the land; he was the person who in his down-to-earth style always told them the truth. If he fucked up or some program wasn't working, he wouldn't pretend; he'd tell it the way it was and do his best to fix it. When he did a fireside chat on television, they listened because he came across as another member of their family. Jacko had a saying, "don't insult, consult," and the public felt he was seeking their permission to proceed. Which he was.

It's probably true to say that trust is a two-way street, and the Australian public felt as strongly as Jacko did about the issues of the day, because they were educated and informed about them like never before.

Jacko failed to understand the public idolatry in which he was held because he had absolutely no ego. He was the most genuinely modest person I've ever known.

When the tragedy happened, there was an outpouring of rage and grief at home and around the world that changed our country forever. To do that to anyone in public life was bad enough, but to do that to their Jacko was unthinkable.

WE MIGHT have appeared to have been Camelot re-created, but we weren't.

We had our disagreements, just like any couple does, yet to his credit he knew when he'd been a prick and he always made up for it. He knew I loved flowers, and a bunch would arrive at home or at uni, but then I often found them at our bedside just because he wanted to communicate he was thinking of me and that he loved me.

Power has always been an aphrodisiac to many people, but never to Jacko. He never saw himself as a head of state, but simply an ordinary bloke, elected by the people to do a job, because at the end of the day all he wanted to do was to come home to me and the kids.

And Mum and Peter, who are still such an integral part of our family.

Yes, I loved him. If it's possible for a kid at ten years of age to fall in love, that was me. I remember knocking on the Smiths' door to be introduced to my pupil, and even then he took my breath away. And of course we'd walk to school hand in hand every day, just like we did down the aisle at our wedding.

It nearly didn't happen. I overreacted to his sexuality—not that he was overtly heterosexual, but I was street-smart enough to look after my feelings. Nothing worse than a gay guy falling for a straight man. Unrequited love was the last thing I needed.

But I nearly ruined Matt's early life by starting a relationship that I found I couldn't sustain because I had to admit I was in love with Jacko.

As with most Western nations at that time, young Australians felt less pressure to conform to a stereotype than ever before, and Jacko was a case in point. Jacko had grown up having sex with women, but he clearly loved me. In his case love had grown from a deep friendship that was central to both our lives, to something he just had to express as a matter of urgency! The biggest surprise for me was how easily intimacy blossomed between us, and I started to relax, but I still didn't want to be part of some ménage à trois in the future, so I held something back. But he understood me more completely than I'd ever realized, and he stunned me by proposing a few days later. He'd known what he'd wanted for a long time and made absolutely sure he got it.

All I can say is that I'd rather have had the nearly twenty years with Jacko than ten lifetimes with someone else.

I agree with his words in chapter one, and I quote: "So I hope our yarn reminds people that hope is a finer emotion than despair. Why? Because of life's most precious emotion, the true regard of one human being for another—love."

Chapter 67
The New Australia,
Written by Sammy Collins-Smith

I'M SITTING here just staring out the huge floor-to-ceiling windows, quite a peaceful, almost bucolic scene. Suddenly there's a high-pitched whine like a jet engine as the very latest of Indonesian garden and lawn care sweeps into view with the president driving. Surprise, surprise.

A group of bemused gardeners are looking on as he sweeps past the windows, waving to me with a huge grin all over his face.

The child is still there, the wonder of things mechanical, particularly those related to his first job, all those years ago at the City. And his love of talking to the workers. "Our mates," he calls them, and it's not hard to understand why everyone regards him as *their* special mate.

There's some gray at the temples now, which makes him look even hotter, and while he appears to be a little thicker around the waist, he's not even a kilo heavier—not bad for a forty-five-year-old. He won't ever be 100 percent again; his left shoulder was smashed so badly it took surgeons five operations to reconstruct and rebuild it. Most people wouldn't notice, but I do. He carries himself a little differently when he walks, and he just can't swing his left arm as far as he should.

But as he says, he's still here and continuing to give everyone buggery, as it were.

It's now nearly three years since the tragedy; we regard it as such because it was a turning point in history where we finally had to say "enough is enough"—politicians and honored visitors shouldn't feel threatened in any way, let alone risk their lives because a tiny minority doesn't agree with the majority. The Army and our security retaliated swiftly and two people died that day: Andrew Fitch and Jeremy Lowther. Both of them had grudges against Jacko; Lowther was retired early because of his blatant homophobia, and Fitch, who was defeated by Jacko in Hinchcliffe, was mentally ill and allowed to roam unchecked, conning his way around his medical contacts to stay out of institutions.

Both were embroiled in Australia First, blindly swept along in a shared hatred of minorities, particularly same-sex couples and Asian people.

The National Capital Private Hospital was front and center on everyone's television screens that day, with one channel providing a round-the-clock commentary, even through the night.

Mine was a flesh wound, even though it hurt like hell, but Jacko was in a bad way. His shoulder was literally in pieces, he'd lost a lot of blood, and was put into an induced coma so they could stabilize his overall condition. I remember the kids coming in with Mum and Peter. Max was so frightened, but Kate was seething—so far as she was concerned, the people who tried to murder us were better off dead. I think she would have dealt with them herself.

Ferdinand and Raina were inconsolable, but it was Angela and Christina, together with Paul and Joan Sinclair, who stepped up and took over. And dear Jenny. Suddenly situations were reversed and she hadn't forgotten.

She stayed close by me as I'd been able to do for her when she lost her husband. She wanted me on my feet as soon as possible, because of the kids. "Once they see you upright, they'll relax," she said, and she was right.

THE SHOCK and disbelief around the world reflected in the press at home and overseas. It was referred to as an assassination attempt, which it was, albeit carried out by two amateurs whose mental health in both cases was highly suspect.

But it was enough, and Angela was determined.

Jacko, finally conscious twenty-four hours later and able to comprehend her request, told her to do it.

"No," she said, and I smiled, guessing what was coming. "I can't take this legislation to the JPR and then the parliament without telling the people what's going on and why. I need to do a fireside chat. Do you approve?"

I knew my husband was going to be okay as he turned his head and smiled at Angela. "You silly bitch, you don't need my permission, just fucking do it."

She leaned over and kissed him on the cheek. "Okay, boss, don't get your knickers damp. I'll just make sure they give you a telly in here tomorrow night."

The following evening Angela Chan as deputy prime minister gave the nation an update on Jacko's health and told the nation the government under the circumstances was preparing to tighten legislation much further to outlaw any individual or organization who threatened national security, such as Australia First. Membership of such an organization would mean immediate imprisonment for up to one year, whether or not those arrested had committed any crime. Membership and/or association was enough.

"This is extreme legislation directed at extreme people, and I don't need to tell you it crosses the borderline between democracy and anarchy. If it makes you all feel any better, I asked the prime minister in a lucid moment and he agreed.

"This time not only was his life threatened, but also that of his husband, so the perpetrators made the decision for us. Our leaders and their families need to go about their business in safety. Being elected as your representatives shouldn't mean we have to risk our lives doing what you've paid us to do. It is also vital that leaders of foreign nations, especially our friends in Asia, should feel they can visit our nation at short notice, particularly if they want to do business with us. Recent events could have ruined our relationship with the ASEAN nations, but I know they will support us in what we must do. Support for us around the world has been extraordinary, and the prime minister's room isn't large enough to accommodate all the flowers and chocolates that have arrived. He asked me to assure you that he will be some months recuperating, but I intend consulting with him daily as he progresses. He thanks you all for your best wishes but asks that you focus on two things, luck and love, because if it hadn't been for his husband's foresight and bravery, he wouldn't be alive today."

I SUPPOSE the most notable event in Jacko's recovery occurred about eight weeks later, purely and simply because it was the first time people had seen him in public and upright since that fateful day.

Christmas was almost upon us, and it was customary for the party leaders to put away their differences and focus on the impending holiday season, family, friends, and a relaxed break before the autumn session of parliament.

Jacko was walking well but needed my assistance to get around because the tightly strapped shoulder was awkward to manage and he bumped into things, swearing profusely as he did so.

I was allowed into the House because he needed assistance, slipping him unobtrusively into his seat on the front bench, the Speaker suddenly acknowledging his presence.

"The prime minister," said Joe Green, the Speaker, as I helped Jacko to the dispatch box to speak.

"Mr. Speaker," Jacko began, and the place erupted. Members stood applauding, even yelling out, as Jacko looked around at Angela, clearly shocked.

"You silly tart, Jacko, we've all missed you. Lap it up while it's happening."

The Speaker smiled, and eventually called for order. "Order, order, the prime minister."

"Mr. Speaker, I didn't want to miss this opportunity to wish everyone a happy and safe festive season, and assure those of us here at home and abroad that even with the dire events of two months ago, Australia remains on track and open for business. I want to thank all those who have wished me and my family well during this time. And your lovely welcome back to this place is much appreciated."

There was more polite applause as I helped him back to his seat.

Paul Sinclair then addressed the speaker. "Mr. Speaker, permission to make a statement."

"Permission granted, the Leader of the Opposition."

"Mr. Speaker," Paul began, and immediately burst into tears, much to his own discomfort, but I detected no one else in the chamber minded that day, because Paul became the voice of the parliament.

"Mr. Speaker, how wonderful it is to have the member for Hinchcliffe alive and well, back where he belongs. We thought we'd lost you, Jacko," Paul continued. "Life as we know it wouldn't be the same without you." He paused again, still battling his emotions. "Mr. Speaker, with the events that very nearly cost this nation its elected leader, it behooves us to remember what has progressively happened to this place, and in this place since the honorable member for Hinchcliffe was first elected. I submit, Mr. Speaker, that no one since Federation has had such influence on politics and politicians, and to have that influence removed by force was more than our nation could tolerate. I know I would embarrass the prime minister, so I won't detail every little accomplishment of his, except to reiterate what a marvelous day this is for us all. We wish you and your lovely family a wonderful festive season full of the love and concern you've given to so many others. May it be returned in full to yourselves."

There was more applause as parliament was adjourned.

Chapter 68
The Last Gasp from Jacko — 2035

I DECIDED I'd better finish this story or risk spending the rest of my days without nooky. I'd put the manuscript away some time ago, not intending to continue for various reasons, but Sammy dragged it out again, reminding me there are many young people around the world who will feel uplifted and empowered by my story, and I actually agreed without having to bargain away my conjugal enjoyment. Because, as usual, he made perfect sense.

Sammy writes very well, and he did capture the drama around the attack on our lives and immediately afterward, when my desire and ability to write dropped to zero because of my mental and physical impairment after the shooting.

But what the whole nasty episode did to us was to force us to question life in politics for me and for our family, and whether it was worth continuing at all.

We worried about Kate and Max; little visible effect remained, they'd moved on, accepting what had happened as part of their parents' public life and service to the community. Kate is seventeen now and Max fifteen, nearly sixteen, and people sometimes give me odd looks when they ask what has been the most noteworthy thing that I've achieved in my lifetime, and I point to our two children.

In raising kids it's never just parents of course. Sammy and I did our best, but Dad and Isobel were always the second line of nurturing, particularly since I entered politics. We think our kids are perfect. All we did was to include them in everything that was going on, making sure they were handed some ownership of events, but above all, we tried to set an example and they followed, without drama or discussion; they just trusted us to point them in the right direction—with Dad and Isobel helping, of course.

Inevitably people holding high office are more senior in years than Sammy and me, with grown-up families, so the kids were among the youngest tenants ever at the Lodge and now here in their new home, they certainly are.

Kate is already a beautiful young woman, if a touch intimidating intellectually. She doesn't suffer fools gladly, can't stand vacuous idiots, particularly those who want to crawl to her because of the place her family occupies in Australian society.

And Max. Max is as intense as ever, reads my mind in a frightening manner, and has a boyfriend. A very handsome boyfriend, about two years older, nearly eighteen, called Rueben. Rueben is "totally hot," Max tells me, and I agree. Because the kid has a few brains, and he actually adores Max. He's even asked our permission to sleep over and promises me Max is physically off-limits until he reaches legal age. Sammy and I plan to be somewhere else on that evening. The scenario doesn't cause us any pain except to say we know Max has already made up his mind; he and Rueben are already destined to be life partners. Like two other little boys we know who fell in love as ten-year-olds, only these days life itself and people are more enlightened, and they don't waste time trying to second-guess each other.

SO WITH our family safe and quite content, I agreed to see my term out, nearly two years to go before we had to face the people again. Some of that time would be consumed with ongoing medical treatment, but as time progressed, I felt stronger and stronger, almost back to my old self. Except I wasn't.

I accepted that very few human beings could completely return their lives to normal after such a profound ordeal, and Sammy understood.

What was missing from my existence was my desire to be a leader once again. I was there physically, but I'd lost my way. The spark that had driven me for all these years in public life just wasn't there. I dragged myself around, making all the right noises, mentally flagellating myself for my attitude.

But Sammy insisted my work wasn't yet finished, which mystified me a little because I was usually the one with long-term vision. But even that seemed in the bucket as well. I seemed not to care about what was coming at us, even though my previous feelings had been chillingly accurate.

Ever the teacher, Sammy knew his star pupil had more in the tank, and he gently pushed me along, quietly steering me toward some professional help. It was discreetly done; the psychologist started visiting the Lodge rather than me visiting her, and I wondered how on earth this little middle-aged lady could ever get me refocused on what I was supposed to be doing. I was like the reluctant debutante: my mind had gone through the whole spectrum of rejecting the process. The humiliation of mental illness was something I hadn't experienced before.

Her name was Rosemary Mills. She seemed so quiet and nondescript, a person that wouldn't stand out in a crowd, quite the opposite. Yet she was pleasant enough, and it certainly didn't faze her taking on the duties of official shrink to the prime minister. She made me talk, even if I didn't want to.

I really couldn't be bothered. My mindset was so negative, but I thought I'd better do the right thing as Sammy had organized the process and I somehow knew I wasn't well. Not mad, just off the pace a little, to the point where I couldn't give a shit about anything.

The first few sessions were boring. I must admit she drew me out of myself as I described the events leading up to and including the assassination attempt, but there wasn't any resolution, and I felt just the same afterward.

It was during the fifth session when I snapped at her, excused myself early, running out the door on my way to the JPR, reminding her I had a country to run. She just smiled at me and nodded, which I thought was a bit strange.

It was around two hours later, after I'd been engrossed in a debate in the JPR over university fees that I stopped in midflight with a big smile on my face. I cared! The blackness of depression had lifted, and I was back where I should be! I rang her and apologized, and she laughed at me. "Bingo," she said. "Not everyone is as easy as that. I couldn't stop smiling as you ran out the door. Motivation isn't a problem for you anymore."

"How did you do that?" I asked her.

"You began the process the moment you admitted you had a problem. I wish all my patients were as switched on as you are. No wonder you're prime minister."

As if on cue, my mind awoke again and I knew what had to be done.

As clear as crystal, I could see what had been obvious all along but we'd all ignored it, for varying reasons.

Changing anything takes time and effort, but if the end result makes it worthwhile, then it was worth the effort in the first place.

I spoke to Angela and she agreed without hesitation. Then to the cabinet and 100 percent approval. Then to caucus, where I explained in great detail why I thought such a change would be good for the country. I thought there would be a few old-fashioned souls who wanted to hang on to the old ways and was flabbergasted to find there were none.

As I left the meeting, Frank Gill joined me in the doorway, raising his eyebrows and muttering something hilarious about queens that was for my ears only, but some humor was exactly what I needed. Because there remained a long journey on this issue.

Next it was back to Julio's for an evening meal with Paul Sinclair and a quiet discussion, and, as expected, there would be majority consensus from the Coalition, but with some hysterical opposition from individual members.

We agreed that this had to be the subject of a referendum so every Australian could have their say.

I wanted the referendum to be held with the next general election due in nearly twelve months' time, but Paul disagreed. "Let's do it as soon as the model is agreed to, and give us enough time to communicate that to the public," he suggested. "That way I can sell it to our side of politics, and the Greens would also support us."

"You pricks have been talking, haven't you?" I said, and Paul had the decency to blush. "Of course we have. You taught us."

WE TOOK the model to the JPR and there were no amendments, and the process and timing of the referendum were rubber-stamped by both Houses.

Paul, Jye, and I did a fireside chat and explained what we wanted to do and why. There would be a simple ballot: Australians could vote yes for a republic or no to remain as we were, a constitutional monarchy.

Australia had last voted in 1999, and the referendum was defeated, the majority needed in each state to sustain a yes vote hadn't happened. This time the model had been changed: instead of Parliament electing a president, the Australian people would choose.

Over and over again I'd been warning my fellow Australians that we needed to be seen to be independent from our old colonial ties, enhancing our integration into Asia.

The other issue was security. Forget ISIL, forget all the Middle Eastern influences on local security. The pricks who had given us more grief in recent times were aligned with the monarchy and monarchists. Australia as a republic would send a serious message to those people, like join us or piss off.

SOMETIMES, AS Sammy pointed out, I could be as dumb as dog shit.

Yes, I was the greatest blue sky proponent, always looking to the future, but it was the obvious things, the things at the end of my nose that I missed.

The referendum passed, and we were headed for a general election, now only a few months away at a time of my choosing. Paul Sinclair asked me when I was going to resign, and I looked at him as if he were speaking Swahili.

"What for?" I asked.

"Because you can't lead the Labor Party into the election and stand for president at the same time."

I looked at Paul stupidly, and Sammy's words drifted back to me. "Dumb as dog shit."

I pretended I knew what he was talking about, but the reality hit me like a ton of bricks and I felt really stupid.

The next morning I talked to Angela, who just laughed at me, but she was also sympathetic. "You've had so much shit dumped on you, Jacko, and you think of everyone else before yourself, situation normal for you."

After much consultation, I called the election for mid-November and vacated the seat of Hinchcliffe in time for a new candidate to be approved.

It felt strange and just a little sad that I was walking away from the electorate that had handed me my political life. I knew every corner of it and most of the people who had made me their elected representative. Peter Prentice, who had run the electorate office for so many years, was selected as my successor. Peter was popular and well-known all over Hinchcliffe, particularly in the country areas, and I knew he'd maximize the vote in exactly the same manner that I had.

Sammy and I did a farewell swing through with Peter, not that he needed any introduction, and inevitably we ended up in the dairying part of the electorate with people around me I felt so comfortable with.

The old butter factory was on a second shift, and dairy produce was being fired into wealthy homes in Asia by the planeload. The whole district was booming, but it was the human contacts I so valued. Des Nightingale and Gus Evans had organized a farewell to me and a welcome to Peter, and it looked like a long night ahead. A huge barbecue was at the ready, and there would be many speeches as the beer and wine flowed.

I'd just been handed a nice glass of red when two smiling faces lit up the early evening in front of us: our former driver, Justin, and his now husband, Harry Evans. They'd been a couple almost since the night Sammy and I introduced them. They'd been backed by their families and were milking two hundred cows, and were one of the major suppliers to the factory.

Justin had put on some weight, looking very much at home, while Harry couldn't wipe the smile off his face. Jane, their first child, was asleep in a pram nearby with Harry's mum keeping watch.

"All the kids are breeding, Jacko," said Gus Evans, "particularly the same-sex couples. For years young people simply couldn't afford more than two kids, but since the dairy factory got going, we're going through a population explosion. Five is average size now, and we'll need bigger schools sooner rather than later."

Gus was pensive, and I thought I knew what was coming.

"My late brother would be astonished at all this." He smiled. "Same-sex couples married with kids, and just being part of the community. If you look around carefully, you'll see several other same-sex couples in addition to the Evans family who are also part of the community. Homophobia has disappeared here, and it's happened because our nation's first family have never been shy to tell the world they love each other." Gus pointed to the table of new products on display. "Our district economy booming after so many years of hand to mouth existence, but what's even better is that we've actually learned to get on with each other. Suicide rates for men under thirty have fallen like a stone. You guys must have saved hundreds of lives in the years you've spent in politics, just by showing people it can be done, and done with love and respect. When you're elected president, Jacko, and you will be, just think about the continuing transformation of attitudes here and overseas that you and Sammy will bring to the office. I salute you."

ANGELA CHAN led the Labor Party to victory and became prime minister in the new government with an almost unchanged majority; Paul Sinclair retained leadership of the Coalition, and Jye Chandler continued on as Leader of the Greens. Situation normal at that level of government.

But that's where the normality ceased and the birth of a new country began. What the Australian people did was to elect me as their first president of the Republic of Australia, an amazing honor.

Whether I liked it or not, my name would be forever written into the history books as the first president. What I had to do was ensure I was a good president, someone that the public could point to and say that I inspired people to reach for the stars and be proud to be Australian.

The post required me to be somewhat of a figurehead, my duties not dissimilar to the old post of governor-general.

The administrative details were straightforward, but no one had written the Australian Presidential Owner's Manual, and like pregnancy, I had the job in front of me. I was expected to offer advice to the prime minister of the time, but only after it was requested.

Fair enough, I was the executive arm of government, not the government itself. Furthermore, I was expected to be totally nonpartisan in approach and had resigned my membership of the Labor Party (somewhat sadly), to demonstrate my complete impartiality.

When I asked Sammy what he thought I should do, his response was typically Sammy. "Be yourself, Jacko. That's why you were elected, don't change."

WE BEGAN to look ahead again, as a family and as a country.

The messages flowing from the ASEAN countries on a daily basis were amazing, to look back on that period in office and realize we'd captured so many hearts and minds with some hard work, common sense, and courtesy was reward enough.

I had to be careful however; leaders always wanted to avoid the possibility of red tape and get an instant decision—from me. I had to explain even though I was the new president, I couldn't get involved in the day-by-day decision-making process of government. But I would help facilitate the process for Angela and her ministers by referring our Asian friends to the right person.

Singapore had been the chair of ASEAN for that year, and Jimmy Tan, prime minister and our lovely mate, rang me at Yarralumla. He and Sanjay thrived, despite all the predictions to the contrary. They already had two kids and unwavering support from the Singaporean community. Singapore boomed again when everyone thought it had outgrown itself, but he was particularly happy today, I could hear it in his voice. "What about we hold the annual meeting of ASEAN in Canberra early next year?" he asked.

"That's lovely, mate, but we're not members of ASEAN."

"You will be next week."

My head spun.

This was just such good news, the culmination of all our hard work recognized at last. Our cousins in Asia embracing us because we were finally our own entity, not tied to a former colonial power. Our transition to independence had convinced our ASEAN friends we meant business and we wanted to belong to a new family, the ASEAN family.

Job done, and I actually allowed myself to feel a real sense of achievement. Because it was much more than trade and economic benefits, it was family, where we trusted each other and would grow closer as the years rolled on.

We'd not spoken much of defense in the past, but the inference was clear: if one of our number were attacked, then we'd be there to help. We'd all had both homegrown and imported doses of terrorist activity, but the response from the ASEAN nations immediately after Sammy and I were attacked that fateful day shocked our armed services people. They didn't understand the speed at which our new informal alliances asserted themselves, or the commitment. Our chief of staff took one phone call after another with offers of assistance, hastened no doubt by the perceived severity of our injuries. We didn't need treaties or agreements to look after each other.

I thought back to the day when I nearly lost my life. I had only a vague recollection of events. Sammy was on edge, watching everything around us, but typical of me, I was quite relaxed for a change. It looked like all my black thoughts and dire predictions were for nothing.

But suddenly the fence crashed down and a wall of screaming people ran at us, Sammy shouting "Down!" as he pushed me, covering me with his body. Just as I was about to lecture him about overreacting, something hit me like an express train, and I didn't remember much until about a day later when they woke me out of an induced coma.

There was no doubt my husband saved my life. In fact, he unselfishly risked his so that I might be saved.

And it was indeed fortunate that Charlie Lim took out Andrew Fitch who, as a consequence, only inflicted a flesh wound on Sammy.

Charlie was adamant, Sammy had saved my life, and that act should be recognized. Sammy disagreed of course, but the matter was out of our hands. The Australian Bravery Decorations Council made a unanimous decision that Sammy should receive the Cross of Valour, the highest award for bravery in the nation.

To be presented by the new president of course, the bloke whose life he'd saved, and the first investiture of any type since Australia became a republic.

As A family we were suddenly in the spotlight all over again. Kate, Max, Dad, and Isobel were in the front row with Sammy. My brother and sister and their kids were in the next row, and right behind were Matt, Scott, and their tribe. Dear Chart and Solada sat quietly with the special guest from Bangkok, quite incognito but certainly very pleased to be in attendance. Lucas and Jonathan were home from Singapore with a newly retired Barbara Shields and Ted on one side and Jenny Bellamy on the other.

The uniqueness of the event was considered newsworthy, so there was an international electronic hookup broadcasting to the world.

It was Sammy's day. Without his loyalty, bravery, and determination, I wouldn't be there, history would have been rewritten, for better or worse.

Nearly fifty people had earned awards. I made sure we did those presentations up front, and that they received the degree of courtesy their bravery deserved.

Finally it was Sammy's turn as he walked toward me with a big smile on his face. I pinned the medal on his suit coat, and for once he was quiet. It was a handshake, a smile, and a few words from me to reiterate his enormous bravery in the face of imminent danger. Then we turned, and in front of the world, we kissed each other. It wasn't intended, but it happened because that's what loving couples do.

Then my bloody brother and sister, together with their spouses and kids, jumped to their feet and applauded us, just as they'd done at our wedding. And every other bastard did the same. Totally embarrassing but lovely.

Kate and Max flew over to be with us, followed by Isobel and Dad.

I HAD an epiphany of sorts. Every time I felt that my career had reached its zenith, Sammy had insisted I had more in the tank and I should press on.

I finally had a feeling I'd see out maybe a second term as president, then slip away into the night with Sammy. We'd probably be grandparents by then, and he agreed. We'd been so lucky; things had fallen our way so luck had a lot to do with our success.

But we were a team, undeniably so. If we hadn't met up as little kids, and if I hadn't eventually followed my instincts, politics over the last decade or so in Australia may have been quite different.

Sammy had set about unlocking my ability, always convinced I could push further, always full of encouragement—and love.

As I said previously, when my life changed for the better, love made it happen. Love was both the catalyst and the motivation, and I don't want anyone to forget it. Least of all myself.

Love has no boundaries and no rules; it's perfect the way it is.

Love inspires us to rise above our ordinary lives. In fact love is never ordinary.

Love is the only imperative we should teach our children, because the lessons of life won't work without it.

In our case love was waiting for us when we least expected it. And we realized our former lives had just been a rehearsal. But having received the gift of love, reality told us we had to work at it. Just like any living thing it needs a good feed every day. A kind word, a knowing wink, a plaster on a cut finger. And a responsibility to share our good fortune and experiences with others.

Leonardo da Vinci, Albert Einstein, Alexander Graham Bell, Sir Richard Branson, Walt Disney, Jay Leno, Whoopi Goldberg, Nelson Rockefeller, Agatha Christie, Steven Spielberg, Harry Belafonte, Winston Churchill, Richard Strauss, Jackson Collins-Smith.

Glossary of Australian English

AFP: Australian Federal Police.

ASEAN: Association of Southeast Asian Nations.

biff: A punch or blow.

bling: Sparkling jewelry.

bludger: Lazy.

buggery: Noun originally meaning anal intercourse, used colorfully. For example: overloaded to buggery, give everyone buggery, etc.

Centrelink: Government agency that helps to deliver services, support, and financial assistance to those in need, for ten Australian governmental departments.

chucked a wobbly: Losing one's temper.

Coalition, the: A coalition between the Liberal and National Country Parties in Australia.

fair dinkum: Famous Australian expression for being serious about something.

farang: A Thai word for "foreigner."

flat-out like lizards drinking: Busy. Very bloody busy.

flat strap: Very busy, up to maximum capacity, no time for anything else.

garbos: Workers on garbage trucks.

God-botherers: Religious extremists.

granting a pair: An informal arrangement between government and opposition to abstain from voting while a member of the other party needs to be absent from the House.

hard yakka: Hard work.

having a run in the lower paddock: The potential for male-male intercourse.

keep one's powder dry: Wait and watch before acting.

kinder: Kindergarten.

Labor caucus: Formed by all elected Labor Members of Federal Parliament in both Houses.

little tacker: Young child.

mine host: The landlord or landlady of a pub.

NCP: National Country Party. The Nationals, as they are now called, were called the NCP between 1975 and 1982.

ocker: Typically Australian in attitude, laid-back, loves a beer, doesn't show affection.

peci: A traditional hat worn widely in Southeast Asian countries.

poddy calves: Newborn cattle.

Poms: A usually disparaging term for English people.

poofter: Old-fashioned derogatory term for a male homosexual.

rorting the system: Using the system for corrupt purposes.

run up a dry gully: To have or receive no sympathy.

scrutineers: Political party appointees supervising the official counting of votes.

short fuse: Quick temper.

singlet: Undershirt.

sparky: An electrician.

spit the dummy: Have a tantrum or lose one's temper; stop cooperating.

stoush: To fight or have a disagreement, verbally or physically.

stubbies: Small bottles of beer.

TattsLotto: An Australian (Victorian) lottery.

toey: Impatient.

wai: A greeting with the hands pressed together. Used throughout Asia, particularly in Thailand.

whatsit: A souvenir.

Author's Note

THE TITLE of chapter 41, "The moving finger writes; and, having writ, moves on," is taken from *The Rubáiyát of Omar Khayyám*, translated by Edward FitzGerald.

JOHN TERRY MOORE and Russell Baum, his partner of thirty-three years, live in Geelong, Victoria's largest regional center, one hour from Melbourne, Australia. Many factors influenced John in the writing of this novel, not the least of which has been Russell's dyslexia, including how it affected him as a young person and how it has played out in his subsequent life. John's interest in same-sex partnerships, economics, politics, and Asian affairs also played a major role in the storyline.

John and Russell have traveled extensively throughout Asia for many years. Studiously avoiding Western tourists, they have inserted themselves into the culture and the daily lifestyles of the local people and consequently have a unique overview and understanding of Asian nations (ASEAN in particular), and the relationships those countries have with Australia.

John completed his education at Hobart Matriculation College and held a number of senior positions in the automotive industry over a thirty-five-year period, working separately for three Asian motor companies.

He was a civil marriage and funeral celebrant for many years (now retired), witnessing firsthand rapidly changing Australian public opinion, questioning traditional family structures and Australia's place in the world. Australia remains tied to the British Commonwealth, yet with the fastest-growing global economies only a few hours away in Asia, the messages Australia sends to its neighbors sometimes appear confusing and unhelpful.

John is a passionate advocate of same-sex marriage and equal rights for same-sex parents and their children, encouraging, supporting, and driving the push for marriage equality in Australia. He believes that LGBTI people should finally be embraced as an integral part of society, removing the scourge of homophobia and the risk of self-harm, replacing it with humanity, commonsense, and love. Only when everyone is treated exactly the same under law will society begin to heal itself.

BLACK DOG

JOHN TERRY MOORE

Australia is a nation in transition. Marriage equality looms but homophobia still rules. Depression and suicide are commonplace as Dean Prentice and his lover, Danny, grow up together in country Victoria. When Dean moves to a nearby regional center to study veterinary science, he finds acceptance and love when reunited with Danny. Profound tragedy visits Dean's life and he grieves, moving on through a series of lovers both male and female and struggling to focus on his studies and his dream of becoming a veterinarian. He graduates and specializes in equine work.

With long hours and unrelenting pressure, he misses the support of a full time partner. The only constant in his life is his loyal Kelpie, Bruce. Then he meets Neil Andrews and falls in love. Neil is a stunning widower in his forties with children and grandchildren, and Dean realizes he wants kids of his own.

But Neil is still deep in the closet and while their relationship is passionate, it's going nowhere permanent. They separate, and Dean contemplates marrying a woman for company and friendship. For the second time in Dean's young life, depression reveals its ugly presence; this time there are medical professionals at hand and he might have a chance for love at last.

www.dreamspinnerpress.com

www.ingramcontent.com/pod-product-compliance
Lightning Source LLC
Chambersburg PA
CBHW050032030726
47506CB00001B/237